WALKING
THROUGH
THE
FIRE

BONITA M. HULLENDER

ISBN 978-1-63630-314-7 (Paperback)
ISBN 978-1-63630-315-4 (Digital)

Covenant Books, Inc.
11661 Hwy 707
Murrells Inlet, SC 29576
www.covenantbooks.com

DEDICATION

I dedicate this book to my husband, Joel. Not only is he my best friend and better half, but he is the love of my life. Many hours of "together time" was sacrificed to fulfill my life-long dream of becoming a published author. But thanks to my husband's love, support and understanding, my dream became a reality. I will forever love you.

I would also like to dedicate this book to my parents, Arthur and Margaret Martin, and my grandma Mary Wylie. From an early age, they taught me about God and the importance of family. My mom and dad taught me, by example, to have unwavering faith, no matter how difficult the circumstances. Each loved me unconditionally and encouraged me to be all I could be. Mom, Dad, Grandma may you Rest In Peace until we meet again.

CONTENTS

Chapter 1:   "Go Ye…" 7

Chapter 2:   How It Started 12

Chapter 3:   An Old Friend..18

Chapter 4:   The Argument..22

Chapter 5:   The Pictures 32

Chapter 6:   The Party 44

Chapter 7:   The Accident..55

Chapter 8:   The Decision..63

Chapter 9:   The Operation 75

Chapter 10: Wyatt Kingsley..93

Chapter 11: A Night without Mom 101

Chapter 12: One Step at a Time 110

Chapter 13: A Locked Door 121

Chapter 14: A Parent's Worst Nightmare 129

Chapter 15: There's No Place Like Home 139

Chapter 16: But for the Grace of God.............................157

Chapter 17: The Love of God 167

Chapter 18: The Mystery Unfolds 174

Chapter 19: The Visitor...182

Chapter 20: Thanksgiving Day 193

Chapter 21: Another Surprise Visitor..............................201

Chapter 22: Then Came Sunday......................................211

Chapter 23: Back to School 222

Chapter 24: You Can Thank Me Later.......................................230
Chapter 25: Secrets Revealed 240
Chapter 26: Love—Sometimes a Complicated Thing 246
Chapter 27: God's Hand Is Not Shortened 252
Chapter 28: Game Time! 256
Chapter 29: Making Amends..264
Chapter 30: The Letter 274
Chapter 31: Jesus Calling...281

Epilogue...284
Afterword...290

CHAPTER 1

"Go Ye..."

Addison McNeely sat on the edge of the cold metal chair. Her entire body shook as she bounced the ball of her right foot and tried to concentrate on taking slow deep breaths. Sitting next to the glass podium, she watched from the far end of the basketball court as hundreds of high school students entered through two sets of double doors and filled the wooden bleachers of the gymnasium. Her sweaty and tightly clasped hands held firmly to the speech she had stayed up half the night preparing. Every minute she grew more anxious, knowing she was about to stand and speak before a group of energetic teenagers. In her heart, she knew the testimony she was about to give was what the Lord wanted. However, she had always hated public speaking, and that was not about to change. Occasionally, loud shouts echoed across the gym as some of the students yelled to one another from one end of the large gymnasium to the other. The constant drone of voices reminded Addison of the many hours she had spent as a little girl listening to the buzz of wild bees in her grandmother's garden filled with daisies and marigolds.

After several more nail-biting minutes, the students were seated, and the double doors leading into the school's gymnasium were closed. The huge clock hanging above the doors read 3:30 p.m. as a petite Chloe Wilson stood from the front row of the bleachers and approached the podium. Chloe, a senior, was president of the Fellowship of Christian Athletes at Iron City High School where today's FCA meeting was being held. Getting the attention of the students, she called the meeting into order; and after a few minutes of FCA business, Chloe enthusiastically introduced Addison.

"Let's give Ms. McNeely a welcoming round of applause," she said as she put her hands together and nodded her curly blonde head toward Addison.

Swallowing the lump in her throat, Addison rose slowly from the chair. She approached the podium and noticed etched in gold on the front glass was the face of a ferocious-looking wildcat, the mascot of Iron City High School. Some of the gold paint had chipped away in a couple of places, but the wildcat's large snarling teeth were still intact.

As she stood behind the podium, she never thought she would be standing before a crowd about to make a speech, let alone give her Christian testimony. All high school students in Cherokee County had been invited to attend the Fellowship of Christian Athletes' sponsored meeting, even if they were not members of the FCA. As an incentive to attend, the students had been offered extra credit in their English classes. Realistically, Addison knew the offered incentive was the only reason the majority of students had attended.

Glancing around the gymnasium, she was a little disappointed. There appeared to be close to six hundred students in attendance; that was less than half the schools combined. Iron City High had approximately six hundred students enrolled, and Indianville High had a little over two thousand enrolled. It wasn't that numbers were all that important to her, but souls were. As the applause came to an end, she carefully placed the written speech on the podium. Looking into the faces of the students, she tried to appear more confident than she actually felt.

"Hi, my name is Addison McNeely," she began. "Boy, do I have a testimony for you!" she said, a little more enthusiastically than she intended. *Good grief, did I really just say that?* The words sure looked better on paper than coming out of the mouth, she thought. She felt her face and neck flush and hoped no one had notice since they were watching from a distance. Clearing her throat, she continued to read from the speech she had prepared. "There are parts of this testimony

I am not particularly proud of. Nonetheless, it is important I tell the events exactly as they occurred."

Taking a deep breath, she looked into the faces of mostly disinterested students. She was trying to speak clearly and distinctly, but her shaky voice sounded almost muffled; her dry mouth feeling as though it was stuffed with several balls of cotton. Nervous and a little frustrated, she wondered why in the world she had let Maggie and Chloe talk her into this. Along with Chloe, her pastor's wife, Maggie Peters, who taught English classes at the school, had arranged today's meeting. Addison's not-so-grateful thought made her feel a little twinge of guilt. She knew this was the will of God and that Maggie and Chloe had only been instruments God had used to help bring this moment to pass.

"My story begins in my senior year of high school," she said as she held tightly to the podium with two hands. She cleared her throat and reached for the glass of ice water that had been placed on the pedestal next to the podium and brought the glass to her lips. She took a large swallow and prayed silently that she would not bolt and run. Looking over the rim of the glass, she swallowed gulp after gulp of the ice-cold water. Since she was wearing one of those hands-free microphones that fit over the ear and came around to the mouth, she was positive everyone could hear every swallow.

School spirit and pride were depicted everywhere. Numerous banners of black and gold, the school colors, hung proudly on the gold-colored cement-block walls. The banners displayed the words: *Go, Iron City Wildcats! Go, Team! Fight Cats Fight!* Championship banners displayed the year various sports had won the ultimate showdown. In fact, today, in honor of her alma mater, she had worn a black pair of dress slacks and a shiny gold buttoned-down long-sleeved blouse. Adorning her long slender neck was a black-and-gold striped silk scarf. In her opinion the colors in the scarf complimented her almond-shaped dark-brown eyes and shoulder-length black hair.

Seeing all the banners caused a feeling of nostalgia to momentarily sweep over her. Almost four and a half years earlier, Addison had graduated from Iron City High. Having been a cheerleader, she stood thinking of all the cheers she had performed on the very same court she was now standing on. Addison returned the glass of water to the pedestal, then looked at the perfectly prepared speech she had written—at least it seemed perfect at the time she had written it. She thought about as a student how she had hated hearing teachers read word for word from a textbook, especially if they had read in one of those tiresome monotones. Turning the papers facedown, she once again cleared her throat and took a deep breath. She sensed the presence of the Holy Spirit as He urged her to forget the prepared speech and to speak from her heart.

"Right now most of you are probably wishing you were anywhere in the universe but here." She received a few claps and cheers with that statement, but ignoring them, she continued, "You want to know something? A few short years ago, I sat in those very same bleachers, and had that very same thought." She moved to the side of the podium, beginning to feel a little more at ease and noticed she was able to steady herself with one hand instead of two.

"Near the beginning of my senior year, a dear lady named Margaret Beckel was invited to speak to students on the negative effects drugs and alcohol can have on a person's life. You see, I was a Christian, but I was also a social drinker. I didn't want to hear how alcohol might have an effect on me. After all, I only drank socially. It wasn't like I was an alcoholic. As I halfway listened that day, I remember thinking Margaret Beckel was one of those old-fashioned Christians who desperately needed to catch up with modern times."

To the right of her, a small group of rowdy students, upon hearing Addison's last comment, erupted into cheers and applause. Out of the corner of her eye, Addison saw Maggie walk over and say something to the students as the cheers and applause quieted.

"I'm here today to share my testimony of how alcohol affected my life and the lives of those around me. I'm also here to share about God's grace and to let you know He is always with us. As Christians, we will occasionally have to walk through the fires of life. There is no escaping it. Test and trials come to us all, and although it is sometimes our own doings which put us in that fire, God is still faithful and full of mercy. Some of you are walking through the fire right now, I have no doubt. You're asking, why, God? Where are You, God? I'm sorry to say I cannot answer the age-old question of why, but I can tell you where He is. Just as He was with me in the fire a few years ago, He is right there in the fire with you. You just have to trust Him."

Studying the faces of the students, she noticed more of the disinterested students now appeared to be a little more interested in what she was saying. As she wondered how she was going to capture the attention of the remaining students, a most unusual thought came to mind. With one hand, she reached and grabbed the metal chair she had sat in earlier and walked to the front of the podium. She positioned the chair, sat, and then proceeded to slowly roll up her left pant leg. Without looking up, she removed her artificial leg and carefully laid it on the floor beside the chair. She heard a few gasp as she quickly scanned the faces of the students as they looked on wide-eyed at what they had just seen. She did not see one disinterested face among them. All eyes were staring at her and the artificial leg lying on the gym floor. Even Chloe, who had been leaning against one of the wooden bleachers, straightened up and stared at her in disbelief. Addison began her testimony.

CHAPTER 2

HOW IT STARTED

Alayna sat next to her best friend on the back pew of New Haven Church of God and softly prayed. "Lord, please draw Addison to you today. As you know, she is not a bad person, but she has never invited You into her heart as Lord and Savior. Please save her today. Let her realize the great love You have for her and that she needs You to be a part of her life. In Jesus's name I pray, amen."

Alayna Thomas had been attending New Haven for almost two years now, but at the moment, she felt a little out of place. She usually sat on the third pew from the front on the left side of the church, but not today. The only way she could talk her best friend into coming to church this morning was to promise to sit on the back pew. Since her attention span was not the best in the world, Alayna usually sat up front where there were fewer distractions. From the back pew, she could see too many people, which meant too many distractions.

She stared straight ahead and leaned against the side of the comfortably padded moss-green pew, twirling her thick auburn hair between slender fingers.

She noticed every little movement from Johnny Upchurch, a retired schoolteacher scratching his round gray head to his wife, Doris, checking out the huge gold chandeliers. A couple of teenagers were texting on their phones. Louise Tully must have been having hot flashes even though the air-conditioner was wide open because she sat frantically fanning her face with the church bulletin. Nevertheless, having to promise to sit on the back pew had been worth it as Addison now sat beside her.

Alayna, having received Jesus at a youth meeting almost two years earlier, was eager for Addison to do the same. One of their mutual friends, Reese, who had since moved to another state, had invited them to the youth meeting at New Haven on a Sunday night. Alayna had attended church with Reese and ended up surrendering her heart to the Lord. Addison, however, had backed out at the last minute, saying she had a terrible headache. Alayna was almost positive: although she could not prove it, the headache had just been an excuse for her friend not to come.

From the very beginning, her relationship with Jesus had put a strain on their friendship. She had honestly thought that when Addison heard about her experience with the Lord, she would have leapt at the opportunity to accept Jesus into her life as well. Instead, Addison had told her she had become a Jesus freak because all she wanted to do was talk about Jesus and church. At the time, Alayna had felt both hurt and angry over the comment, but with Maggie Peters help, she had come to realize she just needed to keep loving and praying for Addison unconditionally. Her pastor's wife had helped her to understand that no matter how much she wanted Addison to get saved; no one could force her. Maggie had encouraged her to just pray and let the Holy Spirit do His work.

After that, the strain on their relationship improved, and things were pretty much back to normal. The major difference was, Alayna would be in church on Sundays and had quit sneaking and drinking alcohol. On rare occasions, like today, Addison would visit with her at New Haven.

Alayna's attention was suddenly drawn to Mr. Wille sitting a couple of pews in front of her. Here was yet another distraction. She smiled as she observed him struggle to stay awake. She watched as periodically his heavy eyelids would give into sleep, causing his head to fall forward. He would then quickly jerk his head straight up, looking around very inconspicuously to see if anyone had noticed.

After a few minutes poor Mr. Wille would repeat the whole process. Once in a while, Mrs. Wille would catch him beginning to nod off and give him an elbow to the ribs. It wasn't that Bryce Peters, mostly referred to as Pastor Bryce, was boring. In fact, he was quite the contrary. Alayna was certain Mr. Wille's need to sleep was because his body had grown accustomed to sleeping during the day due to him working the graveyard shift at one of the local plants.

Turning her attention to her friend, she noticed that Addison genuinely appeared to be hanging on to every word Pastor Bryce was saying. As a matter of fact, she thought she saw tears in her eyes, but couldn't be sure. Normally, her best friend would be checking her watch every few minutes, but not today. It was nearing time for the altar call. Bowing her head, she again prayed for the Holy Spirit to work in the life of her friend.

* * * * *

Addison and Alayna had been best friends since fifth grade and were almost inseparable. Because Addison loved her friend dearly, she had promised to come to church today. For almost two years, Alayna had tried to talk her into confessing her sins and accepting Jesus as her Savior. It had almost ruined their relationship until Alayna finally eased up a little, now only occasionally bringing up Jesus or church. This weekend was one of those moments. Because it had been a while since she attended church with her friend, she had decided to appease Alayna and come today.

Honestly, she just couldn't understand why Alayna felt it so necessary to "confess our sins." *Besides, I'm not a bad person,* she reasoned with herself. *I try to be good to people—well, most of the time. I come to church, sometimes. I've never killed anyone, thought about it—well, not really.* Her mind went on and on trying to justify why she did not deserve to go to a place called hell. Surely Pastor Bryce was talking about really bad people like murderers, child molesters, and rapists, people like that. No way would God send someone like her to a place of eternal damnation. *I mean, I'm not perfect, but I'm a good person. I don't deserve hell.*

Suddenly her stomach let out a low rumbling growl, and her mind drifted to food. After church, the two of them were going to eat at S&P's Homecookin' Restaurant, which was owned by Alayna's mom and dad, Shannon and Patrick Thomas. She was thinking maybe fried chicken today. Even now she could almost smell and taste the crunchy yet juicy, succulent chicken.

Something Pastor Bryce was saying caught her attention.

"All of us have sinned and come short of the glory of God. No one can come to the Heavenly Father but through Jesus. He is the only way." She could have sworn he was looking straight at her with his kind but serious blue eyes when he said, "God's Word says He so greatly loved the world and you that He gave His only begotten Son, that whosoever—and that means you and I—if we will confess our sins and believe on Him, shall be saved."

She had heard those familiar words many times from her BFF, but today something was different.

"Preaching under the anointing," as Alayna called it, Pastor Bryce moved from one end of the platform to the other. Even with the cool air blowing into the sanctuary, he would occasionally walk back to the pulpit just long enough to take a white handkerchief and run it over his oblong face, the back of his neck, and then over his bald head.

Although Pastor Bryce was on the skinny side and somewhat short, he was a ball of fire today, unstoppable under the anointing. Addison felt a lump begin to form in her throat as Pastor Bryce continued to preach. She was desperately trying to hold back the tears but felt as if she was going to lose that battle and burst into an uncontrollable flood of tears at any moment. Not only that, but her heart was beating so hard and fast it felt as if she had a jackhammer in her chest. She looked down and noticed her knuckles had turned white from holding on to the edge of the pew so tight.

"Remember, God does not send anyone to hell," Pastor Bryce said, as if he knew what she had been thinking earlier. "We send ourselves by rejecting His Son, who died on the cross for our sins."

Out of the corner of her eye, she saw Alayna glance her way. Addison felt the tears start to form in her eyes. She tried to think of other things, but she just could not shake the conviction she was under. Would she really be left behind if Jesus returned today? Could she really be on her way to hell? Did she really need Jesus? She was a good person!

"Scripture tells us there is none righteous, no, not one. There is none that doeth good." Pastor Bryce was right on cue, she thought.

As much as she was feeling conviction, she was also feeling an overwhelming sense of love like she had never felt before. Love was drawing her to Jesus. She was beginning to realize God was love and that He really did love her. He wasn't mad at her; He wasn't seeking to harm her or to punish her. He wanted a relationship with her. Addison finally realized she needed Jesus in her life.

Pastor Bryce was now beginning the altar call as his wife, Maggie, approached the grand piano. Callaway, their thirteen-year-old son, made his way to the drums. Maggie began playing softly as she sang a song performed by one of Alayna's favorite gospel groups. The song told of not everyone being ready when Jesus called His church home. She was familiar with the song because Alayna would play the group's CD over and over in her car and at home. Addison would always switch to another song or leave the room when this song came on; maybe even then the Lord was trying to draw her to Himself. The sad words to the song rang out over the entire congregation, causing her to really think about her eternal future. Where would she spend eternity if she died right now? she thought.

Addison turned toward Alayna, who had her hands clasped together and her head bowed. She knew her friend was praying for her. Finally, she couldn't fight the gentle tugging of the Holy Spirit any longer. She touched Alayna lightly on the shoulder.

"Would you please come with me to the altar, Alayna?" she whispered. "I need Jesus."

By this time, the tears were starting to stream uncontrollably down her cheeks. Alayna's round blue eyes became big as saucers as she looked into the tear-streaked face of her best friend. Alayna reached and hugged her so tight Addison could hardly breathe. Taking Alayna by the hand, Addison took the most important steps she would ever take in her life. Both could barely see through their tears as they walked down the green carpeted aisle arm in arm. Maggie continued to sing softly as Addison knelt at the altar and gave her heart and life to Jesus. As she prayed, she felt as though the weight of the world had been lifted from her shoulders. She was no longer afraid of being left behind. All was well, for now.

CHAPTER 3

AN OLD FRIEND

Addison ran and leaped onto her queen-sized bed. She reached and turned off the lamp beside her bed and then lay back on her pillow with her hands folded underneath her head. Her mind played over and over the events of the past few weeks. It had been a month since she had given her heart to the Lord. She was attending church faithfully every week now and loved going to the youth meetings on Wednesday and Sunday nights. She now understood how Alayna felt when she had given her heart to the Lord. It seemed in the past month they had grown closer than ever—until today.

It all started a few days after the twenty-fifth of October, the day Addison turned eighteen. The two were supposed to get together with a few of their mutual friends the following Saturday on the banks of the Broad River and celebrate the occasion, at least that's what Addison had thought.

One of those friends was Isaac Darnell, an old friend from high school. His birthday was the same day as Addison's; only, he had just turned twenty-one. Isaac was a junior at Williamston College located in Indianville, South Carolina, just minutes from Iron City. He had been fortunate enough to land a full ride on a football scholarship and worked part-time at one of his father's dry-cleaning stores. This enabled him to afford a small apartment of his own. However, the biggest part of his time was spent practicing and playing football for the Williamston Warriors. In his freshman year, she and Alayna had watched him practice football a few times after school and attended a few of his home games. During his high school years, Isaac had been the Wildcats' quarterback and helped lead the Wildcats to two state championships. Sadly, the Wildcats had not won a state championship since he graduated.

It was the Friday after her birthday when the two had run into Isaac at Fletcher's Groceries. The grocery store was located in Indianville, where most people in Iron City traveled to shop and dine.

Indianville was only about a fifteen-minute drive from Iron City, and although it was not a large town, it was still larger than Iron City with more places of entertainment. The two towns were separated by the Broad River. On one side of the Broad River Bridge leading into Indianville were two small gravel roads that ran alongside the river, one to the left and one to the right. The wooded areas along the river were ideal sites for camping and fishing, but it was also a popular site for partying late at night. Miles of heavily wooded areas surrounded the river on all sides. Once you left the narrow gravel roads that ran along the river, you would have to walk to get to the actual river. The banks were low lying, and the waters were usually mysteriously dark and murky, except after a torrential downpour in which they became an obscure muddy color. On rare occasions, after days and days of those torrential rains, the river would overflow, and the gravel roads on each side of the river would have to be closed. This well-hidden wooded area was where the party was to take place Saturday night.

Addison knew in her heart the upcoming party wasn't the best place for her to be, but no way could she come across as not being cool about it.

Turning in the bed from one side to the other, she tried to get comfortable. Finally, she fluffed the queen-sized pillow with her fist and tucked one arm underneath it, giving her head a little more elevation. Her thoughts returned to earlier in the day when she and Alayna had encountered Isaac at the grocery store.

The two of them had not seen or spoken to him in almost ten months. They were tossing a couple of tomatoes into a plastic bag and discussing an upcoming youth retreat when they heard, "Hey,

Addie! Hey, Laney!" Addison had known who it was before she even looked up from the red ripe tomato in her hand. Only one person called them by those names.

"Isaac!" she exclaimed, genuinely surprised to see him as she turned and saw him standing across from them on the other side of the produce counter.

"Long time no see," she said.

Isaac Darnell was even more handsome than she remembered. The dark-golden tan he had acquired gave him a kind of outdoorsy look and complimented his light blonde hair. His piercing blue eyes were almost mesmerizing. Isaac had always been one to work out, and she found herself staring at his arm muscles bulging under the tight-fitting pullover he was wearing.

He caught her staring at him like some moonstruck high school girl, and she felt her face blush. How embarrassing, she thought. She was trying to think of something to say to get past the awkward moment, but no words came to mind. As a matter of fact, she was still gawking at him. Seriously! she thought.

Finally, she looked away from him just as Alayna leaned into her and whispered with some irritation, "Will you stop gawking at Isaac like some moonstruck schoolgirl?"

Oh my gosh, she thought, as she stared at the tomato she was holding in her hand, even Alayna had noticed.

"By the way, Addie, happy belated birthday," he said, ending the awkward moment. When he smiled, Addison noticed his perfectly aligned white teeth.

"Happy belated birthday to you too, Isaac," she said as she looked again at the tomato in her hand and turned it over, pretending to inspect it. Alayna mumbled a halfhearted happy birthday as she looked at the beer in Isaac's buggy. Addison tossed the last tomato into the plastic bag and laid it in the buggy.

After a few minutes of discussing how things were going for him in college, he asked if they would like to come to his birthday get-together the following night.

Addison could tell Alayna was wishing they had not run into Isaac. It wasn't that Alayna didn't like Isaac. It just seemed to bother

her a little more that he loved partying, especially if alcohol was involved.

"As a matter of fact, we'll make it a double-birthday celebration," he added. "Yours and mine, Addie. How about it? It'll be fun."

"Well, I really don't know if…if we should," Alayna spoke up.

Isaac picked up a tomato from the bin, looked it over, and then gave it a slight toss in the air before returning it to the bin. "Come on, you two. Don't be party poopers. You won't be the only high school kids there. I've invited a few other high schoolers as well as my college buddies."

Did he just say kids? Addison felt herself start to fume.

"Of course, we'll come to your party," she piped up. "We wouldn't miss it for the world. Thanks for the invite."

If looks could kill, she would have been dead at that moment. Alayna was not happy that she had agreed to go to the party.

After giving details of when and where the party would be, Isaac left, pushing a buggy full of beer, chips, cookies, and other junk foods.

"You know there will be drinking and such," Alayna told her as they placed their groceries on the checkout counter. "You saw all that beer."

"So what? Just because someone else is drinking doesn't mean we have to," she spat back defiantly.

Alayna started to say something else, but Addison interrupted her when she noticed the cashier hanging on to their every word.

"We'll discuss this later," she said with a nod toward the cashier as the cashier looked sheepishly away.

However, there had been no further discussion. Alayna had given her the silent treatment the entire ride home. The only time Alayna spoke was when Addison asked a question.

Fluffing her pillow again, she turned to the opposite side. Addison hated when she and Alayna disagreed on something. It was almost two o'clock in the morning when she finally drifted off into a restless sleep.

CHAPTER 4

THE ARGUMENT

Addison wasn't sure if it was the simultaneous clap of thunder or the buzzing of the alarm clock that woke her. Rolling over, she removed the pillow from over her head and looked toward the bedroom window. Through the thin ivory panels, she could see the steady rain coming down outside as she listened to the gentle pitter-patter it made against the window. Moaning, she placed the pillow back over her head and rolled over facing the alarm clock. I just need five minutes more, she thought. She started to reach for the snooze button when the door to her bedroom burst open. It was Ayson, her twelve-year-old brother.

"Get up, sleepyhead. It's almost time to go," he announced, dropping on the edge of the bed.

Still half asleep, it took a few seconds to realize what he was talking about. Then it dawned on her: he was spending the night with Caleb, and she had promised to drop him off on her way to cheerleading practice. Caleb Garrison and her brother had been best friends since kindergarten and, much like her and Alayna, were almost inseparable. Although it was Saturday, Ms. Redmond, the cheer coach, had called an additional practice. Addison let out another moan. Not only did she have to drop Ayson off at Caleb's, but she had to swing by and pick up Alayna.

"Come on, Addison, get up. It's already ten after eight," her brother pleaded as he began to pull the warm comforter from over her shoulders.

"Stop it, you little pip-squeak!" she yelled as she jerked the warm comforter from his hands and quickly pulled it over her chilled shoulders.

Ayson jumped from the bed and ran to the doorway. "Mom, Addison won't get up!"

"Addison, it's time to get a move on, young lady!" her mother yelled from the foot of the stairs.

Rolling her eyes, Addison threw the comforter back and sat on the edge of the bed. Through half-opened eyes, she glared at Ayson, who was still standing in the doorway grinning with a triumphant smile. Grabbing her pillow, she picked it up and threw it. The pillow barely missed him as he ran through the doorway. Sticking his head back inside the door, he stuck out his tongue then took off running as she leapt from the bed and started toward him. By now it was 8:15 a.m. She really had better get a move on.

Fifteen minutes later, she hurried through the kitchen, almost tripping over Chip, their Chihuahua—Jack Russell mix who was sitting patiently next to the table hoping for a dropped bite of anything. She quickly grabbed a piece of dry toast without stopping and motioned for Ayson to follow. Gulping the last of his milk, he reached and gave Chip a quick pat on the head before grabbing his duffle bag.

"Bye, Mom," they yelled in unison as Ayson caught up with his sister at the door.

"Be careful, you two," their mother yelled from the hall bathroom. Her voice sounded a little slurred and muffled. She was probably in the middle of brushing her teeth, Addison thought. Ayson slammed the door behind them just as they heard their mother call out.

"Don't slam the doo—!" Addison gave her brother an eye roll and shook her head.

"Oops," he said as he shrugged and headed for the red Ford Focus parked underneath the carport.

"Don't forget to grab an umbrella," Addison told him as she grabbed a pink neon umbrella from the container located next to the door. She slid onto the leather seat of the car and gave a slight shiver as she waited for Ayson to grab his umbrella. Reaching for the heater control, she turned the heater on low to knock off the chill of the cool rainy October morning. Ayson grabbed a black umbrella and jumped into the back seat of the car, knowing he would have to give up the front seat to Alayna when they arrived at her house. It was much drier to crawl in the back seat now under the protection of the carport than having to switch in the pouring rain.

The two rode in silence on the way to Alayna's house. Addison adjusted the rear-view mirror and caught a glimpse of Ayson looking out the window. Ayson could be the source of a splitting headache sometimes, but still he was her little brother, and she loved him. She was beginning to feel a little guilty for the way she had treated him earlier. When her parents had brought him home from the hospital, she had been so excited to have a baby brother. He had definitely made life a little less boring.

Though they were full-blooded brother and sister you would never know it by looking at them. She, with her black hair and dark-brown eyes, favored their mom. The only resemblance to her dad, other than her broad smile, was the light dusting of tan freckles across her nose and cheeks. Ayson, on the other hand, was the spitting image of their dad with his sandy-blond hair and deep-set hazel eyes.

"I'm sorry I yelled at you this morning," she apologized as she watched him in the rear-view mirror. "It's the pits having to get up early on a Saturday morning," she tried to explain, "especially a rainy Saturday morning."

A warm smile played across her brother's face. "I'm sorry too," he said, meeting her eyes in the mirror. Once again, at least for the time being, all was well between brother and sister.

A few minutes later, they pulled into the driveway of the Thomas' ranch-style home. Addison showered down hard on the horn. Alayna ran from the house holding a light-blue umbrella over her long auburn hair. The rain was coming down harder, and the wind had picked up, causing some of the rain to blow into the car as she opened the door.

"Gosh, it feels like winter out here," she said, throwing her bag on the floorboard and sliding into the front seat. "Hey, squirt," she told Ayson as she turned and laid the folded umbrella in the back floorboard. Ayson hated it when Alayna referred to him as squirt, but in spite of his objections, she continued to call him that. He had finally resigned himself to living with it. Before he could return her hello, Alayna looked seriously at Addison.

"We've got to talk."

Addison knew what Alayna wanted to talk about, and she was dreading the subject.

The trio rode in silence until they pulled into the circular driveway of the Garrison's two-story brick home. Fortunately, Caleb only lived a couple of blocks from Alayna, which was a big convenience, especially since they were pushing it to get to practice on time. Caleb must have been watching for them because as soon as she pulled into the driveway, he swung open the wooden door and stood looking out the glass storm door. He was wearing a dark hunter-green shirt, which made his fiery red hair stand out even more than usual. Addison smiled as she remembered Shannon Thomas once saying she had always wanted a red-headed, blue-eyed, freckled-faced boy because they were so cute. Shannon was always embarrassing Caleb by telling him how cute he was as she would tousle his red hair every chance she got.

Ayson grabbed his bag, opened the car door, said his goodbyes, and went running toward the front door in the pouring rain. Addison started to yell at him to get his umbrella, but it was too late. Truth be known, he had intentionally forgotten it. No way was his friend going to see him sporting an umbrella. He was way too cool for that.

Putting the car in gear, Addison drove to the end of the driveway. Stopping to look for oncoming traffic, she glanced at Alayna, who was staring straight ahead with her arms crossed.

"Okay, Alayna, let's get this over with," Addison said with a long, exaggerated sigh. "What do you want to talk about?" *As if I don't already know.*

Alayna was a little hesitant, but finally blurted out what was on her mind. "I-I don't think we should go to Isaac's birthday party tonight."

Pulling onto the highway, Addison let out another long sigh and prepared for the worst. "Alayna, we've already had this discussion, and as the saying goes, there's no need to keep beating a dead horse."

"I know, but I just thought after hearing Margaret Beckel's speech earlier in the week about drugs and alcohol that you might change your mind."

Addison pressed the gas pedal a little harder, then thought better of it and eased off the pedal. "Well, I haven't!" she huffed. "Besides, Margaret Beckel is just old and too old-fashioned. She must be, what, in her forties?"

Alayna frowned. "Forty is not old, and she is not too old-fashioned," Alayna responded defensively. "She's a Christian, and what she told us is the truth."

"Look, Alayna, I know you think it is wrong to have a social drink, but that is your conviction, not mine. I don't think because a Christian has one drink, they are going to hell."

Alayna sighed in frustration, yet continued, "But think about what you're doing. You're hurting your testimony. Besides, you know there will be more than just social drinking. I'm sorry for what I'm about to say, but you're acting no different than those who profess *not* to be a Christian."

Addison tried to ignore Alayna and just let her talk, even though she felt Alayna was saying some pretty harsh things. She was glad to finally be pulling into the gym parking lot a few minutes later. The downpour of rain had turned into a light drizzle within a matter of minutes. At the moment, it was stormier inside the car than it was outside.

"And every alcoholic started with one drink," Alayna was saying.

Annoyed and unable to keep silent any longer, Addison shoved the gear stick into park, turned the motor off, and stared into Alayna's clearly concerned face. "I can't believe what you're saying. You've practically made me into a booze head, Alayna!" She realized she was almost yelling at her friend, but she didn't care at this point. Alayna had no right to say these things to her and about her. Addison reached into the back seat for her duffle bag; then lifting it across the front seat, she turned back around to open the car door.

"I'm not going with you tonight," she heard Alayna say softly and with a hint of sadness.

"Fine, don't go. You would probably ruin everyone's good time anyway."

Addison pushed open the door, then slammed it so hard the car rocked. She ran toward the gym without giving Alayna so much as a second glance.

Alayna felt the tears beginning to well up in her soft blue eyes as she opened the car door and walked slowly toward the gym. She didn't even care that it was still raining. All she could think about was whether or not she was going to lose her best friend.

* * * * *

The Wildcat cheerleaders had just begun to run laps when Alayna came through the double doors leading into the gym. Dropping her bag on the floor, she quickly pulled her long, thick hair into a ponytail. She waited for the last of the girls in the squad to run past her then fell in behind them. A few more laps and stretch warm-ups, and they were ready to practice the pyramid.

Since Alayna was the tiniest on the squad, she was the one Coach Redmond had chosen to be on the very top of the pyramid. Last year, the squad had accidently dropped her during one of the practices, resulting in a sprained wrist. There had been some discussion among concerned parents of putting a stop to the pyramid, but the cheerleaders had protested, and the discussion was soon dropped.

After forty-five minutes, Coach Redmond blew the silver whistle she always wore around her neck and called a fifteen-minute break. Alayna watched her coach grab a towel and wipe the sweat from her eyes and face and then fling the towel around her neck. Kaye Redmond was in her early thirties and had never been married. She was tall and slender with chocolate-brown hair and sad brown eyes. Alayna thought her coach was rather pretty and couldn't figure out why she was still single. She did vaguely remember hearing her coach had been engaged at one point, but a week before the wedding, her fiancé had been killed in a plane crash. Rumor had it she had never worked through losing him. Whether or not that was true, Alayna had no idea.

The exhausting practice had left Alayna feeling extremely thirsty. Addison, along with Karlie Adams and Maddie Watkins, was standing next to the water fountain laughing when she arrived to get a drink of water. She was surprised to see Addison with Karlie as Karlie didn't particularly like Addison for some reason. Jealousy, perhaps? But Alayna couldn't really see that as the reason.

Karlie was one of the most beautiful and popular girls in school. She had silky waist-length ash-blonde hair and beautiful jade-green eyes with thick long lashes. She had a cute, slightly turned-up nose, which only added to her sometimes arrogant attitude, which was most of the time. She was the captain of the squad and the envy of most of the girls in the school. It wasn't only her looks they envied but the fact that she was dating the captain and quarterback of the Wildcats football team, Jonah Medley.

"Oh, hi, Alayna," Karlie said in her usual peppy voice as Alayna bent to get a drink of cold water from the fountain.

"I was just about to ask Addison if you two were coming to Isaac's birthday bash tonight."

If truth be known, Karlie was probably hoping they had not been invited. She would have loved to rub in the fact that she and Maddie, her best friend, had been invited to the party and the two of them had not. But before she could answer, Addison spoke up.

"I am, but Alayna isn't. She's too good to come to the party."

Karlie looked at Alayna with sincere surprise in her face and in her voice. "Really? Why on earth would you pass up this party? I mean, look at who is inviting you. I mean, this is basically a college party. I mean, what is wrong with you, girl?" Karlie was talking so fast she didn't even bother to take breaths between "I means."

Alayna finished gulping down the water then stood for a brief second looking at Addison, wondering why in the world she would give Karlie Adams any kind of ammunition. Everyone, including Addison, knew Karlie could be a nasty and cruel person at times.

She would smile at you to your face, then stab you in the back if she thought it would benefit her. She turned to Karlie, who was really starting to get on her last nerve.

"I mean it's personal," she said sarcastically as she walked between Karlie and Addison, giving Addison a slight brush with her shoulder.

Karlie looked at Addison and shrugged. Karlie, Maddie, and Addison headed back to the gym as they discussed what to wear to the party.

Addison felt bad as she watched Alayna walk to the gym in front of them. She wished she hadn't said anything about Alayna when Karlie asked if they were going to the party. Now watching her best friend walk alone made her regret the whole morning of events. Usually it was the two of them walking side by side. Even if she didn't agree with Alayna, she shouldn't have been so hateful to her. First she had been hateful to Ayson, and now Alayna.

Karlie stopped suddenly and put her hand out to stop her.

"You said Alayna was not coming to the party because she was too good to come. What did you mean by that?"

Addison gave a defeated sigh and started again for the practice area. She knew Karlie wouldn't give up until she answered her.

"It's her Christian beliefs. She doesn't want to be around people drinking alcohol and doing drugs. She just doesn't want to hurt her testimony, and it's her conviction that as Christians, we shouldn't drink alcohol, even socially."

The shrill sound of the coach's whistle alerted them that their break was over and it was time to get back to practice. They picked up their pace and headed back to the main part of the gym.

"You're kidding, right? I mean you're a Christian," Karlie said. "You don't see anything wrong with it, do you? I mean, what's a harmless drink or two? I mean, is Christianity really that boring? Because if it is, then I don't want any part of it, you know what I mean?"

Does this girl ever take a breath? Addison thought.

"Alayna just doesn't want to hurt her testimony, that's all," Addison said, finding herself coming to her best friend's defense.

She could take it no longer. Entering the practice area, she spotted Alayna doing leg stretches. Joining her, she apologized for being such a jerk. She could see Alayna felt as relieved as she did. After another hour of practice, it was time to go home. The two of them were so tired they decided to wait until they returned home to shower.

The rain had finally stopped, but the heavy rain had left large puddles of water in the potholes of the graveled parking lot. The school board had recently voted to repave the gym parking lot, but not before the upcoming summer.

On the south side of the gym where she had parked, there were twelve steps leading from the top of the gym to the parking lot. Addison and Alayna stood on the small concrete porch looking down at the long flight of steps, dreading the long walk. It hadn't been so bad when they had arrived earlier in the day before they were so tired and sore. Karlie was already on the bottom step. Maddie Watkins gave Addison and Alayna a vague smile as she walked past them, but did not bother to speak. As she walked briskly down the long flight of steps, her chestnut-brown ponytail swayed side to side.

"See you later, Karlie!" she yelled.

Karlie turned and waved. "Yeah, Maddie, see you later!" Then noticing Addison and Alayna standing at the top of the steps, she yelled, "See you at the party tonight, Addison! Too bad you can't be there too, Alayna. But after all, we wouldn't want you to ruin your testimony!"

Laughing, she turned again and started to step off the bottom step onto the parking lot when Alan Stellar came barreling past her in his truck. The truck hit one of the large puddles of water, causing the dirty water to splash Karlie and drench her from head to toe. Even her duffle bag which she had thrown across her shoulder was drenched. Karlie screeched and threw her hands into the air, and for a moment, she stood frozen in disbelief. Addison was trying hard not to laugh. She looked at Alayna, who just stood staring ahead at Karlie.

"God doesn't like ugly," Alayna said, barely above a whisper and without cracking a smile. Alayna's comment was funny, but the straight-faced expression as she spoke made it even funnier.

Addison lost it. She began laughing almost hysterically, which in turn seemed to snap Alayna out of her almost trancelike state. She too began laughing. Their laughter was so loud and out of control that Karlie turned around and, placing her hands on her hips, gave them a killer stare.

Alan, who had come to pick up his sister Louanne from practice, didn't even hit the brakes. As a matter of fact, he just blew the horn, stuck his long arm out the open window, waved at Karlie, and kept on trucking, as they say.

Addison wasn't really surprised at his action—well, maybe a little. Alan, a wide receiver for the Wildcats, and Karlie had dated for almost a year. However, she had broken up with him over the summer to date Jonah Medley, From what most people heard, it had not been a civil breakup. But what Addison couldn't understand was that Alan and Jonah seemed to have no problem with each other. They remained friends in spite of the situation. Alan appeared to blame only Karlie for the breakup. Just one more reason she didn't understand the male species.

As she and Alayna continued to laugh uncontrollably, Karlie finally stomped across the parking lot with Maddie running after her, asking if she was okay.

"Come on, Alayna. We need to head home. I'm getting hungry."

During the ride home the two called a truce on the subject of the party. Alayna again realized she wasn't God, and she could not change Addison, or anyone else for that matter. She would continue to pray for Addison and let God do His work in her. She realized God was doing a work in her as well. She was beginning to realize she could sometimes be too judgmental, and it was not pleasing to God. She had been called to love people, not judge them, even when she didn't agree with them.

Ten minutes later, Alayna stood in the driveway and watched Addison drive away. Pulling her Wildcats windbreaker tighter around herself, she shivered from the chilly October air, or could it be she was shivering from the uneasy feeling she had been having every time she thought of her friend? As she quickly walked into the comforting warmth of her home, she began to pray.

CHAPTER 5

THE PICTURES

Kyndal McNeely threw a load of white towels into the washer and wished she could have just one day to relax and not do anything. When she wasn't working the day shift as a nurse at Cherokee Memorial Hospital, she was busy doing housework. Now that the children were older, they would sometimes pitch in and help with the household chores, but they too seemed to stay busy with school activities and friends. Pushing her dark uncombed hair out of her eyes, she closed the washer lid and set it to the large setting. The water began to fill the machine as she made her way from the laundry room to the kitchen and sat at the small round table covered by a warm yellow tablecloth. Now that Addison had given her heart to the Lord and started to church, she was involved in even more activities. Church activities kept her busy when school activities didn't. Sometimes Addison was busy with both, and now Ayson was starting to get involved in church.

A couple of weeks ago, he had asked if he could go to church with Addison. Of course, she had allowed him to go. One thing she would never do would be to tell her children they could not go to church. Ayson was also becoming fast friends with Callaway Peters. It seemed music was something they both had in common. Callaway played the drums, and Ayson played guitar. Recently, Callaway had spoken to his parents about Ayson playing the guitar at church. The two had agreed and had approached Ayson to see if he would be interested. He had been beyond excited and was to start practicing with the music ministry next week. Playing his guitar at church was not the only thing he had been excited about. She couldn't get it out of her mind how happy and excited he had been when he had returned home one Sunday from church. He too had given his heart to the Lord. Now he was begging her to go to church.

It wasn't that she didn't believe God existed; she just didn't believe He was a good God. Besides, she worked every other weekend; and on her weekends off, she just wanted to sleep in. At least that was the excuse she gave to her children and everyone else. But she knew she was not fooling anyone, especially herself. The truth was, she didn't want to sit and hear someone preach about a merciful and loving God.

Over the years, as far as she was concerned, God had not shown her or her family anything close to mercy or love. He had taken her mother and father in a car crash when she was only nine years old. At age eighteen, the aunt she had been living with passed away with a massive heart attack, leaving Kyndal with no family until she met and married Josh. God had only shown her and her family loss, hurt, grief, loneliness, and most of all, emptiness. Her husband, Josh, had passed away almost four years earlier with colon cancer at only forty-three years of age. Where was God's love and mercy in that?

Her friends and coworkers kept telling her she needed to get out more, but who had the time or the energy? She most certainly did not. Plus, none of the men her friends and coworkers wanted to set her up with could measure up to Josh. He had been one of a kind and the love of her life. After his death, it had been her children and a few close friends who had kept her going, not God.

The washing machine was beginning the rinse cycle as she slid her chair away from the table. This weekend had been long awaited. Rarely were the children away from home at the same time, but tonight Ayson was staying with Caleb, and Addison was going to a birthday party with Alayna. If she could get all the housework done this morning she might actually have time by the afternoon to curl up on the sofa with a warm throw, a hot cup of cocoa, and a good romance novel.

Walking to the window above the kitchen sink, she pulled back the yellow rooster-patterned curtain and looked toward the huge oak tree located in the backyard. The old oak welcomed autumn as it flaunted its leaves in color combinations of coppers and yellows mixed with a sprinkling of bright reds. Josh's favorite time of the year had been spring "because everything is springing to life," he would always say. However, she had always loved the fall season. She loved the changing of the leaves and the cool crispness of the air. She also loved rain, which they had been getting a fair amount of lately. For most people, rain was depressing; but to her, it was rather relaxing.

Turning to the cabinet next to the window, she grabbed a mug and poured herself a large cup of steaming black coffee.

Pulling her well-worn robe tight around her, she sat at the kitchen table and picked up the morning paper. As was her usual routine, she began reading the obituaries first. She was relieved to find there was no one she knew, but felt for the families and friends of those who were listed. She continued to read world and local news as she debated whether or not to mop the kitchen floor since it was raining outside. She finally decided against it.

"Well, I'm not getting anything done just sitting here," she mumbled, swallowing her last sip of coffee. Her dark-brown eyes started to fill with tears as she headed for the hall closet. She grabbed the vacuum cleaner out of the closet and wheeled it toward the den. She missed Josh terribly. His death had left such a void in her life—and heart. Even when she was in a room full of people, she still felt alone. As she entered the tiny den, her eyes went to the family portrait hanging above the piano. Walking up to the portrait, she ran the back of her fingers softly across the face of her husband. Almost without realizing it, she spoke aloud.

"If God is such a good and loving God, then why did He take you away from the children and me?"

Josh had been a devout Christian and had tried to persuade her to accept Christ as her Savior for years. When he was alive, he would take the children to church with him, but could never talk her into going with them. After his death, she would drop the children off at church, and someone from the congregation would bring them home. Little by little, she took the children less often until eventually they didn't go at all. She was grateful Josh had not made her promise to take them. She knew he would be disappointed that she had not consistently taken the children to church, but after his death, she wanted even less to do with God. She had often wondered why God would take the one who served Him and leave behind the one who didn't want anything to do with Him.

She could not hold back the tears. Slumping into the oversized beige recliner her husband loved to sit in, she buried her face in her hands and let out the gut-wrenching cry she had been trying to hold back.

"Will I ever know happiness again?" she wondered aloud.

Soon she felt Chip on her lap and the gentle nudge of his cool nose against her hands. She grabbed Chip and held him tight.

"I know you miss him too, little fellow," she said as she continued to cry. As if he understood and was trying to wipe away the painful hurt, Chip gently licked her tear-stricken cheeks. Kyndal could see by his actions and his soft tender eyes that Chip somehow sensed the hurt behind every tear.

She tried to smile as she thought about when she first met Chip and how he had just shown up at their house one morning. He had a black collar around his neck that went well with his beautiful brown coat sprinkled with bits of black fur throughout. There had been no tag on the collar and no chip for identification. After days of trying to find the owner without success, Josh had decided he wanted to keep him. Kyndal had not been keen on the idea, but finally gave in, especially after realizing Chip was already housebroken. Of course, the children were more than overjoyed, promising to help take care of him. Josh had insisted she be the one to name the new family member. After giving it some thought, she had decided to name the playful pup Chip, given his medium-colored brown hair mixed with black throughout, which reminded her of a chocolate chip cookie.

Sobbing softly now, she felt it was more like Chip who had taken care of them, especially after Josh's death. He had been crazy over Chip and vice versa. Having him around made her feel as though a tangible part of Josh was still here—like now.

"Well, time for my pity party to be over," she said as she looked into Chip's big brown eyes. She spent a few seconds rubbing his soft fur and telling him what a good boy he was and how precious he was. Chip's tail wagged happily from side to side at the attention.

It was a half hour later from when she had first pulled the vacuum cleaner out of the closet that she finally plugged it into the outlet and began vacuuming the outdated gold carpet.

"Mom, I'm home!" Addison yelled as she entered the house and closed the door behind her. She could hear the loud hum of the vacuum cleaner coming from the den. "Mom!" she yelled even louder as she entered the doorway to the den. Chip, happy at seeing her, greeted her with his happy dance as she reached and gave him a gentle scratch behind his velvety ear.

Getting no response from her mother, Addison walked up and gently tapped her on the shoulder. Startled, her mother screamed and jumped, causing Addison to do the same. Chip gave a confused yelp. She saw the look of relief cross her mother's face as she realized it was her daughter and not some intruder. Kyndal turned off the vacuum.

"Don't do that!" she scolded. "You nearly caused me to jump out of my skin."

Addison noticed the red puffy eyes and knew her mother had been crying again because of her dad.

"I'm sorry, Mom. I called out to you several times, but you didn't hear me." She pretended not to see her mother slip the tissue into her robe pocket. Kyndal noticed her daughter trying to pretend not to see the tissue.

"My dang allergies again," she lied, although she wasn't sure Addison would believe her.

"Sorry to hear that, Mom." She saw her mother's face quickly turn a light shade of red, which was a telltale sign to anyone who knew her mother that she was not being truthful. Neither said anything further, feeling it was better to leave well enough alone. The few seconds of awkwardness between the two seemed a lot longer than it actually was before Addison excused herself to take a shower.

Chip returned to his bed beside the fireplace. Running up the stairs, she heard the hum of the vacuum start up.

* * * * *

After grabbing a towel and a washcloth from the upstairs hall closet, Addison decided to take a relaxing bath instead of a shower. The soothing effects of the warm water on her aching muscles were priceless. She had also added some lavender-scented bath oil to the water. The aroma was so pleasant she could have spent hours in the bathtub, but she didn't have hours. Just five more minutes, she thought as she closed her eyes and breathed in slow and deep in order to lavish the aroma of the refreshing lavender. Since her best friend had bailed on her and she didn't have to stop by and pick Alayna up, she could afford to take a few extra minutes to relax. After twenty minutes, she felt a little chilled as the water had begun to cool. Drying off quickly, she slid on her favorite terry-cloth robe before wrapping her hair in a towel and then made her way to the bedroom.

As she reached for the hand lotion sitting on her dresser, she accidently bumped the wooden handcrafted music box sitting on the edge, causing it to tumble to the floor. She let out a gasp and quickly reached to retrieve the treasured box.

"Please, God, don't let anything be broken," she prayed aloud as she cautiously opened the lid. The little ballerina wearing a white tutu with her arms held high above her head began to spin around and around. Breathing a sigh of relief, she softly sang the words to the familiar tune the music box was playing.

"You are so beauti—," she sang before emotion took over and she could no longer get the words out. Her mother and father had bought the beautiful walnut-stained music box with a violin inlay for her fourteenth birthday. However, they had given it to her a few weeks early because her father was afraid he would not live to see her birthday, and he was right. He had passed away exactly one month before her fourteenth birthday.

Reaching into the box with one hand and holding it tightly with the other, she took out a plain white envelope which held several pictures. She had looked at those pictures more times than she could count since her father's death. They were one of her most prized possessions. Her hands were a little shaky as she reached inside the envelope and removed the pictures. Making her way to the bed, she sat and carefully placed the music box beside her.

The first picture she looked at was a picture of her father holding her in front of the camera with his cheek pressed close to hers. She was tucked snuggly inside a pink baby blanket wearing a striped pink-and-white stockinet over her tiny head. Her dad was smiling ear to ear. He was definitely a proud father. It was the first picture taken of her at the hospital after she was born. On the back of the picture, her dad had written a promise to her. Her eyes began to water as she read, "My precious little angel, I promise to always love you unconditionally with all my heart until my dying breath…and thereafter. Love, Daddy." She smiled as she gently placed the picture back in the envelope.

The next picture had been taken at her first birthday party. She was wearing a bright yellow shirt with ruffles around the end of the long sleeves and hem of the shirt. The silver glittered words on the shirt read, "Daddy's Little Princess." She was sitting happily on her daddy's knee as he fed her a piece of chocolate birthday cake. She couldn't help but smile as she looked at the picture which captured her mouth and cheeks covered with delicious chocolate icing.

"What a mess," she said aloud with a chuckle. Addison turned the picture over and began to read, "My precious little princess has just turned one." Still staring at the promise, she reached and wiped away the tear that was beginning to slide down her cheek. "Another promise I give to you today. I promise when life gets messy, remember, together there isn't anything you and I can't handle. You can always come to me with anything. Love, Daddy."

Gently laying the picture aside, she looked at the third picture which had been taken when she was four years old. Her dad had been tossing her playfully into the air and catching her as she came down. Both were laughing, their faces full of joy. Her long straight hair was pulled back into pigtails. The picture was snapped just as her pigtails flew into the air with the toss of her dad's strong, safe arms. From the laughter on her face, she gathered she had not felt afraid at all. She read number three, "No matter how life may someday try and toss you around, I promise to always be there to catch you. Love, Daddy."

The next-to-the-last picture was taken when she was seven years old. She had fallen off a bicycle at a family reunion and scraped her knee. She still remembered her daddy running as fast as he could to get to her. Falling to his knees, he had scooped her into his comforting arms. As they clung tightly to each other, she had cried into his shoulder. She remembered him gently stroking her hair and assuring her with his soothing voice that everything was going to be all right. Still, after all these years, she could remember how comforted she had felt in her daddy's arms and the smell of his fresh spicy cologne. She turned the picture over and read aloud promise number four: "My sweet little Addison, I promise to always encourage you to get back up and try again when life knocks you down. Don't ever give up! I promise if you will always get back up, things will get better. Love, Daddy."

The last promise picture was taken when she was twelve years old at a cousin's wedding. At the reception while the music played, her dad had approached her, bowed, and asked if he could "have this dance."

"Yes, you may," she told him as she curtsied, and he had taken her by the hand. At the time, she thought her dad had been so silly, but she had decided to play along. Hand in hand, her daddy had guided her onto the dance floor. She remembered how they danced ever so gracefully. Her mom had taken the picture as her dad twirled her around and around on the dance floor. Turning over the picture, she read, "My little girl is growing up fast, yet another promise I do make. I promise one day to walk you down the aisle as you begin a journey with your one true love. A beautiful bride I know you will be, but just remember, you will always be my little girl to me. Love, Daddy." Addison took her robe and wiped away a single tear that had fallen onto the picture.

Then she recalled the horrible day her dad had called Ayson and her to his bedside. It was the night before he died. He had asked both of them to bring their "promise pictures," as he called them. As he held the two of them close with now weak and feeble arms, he had asked them to forgive him for not being able to keep all the promises he had made.

"The only one I can keep is the first one," he had told them. "I will always love you until my dying breath and thereafter."

Addison reached and took a tissue from the tissue box sitting on the nightstand beside her bed. The tears were flowing uncontrollably now.

"But I want you to know there is One who will always keep His promises and who will never leave you nor forsake you," he had continued. He had asked Ayson to hand him his Bible as their father's shaky hands turned to the book of Hebrews. He had then asked Addison to read. She remembered reading how God had promised to never leave nor forsake His own. She knew her father had asked her to read the scripture because he had become so weak and short of breath he could barely speak at times. Afterward, the three of them had held tightly to one another and sobbed unashamedly.

"Daddy, please don't leave us," she and Ayson had pleaded.

"I don't want to go," he had told them, his heart breaking as he tried to blink back the tears.

"Daddy, please! Please don't die!" they continued to plead.

"Listen to me," he told them as he looked into their anguished and tear-stricken faces. "There is one more promise I am going to make, and I will be able to keep it. I promise to see you and your mother again someday. I promise, I promise!"

He had grabbed them and held them as tight as he could. Their mother, who had been crying softly in the background, soon joined them as they cried and held one another as a family for the last time.

Josh McNeely died early the next morning. Kyndal and the hospice nurse Mary, along with Pastor Bryce were at his bedside as he drew his last breath. As Addison and Ayson slept in the early hours of the morning, they had no idea they would never again awaken to the sound of their daddy's voice telling them how much he loved them.

However, except for leaving his family behind, Josh McNeely had been at peace with his passing.

Upon their dad's headstone was engraved the last promise he had made to them on his deathbed: "I am in your future. I promise I will see you again." Below that was inscribed "Loving Husband and Father."

Addison was so absorbed in the moment she was startled when she heard her mother calling from downstairs.

"Addison, are you not ready by now? You need to come down and eat something. I've made egg salad sandwiches." Until now she had forgotten she still had not eaten.

"Coming, Mom!" she yelled as she placed the last picture in the envelope and then into the music box. This time, she sat the box well away from the edge of the dresser.

* * * * *

When Addison entered the kitchen, her mom was sitting at the table taking a bite of her sandwich with one hand and pouring a glass of iced tea with the other.

"Tea, water, or Diet Coke?" her mother asked as Addison slid into a chair.

"Tea will be fine," she said, reaching for a sandwich. Until she bit into the creamy egg sandwich, she had not realized just how hungry she was.

"Umm, this is delicious, Mom," she said, taking another bite.

Her mother handed her the glass of tea and took a seat across from Addison. "What were you doing up there? I thought you would have been down before now."

"I was just looking at some old photos," she answered, hoping her mother would not ask which photos.

"Oh," was all her mother said.

Addison figured her mother knew exactly which photos she was referring to. Neither apparently wanting to discuss them turned their conversation to other things, mostly of how cheer practice went. She told her mother about Alan and what he had done to Karlie, which made her mother actually laugh, something her mother seldom did anymore. Everything was going okay until she went to the sink to put away her glass.

"What time are you picking Alayna up for the party?" her mother asked.

The question, as innocent as it was, caught Addison off guard. As she started to turn and face her mother, she noticed a chewy candy bar lying on the countertop next to her. Grabbing the candy bar, she quickly unwrapped it and took a big bite. Chewing slowly and deliberately, she held up her index finger as if to say, *Give me a moment*, like in one of the old candy commercials a few years back. Chewing the same gooey bite over and over, she tried to think of a way to answer her mother's question. She didn't want to lie to her, but she didn't want to tell her mother the truth about why she would not be picking up her best friend. As far as her mother knew Alayna was still going to the party, and Addison was not about to tell her any different. She finally swallowed the bite of candy.

"I don't have to pick Alayna up. We're not riding together tonight."

Her mother had a puzzled look on her face, and Addison could pretty much guess what the next question was going to be.

"Why not?" her mother asked, turning to face her. *Yep, that was the question*. Needing another *moment*, she took another bite of the candy bar.

Finally swallowing the gooey caramel and trying not to choke on the lie, she answered, "Well, we weren't sure if we would want to leave at the same time or not, so we decided to drive separately. We're going to follow each other instead."

She didn't want to lie to her mother, but that is exactly what she did. She felt the Holy Spirit's gentle conviction for lying but brushed the voice aside. Besides, what other choice did she have? If her mother knew she and Alayna had had a disagreement over going to a party, she would want to know why. Anyway, it was just a little white lie. *It's not hurting anyone*, she told herself trying to justify lying to her mother.

For a brief moment, her mother gave her one of those looks that said, *I don't know if I believe you or not*. After what seemed an eternity, her mother turned back around in her chair and didn't say anything further.

Addison felt her face getting warm and knew it was turning red. Like mother, like daughter, she thought. Neither one of them were very good liars, not that there was ever anything good about lying. Afraid her mother would notice her red face, she quickly dismissed herself saying she had to dry her hair and decide on what to wear. She practically took two steps at a time trying to make sure she got away from her mother in case she decided to ask her anything further.

She had told her mother earlier that a group from church was going to a birthday party for one of their friends. It was true that some of the others from the church would be at the party and Isaac was their friend, but she had not told her mother where the party would be and whom it was for. Her mother would never approve of high school students and college students partying together, let alone a party that was not chaperoned at her age. When it came to chaperones, she had not exactly lied about that. Her mother had just assumed there would be adults from the church chaperoning. She had just chosen not to correct her mother on that assumption. After all, it wasn't her fault her mother had assumed wrong, right?

* * * * *

Kyndal heard the sound of the hair dryer from upstairs. She didn't believe a word Addison had said about why she and Alayna were not riding together. She had debated on questioning her daughter further but had decided against it. She assumed since some of the kids from church were going to the party that it must be one of their birthdays. She had not thought to ask Addison whose birthday it was. After thinking on the subject a little longer, she convinced herself it was probably nothing. After all, they were teenagers, and it was not unusual for teenagers, especially teenage girls, to have mood swings. They had probably had some kind of little tiff that would blow over before all was said and done. She felt relieved to know she had finally completed the housework. Soon she would have the rest of the day to relax and do nothing except curl up with a good book. Little did she know her world was about to be turned upside down—again.

CHAPTER 6

THE PARTY

Alayna called Addison one last time to see if she would change her mind about going to the party, but no such luck. Although there was no argument, she could tell from Addison's tone she didn't want to discuss the subject any further. Alayna still could not shake the uneasy feeling something terrible was going to happen. She felt the Holy Spirit prompting her to pray for her best friend. Kneeling beside her bed, she tried to find the words to pray, but her heart was so heavy with concern she could only cry. She was glad God understood tears when words would not come.

* * * * *

Addison could say one thing about her best friend, she was persistent. Cramming the phone into her purse, she checked herself in the mirror one last time. The blue denim skinny jeans tucked inside black knee boots coordinated with a deep purple pullover sweater met her approval. She grabbed the heavy ICHS varsity jacket hanging over the bedpost and headed downstairs.

Entering the den, she saw her mother stretched out on the sofa engrossed in a romance novel with a throw across her lap. Chip was curled on her mother's lap with his eyes closed wearing his gray sweater that read "Spoiled" in red lettering. She smelled the aroma of hot chocolate and marshmallows and noticed the mug sitting on the coffee table.

Her mother looked up from her book when Addison entered the room. Watching her daughter, she had second thoughts about asking whose birthday party she and Alayna would be attending. It was better to know something than just to assume, especially with teenagers.

"By the way, whose birthday is it?" she asked.

Addison felt her heart skip a beat. *Where was that dang candy bar when you needed it?*

"Just a guy from church," she answered, hoping her face wasn't turning red. "You wouldn't know him."

Addison thought she had told more lies in one day than she had her entire life. Again she felt the gentle nudging of the Holy Spirit, and again she brushed Him aside. As they said their goodbyes, she leaned and kissed her mother on the cheek. Chip barely gave her a glance before he closed his eyes again and buried his nose into the warm throw. Addison turned on the porch light and locked the door behind her as she made her way to the car. Saturday night had finally arrived. For some reason, she felt mixed emotions at the moment. Part of her was excited and looking forward to tonight while another part of her felt uneasy. It was Alayna's fault, she reasoned. Why hadn't Alayna just left well enough alone and let her enjoy the night?

* * * * *

The party was starting at eight o'clock at the north end section of the Broad River off River Road a couple of miles from the main highway. There were already a number of cars parked on the side of the road when she arrived ten minutes later. She could see the warm yellowish-orange glow of campfires and lanterns from the road and feel vibrations from car stereos as rap music blasted through the night air. She wondered how anyone could understand the words to any of the music as several different songs played at the same time. Roars of laughter rang out as she parked on the side of the gravel road and began walking toward the party. The air was cold and damp from all the rain they had experienced earlier. She pulled her jacket tighter around herself and continued walking toward the music and laughter.

She wished Alayna had not bailed on her. Although she knew other people who were coming to the party, it just wasn't the same without her best friend. They were used to doing everything together.

She carefully made her way down the beaten, worn path made by years of people trampling their way to the clearing next to the river. A stick snapped loudly under her foot as she approached the cleared area, causing almost everyone who was near to turn and look her way. Karlie was sitting in a lawn chair next to the campfire sipping on a bottle of beer. She turned briefly to look at Addison before quickly turning her attention back to Jonah, who was sitting in a chair beside her. Many students had brought quilts and blankets and placed them on the ground to sit on.

"Great! Why didn't I think to bring something to sit on?" she mumbled to herself. She heard Karlie give one of her "I means" but couldn't hear the rest of the conversation.

"Addie, you made it!"

She turned to see Isaac walking toward her holding a bottle of beer in each hand.

"Hi, Isaac," she said as he handed her one of the bottles. Taking the cold beer, she took a small sip and then smiled at Isaac.

"Glad you could make it," he said. "Hey, where's your sidekick?" he asked, looking around in case he had missed Alayna in the crowd.

Before giving him an answer, she took another sip of beer. "She wasn't able to make it tonight. She sends her regrets," she lied—again.

"Why don't you tell him the truth, Addison?"

She looked over Isaac's shoulder and saw Karlie, Jonah, and Trevor Grant, one of the teenagers from her youth group, walking toward them. Her jaw tightened, and her eyes narrowed as she looked at Karlie, wanting nothing more at that moment than to punch her right in her lovely face. Annoyed and not seeing Maddie, Addison asked, "Where's your sidekick?"

"Unfortunately, her parents made her go out of town with them this weekend," Karlie said, putting the beer bottle to her lips.

Addison further tried to change the subject by commenting on how chilly the night air was, but Karlie would not let it drop.

"I mean, go on," she said again. "Tell Isaac why "*Laney*," she said, making air quotes with her fingers, "really isn't here."

Isaac looked at Addison, waiting for an answer, but instead of giving him an answer, she turned toward Karlie and told her to shut up. From the smug smirk on her face, she could tell Karlie was enjoying the uncomfortable situation she had placed her in. She suspected this was Karlie's payback for earlier when she and Alayna had laughed at her after Alan had given her a mud bath with his truck.

"Okay, Isaac," Karlie spoke up, "I'll tell you why Alayna isn't here, I mean, since Addison won't tell you." Before continuing, she took a big swallow of beer. "Ms. Goodie Two-Shoes Alayna doesn't want to ruin her testimony as one of those stuffy, boring Christians. I mean, can you believe that!"

Laughter rang out from Karlie, then from Isaac, and anyone else within earshot, except for Trevor and Addison. She wanted to run and hide. She felt bad her best friend was being laughed at and mocked for being a Christian. The fact she didn't even have the guts to take up for her friend made her feel sick to her stomach. She wasn't joining in the laughter, but she wasn't exactly standing up for Alayna either. Addison looked around at the laughing faces and wondered why it was so important for her to be accepted by this bunch of morons, but it was. Just as she thought things couldn't get any worse, it did.

"Laney needs to loosen up and be cool Christians like you and Trevor," Isaac announced loudly as he looked at the two. Still holding the beer, Isaac let out a laugh, then reached and tapped his beer bottle to hers. She glanced at Trevor, and their eyes met for a brief moment. He looked about as miserable as she did.

Trevor Grant was the center for the Wildcats and was in his last year of high school as well. Addison thought he looked more suited for basketball than football with his tall height and long arms. He had to be at least six feet, two inches tall. She had spoken to him a few times at the youth meetings, but she really didn't know him that well.

"Hey, everybody!" Isaac yelled, holding up a bottle of beer above his head. "Let's drink to Laney and her not wanting to taint herself by hanging around a bunch of sorry sinners like us."

Sounds of laughter and the clinking of glass beer bottles rang out. Addison listened as a crowd of her peers raised their bottles and simultaneously cried, "Hear, hear!" as they made fun of her friend. Tears began to well up in her eyes. She was not about to give Karlie the satisfaction of seeing her cry. In the distance, thanks to the full moon, she could barely make out a huge log lying next to the river-bank. Pulling her jacket even tighter, she headed as fast as she could for the log.

"Hey, where're you going?" Isaac asked.

She ignored his question and made her way past him. Isaac reeked of beer, and she could tell he was already half plastered.

"Whatever!" he yelled.

Sitting on the damp log, she threw the bottle of beer into the river. She knew she was littering, but right now littering was the fur-thest thing from her mind. It was cooler away from the campfires, and after a few minutes, her toes felt almost frozen. Fighting back tears, she stared into the murky waters of the Broad River. It was darker away from the campfires and lanterns, but the full moon was emitting enough light that she could still see the calm rippling of the water. The continual sounds of the water lapping against the river-bank and the shrill chirping of the crickets were starting to relax her. Occasionally, among all the chirping, she would hear the deep croak of a bullfrog.

She could also hear the laughter and music from the campsite intensifying. The combination of those two things could only mean there were more people piling into the party or more people getting lit, probably both.

Some birthday party this had turned out to be, she thought. There wasn't even a cake. The smell of roasted wieners and toasted marshmallows was making her a little hungry, but she didn't want to go back to the campfires and be around her so-called friends any lon-ger. Alayna was right in not coming. Of course, Addison had known that from the beginning. She had felt the gentle tugging of the Holy Spirit in her heart telling her not to come, but she had ignored Him.

Her thoughts were interrupted as someone yelled to Isaac that some of them were getting low on beer. The party had hardly begun, and they were already low on beer? That was another bad sign. Most of the students at the party were at least twenty-one years of age and legally old enough to drink alcohol, but there were a handful of students who were not of legal age.

Addison jumped at the sound of someone walking up behind her. She turned to see Trevor walking toward her with a paper plate in each hand. Both plates were filled with a hot dog and chips. Draped over his left and right shoulders were a couple of blankets.

"I thought you might be a little hungry," he said as he handed her one of the plates and a canned soft drink he pulled from his coat pocket. "I hope you like mustard and ketchup on your dogs," he said as he took a bite from his hot dog and sat next to her.

"Thanks, Trevor," she said, taking the plate. "I am a little hungry."

Standing up, he handed her his plate. "I brought you a blanket too. I noticed when you came in you didn't have one with you. I happened to have an extra one in the trunk of the car. If you want, I can spread one across the log, and we can throw the other blanket over our legs.

"Sure, that would be great. Thanks again, Trevor," she said as she stood for him to place the blanket over the log.

Trevor Grant had dark-blue eyes and slightly long brown hair with natural golden highlights. He absentmindedly brushed some of his hair from his eyes before spreading the blanket over the log. The thick, dry blanket felt a lot more comfortable and warm than the log alone. For a while, they sat in silence eating their hot dogs and drinking Cokes.

Addison had never seen this side of Trevor before. Usually, he was of the quiet sort and came across to her as being a little on the shy side, unlike tonight. Could it be he just never had anything he wanted to say in the youth meetings, or because he always seemed to be at a loss for words when he was around Alayna? She had once told

Alayna she thought Trevor had a crush on her, but Alayna had just rolled her eyes and said, "Yeah, right." Trevor finally broke the silence with his deep bass voice.

"Listen, Addison, don't pay any attention to Isaac and Karlie. They can act like jerks sometimes. Well, maybe more than sometimes," he said, smiling. His comment brought a smile to her face. It felt nice to have someone to talk to at the moment, especially someone who wasn't trying to make her look stupid in front of everyone and who wasn't putting down her best friend.

"I wonder if we aren't the bigger jerks," she said as she bit into her hot dog.

"What do you mean?" he asked with a puzzled look on his face. She swallowed and took a sip of Coke before answering him.

"Well, you and I both are Christians and belong to the FCA, but look where we are right now. I bet even Jesus thinks we're big jerks."

Trevor thought for a second about what she had just said. "I think the word you're looking for is hypocrites. We're just big hypocrites." For some reason, the use of the word hypocrite seemed to cut through her like a knife. Maybe it was because Jesus had spoken not so kindly about such people.

"I wouldn't exactly call us hypocrites, Trevor. Just because we've attended a party we shouldn't be at and took a few sips of beer doesn't make us hypocrites," she said defensively.

"Maybe, maybe not, but Alayna's right. We are hurting our testimony. Who would ever want to listen to anything we had to say about God? We're acting no different than the world."

She unfortunately found no way to argue his point.

After finishing their food and drinks, they prayed and asked God to forgive them. They asked Him to forgive them for being weak Christians and hypocrites, or at least for being jerks.

Gathering up the blankets and trash, they headed back toward the campsite and vowed never to let themselves get into another situation as they were in tonight.

"Hey, you two," Isaac called to them as they neared one of the campfires. "Where have you been? I've been looking all over for you."

Addison doubted he had been looking "all over" for them; they hadn't been that far away from the campsite.

"You two are missing all the fun!" he exclaimed, his words slurring from his drunken state. Jonah and Karlie were still joined at Isaac's hip. "I sent Tyler for some more beer. He's got connections up the road," Isaac said as he threw an empty beer bottle on the ground. "You two never did answer me," Isaac said upon reaching them and throwing his arm around Trevor's shoulder. "Where were you, man?"

"We were just enjoying the peace and quiet of the river," Trevor answered, trying to change the subject.

"What? Alone?" Karlie asked, "I mean, aren't you two afraid of ruining your testimony?"

Enough was enough. Karlie just wouldn't shut up! If Addison was going to lose her testimony, it was going to be from knocking the living daylights out of Karlie. She had taken all she was going to take from the little bleach-bottled blonde witch.

"That's enough, Karlie!" she said as she threw the blanket on the ground. With her fist clenched tight, she started for Karlie. Karlie looked a little taken aback when she saw Addison move toward her. She moved slightly behind Jonah. Addison was so mad she was nearly in tears. If she had to go straight through him to get to Karlie, she would.

"Catfight!" yelled Isaac, causing numerous others to gather around.

Suddenly she felt someone grab her by the arm.

"It's not worth it," she heard Trevor say. She jerked away from his gentle grip and knew he was right. Sighing, she looked at Karlie, then back at Trevor.

"I'm out of here," she told him.

"That makes two of us," he replied as he bent and picked up the blanket from the ground.

Addison started past Karlie, but Karlie, thinking she would be safe because Trevor had stopped Addison once, took one last stab. The *clucking* sound she let out proved to be one stab too many. Before she had time to think, Addison turned with a tightly clenched fist and swung as hard as she could across Karlie's left jaw. The perfectly placed right hook knocked the dazed Karlie to the ground. With an icy stare, Addison looked cold and hard into the shocked face of Karlie as she lay on the ground propped on an elbow, rubbing her throbbing jaw.

"Whoa!" the crowd of surprised bystanders unanimously yelled, including Trevor. This time, Trevor hadn't tried to stop her, not that he would have had time; it happened so fast. It was either that, or he had had enough of Karlie as well. One last option would be that he was afraid of being the next to feel her fist of fury had he tried to intervene. Without so much as a flinch, Addison, still glaring at Karlie, warned her through gritted teeth and clenched fists.

"Stay down, Karlie! Don't you dare get up!"

Jonah reached to help Karlie to her feet, but she just pulled away from him and kept rubbing her jaw. Apparently, she had decided to take Addison's advice and stay down. He walked away, and so did everyone else when they realized the fight, if that's what you could call it, was over.

She heard Micah Lynn, from her physics class, asking no one in particular when Tyler was going to be back with the beer. Addison gave an eye roll. More beer—just what everyone needs, she thought. She stomped angrily toward her car, not waiting for Trevor.

"Hey, wait up!" Trevor yelled as he caught up to her.

She stopped and looked at him. "I know!" she said, a little sternly than she meant to.

"Know what?" he asked.

"I should have turned the other cheek," she said as she started again for the car. Then she turned, rather abruptly, causing Trevor to nearly run her over. "But she deserved it," she said, looking at him as if daring him to disagree.

Meeting her cool gaze, Trevor made no comment. Getting no argument from him, she once again turned and started to her car. She felt bad for lashing out at Trevor. After all, he had done nothing wrong. *What am I trying to do, start a fight with Trevor?* She still felt as if she wanted to hit someone. She almost wished Karlie had gotten back on her feet.

Finally reaching her car, she took a few deep breaths to try and calm down.

"I'm sorry, Trevor," she apologized. "I didn't mean to take it out on you. Karlie just makes me so mad."

"That's okay," he said. "No harm done."

Trevor was really a nice guy, she thought as she thanked him again for the food and blankets and reached into her jacket pocket for her keys. She unlocked the door, and sliding behind the steering wheel, she cranked the motor and turned the heat on high. Trevor shut her door, and she rolled down the window.

"From what I could see earlier," he said out of the blue, "Tyler was really wasted."

"Surely no one would sell him beer if he's that drunk," she said. Trevor stood with the blankets tucked under his arms and his hands in his pockets. The night air was getting colder.

"Tyler has a cousin who works at LD's Qwik Mart just up the road. You can bet he will sell Tyler the beer no matter how wasted he is. Never mind the fact he is under age. I'm sure that's why Isaac sent him."

Addison knew the store he was referring to. It was owned by L. D. Myers, who was also a member of the town council. She was sure he would never approve of one of his employees selling alcohol to underaged students. She contemplated how more than half the people at the party were going to make it home in one piece. She had never seen so much alcohol and drinking in her life. She was almost positive there were more plastered bodies at the party than there were designated drivers.

She noticed Trevor shivering and his fair-skinned cheeks turning red from the cold and light breeze that had been blowing most of the night. She decided to quit talking so much and let him get to his car. They said their good-nights as Trevor walked to his car.

"See you tomorrow at church!" he yelled over his shoulder. Addison knew she was going to have to eat crow, but she was going to admit to Alayna tomorrow that she was right about Isaac's party: she shouldn't have come.

Rolling up her window, she waved goodbye to Trevor and pulled onto the graveled road. The sound of loose gravel hit the under carriage of her car as she picked up speed. She slowed a little and then proceeded. From the light of the moon, she could see where the river had overflowed the banks at some of the low-lying areas. Some of the grounds leading up to the graveled road had flooded, but fortunately, the actual road had not. After almost two miles of loose gravel and slow going, she pulled onto the smooth top of the main highway. As she headed north on Highway 29, she glanced at the green digital numbers displayed on the car panel. The clock read 9:15 p.m. She could hardly believe she had been at the party for just a little over an hour. It seemed a lot longer.

Now that she was on the main road, she was able to increase her speed, but she still needed to drive carefully. The roads were still wet from the earlier rain, and the shaded areas of the road were especially wet. It had been a long and steady rain. She knew the roads would be slippery, and the rain could cause tires to lose traction. Glancing in her rear-view mirror, she could see in the distance the headlights of a car pulling onto the main highway from River Road. She guessed it was Trevor. For some reason, knowing he was behind her made her feel a little safer. She looked away from the rear-view mirror and turned back to the road in front of her just in time to see headlights coming toward her. She was almost even with the oncoming car when the driver suddenly swerved into her lane and came at her head-on. She showered down on the horn and at the same time attempted to veer her car toward the right of the road to avoid a collision. It was too late.

CHAPTER 7

THE ACCIDENT

The bright lights from the approaching vehicle lit up the entire interior of Addison's car. She wasn't able to see anything except for the blinding lights, but she was able to hear the sound of screeching tires blending with the sound of her terrified screams. She threw her hands over her face.

The strong smell of burning rubber filled her nostrils. She had swerved, but in doing so, it caused the oncoming car to hit near the driver's side of the door instead of head-on sending her car into a tailspin. Not only was her car spinning, but her head as well. She felt dizzy and sick to her stomach as the car finally hit something hard, giving her a terrible jolt and causing the air bag to release. She heard the shattering of glass. At least the spinning had stopped, but what had she hit? Glancing out the shattered window in front of her, it looked as if she had hit some kind of pole.

A terrible pain shot through her entire body, especially her left leg. She tried to move it, but couldn't. The more she tried to raise her head the more light-headed she became. Something warm and sticky was running down her left leg and the left side of her face. She knew it was blood, her blood. She was starting to panic; she couldn't breathe.

"Breathe, stay calm, and don't panic," she told herself aloud. A loud popping noise coming from outside the car wasn't helping her to stay calm. She tried to shift her body so she could look and see where the sound was coming from, but she could barely move. The blood running down the left side of her forehead along with the salty sweat ran into her eye, causing it to sting. The pain in her leg was excruciating with the slightest move. She had been thrown into a somewhat lying position, making it hard to see over the doors and dashboard. She looked around for her cell phone and found it lying on the floorboard of the car on the passenger's side—out of reach. The steering wheel had her pinned at the waist, and her left leg was trapped.

She felt warm tears trickle down her cheeks and mix with the blood and sweat on her face. She tried not to think about that but instead tried to think of how she was going to get out of the car.

Her thoughts drifted to the driver of the other car. Was the driver alive or dead, needing help? Had anyone seen the accident? Wait! Wasn't that Trevor behind her as they were coming down the road? Surely he had seen what happened, so where was he? Why wasn't he helping her? Had he called for help?

She noticed her breathing was becoming more rapid and shallow, and her skin was cool and clammy. She knew these were signs of shock. She tried to lay flatter in the seat, but no way could she elevate her feet higher than her head. She was feeling light-headed. She tried to control her breathing and stay calm, but she knew she was on the verge of panic. "Lord, please help me!" she prayed in desperation. She heard ringing in her ears. No, wait—it was sirens!

* * * * *

Trevor could see red tails lights in front of him as he pulled onto the main highway in his white Nissan. He had washed his car the day before, but now it was a mess from all the rain. He smiled as he thought about how it always seemed to rain every time he washed his car, kind of like having an itch in an area where you couldn't reach. You could always count on both.

He was glad to be going home. It had been a wasted night, but he knew it was nobody's fault but his own. He thought about Addison as well as himself. Why do Christians feel like they still have to fit in with the world, even after they get saved? He thought about the scripture Pastor Bryce had preached on just a few Sundays ago. He began to meditate on the scripture Paul the apostle had written through the inspiration of the Holy Spirit for Christians not to conform themselves to the world but to be transformed by the renewing of their mind. It most certainly wasn't God's will for him to be at that party. He recalled Pastor Bryce saying you renew your mind by reading and studying the Word of God. Reading was not one of his favorite things to do, but that was no excuse in today's world. There were videos, audio tapes, and—

His thoughts were suddenly interrupted when in the distance he noticed the car ahead of him heading toward the side of the road. He then noticed another car had veered into the wrong lane. He watched helplessly as one car went into a tailspin, spinning several times before running off the road. He was close enough to hear the car crash hard against something, but he couldn't make out what. A few seconds later, he reached the accident and pulled onto the same side of the road where the one car had spun off into a field. He could now see the car had hit a utility pole head-on. It didn't occur to him until he saw the large electrical wire dancing all around the red Ford Focus that it was Addison's car.

"Oh God, no, please let her be all right!" he prayed. Trevor could hear the panic in his voice as his heart raced faster and faster. The other car, a blue convertible Mustang, was banged up in front and sitting in the middle of the road. He could see blood on the windshield of the driver's side. It looked as if the airbag might not have deployed.

"Tyler!" He gasped, finally recognizing the car.

"Please God, let them both be all right," he prayed again.

"I can't believe this is happening!" he said aloud as he pulled the cell phone from his pants pocket. His hands were trembling almost uncontrollably as he struggled to dial three simple numbers.

"This is 911," he heard the operator say, "what is your emergency?"

Trevor gave the operator his name and other information she requested. He explained to her about the live electrical wire dancing and throwing sparks around Addison's car. There was no way he could get to her car to check on her. With puddles of water on the poorly drained road, he wasn't sure about getting out of the car to check on Tyler either. He could see the electrical sparks occasionally shoot across the wet road. He knew the water would be a conductor. From where he was parked, he could see Tyler raise his head from the steering wheel. He froze as he saw him trying to push the door open. He knew if Tyler stepped on the wet road, he could be electrocuted.

"No, Tyler!" he yelled as loud as he could. "Don't get out of the car!" Either Tyler couldn't hear him, or he was so dazed from the crash he didn't comprehend what Trevor was trying to tell him. Trevor heard the 911 operator trying to get his attention.

"Trevor! Trevor! Tell me what is happening."

Not having time to explain the situation to her, he hung up. Tyler was still attempting to push the door open to get out of the car. He knew he was going to have to act quickly before Tyler succeeded in what could possibly mean a sure death for him. He turned the key to his ignition, jerked the gear into drive, and gunned the gas pedal as hard as he could. Tyler had finally gotten the door partially opened.

"Please, Lord, don't let Tyler get out of that car," Trevor prayed as he sped quickly to pull within inches of Tyler's car, blocking the door and leaving Tyler unable to completely open the door. Tyler looked half dazed and a little shocked as he attempted to say something, but before he could protest, he slumped over into the seat.

Trevor had never been so glad a few minutes later to see red flashing lights and to hear the welcoming sound of those irritating sirens. The paramedics and utility workers had made it to the scene of the accident within a minute of one another: one advantage of living in a small town. Once the power was cut and there was no longer any danger of being electrocuted, the medical teams rushed immediately to the aid of Addison and Tyler.

In the meantime, he answered, to the best of his knowledge, the questions the highway patrolman asked him regarding the accident.

Earlier while waiting for medical and power personnel to arrive, he had called Pastor Bryce and Alayna. Maggie Peters was going to notify Kyndal McNeely in person, and Pastor Bryce was going to notify Tyler's parents. Trevor remembered seeing Tyler's parents at New Haven, but he had only been attending the church for about four months and did not really know them. It just occurred to him he had never seen Tyler attend church with his parents.

"He's unconscious…and reeks of alcohol," Trevor heard one of the EMS workers say as they transferred Tyler to the stretcher and placed him in the back of the ambulance. Trevor could still see the bright-red blood blending with Tyler's dark hair, even though part of his head was covered with a bloodstained bandage. Tyler had also failed to wear his seat belt, which explained why he had been thrown into the windshield. Upon hearing this, he was surprised Tyler had not been thrown completely through the windshield. He tried to ask if Tyler would be all right, but all he could get out of the EMS workers was that it was too early to tell.

The night was ablaze with flashing red and blue lights from the emergency vehicles and the highway patrol. Trevor heard the siren as the ambulance headed to the hospital with Tyler.

News was now getting out about the accident as curious motorists passing by Tweeted and texted. Some of the other students from the party had made it to the scene of the accident, but they were motioned through to keep traffic moving at a reasonable flow. It's a good thing the officer wasn't stopping cars and checking for DUIs, Trevor thought. He didn't see Isaac drive by, and then remembered Isaac lived in the opposite direction. He couldn't help but wonder what would go through Isaac's mind when he learned Tyler was the cause of the accident. After all, he had known how wasted Tyler was when he sent him for more beer, not that Tyler shouldn't have known better himself.

Trevor had tried to get close to Addison as well, but had been motioned to stay back by the emergency workers. Finally, one of the paramedics came hurrying up the embankment from where her car had left the road. Trevor tried to ask the athletically built man if she was all right, but the man just kept walking as if he didn't hear him. Frustrated and determined to get some kind of an answer, he grabbed the man by the arm.

"Please, sir, she's my friend," Trevor pleaded.

Hunter Stone was about to give the young man a piece of his mind. Couldn't the young man see he was in a hurry and that every second counted? Why couldn't people understand that and just leave them alone to do their jobs? But seeing the fear and concern on the young man's face, and thinking he must be getting soft in his old age, he answered, "Son, I'm going to be honest. She's alive, but we're going to have to use the Jaws of Life to get her out. We'll know more about her condition then."

Hunter, seeing the disbelief in the young man's eyes and watching every bit of color drain from his face, added, "I'm sorry, son. We're working as fast as we can." He sighed and gave Trevor a quick pat on the shoulder as he hurried on his way. After taking a few seconds to absorb what he had been told, Trevor called after him.

"Is there anything I can do to help?"

"Pray!" Hunter yelled over his shoulder without stopping or turning around.

Trevor heard someone calling his name. He turned to see Pastor Bryce, his wife, Maggie, and Kyndal McNeely hurrying toward him. Close behind were Tyler's parents, Bryan and Rebekah Morris. One of the officers had let them through after finding out who they were. Trevor noticed Kyndal, Maggie, and Rebekah all had red swollen eyes from crying. Bryan Morris looked as if he was literally holding his wife up to keep her from collapsing. Trevor filled them in on what he knew, which wasn't much.

"Alayna and her mother had wanted to come," said Maggie. "But I convinced them to stay home and pray for the time being. They finally agreed it was the best way to help their friend and Tyler, but I had to promise to keep them apprised of the situation."

The medical team supervisor refused to let them come near the car, but did give Hunter Stone permission to keep them posted on Addison's condition and how much closer they were to getting her out of the crumpled car.

Bryan and Rebekah Morris, along with Pastor Bryce, left for the hospital upon hearing Tyler was already on his way. Maggie and Trevor stayed with Kyndal, who appeared to look pale and somewhat dazed as if she had just awoken from a bad dream.

* * * * *

Addison kept trying to go to sleep. She was just so tired, but she knew the paramedics wouldn't let her sleep due to the possibility of a concussion. They wouldn't know if she had one for sure until they arrived at the hospital and ran some test. They had given her a blanket through the window, but she was still freezing. Her left leg still felt numb, and she couldn't feel her toes move when she tried to bend them. Her skin wasn't clammy, and her breathing had slowed, so at least that was a plus. She felt tired and sleepy.

"Addison, stay with me. We've almost got you out of here. Addison, my name is Hunter. I'm one of the paramedics, and I'm here to help you. Don't close your eyes, okay? Talk to me. How many fingers am I holding up? What year is it? Who is the current president of the United States?" On and on the questions went. She didn't feel like talking anymore.

"Leave me alone," she tried to yell, but it barely came out above a whisper. Something was on her face. She tried to pull it off, but someone pulled her hand away, telling her not to pull the oxygen mask off. She sensed what felt like a bee sting to her right arm.

"I've got an IV going," she heard a man say in a deep voice.

"We've got her!" she heard someone else yell. It wasn't long before her limp body was being lifted by strong arms.

"Daddy?" she asked, barely above a whisper.

"Lift her onto the stretcher and be careful," she heard the man with the deep voice say. The jarring from the moving stretcher caused the searing pain in her left leg to intensify with the restored circulation. She winced as a flood of tears flowed down her face. The stretcher stopped momentarily.

"Honey, it's me, Mom. You're going to be all right," she said, taking her daughter by the hand and giving it a reassuring squeeze.

"Where did Daddy go?" Addison asked, still sobbing uncontrollably. Kyndal and Maggie looked at each other, then back to Addison.

"Honey, what are you talking about?" asked Kyndal before she was interrupted.

"I'm sorry, ma'am, but we need to get your daughter to the hospital right away." It was that Hunter person again. Addison had heard his voice so many times she would recognize it anywhere. The two women took a step back from the stretcher.

"We'll meet you at the hospital," her mother said, trying to control her quavering voice. "I love you."

The stretcher started rolling again. Addison's vision was a little blurry from all the tears, but she saw Hunter look back over his shoulder. "You're going to be okay, young lady. We're taking you to the hospital."

She was really beginning to feel afraid now. *Why is my leg hurting so badly?* The pain was almost unbearable. She just wanted to sleep so she couldn't feel the excruciating pain in her leg.

She felt herself being lifted into the back of the ambulance and heard the doors slam. A few seconds later, the ambulance started to move and the sirens wailed. Hunter sat in the back of the ambulance and took her by the hand.

"Daddy, you're back!" she said as the tears began to let up, and her eyes closed.

"Stay with me, Addison."

"I will, Daddy."

CHAPTER 8

THE DECISION

Kyndal, Trevor, and Maggie arrived at Cherokee Memorial shortly after the ambulance. Upon entering the waiting room, Maggie wondered why her husband and the Morrises were not there. She was about to call her husband on her cell phone when he came bursting through the door. He gave them a brief update on Tyler. The doctor was only going to keep Tyler for a twenty-four-hour observation period. As it turned out, his injuries had not been as bad as they had first appeared. They turned when they heard the waiting-room door open again. It was the Morrises. Both looked as if they had neglected to comb their hair before leaving home—not that Bryan Morris had much left to comb, and not that you could blame them given the circumstances. They had also just thrown their heavy coats over their pajamas.

Rebekah Morris approached Kyndal, but before she could say anything, Kyndal turned and walked away. Rebekah Morris burst into tears as her husband and Maggie came to her side. Trevor heard Maggie whisper something to Rebekah but couldn't quite make it out. "Give her some time," it sounded like, but he wasn't sure. He saw Rebekah nod as she and her husband made their way to the door. Maggie gave each one of them a hug, and Pastor Bryce walked them out, returning a few minutes later.

"I told Mrs. Morris this was probably not a good time to speak to you," he told Kyndal.

"There will never be a good time for them to speak to me," she said bitterly as she sat in a chair next to a table which provided a pot of coffee and a tray of condiments. Normally, she loved the strong taste and inviting aroma of fresh brewed coffee, but she knew at the moment she would not be able to keep anything on her stomach.

"It's not their fault—" Maggie started to say, but Kyndal stopped her.

"Don't!" she said, standing to her feet.

The door opened once again. This time, it was Alayna and her mother.

* * * * *

"Let's go," Shannon told Alayna upon hearing Addison had been taken to Cherokee Memorial. Alayna was glad her mother had decided to go to the hospital. Both had been on pins and needles since receiving the phone call that let them know about the accident.

The small group had never seen Shannon Thomas look so disheveled. She had no makeup on and her shoulder-length auburn hair appeared to have been barely combed, which was very much out of character for the usually well-groomed woman.

Kyndal observed the panicked look on Alayna's face as she entered the waiting area. Shannon immediately ran to Kyndal, and they embraced as both women began to cry. Alayna noticed there were no strangers in the small waiting room, and for that, she was grateful. Trevor Grant was standing next to one of the windows staring out into the night. She quickly made her way toward him to ask about Addison. However, before she even had the chance to ask, Trevor, still staring out the window, spoke words she did not want to hear.

"It doesn't look good, Alayna," he spoke softly and with such sadness in his voice that she began to tear.

"Am I going to lose my best friend?" she asked, almost in a whisper.

Trevor didn't answer as he turned his gaze away from her worried face. Then looking around and not seeing Ayson, she inquired about him.

"Addison's mom called Mrs. Garrison and informed her of what was going on. Mrs. McNeely asked her to inform Ayson of the accident and to tell him Addison was all right, and that she would apprise them of any changes."

"I'm glad he stayed the night with Caleb," Alayna said. She would not have wanted Ayson to overhear Trevor say things did not look good.

"Mrs. McNeely?" they heard someone say. Alayna turned to see a rather ruggedly handsome doctor glancing questionably around the room as to which one of the women might be Mrs. McNeely. No one seemed to have heard him come in until he spoke.

"Yes," Kyndal said as she walked slowly toward him, her face drained of any color. Shannon and Maggie, one on each side, held her by the arms.

"Mrs. McNeely, I'm Dr. Noah Steelman. I understand, although your daughter is eighteen, that you have medical power of attorney. Is that correct?"

Kyndal nodded.

"Is it okay to speak in front of these people?" he asked.

Kyndal nodded again.

"Please have a seat, Mrs. McNeely," he said, motioning toward a navy wing-back chair.

Alayna knew it was not going to be good news. She could see the sadness in the doctor's deep earthy-brown eyes. Fine lines on his tanned face told her this was not the first time the doctor had had to be the bearer of bad news.

Dr. Steelman waited for Kyndal to be seated before taking a seat across from her. Rubbing the stubble on his square chin, he proceeded to inform Kyndal of Addison's condition.

"For the moment, your daughter is stable, and except for the superficial cut to the side of her face, there are no severe head injuries. She does have a mild concussion and is a little confused at times, not remembering where she is or what happened to her

65

tonight. Fortunately, there doesn't appear to be any organ damage." Dr. Steelman continued as everyone in the room eagerly clung to every word he was saying, "It's a good thing she had her seat belt on and the airbag deployed. Had it not, things could have been a lot worse when she hit that pole. A Higher Power was definitely looking out for her."

Alayna caught the slight eye roll Kyndal gave, indicating that the last comment had not sat too well with her, but she did notice that Kyndal appeared to relax slightly, and her color was returning.

"If the airbag deployed, how did she get a cut to the forehead?" asked Kyndal.

Dr. Steelman reached in his shirt pocket and handed her a small brown envelope. Taking the envelope, she looked inside. Pulling out Addison's diamond-cut princess ring, she noticed the dried blood.

"It looks as if she might have shielded her eyes with her hands before the impact," Dr. Steelman explained.

"You mean the cut came from the ring?"

"I believe so."

"So far, so good," Alayna whispered to Trevor.

"However," the doctor continued, "there has been extensive damage to Addison's left leg. She is in excruciating pain, so we have given her something to ease the pain. Alayna and Trevor looked at each other as if to say she had spoken to soon. "The bones to her lower leg are crushed, and there is extensive damage to the tissue. We need to operate as soon as possible."

"Of course," Kyndal said anxiously as she folded her hands in her lap. "Will she need pins or rods or—"

Dr. Steelman interrupted her before she could continue. "I'm afraid you don't understand, Mrs. McNeely," he said, slightly hesitating. "I'm sorry"—he looked into her inquiring face—"but we need to do a below-the-knee amputation." Getting no verbal response from her, he could no longer look into her disbelieving face. Looking at the floor, he said, "There's nothing we can do to save her leg."

Alayna quickly steadied herself, then sat in the chair she had been standing next to. She felt Trevor's hand on her shoulder and watched once again as Kyndal's color began to pale. She could feel the color draining from her own face, and for a second she felt as if she couldn't catch her next breath. She wanted to throw up.

Kyndal looked as if she was trying to say something, but nothing was coming through her quivering lips. Finally, after what seemed an eternity, she looked at Pastor Bryce with pleading in her eyes. He took the hint.

"Dr. Steelman, I'm Reverend Peters," he said as he reached and shook the doctor's hand. "I'm sure Mrs. McNeely respects what you're saying, but is there any way she can get another opinion? This is such a big decision for her to make without exhausting every possible alternative."

Kyndal finally found the ability to speak. "He's right...maybe there's something you've missed," she said as Dr. Steelman met her eyes once again.

"I've already consulted with two other surgeons, Drs. Webster and Pelham. I will be glad to have them speak with you and your husband if you wish, but I'm afraid they'll both tell you the same thing." Dr. Steelman took a quick look around the room as it just occurred to him he had not heard any response from Mr. McNeely.

Kyndal looked down at the clammy, cool hands on her lap. "My husband passed away a few years ago. I'm afraid this is a decision I'll have to make on my own," she said, looking again at Dr. Steelman as a dark sadness overshadowed her eyes. Trevor and Alayna glanced at each other, then turned to Kyndal as they heard her burst into tears.

"I don't know if I can do this," she said, starting to sob uncontrollably as she placed her face into her trembling hands.

"Mrs. McNeely, I understand how—"

This time, it was Kyndal who interrupted the doctor. Jumping up, she looked at Dr. Steelman as he too stood slowly to face her.

"No, you don't understand!" she yelled. "Addison's a cheerleader and so active. She's a teenager, for goodness sake! This will destroy her!"

Tears were still rolling down her face as she grabbed Dr. Steelman by his blue scrub shirt and held to him as tight as she could. Sobbing and looking into his eyes, she pleaded with him, "Please, please help her, Dr. Steelman. Please, whatever you do, don't take her leg. Please don't take my daughter's leg!"

Dr. Steelman grabbed her as her knees buckled underneath her and gently lowered her into the chair she had been sitting in. Kneeling in front of her, he took her hands in his. "I wish there was another way, Mrs. McNeely, but there is just no other alternative. Believe me, I wish there was."

Alayna saw the defeat in Kyndal's face and the hopelessness in her voice as she told Dr. Steelman to go ahead with the surgery. He nodded his head and was about to stand when he said, "I'm sorry, Mrs. McNeely, but you look very familiar to me. Have we met before?"

Kyndal answered, her voice barely audible, "We've met a few times. I work day shift here at the hospital, in the ER department."

"Of course, now I remember you. I'm sorry I didn't recognize you earlier. I'm still learning names and faces."

"That's quite all right, Doctor," she replied.

Alayna listened as Dr. Steelman took Kyndal by the hand and assured her that everything would be all right.

"No, it won't!" she snapped angrily at him. "My daughter is going to hate me for the rest of my life!"

"I won't lie to you, Mrs. McNeely," he said as he gently patted her hand. "Your daughter will probably be mad at you and say some hurtful things, but only for a short while. She is going to need time to adjust to this, but she will adjust, I promise," he said, emphasizing the word *will* and giving her a reassuring smile. Giving Kyndal's hand one more pat, he voiced he would need to do the surgery as soon as possible before any infection set in. Standing, he informed her he had placed Addison on IV antibiotics as a precautionary measure.

By now, all the women in the waiting room were in tears. The men were trying hard to hold back their tears in order to be strong for the women, but they could not hide the overwhelming concern in their eyes. Dr. Steelman was almost out the door when Kyndal called to him.

"Does Addison know? Can I see her?"

Rubbing his hand through his thick black wavy hair, he shook his head. "I told her, but I doubt she remembers. And yes, you can see her. I'll send for you shortly. By the way, Dr. Pelham will be assisting me with the surgery," he added as he continued out the door.

A feeling of impending doom filled the room as well as their hearts. Kyndal, with red swollen eyes and speaking through broken words, looked up at Pastor Bryce and Maggie.

"I don't care what he says. Addison will never forgive me."

Maggie knelt beside Kyndal and took her by the hands. Pastor Bryce ran his hand over his bald head before asking everyone to join hands and make a circle around Kyndal and Maggie.

Alayna knew it was an odd time to be sizing up her pastor and his wife, but it was like something just occurred to her for the first time. She had never noticed Maggie was almost a head taller than her husband and how opposite they were in appearance. Maggie had salt-and-pepper hair and was a little on the chunky side; her husband was short, skinny, and bald. They just didn't seem to be a couple who would pair together. It wasn't until she felt Trevor take her by the hand that her thoughts returned to the present circumstances. Maybe this time she wanted to be distracted. At least it was better than the reality they had to face.

"Let us pray and take this to our Heavenly Father, who loves us and cares deeply for us, a Father who understands exactly what Kyndal and her family are facing." They were about to bow their heads when Kyndal pulled her hands away from Maggie and jumped up.

"No!" The sudden movement and anger in her voice momentarily startled everyone in the room. They watched as she made her way to the door. Then turning quickly, she pointed to Pastor Bryce; and glaring angrily at him, she warned, "Don't you dare tell me God loves me or cares for me. First He takes Josh, and now He does this to Addison. Does this sound like a loving and caring God to you? Does this sound like a Father, as you call Him, who understands? Well, I don't understand!" She looked as if she was about to say something else, but instead turned and walked out, slamming the door behind her.

Shannon looked apologetically at Pastor Bryce and Maggie. "I had better go to her," she said as she grabbed Kyndal's and her jackets from the coat rack next to the door.

Pastor Bryce nodded in agreement, then turned to the rest of them and bowed his head. "Let us pray."

* * * * *

Noah Steelman leaned back against the wall outside the door of the waiting room. He choked back the tears and the pain that was suddenly trying to overtake him. He knew exactly what Kyndal McNeely was going through, even worse. Three years earlier, he had lost his wife, Taylor, and his one-year-old daughter, Angie, in a horrible car accident, changing his life forever.

He crammed his hands into the pants of his blue scrubs, mainly to steady his now shaking hands. Shaky hands were not a good thing for a surgeon to have, but he knew it was only because of what had just happened.

He had been a top surgeon in Atlanta, Georgia, for many years; but after the loss of his family, he longed for a change of scenery. At first, he had only moved to a different part of Georgia; but three months ago, he had decided to leave the state completely. He had moved to South Carolina and opened a practice here in the small town of Indianville. His practice had really taken off, and he was settling in nicely.

His mind went back to a few minutes earlier when he had given Kyndal McNeely the bad news about her daughter. No matter how many times he had to give someone bad news, it never got easier. The loss of a limb was always devastating, but especially so for a child or a teenager.

"Lord, help me to get through this surgery. You've never failed me in the past, and I know You won't now," he prayed as he lifted his eyes toward heaven. Of course, this was the prayer he always prayed before performing surgery.

Usually, he was pretty good at professionally separating himself from the patient and their family, but for some reason, Mrs. McNeely had gotten to him. Maybe it was the desperation in her voice or the fear and confusion all rolled into one as she pleaded with him with tear-stricken eyes not to take her daughter's leg. Maybe it was the fact that there wasn't a Mr. McNeely to help her through this. She looked so vulnerable, so helpless. At least she had friends. But the truth was, he knew she would still feel alone no matter how many friends surrounded her. No one understood that better than him.

He also knew it had been his faith in God that had helped him keep his sanity after the loss of his family. He missed Taylor and Angie so much it seemed his heart literally ached at times. There was not a day went by that he did not think of them. But God, in His mercy, had given him, in a most difficult situation, the peace that passed all understanding. Whatever the reason for the sympathy instead of the empathy he was taught to have concerning his patients, this case was bothering him. He had also promised her everything would be all right. Why, he wondered, did he promise her such a thing? He often encouraged his patients, but this lady was extremely fragile. He knew there was always risk with any surgery. He was wishing he had made no such promise when he heard the loud angry voice of Kyndal McNeely coming through the door. He couldn't make out everything she was saying through the thick fire door of the waiting room, but he heard enough to know she was definitely mad at God. He didn't feel right hearing words that were not meant for him to hear.

He quickly walked away from the door and started down the hall, not only praying for himself but for the McNeely family and friends as well. As he started to round the corner of the empty hall, he heard the door to the waiting room slam and the loud click of a woman's high-heeled shoes on the tile floor. He could tell from the clicking sound of the shoes that the person was in a hurry. He was pretty sure it was Kyndal McNeely. Shortly after, he heard the faint echo of the sliding doors leading into the courtyard as they opened and then closed again. He continued to pray silently as he opened the door to the small chapel located inside the hospital. No one else was there. He was glad as he knelt at the altar and released all his care to his Heavenly Father.

* * * * *

71

Kyndal noticed Dr. Steelman rounding the corner as she stepped out into the hall. She knew he probably heard her yelling at Pastor Bryce, but at the moment, she couldn't care less. Come to think of it, maybe it wasn't Pastor Bryce she needed to be yelling at. Maybe it was God, the one responsible for all the hurt and confusion in her life. After all, Pastor Bryce wasn't the one who had control over life and death—God did. Neither could he have kept Addison's leg from having such extensive damage that it would require amputation, but God could have. She passed through the sliding doors to the court-yard. She was crying so hard she could barely see the huge oak tree with its beautiful fall colored leaves in the middle of the court. There were several spotlights shining on the tree, giving it a warm soft glow. Looking around, she finally spotted a white concrete bench directly across from the oak. She thought how the oak tree was a symbol of strength, something she didn't have right now. She felt afraid and weak, but mostly alone. She had felt that way for a very long time. Why should now be any different?

Sitting on the cold bench, she wrapped her hands around her arms, partly to warm herself and partly to comfort herself. She had run from the waiting room so quickly she had not thought to grab her jacket. At least she had on a long-sleeved pullover sweater. As she rubbed her arms with her hands, she thought about how much she would love to feel the strong comforting arms of her husband around her at this moment. She turned when she heard the sliding doors open. Shannon came and sat down next to her. She shivered uncontrollably from the coldness of the concrete bench.

"Don't say a word," Kyndal warned through partially clenched teeth.

"I won't," Shannon said softly as she handed Kyndal her jacket and reached and put her arm around her friend. Shannon wasn't Josh, but it did feel comforting to feel the caring arm of someone around her. She looked at Shannon and gave a halfway smile.

The two had been close friends since their daughters had become friends in elementary school. However, since Josh's passing, Kyndal had distanced herself a little from Shannon, as she had with many of her other friends. Maybe she didn't want to feel more pain should something happen to Shannon, or maybe she felt as if she were a fifth wheel. Kyndal and Josh had gone out with Shannon and her husband, Patrick, on many occasions. But now all that had changed. Anyway, it was her doing; and after a while, Shannon had given her the space she needed.

She could tell from the pained look on Shannon's face that she really was concerned for Kyndal and her family. She wanted to say something to ease Shannon's worry, but was at a loss for words. After all, she couldn't even ease her own worry. For a moment they sat in silence, each with their own thoughts.

She was feeling so confused and so angry, especially toward God. On the one hand, she didn't want anything to do with this God who seemed to take everyone and everything away from her and the people she loved. On the other hand, she felt He was the only One who could help her—if He just would. She just didn't understand why He wouldn't. Finally, she broke the silence as she gave voice to her thoughts.

"Shannon, I don't understand why God lets things like this happen. I can understand why He doesn't love me. He knows I don't want anything to do with Him. But what I don't understand is why He doesn't love Addison, or why He didn't love Josh? They believed in His goodness and in Him."

Shannon lightly rubbed Kyndal's arm, mainly because she could feel her shivering from the chilly night air. "Better put that jacket on." She helped Kyndal put on the brown leather jacket Josh had given her for Christmas the year before he died. "Kyndal, I'm not an expert on the Bible, but I do know it's not your understanding that moves God. It's your faith. And you're wrong about Him not loving you. He loves you so much that He sent His Son, Jesus, to die for you. He cares about what you're going through, and even though I don't have all the answers to your situation, Kyndal, God does. You just have to trust Him, not only with this but with your life."

"I can't," Kyndal said, tearing her eyes away from Shannon and shaking her head. "I'm just so angry!"

Shannon was about to say something else when they heard the sliding doors opening again. Kyndal thought the doors were more like revolving doors than sliding doors. They looked up to see Maggie walking toward them, holding a cup of steaming hot coffee.

"I thought you could use this," she said, handing Kyndal the cup of coffee, which immediately warmed her chilly hands.

"Thanks," she said, slowly taking a sip of the hot brew. Kyndal felt her face start to blush from embarrassment. Looking to the oak tree in order to avoid eye contact with Maggie, she offered an apology. "Listen, Maggie, about what just happened in the waiting room. I'm sorry…"

"It's okay," Maggie interrupted. "I totally understand. I know this is a very difficult time for you and your family." She turned and met Maggie's warm, compassionate eyes. Maggie's eyes had always reminded her of the color of the ocean, almost a blue green but with flecks of gold, depending on what she wore. They were somewhere between a hazel color and an amber color. Maggie and her son Callaway were the only two people she had ever seen with that unique color of eyes. She thought Callaway favored his mom, having the same color eyes and round face, but was on the short side like his dad. Tonight Maggie's eyes looked mostly blue from the light-blue button-down blouse she was wearing. Kyndal could see where mascara had run down her face from when she had been crying earlier.

"Thanks," Kyndal said as she stood and gave Maggie a hug. "I tell you what," she said as she held Maggie, "go ahead and pray to your God. Maybe He will listen to you."

As all three locked arms and headed back into the hospital Maggie assured her, "He will listen."

CHAPTER 9

THE OPERATION

Kyndal had spent most of the night and part of the early morning signing several consent forms and other needed paperwork in order for the surgery to be performed. It took every bit of courage she could muster to put her signature, shaky and almost unreadable, on the consents giving the surgeons permission to amputate her daughter's leg.

She had met again with Dr. Steelman before he had left for the night, and also with Sue Johns, the anesthesiologist. Sue Johns, in Kyndal's opinion, looked a little too young to be putting someone to sleep, but she had been assured by Dr. Steelman that she was one of the best. Sue was short and petite with blue innocent eyes and looked as though she had just graduated high school. Wearing her long strawberry-blonde hair up in a ponytail didn't help her appear any older. Kyndal guessed the young doctor had to work really hard at winning the patient and family's confidence. However, she appeared to take it all in stride, given her sunny disposition. To Kyndal's relief, Dr. Johns was very professional and able to answer any questions she threw her way.

Earlier, Addison had been assigned a room, and Dr. Steelman had given Kyndal and one other person permission to stay the night. It was decided Maggie would stay with Kyndal as Shannon needed to get Alayna home. It was almost 1:30 a.m. when everyone left, and the two women settled in for the night.

Addison was still groggy and looked so helpless. Kyndal had tried to explain to her again about the operation, but it was no use. Even when Addison did respond, the words made no sense, and she would soon drift off to sleep again. Kyndal knew the pain medication was keeping her pretty sedated. However, without the meds, she was in excruciating pain. The fact that Addison had no idea about what was about to take place only added to Kyndal's grief. Mothers were supposed to protect their children, not do things that would rip their children's world apart, she thought.

She stepped outside the door of her daughter's room to get some much-needed air. The small hospital room seemed to have sucked up every bit of oxygen. Right now she would give anything to trade places with her daughter. This was no doubt the hardest decision she had ever had to make. It was hard to look at her daughter lying there with no clue as to what was going on. Reaching into her jeans pocket, she pulled out another tissue. She blew her nose and tried to compose herself. Her nose was red and raw from so much wiping she could barely stand to touch it. Her head was beginning to ache, and she knew it was from all the stress and lack of sleep. As she leaned against the wall outside her daughter's room, she reached and gently massaged her forehead. At the moment, she was feeling so overwhelmed.

Addison's surgery had been scheduled for 8:15 a.m. Fortunately, and to her relief, Shannon had offered to stop by the Garrisons and pick up Ayson on their way back to the hospital. Ayson didn't cry, but he had been so pitiful over the phone when she talked to him earlier and told him about the needed surgery. He was still a little too young to quite understand. He had pleaded with her not to let them "cut off my sister's leg." She tried to explain to him she had no choice, but she could tell he had been upset with her. Was it possible both of her children were going to hate her? Ayson had hung up rather abruptly with her, but called back a few minutes later, saying he wanted to be there for the surgery. She had tried to talk him out of it, but he refused to take no for an answer.

Kyndal stuffed the tissue back in her pocket. She reentered the room and noticed Maggie was already asleep. Looking at Maggie's short spikey pixie haircut, she wondered if that cut would look good on her. She might give it some thought in the future, but right now all she could think about was Addison. She walked over to the bed and stood watching her daughter as tears began to fill her eyes. A few times during the night after getting to her room, Addison had tried to speak, but her speech was so garbled neither Kyndal nor Maggie could understand her for the most part. They did understand the word *daddy* a couple of times.

It was out of pure exhaustion that Kyndal finally drifted off to sleep a few minutes later. It wasn't a restful sleep as nurses and the lab tech kept coming in what seemed like every few minutes. Addison's arms were black-and-blue from lab sticks in which it seemed endless tubes of blood were drawn. The traffic finally tapered off around 4:00 a.m. Now maybe she would be able to get a little shut-eye without any interruptions. She wished she could be like Maggie, who hadn't moved a muscle the entire night. Just as Kyndal felt herself drifting off to sleep, again she jumped, being suddenly startled by a loud noise. Realizing what it was, she tried to cover her ears with her pillow, but she could still hear the muffled sounds of Maggie's irritating snores.

* * * * *

Dr. Steelman heard the throaty but sleepy voice come across the intercom as he stood at the nurse's desk looking through Addison McNeely's chart for the last time before surgery.

"Dr. Steelman, extension 1433," the throaty voice repeated. Taking the chart with him, he walked to the small desk next to the medication room, which was the doctor's charting area. He located the phone partially hidden under some papers and called the ER. Thankfully, it was not an emergency, and he was able to handle the situation over the phone. Replacing the receiver, he again turned his attention to Addison McNeely's chart. Everything looked in order including his pre-op orders for type and crossmatch for blood type and other labs. He glanced at his watch. He closed the chart and headed for room 212. He wanted to speak one last time with Kyndal

McNeely in case she had any questions before the surgery. He also wanted to see if there was anything she needed.

Reaching the room, he knocked lightly on the door.

"Come in."

He entered quietly upon hearing the sleepy voice. The bathroom light was on and gave a faint glow to the room from the partially closed door. He noticed Kyndal lying in one of the ugly green hospital recliners covered up to her neck with a white hospital blanket and a pillow over her head. Another woman was sitting partly slumped over in a straight-back chair with her feet propped on the foot of the hospital bed. Her blanket was hanging halfway on the floor, and she was steadily snoring—and pretty loudly at that. He wondered if she might benefit from having a sleep apnea study. Now he understood the pillow over Kyndal McNeely's head. Just as he was about to speak, the woman let out such a loud snort she literally woke herself up.

"What—," she started to ask as she looked around to orient herself. If he was not mistaken, she was the pastor's wife, Maggie Peters. He tried to stifle a grin, but Kyndal had caught him red-handed. He saw a smile play across her tired face. He couldn't help but notice how much younger she looked when she smiled. Thinking back from the time he had spoken to her in the waiting room, he thought this was the first time he had seen her smile. Under the circumstances, it was understandable. The poor woman had encountered nothing but bad news all night.

"Mrs. McNeely, I just wanted to stop by before the surgery to see if you needed anything or if you had any further questions.

"Thank you, Dr. Steelman, but I believe I've run out of questions except for one, and I don't believe you have the answer."

Nodding in agreement, he knew what the question was; and she was right, he couldn't answer the question—*why.* He remembered asking that same question when his wife and little girl died. He too had received no answer to probably the most asked question on earth.

Maggie sat up in her chair, wiped the drool from her mouth, and cleared her throat. Dr. Steelman could tell from the inquisitive look on her face that she was wondering if he had heard her snoring. He couldn't help himself. He gave her an amused look and, without saying a word, gave her a slight grin, just big enough to convey, *Yep, I heard every snort.* Even in the dimly lit room, he could see her face start to blush.

"The transport team will be here for Addison shortly. I will try my best to keep you informed every hour as to her progress once the surgery has begun," he said, turning toward the door.

At first, Kyndal made no reply; but as he placed his hand on the door, she stopped him. "Dr. Steelman," she said as he turned back to face her. "Thank you for everything you're doing."

"You're welcome," he said with a nod. "Let me know if you need anything." Once again, he couldn't resist. Turning to leave, he looked over his shoulder and smiled. "Good day, Mrs. Peters. I hope you slept soundly." Before she could respond, he was gone.

A half hour later, two people from the transport team, both who looked to be in their midtwenties, came for Addison and transferred her onto the stretcher. Kyndal attempted again to speak to her, but again she only mumbled a few unintelligible words. Following behind the stretcher, Maggie held tight to Kyndal. As they exited through the double doors of the ICU, they saw Pastor Bryce, Ayson, Shannon, and Alayna standing together in a small circle. As they neared the tiny group, Pastor Bryce asked the two transporters if they would mind giving them a moment. This time, Kyndal joined hands with the rest of the group and hoped with all her heart that God would hear and answer Pastor Bryce's prayer. Even the young man and woman transporters bowed their heads as Pastor Bryce prayed and asked God to give wisdom to the doctors and nurses and to guide the hands of Drs. Steelman and Pelham as they performed the surgery. Afterward, they watched the two men wheel Addison through the automatic doors leading to the surgery area.

Ayson heard his mother burst into tears as she grabbed him and hugged him so tightly he could hardly breathe.

"She's going to be all right," she told him as they stood in the stark hallway staring at the doors which Addison had just been taken through.

* * * * *

Ayson wasn't sure if his mother was trying to convince him or herself that his sister was going to be all right. He was also wondering what was wrong with him. Today was the first time he had seen his sister since the accident. She didn't look like herself. Her face was slightly swollen, and she looked frail and weak. She had always been the strong one in the family, even stronger than their mother. He wanted his sister back the way she was before the accident. He couldn't stand the way she looked now, yet from the time he had first heard the news about his sister, he had been unable to cry. He felt as if he wanted to, but for some reason, the tears simply would not come. Maybe it was because all of this seemed to be unreal. Why else would he be unable to cry?

Alayna's cell phone rang.

"Oh, hello, Trevor," she answered. "Yes, they've just taken her to the OR."

Ayson's mother finally let go of him and was talking a mile a minute to Pastor Bryce, Maggie, and Shannon. He supposed his mother's nonstop talking was due to nerves.

"How about we all go to the hospital cafeteria and get us a bite to eat?" Maggie said to no one in particular. His mother was about to protest, but Maggie stopped her and told her she needed to eat something in order to keep her strength up. His mother nodded in agreement and, turning, held out her hand toward him. He took her hand as they headed toward the elevator.

Normally, there was no way he would be seen holding his mother's hand, not at his age—how embarrassing! After all, he was twelve years old, almost a teenager, for goodness sake! However, given the state of mind his mother was in at the present, he felt it best to oblige her. His mind drifted back to his sister. Maybe this was all a bad dream, and he would wake up any moment. The gray elevator doors opened, and they piled one by one into the already crowded elevator. Shannon pushed the button to the first floor where the cafeteria was located.

* * * * *

Alayna had a restless night. It was in the early hours of the morning when she and her mother had left the hospital and then returned a little after 7:30 a.m. The drive to the hospital had been a quiet one, partly because she and her mom were still half asleep, and partly because they were lost in their own thoughts thinking about Addison and her family. Ayson had been quiet the entire trip as well. Since hearing Addison was going to have her leg amputated, Alayna wondered how she was ever going to face her best friend. What was she going to say to Addison when she woke up and realized half her leg was gone? What would they find to talk about? What would they have in common? There seemed to be so many unanswered questions racing through her mind.

She wasn't really hungry. As a matter of fact, she was feeling a little sick to her stomach. Alayna looked at Ayson, who looked as if he was almost in a zombie state of mind. She had not seen him cry, or even tear up for that matter. He just kept that weird, almost-blank expression on his face.

Her thoughts turned to the phone call she had received from Trevor. He had called to ask how things were going with Addison but to also inform her that Tyler was definitely going to be released from the hospital later on in the day. She purposely avoided mentioning this to Kyndal. Alayna really was glad Tyler was all right, but it was just so unfair! The accident had been his fault, but he gets out of the hospital practically injury-free, and her best friend ends up losing her leg! It just wasn't right, she thought, as the elevator doors opened, and she stepped out onto the blue carpet of the hospital floor. As they neared the cafeteria, Alayna heard the clanking of dishes and smelled the inviting aroma of bacon, omelets, and fresh brewed coffee. Maybe she was hungrier than she thought as her mouth began to water.

* * * * *

Several other families had gathered in the small surgery waiting area when they returned from eating breakfast. The phone on the wall rang as they sat down. The loud ring startled Kyndal. One man, tall and lanky with a red beard, jumped up from his seat and answered the phone.

"McNeely!" he yelled, holding the receiver in the air. Kyndal glanced at her watch as she hurried toward the phone. It was exactly an hour since the surgery had gotten underway. It was the OR nurse. Dr. Steelman had kept his word about calling to update her regarding Addison's progress.

Alayna noticed a look of relief cross Kyndal's face as she gave them the thumbs-up. Good, everything must be going well, she thought, as she took out her cell phone to text Trevor. He texted back asking her to let everyone know he would make sure Addison's name was placed on the prayer list at church. Pastor Bryce had arranged earlier for the assistant pastor to head up the morning service so he could be with Kyndal and Ayson.

True to his word, Dr. Steelman kept them updated. In between times, they dozed, watched television, or talked with the others in the waiting area. They learned the seven-year-old son of the man who had answered the phone had fallen off the monkey bars at the park the day before and broken his arm in two places. An elderly man's wife was having gallbladder surgery. His tanned wrinkled face had seen many years for the wear, but it was a kind face, one that, at the moment, was filled with worry. The young Hispanic couple was anxiously waiting to hear news about their six-year-old daughter, who was having her tonsils removed.

Finally, after two hours of surgery, Kyndal received a call from the O.R. that Addison was out of surgery and everything had gone well. The nurse informed her Dr. Steelman would be around to speak to her shortly and that Addison was being moved to the recovery room as they spoke. Dr. Steelman arrived soon afterward and spoke to the anxious group. After giving them details of the surgery and what to expect, he suggested they get a bite to eat as it would be another thirty to forty-five minute or so before Addison would be out of recovery.

* * * * *

Since they had eaten a late breakfast, no one was really hungry, so they decided on drinks and a dessert. Again Alayna felt a little sick to her stomach as they entered the cafeteria. It wasn't that anything was wrong with the food, but she knew it was getting close to the time Addison would be finding out about losing a leg. She looked around at the people she had spent the morning with. They didn't seem to have much of an appetite either. Each one sat engrossed in their own little world or making small talk when they heard the page.

"Code blue, 1577," announced the throaty but calm voice overhead.

Kyndal was in a state of panic as she jumped up. "Oh, no!" she said as she took off running through the cafeteria, almost knocking a stunned cafeteria worker off her feet. The woman looked a little annoyed that Kyndal didn't at least apologize for her rude actions. The rest of the gang jumped up and ran after Kyndal.

Ayson accidently bumped into the same cafeteria worker, nearly knocking her off her feet as well. "Sorry!" he yelled as he whizzed past her.

The operator repeated the code two more times. The bewildered group caught up with Kyndal at the elevator as she waited for the door to open. A man in a white lab coat, also waiting for the elevator to descend, stood, next to Kyndal. When the door opened, Kyndal was the first to get on the elevator with the others following quickly behind. The man in the white coat looked a little taken aback by their rudeness, but politely stepped aside. Shannon was holding the door for the last of them to pile in when Kyndal's cell phone rang.

"What? I can't hear you," she said as she made a U-turn in the elevator, pushing her way past them. "What? Yes, thank you, thank you so much!"

By now, Shannon had been holding the elevator door open so long it started to make a buzzing sound. Kyndal burst into tears as Shannon let go of the door, and they all exited the elevator and stood next to her. The man in the white lab coat was momentarily distracted by all the chaos as he watched the small group huddle together in the lobby.

Looking at Kyndal, Pastor Bryce was the first to speak. "What's going on, Kyndal? Who was that on the phone?"

Taking a deep breath, she composed herself long enough to answer him. "It was Dr. Steelman. I had given him my cell number in case I was not in the waiting room and he needed to get in touch with me. He was calling to let us know the code blue was not Addison. He said he knew when I heard the page I would think it was her." Seeing the confusion on their faces, she explained, "The number to the recovery room is 1577. By me being employed here, he knew I would recognize the number."

Upon hearing this, the man in the lab coat turned to step into the elevator, but the door had just closed. He mumbled something, then glanced at his watch and pushed the elevator button. A sigh of relief went through the small group of friends. Kyndal felt both relief and guilt. She was relieved it was not Addison, but felt guilty for feeling relieved it was someone else. She knew somewhere in the hospital someone was feeling what she had felt a few minutes earlier: the fear of losing a loved one.

"We need to pray for whoever this code is for," Maggie said as though she had read Kyndal's thoughts. The truth was, she was feeling the same relief and guilt that Kyndal was feeling.

Pastor Bryce spoke again, "Maggie is right. We need to stop and pray right now. We will thank God Addison is all right and pray for His healing power to touch the person for which this code was called."

Kyndal wasn't sure why, but she bowed her head too, but not before thinking prayer seemed to be all these people did.

After a few days, Kyndal and Maggie learned the code blue had been called, because of the elderly gentleman's wife, who had undergone gallbladder surgery. They had run into Mr. Martin one afternoon at the hospital gift shop. His wife's blood pressure had dropped suddenly, and her heart had stopped beating for a few minutes. However, the doctors and nurses were able to resuscitate her, and she was doing fine. He had inquired of the little girl, referring to Addison. Kyndal informed him that physically she was doing fine, but emotionally she was not coping too well at the moment. He promised to keep her in his prayers, and Maggie promised to do the same for his wife.

After their code-blue scare, the group returned to the surgery waiting room where, shortly afterward, Kyndal received a call from Dr. Steelman. He informed her Addison was waking but still drifting in and out of sleep at the moment. He assured her he would be there to help break the news to Addison when she was fully awake. Ten minutes later, he called again.

"They are taking her to her room now. I strongly suggest there not be a room full of people," he added.

Kyndal relayed the message to the rest of the group and asked that only Pastor Bryce be with Dr. Steelman and her. She felt Pastor Bryce would be a source of strength to Addison when she learned of the surgery. The three of them arrived at the room just as the hospital staff was backing the empty stretcher out of the doorway. Kyndal couldn't remember ever feeling as sick to her stomach as she felt at the moment. They entered the room just as the nurse finished raising the head of the bed. As the nurse left the room, Addison turned toward her mother and smiled. She seemed a little more alert than Kyndal had expected her to be. She tried hard to return the smile, but was unable as she struggled to choke back tears that were threatening to break through at any moment.

"What's wrong, Mom?" Addison asked, noticing the anxious look on her mother's face.

Kyndal suddenly felt as if she couldn't breathe. She took a deep breath and looked at Dr. Steelman. As if that was his cue, he walked over and stood on the opposite side of the bed from Kyndal and Pastor Bryce. "How are you feeling?" he asked.

Although Dr. Steelman was smiling, Addison could tell he was bothered by something. "Okay, I guess. I'm a little fuzzy on every-thing that has happened." Then she turned toward her mother. "Mom, I couldn't feel my left foot just now when I tried to rest my right foot over it."

Kyndal burst into tears and grabbed Pastor Bryce by the arm as he gently reached and placed his hand over hers. Seeing her mother's reaction, Addison screamed.

"Oh my God, I'm paralyzed!"

Kyndal closed her eyes briefly and then opened them again.

Addison again, took her right foot and placed it where her left foot should have been. "Doctor, I can't feel my left foot and lower left leg!" Addison looked frantically at Dr. Steelman.

"Addison…," he began, but before he could finish, Addison threw back the heavy layer of hospital blankets and looked at her legs. She noticed the bandaged nub with the drainage tube and realized immediately what had taken place. She began screaming.

"Oh God, no! Please no! This can't be happening!" She looked at her mother and screamed even louder, "Mom, how could you let them do this to me! I hate you, Mom! I hate you! I hate all of you!"

As long as she lived, Kyndal knew she would never forget the screams and the wild, terrified look in her daughter's eyes. She would also never forget the words "I hate you, Mom!" The tears had finally broken through and ran down her face.

Addison kept screaming over and over how she hated her and would never forgive her. Dr. Steelman attempted to explain to Addison how she couldn't have lived without the surgery, but ended up calling a nurse to bring an IV sedative.

"Get out of here, all of you!" Addison screamed.

Pastor Bryce attempted to talk to her as well, but she screamed at him. "Get out of here! All of you just get out and leave me alone! I hate you! I hate all of you!" Addison burst into uncontrollable, gut-wrenching tears. "You've made me into a freak!" she screamed at Dr. Steelman as the sedative finally began to take effect.

Kyndal wanted to hold her daughter as tight as she could and tell her how much she loved her. She wanted to comfort her and reassure her that everything was going to be fine, but that wasn't going to happen. Addison was so angry with her.

"My daddy would never have let them do this to me," she said as she drifted off to sleep.

"Call me as soon as she wakes," Dr. Steelman told Kyndal as he left the room. Kyndal had never seen her daughter so distraught, but how was she expecting Addison to act given the circumstances?

An hour later, Kyndal had Dr. Steelman paged as Addison began to stir. She cleared the room and asked again that only Dr. Steelman and Pastor Bryce be present when Addison awoke.

* * * * *

Dr. Steelman arrived just as Addison opened her eyes and looked around the room. She was trying to focus and recall the earlier incident. She remembered the nurse administering the sedative, causing her to drift off to a calm sleep. As far as she was concerned, she could have slept for eternity. It would have been better than what she had just awoken to. Her mother and Pastor Bryce came and stood beside her as Dr. Steelman pulled a chair next to her bed.

"How are you feeling, Addison?" he asked.

She didn't answer, and he didn't push for one. He cleared his throat then proceeded to explain the severity and extent of her injury. She had heard few people speak with such compassion. He repeatedly assured her there had been no other choice except amputation. She lay staring at him flatly, giving him no response. "You would have died from an infection or other complications," he explained.

She finally spoke for the first time, "Then you should have let me die." Her voice was filled with absolute hopelessness. She lay on the bed facing him, her pillow bathed from bitter tears that flowed nonstop.

Pastor Bryce stepped forward. "Surely you don't mean that, Addison. You've got so much to live for. You have your whole life ahead of you."

She heard her mother crying softly behind her.

"No, I don't," she told him as she turned to face him. "Please, please, everyone," she said, almost begging, "just leave me alone!" She was sure they could hear the angry undertone.

Dr. Steelman patted her briefly on the hand and motioned with a nod for her mother and pastor to give her the space she needed. In her heart, she knew her mother had made the best decision, but somehow it still didn't help. She regretted having said some really hurtful things to her mother and Pastor Bryce, but what was said was said. She even felt bad for screaming at Dr. Steelman. But she wasn't ready to apologize to any of them at the moment. She wasn't sure if it was pride stopping her or the fact that she needed someone else other than herself to blame.

Dr. Steelman stood, and the three of them headed for the door. Pastor Bryce placed his hand on the knob and was about to open the door when her mother stopped dead in her tracks and faced Addison's bed.

"No. No, I won't leave you alone."

Both men looked at each other in total surprise. Even Addison was surprised at her mother's assertiveness. Her mother approached her bed.

"Addison, you have friends and family who have been praying for you nonstop and who have stayed at this hospital day and night. The least you can do is to see them and show a little respect. I know this is hard on you, but you're going to have to face people someday, and it might as well be now." Her mother didn't wait for a response, and quite frankly, Addison was left speechless.

Kyndal looked at Pastor Bryce. "If you would give us fifteen minutes please," she told him.

He nodded, and the two men left the room. Addison watched as her mother ran cold water over a washcloth and brought it to her. Her mother sat on the edge of the bed as Addison rubbed the washcloth over her face.

"Look, Addison," she began, "I know you are angry with me, but I'm not going to let you feel sorry for yourself. I can't imagine all you are feeling right now, but I love you, and I'm not going to let you give up. If you need to cry, scream, or hit something, then fine—do it. Let it out, but then get on with your life. You have family and friends who love you and will help you get through this."

Her mother reached to brush several strands of hair from her face, but Addison pulled back. She immediately regretted her reaction when she saw the hurt in her mother's eyes, but she was still too upset to apologize.

"You know," her mother said in a quavering voice, "maybe you're not ready for this." Kyndal looked down and began turning the gold band on her finger. "I'm sorry, sweetheart. Maybe I'm pushing a little too hard. After all, this is a lot to absorb in just a few hours. But if you will just talk to your brother, I'll send the others away. I'm sure they will understand." Kyndal started to stand when Addison gently but briefly touched her on the arm.

"No, wait, Mom, you're right. I'm going to have to face people sooner or later. I'd rather start off with my family and friends, so please don't send them away." Addison wiped her face again with the cool washcloth and ran a brush through her tangled hair.

Ten minutes later, Ayson entered the room and walked slowly toward Addison, turning once to face their mother. She gave him a reassuring smile as his hazel eyes grew wide with uncertainty as he neared Addison's bed. Suddenly he broke into a run and threw his arms around her and burst into tears. He lay next to her on the bed sobbing uncontrollably with his face buried in her shoulders.

"I'm sorry, I'm sorry," he kept saying. "I'm sorry this happened to you." Kyndal placed her hands over her face in an attempt to hide her tears as she took a step forward and then stopped.

"Stop it, Ayson!" Addison said in a tone a little harsher than she meant to. Looking into his watery eyes and trying to hold back her own tears, she assured him everything was going to be okay. "Nothing can hold a McNeely down," she told him and wished she could believe her own words. She placed her two index fingers on the corners of his mouth and gave them a gentle push upward. "Come on, little brother, give me a smile," she said as she gave him one of her own dimpled smiles. From then on, everything seemed to go a little easier.

Alayna came in next. It was almost a repeat of the same, but not quite as bad. After her visit with Alayna, everyone else came in at once. She was glad the initial visits were over and that she had decided to go ahead and meet with everyone. There had been a few more tears shed, but seeing friends and family turned out not to be as bad as she thought, mostly due to their outpouring of love and encouragement.

Later that afternoon, when the room was empty of visitors and Addison had drifted off to sleep, Kyndal decided to lay back in the recliner and read for a while. She didn't get far into the magazine before she was sound asleep.

Addison awoke later and heard her mother reposition in the recliner as the magazine she had been reading fell to the floor. Thinking the fallen magazine might wake her mother, Addison turned over in the bed facing away from her and pretended to be asleep. Hearing no sound after a few minutes, she turned back and continued to watch her mother sleep before rolling onto her back. She placed her hands behind her head and stared at the stark ceiling. As a matter of fact, the whole room was stark. Everything from ceiling to floor was white and bare. The only color to the room at all was the heavy burnt-orange-colored drapes with a pattern of gold interlocking circles. At least she had a view of the highway and could watch drivers hurry past as they headed to their particular destinations. Without realizing it, her mother had awakened and was watching her.

"Did you sleep well?" her mother asked.

For a split second, Addison thought about closing her eyes and pretending to be asleep, but it was too late. "I guess so," she mumbled, not really wanting to talk to her mother yet. Her mother pushed the lever on the recliner and sat up. She slid on her shoes and then came and stood over the bed. Addison kept her eyes fixed on the cold white ceiling of the hospital.

"Look, as I said before, I know you're angry with me, but just remember this. You have always been a strong and determined young woman. You have never let anyone or anything beat you, and you're not going to let this beat you," her mother said. "God," her mother said, almost choking on the word, "will help you through this." Although she herself, did not put any faith in God, Kyndal knew her daughter did, or at least she used to.

Addison turned and looked at her mother. "You don't even have faith in God."

"Of course, I do." Kyndal felt her face start to blush.

"I didn't think so," Addison said, noticing her mother's reddened cheeks.

Her mother was determined not to back down. She sighed. "The point is, you have faith in Him," she said, still meeting her daughter's steely eyes.

Addison looked away. She just wanted to think. She wanted answers to her many questions. She felt betrayed by God. Sure, she was wrong in drinking and going to the party. Sure, she should have turned the other cheek instead of hitting Karlie, but did God have to get back at her like this? After all, there were plenty of people at the party who had acted worse than she had, and nothing had happened to them. It just wasn't fair! She was going to be so embarrassed hopping around on one leg. Her cheerleading days were over, and who would ever want to date a girl with one leg? What was she going to do with the rest of her life?

Kyndal was about to say something else when they heard a knock at the door. "Come in," Kyndal called as she sat once again in the recliner. It was Dr. Steelman.

"How's my patient doing?" he asked as he approached Addison's bedside.

"She's doing better," Kyndal answered, although she wasn't exactly positive about that.

"May I sit here?" he asked Addison, pointing to the edge of the bed.

"Suit yourself," she answered coolly as he sat next to her and cleared his throat.

"Addison, I want you to see a psychologist."

Addison's brows furrowed as she pulled herself up in the bed. "You mean you want me to see a shrink?" She couldn't believe what she had just heard.

"Addison, you've already been through a lot these past few days, but you still have a long road ahead of you. I just feel it would help if you had someone to talk to on a professional level."

"Do you think I'm crazy or something? I've lost my leg, not my mind!"

"Honey, of course, he doesn't think you're crazy," said Kyndal, moving closer to the bed.

Dr. Steelman placed his hand on Addison's shoulder. "How you deal with this emotionally, Addison, is going to play a huge part in how well and how fast you recover physically. The psychologist's name is Dr. Tillie Davenport. I'm sure she can help you deal with what has happened to you. I'm asking you to trust me, Addison."

She sensed a hint of pleading in his voice. Yawning, Addison placed her hand over her mouth and then folded her arms across her chest. She knew it would be a moot point to argue with him in the long run.

"Whatever," she mumbled.

"Good," Dr. Steelman said as he stood and smiled at her. She had to admit the doc had a very pleasant smile, one that had the ability to win people over. He informed them of his treatment plan to include physical therapy. "In the meantime, I'm going to order some range of motion to be done two to three times a day. If either of you need anything, let me know," Dr. Steelman said as he left the room and closed the door behind him. As Kyndal turned back to look at Addison, she saw she had nodded off to sleep again, or at least had pretended to.

CHAPTER 10

WYATT KINGSLEY

A week had almost passed. Each day had been extremely busy for Addison between visitors and medical staff. The Physical Therapist had been in to evaluate her and work with her on transferring safely with the use of her crutches while waiting on the temporary prosthesis to arrive. Tillie Davenport had also been in several times to see her. The doctor was soft-spoken and appeared to be somewhere in her midfifties. She had thick brown hair scattered with a few strands of gray that softly framed her heart-shaped face. She wore thick black-rimmed glasses which kept sliding down her slightly pointed nose. Addison couldn't help but smile as she watched Dr. Davenport alternate between writing her notes and pushing the glasses back onto their proper place. This appeared to be so automatic she doubted Dr. Davenport even realized she was doing it.

Although the doctor was nice enough, Addison just did not feel up to talking much about her ordeal, at least not yet. She could see a little bit of frustration in the doctor's face, but she didn't care. She had never been one to easily reveal her feelings to others, except to Alayna, and sometimes not even to her. At present, Regina Harrison, the hospital's prosthetist, had come in to measure and fit Addison for the temporary prosthesis she would soon be getting. She was short, skinny, and all businesslike. Regina measured while explaining about the temporary prosthesis.

"The temporary prosthesis consists of a cushion inset, laminated socket, pylon, and a dynamic-response foot. Your prosthesis has two functions: to allow you to begin walking and to control swelling, which will start the maturing of the residual limb. When the prosthesis is not in use, you will continue to use the shrinker sock as you are currently doing."

Addison was familiar with the use of the sock, which had replaced the bandages a few days earlier. The hospital staff had initially come in and removed the sock three times a day, massaging her stump for ten minutes each time. Recently, the staff had taught her to perform the task.

The more Regina Harrison talked, the more Addison felt her head spinning from trying to comprehend everything the prosthetist was saying. All the medical terminology was like a foreign language to her. She was glad her mother was present for the meeting as Regina continued to explain about the prosthesis.

"You will also be supplied one, three, and five-ply socks so you may adjust your fit as your limb starts to mature." Through the whole process, Regina Harrison had managed not to smile even once.

Please, someone, make her stop, Addison thought while trying to look as if she understood every word being said. Thirty minutes later, Regina handed her mother a mountain of papers and asked if they had any questions. Thank the Lord for written instructions. Addison could tell from the way Regina kept looking at her watch she was hoping they would not ask anything further. They shook their heads.

"Great. Have the nurses contact me if you think of anything later." Having said that, she was out the door in a flash.

Addison looked down at her stump. The nurses, soon after surgery, had started to perform stretching exercises to her leg. Once the prosthesis came in, she would have to start more intense physical therapy. She wasn't sure if she was ready for anything else, but lately she had had to endure a lot of things she didn't feel she was ready for.

* * * * *

Alayna made it through the school week answering questions regarding Addison. Tomorrow was parent-teacher day for the schools, so there would be no school for the students. Alayna had visited Addison every day after school and was feeling more comfortable being around her. Occasionally, there would be awkward moments between them; but for the most part, things were much the same as before the surgery. Kyndal had returned to work, but continued to stay at the hospital at night. She would run home and spend a few hours with Ayson before dropping him and Chip off at the Garrisons for the night. Addison had suggested her mother stay home Thursday night and let Alayna stay with her.

"Not that anyone needs to," she had told her mother. She had run the idea past Alayna earlier and had purposely run it past her mother in the presence of Dr. Steelman during one of his visits. She knew he would agree her mother needed to get some much-needed rest, and she was right. Dr. Steelman agreed it would actually be good for the both of them. Her mother was reluctant at first, but after being outnumbered three to one, she finally gave in to their request. However, the deal was only contingent upon Addison and Alayna promising to call her if anything changed.

She was glad her mother worked the day shift. She knew her mother would be dropping in on the duo all during the night if she were on the night shift, pretty much like she did during her day shift. Addison was looking forward to having Alayna to herself. She knew she could be herself and speak freely to her friend. If the truth be known, most of the time, she felt angry and depressed. It was exhausting trying to put up a brave front for everyone, and though she tried not to show it; she was scared. She was unsure of what the future held, and quite frankly, she did not see herself as having much of one. She glanced at the clock over the sink. Her mother would be getting off work in another three minutes, and shortly after, Alayna would arrive. She picked up the Agatha Christie novel Ayson had brought from home. She was just starting to thumb through it when she heard a knock at the door. She hoped it was the patient-care tech coming to bring her some fresh water.

"Come in," she said, looking up from her book. She saw the door slowly open and could hardly believe her eyes. She actually closed them for a second and then reopened them to see if her eyes were playing tricks.

"May I come in?" Tyler Morris asked, holding the door slightly ajar. She wanted to shout for him to get out. Her mouth was wide open, but no sound came forth. She felt the hardcover book in her hand. Rearing her arm back, she hurled the book toward Tyler with all her might. He ducked as the book flew past his head. Not knowing if she had anything else to throw at him or not, he yelled from the partially closed door he was hiding behind.

"I just want to say I'm sorry!"

Suddenly finding her voice, she yelled, "Get out, Tyler! Don't ever try to talk to me again! You've ruined my life!" She was so upset by his presence that she was having trouble finding the nurse's call button. Finding it, she screamed hysterically when the nurse answered.

"Get him out of here! I'll kill him, I swear!"

It took only seconds for two nurses to arrive. "What's going on?" one of the nurses asked as she opened the door wider and pushed past Tyler.

"Get him out of here! Get him out of here!" Addison repeated.

The nurse looked at the young man with the bewildered look on his face. "Sir, I'm afraid you're going to have to leave."

"I just want to talk to her for one minute, please!" he begged.

"Sir, you're upsetting her. Please leave." Then she added rather sternly, "Don't make me call security."

Tyler mumbled something to the nurse Addison could not make out, then left. It took a few minutes, but she finally pulled herself together and assured the nurses it was okay for them to leave. One of the nurses bent down at the door and retrieved the Agatha Christie book.

"Thanks," she said as the nurse handed her the book. "Please close the door on your way out." She couldn't believe Tyler Morris had the nerve to show his face. Alayna had told her his parents had visited her mother on the night of the accident, but her mother had been less than receptive.

"They felt terrible," Alayna had told her. "They can't help what Tyler did, and I know they would do anything to change things."

She was right. It wasn't their fault. It was Tyler's fault. Of course, her mother was not as forgiving toward them, but at least she had not tossed out the arrangement of flowers they sent a few days later. She looked at the vase of white baby's breath scattered throughout a dozen pink carnations. Pink carnations were her favorite flowers. She wondered if they somehow knew that. As she looked around at all the flowers, she thought for the first time it looked more like a funeral parlor than a hospital room. There were red roses from Coach Redmond and the cheerleaders, a couple of peace lilies from the church and the ER staff, and a mixed arrangement from the school. Alayna's family and the youth at church had sent pink carnations as well. The hospital administration staff had sent yellow roses since Kyndal was an employee. It even smelled like a funeral parlor, she thought, as she started to open her Christie novel again.

She frowned as she heard another knock on the door and heard a male voice ask if he could come in. I don't believe this! she thought as she felt her face begin to get hot from the growing anger. This time, I won't miss Tyler. Picking up the novel, she drew back her arm and aimed the book at the door. The nerve of some people!

"Of course, you may come in," she said with a bit of sarcasm. She watched as the door opened, then hurled the book as hard as she could. However, as soon as she let go, she realized the man at the door was not Tyler. She tried to warn him, but it was too late. Fortunately, he had quick reflexes and reached out with his left hand and caught the book just as it neared his head.

"Whoa!" he said, looking stunned and unsure as to what to do or say next.

"I'm sorry," she said apologetically and a little embarrassed. "I thought you were someone else."

"Agatha Christie," he said, looking at the book. "At least you have good taste." He walked over to the bed and handed her the book. "Addison McNeely?"

"Yes," she said, wondering whom she had just thrown the book at, so to speak. But whoever he was, she was impressed that he was familiar with Agatha Christie. He didn't look to be much older than she was, and most young people had no clue who Agatha Christie was. If it hadn't been for her dad, she would probably have no clue either.

"Well, Addison McNeely, my name is Wyatt Kingsley. I'm a PTA—physical therapy assistant," he added when he noticed the question in her eyes. "I'm going to be working with you for a while so we can get you back on your feet."

"Don't you mean back on my foot?" she asked sarcastically.

Wyatt Kingsley smiled. It was a warm, friendly smile, and she couldn't help but notice the dimple in his left cheek. He also had a small dimple in the middle of his chin. He had short light-blond hair parted to the side and beautiful green eyes. She thought the lean but athletically built therapy assistant rather handsome and could feel herself becoming a little self-conscious about her leg, or lack of one. There was another knock on the door.

"Should I warn whoever that is at the door that they might want to duck?" he asked with another dimpled smile. She didn't answer but returned his smile as her mother entered the room, looking slightly exhausted. After giving it some thought, she decided not to mention Tyler's attempted visit.

"Oh, hello, Wyatt," her mother said, closing the door behind her.

"Hi, Mrs. McNeely," he answered. "You just get off work?"

"Finally!" she said, placing her purse on the foot of Addison's bed and blowing a twig of loose hair from her eyes. "What about you? I thought you would have left by now. And remember, it's Kyndal, not Mrs. McNeely," she said with a smile.

"Be leaving in about ten minutes. I just wanted to check on Ms. McNeely first. I start working with her tomorrow."

Addison felt herself becoming a little bit annoyed. She didn't really like being referred to as Ms. McNeely, especially since Wyatt Kingsley didn't look to be much older than she was.

"Addison," she said in a slightly irritated tone.

He turned toward her with an inquisitive look on his face.

"Addison," she repeated. "Call me Addison. You can't be more than two or three years older than me."

The warm smile he gave made her feel less annoyed and a little ashamed at being irritated with him. "Okay, Addison it is," he said as he took a bow and tipped an imaginary hat. This time, it was she who smiled. After exchanging a few more niceties, he promised to see her the next morning. "Happy reading," he said with a wink as he left the room. She watched him leave and noticed he had a slight limp to his right leg. Afterward, she asked her mother about the limp.

"I don't know," her mother said, digging through her purse for a piece of gum. "I've never asked him. Oh, I remember now," she said finally, locating the piece of gum. "I believe I heard he was hurt in a motorcycle accident a few years back."

Addison made a mental note to ask Wyatt Kingsley about it at some time or another. He had barely left the room when Alayna arrived, bringing with her two peanut butter milkshakes. She was glad to see her friend. It wasn't that she didn't want her mother around, but her mother fussed over her like she was a little child. Was her head raised high enough? Did she need an extra blanket? Did she need her pillow fluffed? Her mother was definitely what one would call a doting mother. Not that it was all bad; at least she knew her mother cared. She also knew it had been hard for her mother to make the decision she did concerning the amputation. It had taken several days to get over being angry with her mother. She especially regretted telling her mother she hated her. The day she had asked her mother's forgiveness, they had held each other tight and cried for what seemed like half the night.

"There's nothing to forgive," her mother had told her. But Addison knew there was. She had spoken hurtful words, words that she would never be able to take back. She had also apologized to Pastor Bryce and Dr. Steelman.

"Addison, are you listening?" her mother asked as she rattled off a list of dos and don'ts.

"Yes, Mother," she answered with a slight roll of her eyes. After a few minutes, her mother reluctantly said her goodbyes, stressing for the umpteenth time that they be sure and call her if anything changed.

Alayna sat on the bed next to Addison as they continued to sip their milkshakes. "Who was that nice-looking guy leaving your room when I arrived?"

Addison took a long sip of her favorite milkshake before answering, "His name is Wyatt Kingsley. He's a PTA."

Alayna looked up from her milkshake.

"Physical therapy assistant," Addison explained.

"Oh," Alayna said, taking another sip of the milkshake.

"He's going to start working with me tomorrow."

"Lucky you," Alayna said, stirring the half-drunken shake with her straw.

"Yeah, lucky me," Addison said softly.

"I'm sorry, I didn't mean…"

"Stop apologizing," Addison said flatly.

Suddenly her favorite milkshake didn't taste so good anymore. She reached and set the cup on the bedside table next to her as the two of them sat for the next several seconds in complete silence. She sat up in bed wrapping and unwrapping the bedsheet around her fingers for no particular reason. Alayna kept sucking non-stop on her milkshake. It was an awkward few seconds, until Alayna made a long, loud slurping sound with her straw. It was so loud and unexpected that the two of them jumped at the sound. They looked at each other, and seeing the surprise in each other's face, they burst into laughter. They laughed so long and hard tears were streaming down their faces.

Addison grabbed Alayna and hugged her around the neck. "I'm so glad you're here," she said, holding tightly to her best friend as she burst into tears. This time, the tears came to release all the hurt, bitterness, and confusion she had been feeling for days. Alayna wept along with her best friend.

Addison continued to cling to Alayna and silently wished things were different. She wished she could somehow turn back the hands of time to before the accident. Wishing—the only thing she could do.

CHAPTER 11

A NIGHT WITHOUT MOM

Dinner arrived and consisted of fish, mashed potatoes, green peas, and a roll. Addison hated fish but was starving for something to eat. She had forgotten to fill out the hospital menu earlier, or she would have requested something different. Alayna was hungry as well and offered to drive to a nearby burger joint and bring back double cheeseburgers and some fries. After she left, Ayson called to see how the two of them were doing. There was no doubt in Addison's mind that her mother had put him up to calling. Of course, after a few minutes of speaking with her brother, her mother had to speak to her as well. She didn't dare tell her mother Alayna had run out to grab them a bite to eat.

"Yes, Mom, I have enough blankets. No, I'm not having any pain. Yes, Mother, my stump is elevated"—on and on it went for what seemed an eternity, although it had only been a few seconds. "Alayna? Oh, ah...she is in the bathroom," she said, rolling her eyes at yet another lie. "Love you too, Mom, and give my love to Ayson."

She was hanging up the phone just as Alayna was returning with their food. The juicy, charbroiled cheeseburger hit the empty spot in her stomach. "This is *sooo* good," she told Alayna, wiping ketchup and mayonnaise from her mouth.

After dinner, they watched TV for a few hours, most of which were reruns. She informed Alayna the principal had talked to her mom and that the school district would be sending a teacher by the hospital every few days to tutor her and make sure she did not fall behind in her studies. The teacher, a Ms. Michelle Windom, would be coming at the start of next week.

They had just finished watching *American Idol* when Alayna went to the bedside table and pulled out a Gideon Bible. She sat next to Addison on the bed and opened it to the book of Psalms. "How about we study the Twenty-Third Psalm for our devotional tonight?" she asked, flipping carefully through the pages of the Bible.

"I can't," Addison said flatly.

"What do you mean you can't? Do you want to study something else?"

"I mean…," Addison said with a slight hesitation, "I don't want to."

Alayna quit leafing through the pages and looked at her. In an instant, Addison's whole countenance had changed, and her eyes were dark with anger. She could see the tightening of Addison's jaw as she clenched her teeth. Even the vein on the right side of her neck was sticking out.

Alayna narrowed her eyes. "What's the matter with you?"

"Nothing is the matter with me," Addison said softly, tearing her eyes away from Alayna's piercing stare.

"Come on, Addison, out with it. I know you better than that."

Determined not to back down from Alayna's stare, this time, she turned to her friend. "All right, if you must know, I'll tell you. I tried God, and it didn't work." The last thing she wanted to do was to start crying. She reached up and brushed away a tear that had begun to roll down her flushed cheek. "Maybe my mom's right. Maybe God isn't a loving and caring God, or maybe He does have favorites. There's no way I'll ever be good enough for Him, especially now."

Alayna gently closed the Bible that lay across her lap as she continued to look her best friend square in the eyes. "Okay, Addison, first of all, God is not an 'it,' and secondly, He doesn't have favorites. Acts 10 tells us our Heavenly Father shows no favoritism, and whoever fears Him and works righteousness is accepted by Him."

More tears ran down Addison's face. Alayna stood up and walked over to the counter next to the sink and retrieved a box of tissues. She walked back and stood beside the bed, feeling somewhat helpless as Addison tried desperately to hold back more tears. Alayna handed her the box of tissues. Addison quickly jerked a tissue from the box and wiped her face, but she couldn't seem to wipe away the tears as fast as they were coming. They were coming nonstop, and she was feeling like such a fool. At this point, Addison looked so beaten down and fragile that Alayna could not hold back her own tears. She reached and took a couple of tissues from the box.

"Alayna, how can I trust God now? Look what He let happen to me. Just look!" She threw back the sheet, exposing her leg.

Alayna wanted to look away, but could not tear her watery eyes from the stump Addison had exposed. Addison's sobs had now turned into gut-wrenching wails. She had her arms folded across the top of her stomach and was rocking back and forth as if trying in some odd way to comfort herself. Alayna turned once again to face her friend. She felt her legs give a little as she heard Addison pray words of desperation.

"Please, God, give me another chance. Let me go back in time. I'll do better, I promise!"

"Oh, Addison," Alayna cried as she reached and wrapped her arms around her friend, trying to comfort her the best way she knew how. "Please don't do this to yourself. It's going to be all right, I promise."

Addison pushed Alayna back from her, but continued to hold onto her firmly as she locked her gaze intently on her friend. "I wish everyone would stop telling me everything is going to be all right! It isn't going to be all right!"

Alayna could hear the anger building in Addison's voice. "Yes, it is," she said, trying desperately to calm her best friend. She noticed the almost wild, distant look in Addison's eyes. Then almost instantly, her expression changed, and her tone of voice was calm.

"You promise?"

"I promise," said Alayna assuredly as she could, "But you've got to promise me something in return. Promise me you won't ever give up on God no matter what."

Addison loosened her grip. Alayna half-expected another outburst.

"I'll try not to give up," Addison said softly. "That's all I can promise." She reached for the cup of water next to her bed and took a sip as Alayna pulled the sheet back over her leg.

"Are you cold? Do you need another blanket? Do you need your pillow fluffed?"

Addison had turned toward Alayna with a mouth full of water just as Alayna asked the questions. Not meaning too, she burst into laughter at the bombardment of *mother* questions and spewed water into the face of a shocked Alayna. She couldn't help it, still laughing.

"No, Mother, I'm fine!" she said, emphasizing the word mother.

"Mother?" asked Alayna as she wiped her face with one of the tissues. The bewildered look on Alayna's face made her laugh even harder. "You're weird," Alayna said as she took the hair dryer and headed to the bathroom to dry the top of her shirt.

* * * * *

The warm air from the dryer felt good as Alayna's shirt began to dry. Maybe she had been too unsympathetic toward her friend. After all, look at all she had been through in the past couple of weeks. Alayna was positive she might find her faith wavering too if it were her lying in that hospital bed with one leg. But why in the world, she thought, did she promise Addison everything was going to be okay? She really had no earthly idea how things were going to turn out. She had overheard, quite by accident, Dr. Steelman tell Kyndal that Addison was not quite out of the woods yet. She continued to run the hair dryer over her shirt when she heard the words deep in her spirit, *Trust Me*. She knew it was the still small voice of the Holy Spirit.

"Forgive me, Lord, for my moment of doubt," she prayed aloud. For a brief moment, she almost felt like a hypocrite. There she was, just moments earlier telling Addison not to give up on God; but less than five minutes later, she had doubted Him. She thought about the scripture in the book of Romans, how all things work together for good to those who love God and who are called according to His purpose. Alayna knew she was going to have to trust God and that everything would work out for the best when it came to her friend.

She glanced at her watch. It was almost 9:30 p.m. Feeling to make sure her shirt was dry, she turned off the dryer and, unplugging it, wrapped the cord around the nozzle. The warm shirt felt good next to her skin. She came through the bathroom door and started to say something to Addison, but she was already asleep. She laid the dryer on the counter then turned and took a step toward the bed.

She reached and pulled the blanket over Addison for added warmth and tucked the blanket around her shoulders. She watched the steady rise and fall of Addison's chest and noticed the peaceful look on her face as she slept. At the moment, Addison didn't have a care in the world. Alayna wished it could be that way in her friend's waking hours as well.

Returning to the bathroom, she reached inside and turned on the light. She left the door slightly ajar in order to allow enough of the soft glowing light to illuminate the dark room once she turned off the overhead lights. Gathering a blanket, she turned off the light and lay back in the recliner. She pulled the blanket tightly around her shoulders and closed her eyes. She started to pray, but drifted off to sleep before she was even thirty seconds into her prayer.

They were awakened early the next morning by the lab tech arriving to draw blood. Alayna reached and turned on the over-bed light. She squinted as she tried to adjust her eyes to the blinding light.

"What time is it?" she asked, still trying to adjust to the light.

"Four thirty," the lab tech answered, checking Addison's wrist band and wrapping a tourniquet around her arm. Addison barely flinched as the tech located a vein and inserted the needle, collecting several tubes of blood. She thanked Addison as she reached and turned off the light, then quietly left the room, leaving the two to quickly drift off to sleep.

A knock on the door awoke them for the second time. The lab tech must have forgotten something to be coming back so soon, Alayna thought.

"Good morning, Miss Addison." It was Wilma from dietary. "Watch the eyes," she said with a chuckle. She turned on the light, causing their eyes to have to adjust once again to the brightness.

"Good morning, Wilma," Addison said, yawning and still a little sleepy.

Alayna glanced at her watch: it read 7:30 a.m. "Gosh," she said. It felt to her as if it had only been a few minutes since the lab tech had left. Wilma placed the over-bed table across the bed and set the breakfast tray in front of Addison. Wilma began to chat nonstop about the cool day ahead and the chance of an afternoon shower. She helped Addison sit up in bed and started to help her fix her breakfast tray.

"I can do that," volunteered Alayna. "But thanks anyway," she said, smiling at Wilma.

"You two have a good day." Wilma chuckled as she left the room.

Wilma Littlejohn had quickly become one of Addison's favorites around the hospital. She was a slightly plump black lady in her late fifties who seemed to laugh all the time, even when there was nothing to laugh about. She was missing a tooth from the top set of dentures, and the empty space in front was easily seen each time she smiled or laughed. "I jus' happened to sneeze one day and sneezed 'em right onto the floor," she had told Addison with a chuckle when they first met. "Broke my dang tooth right off." Wilma's smooth round face was surrounded with gray hair, which she kept pulled back in a hairnet. Her sunny disposition always seemed to cheer everyone up. The inviting aroma of pancakes with maple syrup and bacon made Alayna's mouth start to water as she began setting up the tray.

"Yoo-hoo!"

"Yoo-hoo?" Alayna mouthed to Addison as both girls looked at each other and giggled. "Yoo-hoo?" Alayna asked as her mother entered the room. "Really, Mom?"

Shannon Thomas dismissed her daughter's question with a wave of her hand. "Whatever," she replied nonchalantly.

Alayna noticed the white bag from her mother's restaurant. She was hoping it was something to eat as her stomach had been growling continuously for the past five minutes. Her mother held out the bag to her. "Here, I brought you two: a ham, egg, and cheese biscuit and some hash browns. I thought you might be getting a little hungry."

"You thought right. Thanks, Mom."

Alayna devoured the biscuit and hash browns in a matter of minutes. Addison opted for the biscuit as well. Alayna drank the orange juice from Addison's tray while Addison drank the coffee, even though it was a little stronger than she preferred. She tried to eat one of the pancakes, but was too stuffed to eat more than a few bites.

After finding out how their night went, they listened to Shannon talk about the weather and anything else she could think of.

"Well, girls, I've got to get back to the restaurant," she said a few minutes later, giving them both a hug and then a kiss on the cheeks. "Do you two need anything before I leave?" she asked while holding up a compact mirror and refreshing her bright-red lipstick. The girls looked at each other then shook their heads.

"Okay then. I'll see you two later," she said as she reached for the door. Then turning and waving with her fingers, she gave a cheerful, "Toodle-oo!" Jokingly, she crossed her eyes and stuck out her tongue at Alayna, causing everyone to burst into laughter.

Forty minutes later, Wilma returned for the breakfast tray. "I ran into your mother downstairs, Miss Addison. She said to tell you she'd be here to check on you during her break."

"Thanks, Wilma," she said, lowering the head of the bed.

Wilma collected the tray and hurried off. She was chuckling softly as she left the room, but it was anyone's guess as to why.

True to her mother's word, Kyndal was there to check on her during her fifteen-minute break and again on her lunch break. Both girls slept off and on in between times. They were still sleeping when Wilma brought in the lunch tray.

"Are you two going to sleep all day?" she asked, placing the tray on the over-bed table.

Addison lifted the lid from the plate on the tray and inhaled the mouth-watering aroma of chicken tetrazzini. She looked at the chocolate brownie. "Wilma, when are y'all going to make some of that delicious cherry cobbler? Do you want me to go into withdrawal?

Wilma didn't bother to give an answer. She just shook her head and chuckled on her way out.

Alayna glanced at the clock on the wall. "Gosh, Addison, I've got to get going," she said, gathering her belongings. Although there was no school today, she still had her final regular-season football game tonight.

"Good luck with the pyramid," Addison said as she watched Alayna stuff purple-heart pajamas into her duffle bag.

Alayna heard the sadness in her friend's voice. "I'll be careful," she replied as she zipped the bag. Alayna hated these awkward moments. She never knew quite how to respond and was relieved when they heard a knock on the door.

"Come in," both said in unison. Alayna was sure Addison had felt the awkwardness too, as well as the relief upon hearing the knock. It was Wyatt Kingsley. He came and stood by the bed.

"Chicken again?" he asked with a smile.

"What else?" Addison said, returning his smile. Then she introduced Alayna to Wyatt.

"Nice to meet you," he said, revealing his dimpled smile.

"You too, but if you two will excuse me, I have to go." Alayna grabbed her duffle bag and made her way to the door.

"Go, Wildcats!" Addison yelled after her.

"Go, Wildcats!" Alayna yelled over her shoulder as she closed the door behind her.

Wyatt turned back to Addison. "I hear you're a cheerleader."

"*Was* a cheerleader," she replied flatly.

Wyatt stuck both hands in his scrub pant pockets and started to say something, but then decided against it. "I just came by to let you know that I would be in around two o'clock to take you to the therapy room."

"Sure, that will be great," she said, less than enthusiastically.

"Okay," he said, taking his hands out of his pockets. "I'll see you then." He gave her another smile and was gone.

She again noticed the limp to his right leg and could have kicked herself for not remembering to ask about the motorcycle accident—not that he would share anything with her anyway. He would probably tell her to mind her own business. At least he has a leg to limp on, she thought.

She ate her lunch alone and afterward reached for the Agatha Christie novel. Maybe a good murder mystery will keep my mind off things, she thought. Speaking of murder, that's exactly what she would like to do to Tyler and Isaac. Of course, she wouldn't really go to such an extreme; but all the same, she felt bad for even thinking such a thing. She still couldn't help but feel God had dealt her an unfair hand in life; and for that, she was still angry.

She tried to read, but her thoughts kept turning to Wyatt Kingsley's next visit. She was to try and walk with her temporary prosthesis for the first time. Surely, it can't be that difficult, she thought. Wyatt had informed her earlier that he would have the prosthesis waiting for her in the therapy room. Regina Harrison would also be there to instruct her on how to apply the prosthesis and have her give a return demonstration. She was feeling so overwhelmed and inadequate at the moment. Placing her face in her hands, she began to weep.

A few days ago, she thought she had no tears left; now she wondered if the steady stream of tears would ever end.

CHAPTER 12

ONE STEP AT A TIME

It was past time for Wyatt to show up for Addison's therapy. The downside to him not showing up was that she had sort of looked forward to being around someone her own age; the fact he was cute didn't hurt either. The upside was because she was more than a little nervous about trying her new prosthesis. At ten past two and thinking Wyatt might not get to her today, she heard a knock at the door.

"Come in," she said as Wyatt Kingsley entered her room, pushing a wheelchair. Apologizing for being late, he placed the dark-blue wheelchair close to her bed and locked the wheels.

"It took a little longer with one of my other patients," he said as he carefully guided her unsteady body into the chair.

"No problem," she said as she sat not so gracefully into the chair.

It felt somewhat strange having to be pushed around in a wheelchair. She was embarrassed and wished she could have had an old dried-up prune of a person for a therapy assistant instead of one as handsome as Wyatt. It would have been even nicer to have had a female assistant. At least that way, she wouldn't have to be so embarrassed in front of the male gender. Of course, she had to admit, as unsteady as she was on one leg, she felt more secure in the strong arms of Wyatt Kingsley than she would have a female therapist. She knew she was making an unfair assessment of female therapists because they too had been trained in safe and proper transfer of patients. Since she was no longer receiving any IV therapy, she was able to wear her own pajamas. She was at least grateful for that. She had hated wearing the opened-back hospital gowns.

Wyatt reached and flipped the left leg of her pajamas over her stump. She felt her face blush from embarrassment. However, she noticed he didn't seem to be repulsed or bothered by the touch or the sight of the stump at all. Of course, he wouldn't, she thought. He was studying to be a therapist; at least that was what her mother had told her.

"Are you comfortable?" he asked as he unlocked her chair.

"Yes, thank you," she replied as he opened the door and pushed her into the hall. Wyatt closed the door, then pushed the wheelchair toward the elevator.

They waited quietly for the elevator to reach the second floor, which Addison thought seemed to be taking a lifetime. The elevator finally dinged, letting them know it had arrived at its destination. As the doors opened, Wyatt waited for the elevator to empty of all passengers before pushing her through the stainless steel doors.

The two of them were the only ones on the elevator. Wyatt leaned over to one side of her and pushed the button to the first floor. His nearness made her feel self-conscious about her appearance. She brushed her hands through her thick dark hair and wished it still had the luster it normally had. Since being in the hospital, she had only had bed baths and the use of waterless shampoo. The shampoo kept the oil down a little, but did nothing to give it the shine she was used to.

Another ding of the elevator, and they were on the first floor headed for the therapy room. Neither of the two had spoken much since leaving her room. They had just turned the corner that led down the long hall to the therapy room when she noticed a tall, slim woman in uniform approaching them. As the woman neared, she could see her name tag read "Candace McIntire, RN." She had long straight sandy-blonde hair, a perfectly shaped oval face, and soft light-blue eyes. Addison thought Candace was one of the most beautiful women she had ever seen.

"Hey, Wyatt, I'm glad I ran into you," she said, smiling at him with perfectly straight teeth that were the whitest she believed she had ever seen. "I have the dollar I owe you," she said, reaching into her uniform pocket.

"You don't have to give that back," he said.

Candace glanced down at Addison, her eyes resting briefly on the stump. She quickly turned her attention back to Wyatt when she noticed Addison watching her, but not before Addison caught a glimpse of pity in her eyes. Wyatt must have noticed the sad expression on her face. It was all she could do to keep from bursting into tears.

"Look, I really do need to go," he said as he quickly began to push the wheelchair down the hall.

"But what about the dollar I owe you?" Candace yelled after him.

"Keep it," he yelled back, not bothering to turn around.

Addison was still fighting back tears. She had never felt so humiliated in all her life. Pity was the last thing she needed from anyone. Was that what she had to look forward to for the rest of her life, everyone's pity?

"Knock, knock."

Did Wyatt just say "knock, knock"? She wasn't sure whether to respond or not.

"Knock, knock," he repeated.

"Who's...there?" she asked slowly.

"Orange."

"Orange who?"

"Orange you going to let me in?"

For a second or two, she could only think it was the worst knock-knock joke she had ever heard—not that there were any good knock-knock jokes as far as she was concerned. She burst into laughter; she couldn't help it. The fact that Wyatt Kingsley even dared tell such a corny knock-knock joke struck her as being funny.

"I'm glad you liked it," he said as the automatic doors to the therapy room opened. His comment made her laugh even harder as he wheeled her over to an area where there were a set of two long parallel bars. Surely he didn't think it was the joke she found so funny. Wyatt locked down the wheelchair and then pulled up a chair and sat in front of her. "Feel better?" he asked, smiling at her. She knew what he was referring to.

"Yes, thanks," she said as she nodded and then turned her face toward the parallel bars. "I still feel so emotional at times."

Wyatt's smile faded, and his expression turned serious. "Look at me, Addison." She turned slowly and faced him. The seriousness of his face almost frightened her.

"I give you my word, right here and now, that your life will get better. I know you don't think so, but it will." She started to protest, but he placed his finger gently over her lips. "You've got your whole life ahead of you, a good life. Addison, God did not do this to you, but He knows all things, and He knew this was going to happen."

She felt herself getting angry. She wished everyone would quit talking to her about God. She pushed his finger away from her lips. "You're right! He does know all things, so why didn't He stop this? Why!"

"I can't answer that," he said with a sigh. "All I know is that He promises to never leave us nor forsake us. I know you feel alone at times, but you're not. Even now He's here—because He's *here*," he said, pointing to her heart.

Addison felt some of the anger leaving. "What happened to you?" she asked softly.

He looked at her as if he didn't know what she was talking about.

"You limp. Why do you limp?"

"Oh, that." He smiled. "I was in a motorcycle accident a couple of years ago. Messed up my foot pretty bad. A man pulled out in front of me at a stop sign, said he never saw me coming. I ended up having to have three toes amputated on my right foot."

Not expecting to hear something like that, Addison didn't quite know how to respond. "I'm sorry," she said, glancing back at the set of bars. "Do you still ride?"

"Nah, not anymore," he said. "That kind of did it for me."

Addison apologized again.

"No need for apologies. I've a good life now and a good life ahead of me."

"What makes you so sure you have a good life ahead of you? You don't know or hold the future." Her anger was beginning to sneak up again.

"You're right, Addison. I don't know everything my future holds, but I do know the One who holds my future. In the Bible, Jeremiah tells us the Lord knows the thoughts and plans He has for us, thoughts and plans for welfare and peace and not for evil, to give us a hope in our final outcome."

"Sounds good. I just wish I could believe that."

"You will," he said, standing. "You will."

She was about to say something else when Ms. No Smile, a.k.a. Regina Harrison, made her way over with the prosthesis. After twenty minutes of showing Addison how to put on and remove her prosthesis and having her demonstrate the same, Regina left her to work with Wyatt. He pushed her over to the bars she had seen earlier and locked the wheelchair.

"Let's get started."

She felt awkward and clumsy as Wyatt helped her into a standing position. She had no idea until then just how much a person depended on two legs. Her arms were weak, and her good leg had not seen much standing lately—and now Wyatt Kingsley was expecting her to walk as if she had two good legs. The prosthesis felt heavy and awkward.

"Walk toward me," he said, motioning with both hands for her to walk forward.

Holding tight to the bars on each side of her, she walked toward Wyatt. She would take three or four steps, almost reaching him, before he would move further back and tell her again to walk toward him. She broke out in a sweat, and her arms were burning and stinging from having to carry most of her weight.

"Let your weight fall on your lower extremities, not your arms," said Wyatt as he continued to encourage her to move toward him.

"I can't do this!" she finally yelled, feeling frustrated. Her arms hurt so much she could no longer hold herself up.

"Addison, you can bear weight on your prosthesis," Wyatt reminded her.

She felt her artificial leg give way as she started to fall to the floor. She began to panic and was helpless to stop herself from falling. Suddenly she felt a pair of strong arms around her.

"I've got you. I won't let you fall," she heard Wyatt say.

She began to cry as he lowered her to the floor. She felt both relieved and frustrated at the same time. She noticed some of the other patients watching her. She wanted to scream as loud as she could for them to stop staring, but all she could do was sob. She buried her face in her hands, too ashamed to look Wyatt in the face. She sat on the floor next to him, sobbing uncontrollably.

Still sobbing, she looked up when she heard a clanking noise. A young man who appeared to be in his early to midthirties was approaching them. He had long dark hair midway down his back, which he had pulled back in a low ponytail. He was wearing a sleeveless white T-shirt revealing tattoos from the top of both arms all the way down to his hands. Most of the tattoos looked like military tattoos with eagles, tanks, USA flags, and rifles. The one going down his right arm read, "God and Country." He was steadying himself with two metal crutches and wearing navy-blue shorts, revealing bilateral artificial legs from the knees down. When he got to where she was curled up next to Wyatt, he didn't even bother to introduce himself.

"Miss, if I can do it, I know you can. You just have to be determined. This setback is not going to beat you. If you fall, get back up. There's no shame in falling, but there is shame in not getting back up."

His words reminded her of one of her dad's promises. He started to walk away, but then stopped and looked at her again. "Get a fighting spirit, young lady, and nothing will be able to hold you down.

She watched the man walk away, not knowing quite what to make of him. The large gold chain bracelet he wore around his right wrist beat against the metal crutch, making a clanking sound as he walked. She realized she had stopped crying, and for some reason, she didn't even feel offended at what the stranger had said. Maybe it was because she didn't see pity or disgust in his eyes when he looked at her; she didn't even see compassion. It was more like a look of, *Suck it up, buttercup, and quit feeling sorry for yourself.*

Wyatt's voice snapped her from her thoughts. "That was Mason Orbach. He lost both his legs a few years ago while serving in Afghanistan. He's a volunteer now at the hospital."

"You mean he works here?" she asked, surprised at the information.

"Volunteers," Wyatt emphasized, "But yeah, I guess you could say in a way he works here." Suddenly realizing she had reached and grabbed hold of Wyatt's arm, she quickly let go and asked him to help her stand.

"He's right," she said, holding her chin up. "I'm tougher than this. I'm ready to try again."

"Tomorrow," Wyatt said, lifting her to a standing position.

"No, now!" she said, determined not to give in.

Hearing the determination in her voice, he knew it would be pointless to argue. "Okay," he said, smiling. "Go for it!" Truth was, he really was proud of her sudden determination.

Addison struggled again to hold herself up, but this time, she didn't cry when she started to fall. She knew Wyatt would catch her—much like her daddy had done when she was a little girl. For a split second, she had a vision of her dad throwing her into the air and catching her like on her promise picture. She laughed as Wyatt lowered her to the floor.

"You made it further this time," he said excitedly.

"And I'll go even further tomorrow," she said, trying to catch her breath. She looked up and saw Mason watching from across the room. She gave the thumbs-up sign, and he gave a nod of approval.

She was totally exhausted by the time she returned to the room. Her mother was already off work and waiting for her.

"Well, how did it go?" she asked as Wyatt rolled Addison into the room.

"It went great! Your daughter's a real fighter," Wyatt said proudly.

Addison felt her face flush, but nevertheless, she was thankful for the compliment. After she was situated in bed, Wyatt said his goodbyes and told her he would see her tomorrow around the same time.

Her mother lay back in the recliner, kicked off her shoes, and picked up a crossword puzzle. Watching her mother, Addison could see she wasn't the only person who was exhausted.

"Mom," she said, hesitating, "I...I don't want you to stay tonight." She could see the big question mark in her mother's expression.

"Why on earth would you not want me to stay?"

"I can give you three good reasons: Number one, you're exhausted. Number two, Ayson and Chip need you. And number three, I'm perfectly capable of staying by myself. If I need anything, I can call a nurse."

Kyndal sat up in the recliner. Addison could see her mother was a little hurt, but she was determined not to give in. "Mom, this is something I need to do for myself. I want to stand on my own two feet." She realized the words she spoke as soon as the words left her mouth. Her mom looked like she wasn't sure how to respond.

Addison gave a slight smile. "Well, maybe I'll just stand on my own foot."

Her mother looked relieved that she had made light of the slip instead of bursting into tears. Addison could see her mother was debating whether or not to leave, but she also noticed when her mother moved her neck from side to side and winced from the tightened muscles. She was also certain her mother was feeling guilty for leaving Ayson and Chip at the Garrisons so often because of all the phone calls she made to him every time she spent the night at the hospital.

"Okay, but—"

"I know. Call you if anything changes," Addison sighed.

Kyndal lightly massaged her feet before sliding her shoes on and gathering the rest of her things. She leaned and gave Addison a kiss on the cheek. "Do you need your head raised, or your pillow fluffed before I—"

"Mom!"

"Okay, okay, I'm out of here," she said with a wave of her hand. "Love you."

"Love you too, Mom."

After her mother left, Addison felt a little less smothered, but she did have a few boring moments. After supper, to help pass the time, she watched a Lifetime movie on TV for a couple of hours and then read some more of her Christie novel. At the moment, she was busy working a crossword puzzle in the newspaper.

"Four-letter word for walk at a steady and consistent speed," she said, thinking aloud.

"Try the word pace." The deep voice startled her, causing her to jump. Dr. Steelman noticed her jump as soon as he spoke. "Sorry," he apologized. "The door was open."

"Thanks," she said, turning back to the puzzle and filling in the answer he had given her. Finishing the four-letter word, she laid the puzzle aside. She glanced at the clock, then back at Dr. Steelman.

"You're working late tonight. Are you on call?" she asked.

"No, just had a lot of patients to see, but you're my last."

"Saving the best till last, are you?" she asked with a smile.

"Of course," he said, returning her smile. "I heard you had your first therapy session using your prosthesis today. How did it go?"

Addison folded her hands on her lap and put on a positive face. "It went really well…after the first try. I am determined to beat this thing, Dr. Steelman."

Maybe Tillie Davenport was right, she thought. Maybe she was starting to accept her situation, as she thought about the five stages of grief and loss—acceptance being one of the stages. If nothing else, Dr. Davenport had caused her to understand the feelings of confusion and the emotional ups and downs she was having.

"That's the spirit," Dr. Steelman said. She could tell he was trying to get a read on her as to whether or not she was telling the truth or if she was just telling him what she thought he wanted to hear.

"Where's your mother?" he asked, approaching the bed.

"Believe it or not, I convinced her to let me stay alone tonight. She left a few hours ago."

Dr. Steelman gave a slight nod. She couldn't really swear to it, but she was almost positive she saw a hint of disappointment in his somewhat tired eyes upon hearing he had missed her mother.

"Okay, young lady, let's have a look at that leg." Pulling back the sheet, he gently pressed on her stump and examined it carefully. Satisfied that everything was healing as it should, he bid her goodbye. "Tell your mother I'm sorry I missed her," he said as he left the room.

She frowned. *What's going on here?* she wondered as she picked up the paper again.

After finishing the crossword, she wasn't sure what she wanted to do next. She was bored with watching TV, and she really wasn't in the mood to read more of her novel. She sat twiddling her thumbs for a few seconds while she looked around the room. Her eyes fell on the Gideon Bible.

I definitely do not want to read that, she thought.

She looked at the clock. Another forty-five minutes, and Alayna would be jumping and doing back flips and cheering the Wildcats on to hopefully another victory. She felt the tears begin to well up in her eyes. Maybe staying alone tonight wasn't such a good idea after all. At least with someone to keep her company, she could keep her mind occupied.

Now all she could do was sit and think about the sorry hand life had dealt her. She reached and brushed away a tear. Her hand moved toward the Bible lying on the bedside table, then she quickly pulled it back as if she had almost picked up a lump of hot coal. She turned on the TV instead. She turned it to the game-show channel and watched several games.

Before long, she drifted off to a restless sleep. She kept dreaming crazy dreams all during the night. In one dream, she was in church wearing a bikini with huge rollers in her hair and cold cream on her face. In another dream, she was surrounded by snakes and was trying to beat them off with a stick. In yet another dream, she was being chased through the woods by some kind of enormous hairy monster with humongous fang-like teeth. She finally woke up in a cold sweat when she was about to fall off a fifty-foot cliff.

The clock read 3:27 a.m. She reached for the cup of ice water next to the bed and took a drink to try and soothe her dry mouth. The cold water felt refreshing as she practically gulped the entire cup of water at one time. She placed the cup back on the table. Once again her eyes fell on the blue Gideon Bible.

"Lord, if You really do love me," she prayed, "then show me something in this Bible that would prove it to me right now". She picked up the Bible, closed her eyes, opened it up, and pointed blindly with her index finger. She looked eagerly at the scripture her finger had landed on. She began to read aloud from the book of Hebrews.

"Do not harden your hearts as in the rebellion, in the day of trial in the wilderness."

She slammed the book shut. Great.

"Somehow that doesn't make me feel much loved," she complained aloud. "I knew You wouldn't listen to me. You won't even do something as simple as letting me know how much You love me. It's because You don't." She was beginning to feel angry again. She looked toward the heaven.

"I made a mistake, okay! I went to a party, I drank a little, and I hit smarty-pants Karlie. If I needed to be punished, okay! But why this?" she said, raising her stump off the bed.

"What's the use?" she mumbled as she laid the Bible back on the table and rolled over.

She was trying hard to keep her promise to Alayna and not give up on God, but He was making it awful hard. Thirty minutes later, she finally drifted off to sleep on a tearstained pillow.

CHAPTER 13

A LOCKED DOOR

It was Saturday, and Addison had a room full of visitors. Her mother, Ayson, and the Garrisons had arrived earlier around 9:15 a.m. From then on, one person after another had arrived. Alayna and her mom came, then Pastor Bryce and his family, and then Trevor Grant.

At the moment, Ayson was telling her about a new computer game he and Caleb were now into. Alayna was simultaneously telling her about the Hail Mary the Wildcats had thrown during the last three seconds of the game. They had won 13–7, clinching them a spot in the playoffs. Her mother, Shannon, and Pastor Bryce and Maggie were engaged in conversation about antique furniture. Listening to their conversation made Addison think about the flowered sofa at home. It really wasn't an antique, but it was definitely outdated. Having had a restless night, all the talking at once was beginning to wear on her nerves. She was about to the breaking point of yelling for everyone to be quiet when she heard someone lightly rap on the door and ask if he could come in. It was Dr. Steelman. The small gathering echoed their greetings before he asked that everyone leave the room so he could check her leg. He cleared his throat.

"Would you mind remaining, Kyndal?" he asked as he walked toward the bed.

"Okay, Noah," her mother replied.

Kyndal, Noah? Addison frowned. Since when were her mom and Dr. Steelman on a first-name basis? Something weird was going on.

Dr. Steelman pulled back the sheet to check her stump. The staples had been removed about a week earlier, which she was thankful for. With the staples removed, the incision didn't feel quite as tight. After a couple of minutes, he pulled the sheet back over her leg and asked how she was feeling. Other than having to deal with some occasional phantom pain, she was doing pretty well, she told him. Dr. Steelman sat next to her on the bed. She could tell from the expression on his face he was about to discuss something of a serious nature.

"Addison, you've been here a little over two weeks now," he began. "I think we should look at you going home in another day or two. Too be honest, I really should have already released you." He gave a look toward her mother, who quickly turned from his gaze. "I'm running out of reasons to keep you here, and to be honest, the hospital, as well as the insurance company, is not too happy with me at the moment," he said with a long sigh.

The news totally caught her off guard.

"But what's going to happen with my therapy? I've just started making great progress."

"You'll have another few days here, and then I will arrange for outpatient therapy or perhaps home health for a few weeks."

She felt happy to be going home to her family, but afraid of what awaited her outside the four walls of the hospital. The hospital, in a way, had become a safe haven for her.

"What about my tutoring? Will Mrs. Windom still be allowed to tutor me on my schoolwork?"

Michelle Windom had been coming to the hospital twice a week for the past week to tutor her, and so far, she was caught up with the rest of her class.

"All of that will be arranged," he assured her. "You know, Addison, there is really no reason you can't attend school." Dr. Steelman could see the apprehension in Addison's face. Then he said those inevitable words that absolutely drove her crazy. "Everything will be all right. You'll see." After giving her a pat on the hand, he turned to her mother and smiled. "It will be all right," he repeated for her mother's benefit.

Her mother forced a smile and nodded in agreement. "Of course, it will," she said, although Addison didn't think her mother sounded too convinced.

Addison forced a smile as well. Dr. Steelman and her mother stepped outside the room. She knew her mother was voicing her concerns and did not want her to hear the conversation. A few minutes later, her mother came back into the room, followed by the rest of the gang. Pastor Bryce and his family and Trevor were the first to leave about thirty minutes later, followed by Shannon, the Garrisons, and then her mother and Ayson.

Alayna was staying the night again, mostly to keep Addison from being bored. She had told Alayna she didn't have to stay, but Alayna insisted on staying anyway. Addison didn't want to put a damper on her friend's social life and had told her as much. Alayna made sure to stress the fact that she had no social life by making a sad pouty lip while trying to hold back a smile.

At the moment, Alayna sat on the edge of the bed, catching her up on all the school news. The big news at the moment was Jonah Medley had dumped Karlie Adams Friday night after the game for Aliyah Dodd, a member of the Wildcats color guard. A part of Addison wanted to gloat a little over the news, but she was too caught up in thoughts of having to leave the hospital. At least here, she didn't have to endure the stares and whispers of her peers.

Alayna was on a roll now, first one thing then another. She heard Alayna mention Aliyah's name again but didn't catch what she was saying. She just nodded as Alayna talked. Every now and again, she mumbled words of agreement as if she were hanging on to every word. Truth be told, she was barely listening. The thought of going back to school was really rattling her.

Alayna glanced at the clock. It would be a little over an hour before dinner arrived. She pulled out her cell phone. "Hey, Addison, let's see what news is on here. Maybe there's an update on the Jonah,

Karlie, and Aliyah saga," she said cheerfully. Alayna was definitely gloating.

"Sure, why not?" Addison said.

* * * * *

Tyler Morris didn't want to be bothered right now. He locked the door to his bedroom and sat on the unmade bed. He just wanted to be left alone to think about how he had been the reason Addison McNeely had lost her leg. He shuttered at the thought that it could have been worse: he could have killed her. Now, on top of that, he was facing jail.

Tyler didn't really know Addison well, but he knew she was a cheerleader and very active in school activities—and she was a Christian. He ran his shaking hands through his unkempt hair.

"Addison, what were you doing at that party?" he asked aloud. He had wanted and tried to blame Addison for the whole mess. She had no business as a Christian being at that party. But he knew in his heart as true as that might be, Addison McNeely was not the one to blame. She had not been the one driving drunk behind the wheel.

He looked toward the single window in the small bedroom. The warm glow of sun streaming through the partially opened blinds formed several honey-colored streaks on the beige carpet. Today the warmth of the usually comforting sun failed to bring even the slightest feeling of comfort.

He looked around at the numerous football posters on the walls, as well as the large collection of football trophies he had accumulated over the years. A lone tear slid down his face and fell onto his lap.

"I messed up," he said, barely above a whisper as another salty tear ran down his face.

It was now the first week in November. This was usually the time of year he looked forward to football games and holidays, but not this year, not since that stupid accident. Before the accident, he had it all.

He was a football star at Williamston College, and he could have just about any girl he wanted. He was tall and muscular and had been told by a number of the female population that his jet-black hair, full lips, and dreamy blue eyes—whatever that meant—were his best features. Some said he favored Elvis.

Now he and his cousin Jude from LD's Qwik Mart were facing criminal charges. He had not been surprised to hear L. D. Myers had terminated Jude upon hearing he had sold alcohol to an underaged student, especially after it resulted in an accident. The incident had also put the store's liquor license in jeopardy, something else Mr. Myers had not been happy about. There had been some talk of Isaac possibly being charged for providing alcohol to minors, but most of the students at the party had provided their own alcohol. However, the few minors who hadn't were reluctant to snitch on Isaac, including Addison. He had heard through the grapevine that Addison, much like the others, felt no one had twisted their arms to drink.

Tyler rested his head in his hands. He knew his football career and his days at Williamston College were pretty much over.

Lately tormenting thoughts had plagued his mind nonstop. He had hurt someone badly, both physically and emotionally, not to mention numerous others who had been affected emotionally due to his irresponsible actions. His own mother and father were among those he had hurt.

He had wanted to tell Addison how sorry he was, but she wouldn't even let him get near her, let alone apologize. Not that he could blame her. He had asked Isaac to try and convince Addison to talk to him, but Isaac didn't even have the guts to see her himself.

Tyler was sure he had no future, at least not one worth living for—no way was he going to rot in jail. He picked up the .32 caliber revolver lying next to him he had retrieved by breaking into his father's gun cabinet.

If only he could have just quit drinking. He had tried to give it up a few times, but he just couldn't put the bottle down. He had always liked to party, and he liked the way alcohol made him feel, at least until the hangover kicked in. Now look where it had gotten him.

He stared at the revolver in his sweaty hand.

"It wasn't worth it," he said aloud. "Now it's too late. I'm a failure, and I always will be."

He knew his parents would be devastated at what he was about to do. Once more he would be a disappointment to them, but at least it would be the last time. His parents had a strong and unwavering faith in God. If there really was a God, He would help his mother and father get through this.

In recent years, he had often wondered if there really was a God. His parents had taught him at an early age to believe in God and His love for mankind, to believe God had sent His only Son to die for the human race and for him. As a child, he had been taken to church and often sang in the children's choir. It wasn't until he was in his teens that he had begun to doubt the existence of God. Scientifically, it was easier to believe in evolution than to believe a higher authority had created man from dust and woman from a rib.

"That's where faith comes in," his father had told him the first time he told his parents he wasn't sure about the existence of God. His mother had burst into tears, and his father had simply shaken his head in disbelief. He remembered how his father had reached and hugged him and then looked him boldly in the eyes and said, "Son, we have trained you up in the way you should go. God's Word tells us if we do that, then when you are old, you will not depart." His father had put his arms around his wife of twenty-two years and smiled at her before turning back to him. "We did our part, son, and now we're going to trust God to do His part. Your mother and I are not giving up on you."

Now, the tears were coming fast, so fast he could barely see the gun in his hand.

"You can finally give up on me," he whispered through broken words and bitter tears.

Raising the gun to his temple, he wrapped his index finger around the trigger. His hand was shaking violently as beads of moisture formed on his forehead. His heart was hammering so hard and fast he felt as if it were going to explode into a million pieces. He heard the constant pounding in his ears as turbulent blood rushed through his vessels. His chest felt tight, and it was getting harder to breathe. Tyler closed his eyes as tears streamed down his cheeks. He felt fear surging through every fiber of his being. Once he pulled the trigger, there would be no turning back. He knew this was going to hurt, but hopefully for only a split second. But what if he didn't die instantly, then what? Fear was mounting with every breath he struggled to take. If he didn't quit contemplating the what-ifs, he knew he would talk himself out of what needed to be done.

Just pull the trigger, he told himself.

Pull it now! an evil presence screamed inside his head.

Without further hesitation, he squeezed the trigger and fell to the floor. A warm sticky substance oozed from his head. The warmth of the blood and the warmth of the sun-streaked carpet mixed as the carpet began to soak up the pool of red liquid. For a brief second, Tyler thought he heard yelling at the door, and then there was silence and darkness, cold darkness.

* * * * *

Addison sat straight up in bed. She could tell from the expression on Alayna's face that she had read something disturbing on her phone. Every bit of color had drained from her face, and her mouth was opened in utter disbelief. She saw Alayna's hand begin to shake and her eyes fill with tears.

"What is it, Alayna? What's wrong?" she asked, curious to know what had disturbed her so.

Alayna looked at her and shook her head. "It's Tyler Morris. He shot himself!"

"What!" Addison's hands flew to her mouth as she let out a gasp. "He's dead?"

"No, but he's in critical condition." She handed Addison the phone. She read how Tyler's parents heard the gunshot and ran to his bedroom. His father, having to kick the door in, found him lying on the bedroom floor, soaking in a pool of blood.

A few minutes later, Alayna's phone rang. It was Trevor.

"Yes, we just heard," she told him as she walked toward the door. Alayna continued to converse with Trevor on the phone, but

Addison was so lost in her own thoughts she barely heard anything Alayna was saying.

"What if he dies?" Addison asked softly to no one in particular. Why didn't she let him come in and talk to her when he had come to visit her? "What have I done?" she said louder.

"Talk to you later," she heard Alayna say. "Keep us informed." Alayna walked back to the bed and sat on the edge. She shook her head. "Trevor said he spoke with Isaac. It doesn't look good."

"Alayna," she said somewhat slowly, "Tyler came to see me the other day. I wouldn't let him in. I even threw a book at him."

"What!" Alayna exclaimed.

Addison told her the whole story. "Alayna, did they bring him here?" she asked after she had finished updating her on Tyler's attempt to see her.

"From what Trevor told me, EMS brought him here just long enough to stabilize him, and then he was airlifted to Charlotte, North Carolina."

"Please, God," Addison prayed aloud, "don't let Tyler die."

It was the first time in weeks Alayna had actually heard Addison pray about anything. She reached and took Addison by the hand. Addison looked out the window. It was beginning to get dusky dark.

"I feel so guilty for not letting Tyler talk to me. Could I have prevented this? Is this my fault?" Addison asked.

"This is not your fault," Alayna answered, somewhat sternly.

Addison tried not to think about the times she had wished Tyler dead and the time she had threatened to kill him when he had come to apologize to her at the hospital. Addison's hospital phone rang. It was her mother.

"Yes, Mom, we heard a few minutes ago. Yes, I'm fine," she told her mother, although she wasn't sure if she was or not. For some reason, the sound of her mother's voice brought a feeling of comfort amid all the disturbing news. Maybe she needed her mother more than she realized.

CHAPTER 14

A PARENT'S WORST NIGHTMARE

Dr. Arthur Linski was waiting in the trauma center of Faith Hospital when twenty-year-old Tyler Morris was brought in with a self-inflicted gunshot wound to the head. Earlier, Dr. Linski had received a verbal report from the ER doctor at Cherokee Memorial and had been expecting the young man. Earlier he had spoken with Mr. Morris by phone to get a verbal consent for surgery. He had also spoken to him regarding Tyler's surgery and everything the surgery would entail. He had taken great care to explain every detail and answer any questions so that Bryan Morris and his wife would know what to expect. He was busy reading the faxed report when he heard the buzz of the entrance doors. He looked up from behind the nurse's station and saw Joel and James pushing a stretcher through the first set of automatic sliding doors. Standing, he made his way around the U-shaped nurse's station and met the two men as they entered quickly through the second set of wide doors.

"Take him to OR 3," he instructed. He glanced at the almost lifeless young man as he followed the two men to the operating room. Tyler Morris was alive but nonresponsive.

"We almost lost him once, Doc," said Joel Kellerman, the flight paramedic. Dr. Linski could see the relief on Joel's face that he and his coworker James had finally arrived at their destination.

"Yeah, Doc, he gave us quite a scare," said James, the flight nurse.

"He was stable when we left Cherokee Memorial with him," Joel said as they hurriedly wheeled the stretcher to OR 3. "But then he took a turn for the worse on the way here."

"We were almost here when he coded," continued James. "But we were able to get him back." As they reached room 3, the door opened.

"We'll take it from here," said one of the OR staff as he rolled the stretcher into the cold operating room.

Arthur listened intently as Joel finished giving report as the OR staff scrambled to their stations for surgery. The head nurse over the unit signed the receiving papers, relieving James and Joel of any further responsibility. Dr. William Kelsey, who would be assisting with the surgery, and a nurse were heading to room 3 just as the men were leaving.

"Good luck, Doc," Joel said as he and James passed the doctor and the plain but rather pretty nurse.

"It's going to take more than luck. It's going to take a miracle," Dr. Kelsey said.

"I'm getting too old for this sort of thing," Dr. Linski mumbled as he began the delicate surgery.

Arthur Linski was in his late forties but appeared a little older. He had been chief of staff for the past four years at Faith Memorial and was one of the leading neurosurgeons in the area. He felt his face grow warm and knew it had probably turned red as well. He felt the anger rising inside of him. Here was a young man who had his entire life ahead of him.

"What drove him to this point?" he wondered, not realizing he had spoken aloud.

"I heard he caused an accident while driving drunk, resulting in a young girl losing her leg," stated Dr. Kelsey as they continued to work.

"His blood pressure is dropping—we're losing him!" he heard the anesthesiologist say with urgency in his voice.

"Jesus, help us!" prayed Dr. Linski. "We've got a bleeder somewhere. Show us, God, where it is!"

"Here it is!" cried Dr. Kelsey.

"Clamp!" Dr. Linski yelled as the surgical nurse quickly slapped it into his waiting hand.

"His blood pressure is coming back up!" the anesthesiologist said with relief in his voice. Both doctors breathed a sigh of relief, along with everyone else.

"Thank You, Lord," Dr. Linski said as he looked toward heaven, then back at his young patient. Finally, the bullet had been removed. Dr. Linski could only imagine what Tyler's parents were going through. He was sure they would have arrived at the hospital by now—wondering, waiting, and praying for the life of their son.

* * * * *

Tyler's parents, as well as a few other family members, arrived twenty minutes after Dr. Linski had begun surgery. Although other people were in the surgery waiting area, Bryan and Rebekah Morris felt no embarrassment as they knelt in front of their chairs and began to silently pray.

April Linski, the nurse manager for the intensive care unit, was passing by when she noticed the couple. She had heard about Tyler Morris and was pretty certain the couple she saw kneeling was his parents. The TV was turned to a talk show, but the volume had been turned to low. She stuck her head through the door and heard a few whispers, but most of the onlookers were silent as they showed their respect. Some were even wiping tears from their faces.

She hesitated for a few seconds before approaching Rebekah Morris, who had not even taken the time to pull off her heavy gray coat. April gently placed her hand on the woman's shoulder, causing Rebekah to look up. April, upon seeing the mother's sad swollen eyes from hours of crying, had to fight back her own tears. She couldn't even begin to imagine what the woman and her husband were feeling at the possible loss of a child. She had been a nurse for twenty-three years, yet this kind of situation had never gotten any easier.

"Mrs. Morris…"

But before she could finish, she saw the fear in the woman's eyes and noticed that every bit of color had drained from her face.

"Oh God, no!" Rebekah screamed. The outburst caused her husband to turn and look at his wife and then at April. It took April only a second to realize what Rebekah and Bryan Morris were thinking.

"No, no!" April said quickly. "Your son is okay! Everything's fine." She saw the look of relief and the color start to come back into Rebekah's face. Bryan Morris stood and helped his wife to her feet. Since April was not approaching them about their son, he concluded she must be approaching them about praying in the waiting room.

"We didn't mean to offend anyone, Ms. Linski," he said, glancing at her name badge. "We just wanted to pray for our son," he explained.

April felt a little uncomfortable as she looked around at the angry glares she was getting from the people in the waiting room. "Oh no, Mr. Morris," she hurried to explain. "I just saw you and your wife praying, and I thought you might like to have more privacy. I would be glad to take you to our chapel if you wish. However, if you prefer to stay here, that is perfectly all right as well." She glanced around the room and actually saw a few smiles come her way.

"We don't want to miss the doctor should he call with any news," Rebekah said, looking at her husband.

Bryan Morris shook his head in agreement.

"I can arrange it so you won't miss any calls from the OR," April assured them, pointing to the receptionist near the door. "I'll make sure Rosalie calls me if there is any news about your son, and I will personally see the message gets relayed to you."

They turned toward the receptionist, and she nodded, giving them a warm and friendly smile. The Morrises agreed they would feel more comfortable praying in the chapel.

The chapel was only a few yards around the corner to the left. Bryan Morris apparently felt he needed to explain further, or maybe he just needed to drown out the awkward silence as they made their way to the chapel. "We just feel led to pray the whole time Tyler is in surgery. I guess you think we're just being silly."

April looked into the weary blue eyes of the man walking beside her. "Quite the contrary, Mr. Morris—"

Mrs. Morris interrupted her, "Please, dear, call us Bryan and Rebekah."

"Only if you call me April," she said smiling at the exhausted couple.

As they made their way to the chapel, April wondered how old the Morrises really were. She was almost willing to bet they appeared a little older than they actually were. As she looked into the kind eyes of the woman walking arm in arm beside her husband, she couldn't help but notice the most beautiful eyes she had ever seen. They appeared to be green with gold flecks, or were they brown with green flecks? April couldn't really decide. It all depended on how the light reflected in them.

Reaching the chapel, she opened the door and waited for the couple to enter the small but peaceful sanctuary.

Rebekah finally took off her coat and placed it on the back of the wooden pew. She was slimmer than April had originally thought due to the heavy coat she had been wearing. Her strawberry-blonde hair with the tapered short haircut flattered her oval face. April could tell even through the puffiness and red splotches on her face from crying that Rebekah Morris was a beautiful lady. Her husband, Bryan, was of average height and built and had mousy brown hair fashioned in a crew cut. He was just beginning to show a little gray, mostly around the temple, making him look rather distinguished, April thought.

The couple thanked her as they joined hands and walked to the altar at the front of the sanctuary. Kneeling side by side, they began to pray for their beloved son. April started to turn and leave, but instead she approached the altar, knelt, and took Rebekah by the hand.

"Rebekah," she whispered, "may I stay and pray with you and Bryan for a while?"

Rebekah and Bryan's eyes began to fill with even more tears.

"Of course, you may," Rebekah said as she gently squeezed her hand. "By the way, I noticed you have the same last name as Dr. Linski. Are you of any relation?"

"He's my husband, and the best neurosurgeon your son could possibly have." Rebekah smiled and bowed her head. April Linski, mother of three, returned the warm smile and bowed her head as well. She began to pray as she resigned herself to skipping her lunch.

* * * * *

April had relayed a few messages to the Morrises regarding how the surgery was going upon getting updates from Rosalie. Since everything had turned out okay with the bleeder, she had decided not to relay that part. No need in worrying the couple unnecessarily. Earlier she had been asked by the Morrises if she could be present when Dr. Linski updated them on their son's condition after surgery. Rosalie was to call the OR and ask Dr. Linski if it would be okay. Finally, she received the call she had been anxiously awaiting. Tyler was out of surgery, and her husband had approved her sitting in when he updated the family on Tyler's condition.

"Dr. Linski is headed to the chapel right now to update them on Tyler's condition," Rosalie informed her.

April pushed back the black leather chair she was sitting in behind her desk and grabbed her purse. She turned the light off and locked the office door, then quickly made her way down the long hall. It was perfect timing. Her shift would be ending shortly. She hurried to the elevators and pushed the down button.

"Hurry, hurry!" she mumbled as she tapped her foot impatiently while waiting for the elevator to arrive. Arthur was a busy man and would not like to be kept waiting, even by his wife. She watched the light above the elevator door indicate on which floor the elevator was stopping. She continued to tap her foot anxiously as she watched the elevator slowly descend one floor at a time.

"Geez!" she said, irritated, and louder than she intended to. A young man with a goatee had walked up next to her and was holding the hand of a little boy who looked to be about three or four years old. The man looked at her and smiled. She felt her face blush.

"These things never seem to get in a hurry when you're in a hurry," she said, trying to sound a little less irritated.

The man smiled again, but made no comment. At last she heard the welcome ding of the elevator as the door opened. She started to hurry onto the elevator, but then had to step back and let people on the elevator exit before she could enter. As the last passenger exited, she slid past the man with the goatee and grabbed the door. She held it open for him and the little brown-haired boy.

"Daddy, I don't want to get on," the little boy yelled. The man was trying to pull the little boy into the elevator, but his young son kept pulling back in a game of tug-of-war. This time, it was the boy's father who was blushing. April tried to smile and not appear impatient, but she had never been good at hiding her feelings. A person could read her like a book. She definitely did not have a poker face. She glanced at her watch, then back at the man. He was fighting a losing battle. She wanted to shout to the man that he was the father, and he needed to just pick up his son and get him in here! As if suddenly reading her mind, the man reached down, picked his son up, and entered the elevator. By now the little boy was kicking and screaming. April's ears were still ringing when she finally stepped off the elevator onto the third floor. She could still hear the little boy screaming as the elevator descended to the next floor.

Fortunately, her husband was just entering the chapel as she rounded the corner. She picked up her pace and arrived just as he was about to close the door. She was out of breath and was glad when Rebekah motioned for her to come and sit next to her. Bryan was sitting to the left of his wife and was nervously shaking his right leg, causing the whole pew to shake. Rebekah, without saying a word, gently placed her hand on his leg. He read her unspoken words and quit shaking his leg for about five seconds. Bryan Morris didn't bother to introduce anyone.

"How is our son, Doc? Is he going to be okay?"

"Mr. Morris, I'm going to be honest. Right now Tyler is stable, but the next two or three days are going to be crucial, especially the next twenty-four hours. He has had a lot of swelling and blood lost. The good news is that the bullet only nicked a small part of the brain, and we were able to remove the bullet."

"How soon before we can see our son?" asked Bryan.

"You can see him in a couple of hours, but he won't be able to talk to you as we have put him into a medically induced coma."

Rebekah gasped. "Why would you do that?" she asked, confusion showing in her face.

"The coma will help rest Tyler's brain by reducing swelling and pressure, which can cut off blood flow to the brain," Dr. Linski explained. "Try not to worry," he added. "Tyler will be closely monitored during the induced coma."

Rebekah Morris squeezed her husband's hand.

"How long will he be in a coma?" Bryan asked.

"It could be a few days or maybe even a few weeks." Arthur cleared his throat, and April could tell from the sad countenance on his face and the slight hesitation in his voice that he was about to tell them something they would really rather not hear.

"Also, when he does come out, you need to prepare yourselves for the possibility of permanent brain damage, or even paralysis as a residual effect from the trauma to the brain. We'll just have to wait and see. Take one day at a time."

No one commented nor asked anything further. Rebekah looked at April with questions in her eyes, but there were no answers; only time would tell. April half-expected Rebekah Morris to burst into more tears at hearing the news, but she looked to be more in a state of disbelief than anything.

"Nurse Linski, may I see you for a minute?" her husband asked. "Let me know if you think of any further questions," he said to the Morrises before turning to leave. The look of disbelief and confusion on their weary faces told him the two were going to need more than a little time to absorb everything he had just told them. The silence in the chapel had become slightly uncomfortable, and April was glad for the opportunity to leave the room.

She and her husband stepped outside the tiny chapel and closed the door gently behind them. Her husband leaned against the wall.

"April, I know you've had a long day, but before leaving, would you please see if there is anything the Morrises need?"

"Sure," she answered. "They seem like such a nice couple. I wish they were not having to go through this."

"Me too," he said as he stood still leaning against the wall with his feet and arms crossed and his head bowed. April noticed her husband staring intently at the tiled white-and-gray checkered floor as if he might somehow find some answers in them. She understood why her husband looked older than his forty-four years. He had performed many surgeries throughout his career, but it was the few who didn't pull through for one reason or another that had added years to him. She could tell he was wondering if Tyler Morris was going to be among those few.

"Did you know the whole time their son was in surgery, they were on their knees praying for him nonstop?"

"I'm glad," he said as he looked up into the concerned face of his wife. "We were afraid at one point that we had lost him."

She took her husband by the hand. "I heard. Arthur, I'm so sorry. But do you know what I think?" she said with a smile. Before he had time to answer, she proceeded to tell him, "I believe the fact you and your team were able to bring Tyler back is a sign. I believe the Lord is letting you know between Him and all the prayers, and you and the OR team, that Tyler is going to be all right."

Smiling, Arthur took his wife by the hand and looked into her beautiful dark eyes. The Lord had truly blessed him to have given him such a beautiful, understanding, and compassionate wife, not to mention one full of wisdom. It was her love and devotion to him that had kept him going all these years. She seemed to always know when and what to say to help encourage him—like now. He reached and hugged his wife, giving her a quick kiss on the lips.

"I hope you don't treat all the nurses this way," she said with a twinkle in her eyes.

"Not on your life," he said with a chuckle. "I'll see you tonight."

She pushed back a wisp of black hair from her eyes and watched her husband all the way to the end of the hall. His shoulders appeared less slumped and weighty and his steps a little livelier. When her husband reached the end of the hall, he turned, looked back, and waved before disappearing around the corner.

Taking a deep breath, she reentered the chapel. As she closed the door behind her, she heard the unmistakable fruity voice of Jackie Granger, one of the registered nurses, page overhead.

"Dr. Arthur Linski, please call extension 1544. Dr. Arthur Linski, extension 1544."

It was the ER. April wasn't so sure if she would see her husband tonight or not.

* * * * *

Arthur Linski stopped at the third floor nurse's station and called the ER. Jackie, a longtime veteran of the ER, informed him that Dr. Kelsey wanted him to take a look at a little five-year-old girl who had just come in. She had fallen off her bicycle and hit her head on the sidewalk. "She had not been wearing a helmet," Jackie reported. "Dr. Kelsey would like you to consult."

Hanging up the phone, he headed toward the ER. As he came through the automatic doors to the ER, he heard the shrill screams of a child. There was no need to ask which room the injured cyclist was in. Opening the door to room 4, he looked into the terrified face of the little five-year-old girl. The parents and Jackie Granger were trying somewhat unsuccessfully to calm the frightened child. As Arthur Linski entered the room and closed the door behind him, he wondered if he would be seeing his wife and children any time soon.

CHAPTER 15

THERE'S NO PLACE LIKE HOME

It had been two days since the news of Tyler's attempted suicide. The information gathered from friends was that he was still in an induced coma, but in stable condition. Addison was still feeling down from the horrible news. She was surprised she wasn't feeling as though justice had been served—after all, look what Tyler had done.

Dr. Steelman had come in earlier in the morning and given orders to discharge her. At least she would not be returning to school until after Thanksgiving. In the meantime, Michelle Windom would come to Addison's home and continue to keep her abreast of schoolwork.

She had been pleasantly surprised when Wyatt Kingsley stopped by earlier in the morning to tell her goodbye. "You're going to make it through this, Addison," he had told her. "You just wait and see."

She had never been good at waiting. Patience definitely was not one of her virtues. He had even told her she was going to do great things for the Lord someday.

"What makes you so sure, Wyatt Kingsley?" she had asked, a little irritated at him. "You act like you know me better than I know myself."

"Maybe I do," he said as he left her room with a smile and what she felt was a smug attitude.

She glanced at the clock. Her mother would be here soon. Earlier, the nursing assistant had helped her pack everything and brought in the wheelchair she was now sitting in. She hated having to ride in a wheelchair, but it was the hospital's policy that all discharged patients be transported out by wheelchair and a hospital employee.

She sat twiddling her thumbs and thinking how far she had come in a few short days with Wyatt's help and encouragement. She hoped she liked the therapist at outpatient as much as she liked him, though she doubted it. Mason had also been a big source of encouragement as well. He sure knew how to push her buttons. No way could one feel sorry for themselves around him, at least not for long. The hospital could use more volunteers like him, she thought. She was going to miss Mason, and as much as she hated to admit it, she was going to miss Wyatt Kingsley.

Getting bored waiting for her mother to arrive, she took a look at the lunch menu lying on the over-bed table. "Dang!" she said. The kitchen was serving cherry cobbler, her favorite, and she would be gone before lunch. Her mouth was beginning to water when she heard a knock at the door.

"Come in!" she yelled, returning the menu to the table. It was Wilma Littlejohn.

"I brought you something, Miss Addison," she said with a chuckle.

"Oh, Miss Wilma, thank you!" she said as she took the bowl of warm cherry cobbler from Wilma's hand. Closing her eyes, she inhaled the tantalizing aroma of the cherry cobbler. She could almost taste the sweet yet slight tartness of the delicious fruit and the buttery golden brown crust.

"I knew how much you loved cherry cobbler, so I slipped you some," Wilma said, chuckling.

"Oh, Miss Wilma, I'm going to miss you something terribly."

Wilma reached and gave her a hug. "I'm going to miss you too, Miss Addison." Wilma finally let go. "You gonna to be all right, Miss Addison. You just wait and see," Wilma said. This time, there was no chuckle as she left the room.

Addison took one more whiff of the cobbler before digging in. Her mother entered the room just as she was finishing the last bite.

By the time the hospital completed all the discharge teaching and paperwork, they didn't arrive home until around lunchtime.

Addison had grown so accustomed to the hustle and bustle of the hospital that the house felt quiet and empty as she made her way to the flowered sofa. She had just dropped onto the seat when she heard Chip bouncing down the stairs. Running toward the sofa and without hesitation, he did a flying leap and landed on her lap. His tail was wagging fast and furious in his excitement to see her. She felt his warm, sloppy, but welcomed kisses all over her face. She couldn't help but laugh as she tried to calm him.

"Did you miss me, precious? I sure missed you!" She squeezed him tight and returned his kisses. Eventually, he calmed down. Making a couple of circles on her lap, he finally found the perfect spot and settled down contended to have her home.

She watched as her mother brought in the last of the luggage and shivered at the gust of wind as her mother closed the door. The days were much colder now than when she had first been admitted to the hospital. The autumn leaves on the trees were beginning to fall, leaving a colorful patchwork of leaves on the ground. It was especially cold today due to the rain and frequent strong gusts of wind.

At Wyatt's insistence, she had ventured out into the courtyard at the hospital a few times on some of the warmer days. "You can't stay cooped up all the time," he had told her. He had been right, though, because she felt less depressed after going outside and experiencing the warm sunshine on her face. The fresh air had made her feel less stressed and more energized. Today, however, though she was glad to be home in familiar surroundings, she was feeling a little down and alone. The old worn-out sofa didn't do much to lift her spirits either. She really wished her mother would get something a little more updated; but a few years earlier, her mom and dad had picked out the flowered monstrosity together. It would be years before her mother would let it go, maybe never.

"Do you need anything right now?" her mother asked.

"Don't think so," she answered as Chip gave a gentle nudge to her hand. This was his way of saying, *How about giving me a rub?* She smiled as she started to rub his back then watched as he flipped over onto his back so she could rub his tummy.

"You are so spoiled!" She laughed while rubbing his little round tummy. She could have sworn she saw him smile.

"In that case, I'll make us a sandwich," her mother said, making her way toward the kitchen. "How about I make us a BLT?"

"Sounds good, Mom," she answered as she reached for the TV remote and tuned into the local news channel.

Twenty minutes later, her mother brought out the sandwiches and two glasses of iced tea. She placed them on the coffee table in front of Addison and took a seat beside her.

"Mom," she protested as she sat up straighter, "you didn't have to bring the food to me. I am well capable of coming to the table."

"Enjoy this while you can," her mother said, ignoring her protest and grabbing the remote from the coffee table. "Are you watching this?" she asked, pointing toward the TV with the remote.

"No, not really," she said, reaching for her sandwich. "But there really isn't anything else on." Kyndal changed the channel and flipped from one program to another, trying to find something to watch. Addison was right; there was nothing worth watching.

"What if we just turn the TV off and enjoy our sandwiches?"

Addison nodded in agreement as her mother clicked off the TV, and they both bit into the crispy BLTs.

Of course, Chip wasn't going to be denied as he moved between the two of them enjoying the spoils from each. Addison savored every bite of the BLT. Turned out she was hungrier than she had realized, and boy, had she missed her mother's tea. No one and no restaurant could match her mother's sweet tea. They mostly ate in silence as they devoured their sandwiches in a matter of minutes.

"Thanks, Mom, that was delicious," she said as her mother stood to take the empty plates and glasses into the kitchen.

Returning a few minutes later, Kyndal found Addison fast asleep on the sofa with Chip curled next to her. As she reached and threw the black-and-burgundy throw over the both of them, she felt the hardness of the artificial leg. As she tucked the throw around her little girl, tears filled her eyes.

"If only I could fix this for you," she whispered as she bent and kissed her daughter on the forehead. Retreating to the kitchen, she began loading the dishwasher.

"Maybe I'll mop the kitchen floor," she said aloud. She had to do something to keep her mind occupied.

Addison awoke when she heard the front door slam and Sarah Garrison pulling out of the graveled driveway.

"Addison!" her brother yelled when he saw her lying on the sofa. "You're home!" Ayson quickly dropped his bookbag on the floor as he ran and grabbed hold of his sister.

"Wow! This is some bear hug," she said, hugging him just as tightly.

"I'm glad you're home," he said as he let go and stood beaming ear to ear. She saw the sparkle in his big hazel eyes.

"I'm glad to see you too, little brother," she said, smiling at him. Chip was doing the happy dance while waiting for Ayson to notice him too.

"Sis, I can't wait for you to see my new video games," he said enthusiastically as he reached and scooped Chip into his arms. "They are awesome!" Without taking a breath, he asked where their mom was.

"I'm not sure. I fell asleep, but try the kitchen."

He took off to the kitchen with Chip giving his face a barrage of sloppy kisses.

"Be careful!" she heard her mother tell him as he started through the kitchen door. "The floor is still wet. Give me a minute, and I'll bring you a snack."

"Okay, Mom," Ayson said as he stopped, then turned and hurried up the steps to his room still carrying Chip. A few minutes later, his mother came through and stood at the bottom of the stairs and yelled for him to come get his sandwich. He was down in a flash. "Thanks, Mom," he said as he took the plate and ran back up the steps.

Addison looked at all the stuff brought in from the car sitting just inside the living room door. Until this moment, she had not realized just how much stuff she had accumulated while in the hospital. It was a good thing her mother had brought some of the flowers home after each visit. She hadn't noticed earlier, but now as she looked around the room it appeared a little larger for some reason. Then it occurred to her: the beige oversized chair that usually sat in front of the fireplace was missing. She was about to yell for her mother when her mother came through the kitchen door.

"Whew, I'm glad that's done," she said as she wiped the moisture from her forehead with the hem of her blue checkered apron. She gave a tired sigh as she looked at all the things brought back from the hospital. She had completely forgotten to put the things away.

"Ayson!" she yelled. "Could you please come down and help me a minute?"

"In a minute," he yelled back. "Gotta couple more bites left of my sandwich." Addison was pretty sure he would have already finished the sandwich had he spent more time eating and less time on his video game.

"Never mind, Mom," she said, getting up from the sofa. "I can help."

"Are you sure?" Kyndal asked a little hesitantly. "I mean, I don't want you to hurt yourself."

"I'm fine, Mom, really." After several minutes, the last thing to be put away was a clear vase which held a dozen pink roses with yellow tips and baby's breath.

"Mom, where do you want to put this vase of roses?"

"Just set them on the coffee table," Kyndal said, once again wiping her forehead with the hem of her apron.

"It was nice of the nursing staff to buy you those roses, Mom," Addison said as she placed the roses in the middle of the coffee table and returned to the sofa. For some reason, the pink roses seemed to warm up the room and even made the outdated sofa look better.

"Yes, it was," her mother said as she walked over to the coffee table and studied the placement of the roses. "I was pleasantly surprised." Addison watched as her mother moved the vase of roses from one spot to another. Finally, she placed them to her liking, right smack in the middle where they were to begin with.

Addison had known earlier the staff of the orthopedic surgery care unit on which she was a patient was buying the roses for her mother. Lauryn Jacobi, one of the nurses, had recently transferred from her mother's department to the unit, taking the position of nurse manager. She had informed Addison of their intentions one day when she came to her room to inquire of her mother's favorite flower. Over the years, according to Lauryn, most of the nurses on the unit had worked with Kyndal at one time or another. She said the nursing staff just wanted to do a little something to let her know they loved her and were praying for them. Today when her mother had arrived at the hospital, Lauryn had brought the vase of flowers in along with a card signed by the orthopedic nursing staff. Addison had seen tears in her mother's eyes as she and Lauryn hugged, being genuinely touched by the warm gesture of the nursing staff.

"The roses look beautiful, Mom," she said, admiring the arrangement on the glass-topped coffee table. Then it occurred to her to ask about the missing chair.

"Oh! I thought maybe it would give you a little more room to move about if the chair was out of the way. I'm also thinking about removing the coffee table as well. We don't really need it. We've got too much clutter as it is," her mother said, bending over to smell one of the roses.

"Mom, you don't need to move everything out of the way. As a matter of fact, if I start to fall, the chair would give me something to hold on to." Addison knew her mother was trying to remove as many obstacles as possible to keep her from hurting herself should she take a tumble. "Please put the chair back," she said softly, "and leave the coffee table alone, okay, Mom?"

Kyndal studied her daughter for a few seconds and realized too many changes might not be the best thing right now. "Okay, Addison. I'll put the chair back tomorrow." They turned when they heard footsteps on the staircase.

"Okay, Mom, what do you need me to do?" Ayson asked.

Mother and daughter burst into laughter just as there was a knock at the door. Ayson, not certain of what was so funny, ran to answer the door with Chip following at his heels. It was Pastor Bryce and his family. Kyndal felt a little embarrassed at her appearance and kept overly apologizing as she led them into the living room. Motioning for them to have a seat on the sofa, she offered them something to drink.

"I'll take a cup of hot chocolate, Mrs. McNeely," piped Callaway. "It's cold outside."

"I'll have a cup too, Mom," Ayson said as he invited his friend upstairs to see his new video games. The two boys, followed by Chip, took off running up the stairs.

"Make that three hot chocolates," said Addison.

"How about I get the rest of us a cup of strong hot coffee?" Kyndal said as she removed the elastic ponytail holder from her hair and neatly pulled it back again.

"Sounds like a winner to me," said Pastor Bryce, smiling.

"What lovely flowers!" Maggie exclaimed.

Kyndal explained the kindness shown to her by Lauryn and the orthopedic nursing staff.

Maggie turned to Addison, who was sitting next to her. "Well, young lady, I guess you're glad to be home. It won't be too long before you're back at school with all your friends."

"I guess so," Addison replied, barely above a whisper as she glanced down at her hands and began purposely twiddling her thumbs.

Maggie looked at her husband and then at Kyndal, who was shaking her head, giving Maggie the hint not to pursue the topic of school any further.

"Kyndal, how about I give you a hand in the kitchen?" Maggie said as she rose to her feet.

Addison heard her mother whisper something to Maggie as they went through the kitchen doorway. Pastor Bryce cleared his throat. She didn't look up.

"Addison, would you please look at me for a moment?"

She raised her head and faced Pastor Bryce as she continued to twiddle her thumbs. He looked intently at her for a few seconds without saying a word. He then slid to the edge of the sofa, letting out a long sigh. "Addison, I know you're going through a lot right now and that you're a little upset with God."

Little was not quite the right word, she thought, as she looked at him. Try *a lot upset*. She turned her attention back to her fingers as he continued.

"I can't even begin to understand everything you must be feeling. You must be hurt, feeling abandoned by the Lord, frustrated, and naturally angry."

He was right. She felt all those things rolled into one. Her eyes started to tear. He must have sensed the question she wanted to ask.

"Addison, I can't answer why this has happened to you and why you have to go through this—but I can tell you that you are not walking through this fire alone. You're going to come through this stronger than you could ever imagine."

They sat for a few minutes in thoughtful silence when she finally looked again at her pastor. She felt herself wanting to scream at him to just leave her alone, and to tell him she didn't want to hear anything he had to say. However, when she looked into his kind eyes and saw such sincere concern and genuine compassion, she remained silent. She knew he was only trying to help—not that he could, not that anyone could.

"I'd like you to come to church Sunday," he finally said.

"Pastor Bryce, I…I really don't know if I'll feel up to it or not."

"There's a new couple I'd like you to meet, Michael and Jennifer Scobie."

Before he could say anything further, they heard the two women laughing as they entered from the kitchen. They placed two trays of coffee, hot chocolate, cups, creamer, and sugar on the coffee table. Maggie handed Addison a cup of hot chocolate. She then poured her husband, Kyndal, and herself a cup of hot steaming coffee before sitting down on one side of Addison. Maggie and Pastor Bryce waved Kyndal off when she offered them cream and sugar. She added cream to her own coffee before making her way to the foot of the stairs and yelling for the boys. Ayson and Callaway hurried down, grabbed their cup of chocolate, and were off again. Kyndal sat in the solid burgundy glider rocker across from Addison.

"I was just about to tell Addison about our new youth pastors," Pastor Bryce said as he blew on his cup of coffee. "Mmm," he said, "you just can't beat the aroma and taste of fresh brewed coffee, especially on a cold day like today."

As soon as he mentioned youth pastors, Addison remembered where she had heard the names Michael and Jennifer Scobie. Alayna had mentioned to her a few days ago that New Haven had hired two new youth pastors, Michael and Jennifer Scobie.

"I'm so glad we're not going to have different volunteers every week to lead the youth class," said Maggie as she sipped slowly and carefully on the hot coffee. "We are so grateful for all the volunteers. They have done a great job since and Keith and Catherine moved away this past summer, but—"

"It's always best to have the same people work with the youth," Pastor Bryce interjected. "That way, trust can be built between the teens and their youth pastors."

"I agree," said Maggie, leaning forward and placing her cup on the wooden coaster.

Kyndal and Addison made no comment one way or the other. Pastor Bryce and his wife let the subject drop. They were both aware it was not only Addison who had issues with God.

Kyndal McNeely had not stepped foot inside the church since her husband's funeral, although Maggie had invited her to visit on several occasions. She had, however, since Addison had been in the hospital, dropped Ayson off at church on the Sundays she was off work. Every other Sunday, he would catch a ride with Alayna and her parents.

The rest of the Peters' visit consisted of current news and politics—boring stuff as far as Addison was concerned. Forty-five minutes later, Kyndal went to Ayson's room and informed Callaway his parents were ready to leave. Ten minutes later, Maggie went to the foot of the stairs.

"Callaway," she yelled, a little more sternly, "you need to come down now!"

"Okay, Mom, I'll be right there!"

Less than a minute later, they heard what sounded like a stampede of cattle running down the stairs. Several goodbyes later, the Peters family was gone, and both women were left with their feet kicked back on the edges of the coffee table.

Addison stared at her temporary artificial leg; her mother was trying not to. It would be anywhere from two to six months before she would be fitted for her permanent leg. Not that she really cared. It wasn't like it was something to look forward to.

Another knock on the front door interrupted the awkward moment. It was Michelle Windom.

"I'm sorry to be stopping by so late," she apologized.

"It's quite all right," Kyndal replied.

"I just needed to drop these assignments off. Please let Addison know I will be stopping by tomorrow to help her with them, and I will call before I come. In the meantime, she can be looking these over."

Addison heard her mother invite Michelle Windom in, but she declined, saying she had one more student to deliver assignments to. Closing the door, her mother came and laid what looked like a ton of schoolwork on the sofa next to her.

"Ms. Windom said to tell—"

"Yes, I heard."

Her mother gave a tired sigh as she sat down and rested her head against the back of the rocker. Soon after, Ayson came running down the stairs.

"Mom," he said, trying to catch his breath, "can Callaway and Caleb spend the night this Saturday?" he pleaded. "Pleeeease!" he added, holding his hands under his chin in prayer position.

Her mother sighed, throwing her hands in the air. "Why not?" she said, smiling. "As they say, the more, the merrier!"

"Thanks, Mom, you're the best!" he said, throwing his arms around her neck. Apparently, this was something Ayson and Callaway had cooked up before the Peters had left for home.

It had been a long and tiring day. Next week was Thanksgiving, and it seemed there was a lot of schoolwork that needed to be crammed in before the holidays. Alayna would be over tomorrow.

Together they could work on the school assignments, hopefully before Michelle Windom arrived. Addison's outpatient therapy was to begin the next day as well. She was beginning to feel a little overwhelmed.

As she did not quite feel comfortable with the stairs yet, she decided to sleep on the sofa. Her mother had wanted to bring a bed downstairs, but she refused. "No way, Mom!" she had protested.

Her mother had finally relented; however, Addison still ended up having a restless night. It was too quiet, and she was still anxious about starting back to school. It was close to 1:00 a.m. before she was finally able to sleep.

* * * * *

The next morning, Kyndal and Ayson tried to be quiet before leaving for work and school, but that didn't quite work out. Her brother couldn't find one of his shoes. Naturally, it was underneath the sofa. Her mother kept banging pots and pans while making breakfast. Plus, she could hear her mother shushing her brother every now and then to be quiet. She thought it would have been quite comical had she not had such a restless night. Chip lay on his doggie bed next to the fireplace, unfazed by any of the commotion going on. Finally, her mother left for work, and Alayna arrived a short time later to pick Ayson up and drop him off at school. She heard him gently close the door behind him after hearing Alayna shower down several times on the car horn.

It was not long before she drifted off to a deep sleep. She awoke an hour and a half later. She had not meant to sleep that long. If she didn't get a move on, she would be late for her first outpatient therapy appointment. She hurriedly jumped up and almost fell, forgetting upon awakening that she only had one good leg to stand on. She quickly attached the artificial leg to her stump, stood, and then folded the bedlinens, laying them neatly to one side of the sofa.

Walking a little unsteady, she made her way to the downstairs bathroom, brushed her teeth, and then combed her hair. She threw on a pair of blue jeans and an old white sweatshirt her mother had brought from upstairs. She quickly made her way to the kitchen and set out a bowl of food and freshwater for Chip. Passing the hall mirror and seeing her reflection, she decided to pull back her thick mass of hair. She was just twisting the last loop of the black hair tie around her hair when she heard someone at the door.

"Great," she said aloud. "That is probably Shannon coming to drive me to my therapy appointment, and I haven't even had a chance to eat breakfast."

Her mother had offered the night before to prepare breakfast for her, but she had been adamant that she wanted to prepare her own breakfast. "I've got to do some things for myself," she had insisted. Her mother had reluctantly given in. No way was she going to let her mom know she had overslept and skipped breakfast. She looked through the peephole to see Shannon Thomas standing on the other side of the door clutching a white paper bag from her restaurant. Please let that be my breakfast, Addison thought. She flung open the door and looked at Shannon hopefully.

"Here's breakfast. Hope you're hungry," Shannon said, holding the bag out in front of her.

"You bet I am!" Addison said as she grabbed the bag and gave Shannon a hug. "I overslept and didn't have time to fix anything."

"Your mother thought you might." Shannon smiled.

Addison gave a sheepish grin. Good ol' Mom, she thought.

"Come on, you can eat on the way. The coffee is in the car."

Addison grabbed her jacket and looked at her best friend's mom. Shannon Thomas looked classy and sophisticated. Every strain of auburn hair was in place loosely framing her oval face. As always, her minimally applied makeup was perfect. Today her long natural nails were polished a deep red and perfectly matched the red jacket she was wearing. The slightly below-the-knee black dress and five-inch black stilettos, along with her glitzy jewelry, finished off the polished look. Addison looked down at her jeans and sweatshirt. *Talk about feeling underdressed.*

She closed the door, and it wasn't long before she was on her way to her first therapy session. Fifteen minutes later, they arrived at a big white building with the words Therapy Inc. inscribed in large blue letters on the front directly above the glass entry doors. Never in a million years did she think she would be entering this building for any kind of rehabilitation at her age. Walking to the receptionist's window, she signed herself in.

"Surprise!" she heard Shannon yell as she was about to turn away from the window.

What in the world is wrong with Shannon? Addison thought as she turned around. She could hardly believe her eyes. She watched, speechless, as Wyatt Kingsley quickly made his way toward her.

"What are you doing here?" she asked in disbelief.

"What? They didn't tell you?" he asked as he came and stood next to her.

However, before she could answer, Shannon spoke up, "Your mother and Noah—I mean Dr. Steelman—wanted it to be a surprise."

"Well, I am definitely surprised," she said, looking at Shannon, who was still grinning.

Addison couldn't believe her mother had known Wyatt was going to be here and didn't tell her. Even harder to believe was the fact her mother had laid out the not-so-flattering outfit she had on. The bulky white sweatshirt even had a yellowish stain on one of the sleeves.

"I'll just go and sit in the waiting area," Shannon said as she made her way to a seat next to an end table filled with magazines.

"Addison, this isn't a problem for you, is it?" Wyatt asked.

"Of course not. Why would it be?" she replied, surprised at his question.

Wyatt shrugged. "In that case, let's get to work."

She placed her hand on his arm. "Wait. I don't understand. I mean, I'm really glad you're here, but I don't understand *how* you are here. What about your work at the hospital?"

"I'm still there, but I work here prn...as needed," he added, seeing the question in her eyes as to what *prn* stood for. "I hope you don't mind, but I requested to work with you. You were doing so well at the hospital. I just wanted to see you—I mean, I just wanted to see you through this."

"Of course, I don't mind. I'm actually glad. I have been so worried about having to work with someone who might not tolerate me as much as you have."

She looked down and realized her hand was still on Wyatt's arm. Somewhere along the conversation, his hand had come to rest over hers. She gently removed her hand from beneath his. She saw his face flush slightly before clearing his throat.

"Enough said, let's get to work on those stairs." Wyatt led her to a long staircase. Fortunately, he didn't make her walk the entire staircase. What she once dreaded didn't seem so bad after all. Wyatt worked with her a while before letting her walk up and down the stairs for about five minutes with only standby assist. "You did great!" Wyatt said afterward as he sat on the edge of one of the steps to complete his paperwork. "Mason would be proud." A few minutes later, he stood and smiled. "I'll see you again Monday."

"Thanks, Wyatt. See you then," she said, making her way to the waiting room to find Shannon.

After leaving, the two talked for a few minutes about how the first day of outpatient therapy went. After that, they rode in silence for a few minutes before Shannon spoke.

"Tell me what you think of Wyatt."

But Addison wasn't listening. Her mind was on Wyatt Kingsley.

"Well?" Shannon said as she turned onto Walnut Drive.

"Well, what?" Addison asked, finally realizing Shannon was speaking to her.

Shannon rolled her eyes and sighed. "What do you think of Wyatt Kingsley?"

"Oh, him. He's okay, I guess," she said as she turned and looked out the window. But she knew in her heart Wyatt Kingsley was more than okay. He was beginning to mean something to her. Sure, he was nice enough to her all right, but he would never love her. He would probably end up falling in love with someone like Candace McIntire, the beautiful nurse at the hospital who had looked at her with such pity. She felt another pity party coming on, but in her opinion, she deserved it, given the unfair hand life had dealt her.

* * * * *

153

Wyatt Kingsley sat in the break room eating a ham on rye sandwich thinking of Addison McNeely. She had been on his mind a lot over the past few days, and it wasn't because of her therapy. He was beginning to care for her and to care for her on a more personal level—maybe he was even falling in love with her. He wondered if that would only complicate things for her. Besides, Addison McNeely had shown no personal interest in him at all. He gave a long sigh and then gulped down a couple swallows of Coke before taking another bite of his sandwich. Maybe requesting to work with her hadn't been such a good idea after all.

* * * * *

Alayna stopped by immediately after school and helped Addison worked on the mount of schoolwork delivered the night before. Addison told her about Wyatt working at the therapy place, but of course, her mother had already told her and made her swear to keep it a secret.

Earlier, the school had phoned Kyndal at work. Ayson had a toothache, so she had left work early and picked him up. Fortunately, she was able to get him a dentist appointment on short notice. It was a late-afternoon appointment, but she was just grateful the office had been able to work him in on the same day.

The girls watched in amusement as Ayson slid his arms into his coat, and his mother wrapped a scarf around his neck and mouth. They couldn't help but giggle when they saw Ayson roll his eyes at his mother's excessive doting.

"After all," he was telling his mother, "I'm twelve years old. I can dress myself."

Ignoring him, Kyndal stood back with her hands on her hips and examined him so as to make sure he would be warm enough. Then looking around, her eye caught a toboggan lying on the hall table next to the door. She shoved it over his head and ears. "Gee, Mom, it's just cold outside. We're not having a blizzard!" they heard him say in protest as he and his mother started out into the cold November air.

"A mummy couldn't be wrapped any tighter." Addison laughed as she and Alayna bade them goodbye.

An hour and a half later, they returned with Ayson being all smiles. The dentist had given him an antibiotic and something for pain. He was to go back Wednesday for more dental work.

Michelle Windom arrived about the same time as they had and was now tutoring various subjects and delving out more assignments. After an hour and a half, she left followed by Alayna thirty minutes later.

Addison sat in the oversized chair in front of the fireplace and listened to her mother explain Wednesday's agenda. In order for her not to have to miss another day of work, Sarah Garrison had offered to take Ayson to his dentist appointment. Kyndal was thankful for her friends, friends she had pushed away at one time or another in her life. However, they had remained faithful and given her the space she needed, the space she still sometimes needed.

* * * * *

Saturday came, and the house was a lot noisier with three boys. The boys were constantly running up and down the wooden stairs. All morning sounds of laughter echoed through the house. Chip, not to be left out, made sure he was right in the middle of the action running and yelping behind the boys.

Earlier, Callaway and Caleb had decided to closely examine and touch Addison's artificial leg. Between the two, they must have asked about a hundred different questions, Addison thought. She was actually a little surprised that all their staring and questioning had not bothered her. Then again, they were only kids. It was her peers she was dreading to face, especially certain ones.

She was jolted from her thoughts when she heard another unanimous sound of laughter resonate from upstairs. Even through the closed bedroom door, she could hear the excited voices and laughter as each of the boys were challenged by the numerous video games. Sitting in the oversized chair, she tried to concentrate on her Christie novel; but with all the noise, it was almost impossible. The phone rang as she closed the book.

"Hello. Yes, this is she. Well, I-I guess that will be all right. See you around ten," Addison heard her mother say before hanging up. Wonder who that could be? she thought.

Addison knew Alayna was supposed to be coming, but she wasn't due to arrive until after cheerleading practice. Coach Redmond had called another Saturday practice wanting the squad to learn a couple of new cheers since the Wildcats had made the playoffs. Her thoughts drifted to her last Saturday practice, the one when she had two good legs and had argued with Alayna. Why hadn't she listened to her friend? She quickly tried to get her mind on something else.

Glancing at the clock above the stone fireplace, she noticed it was only nine o'clock in the morning. She attempted to read again as it had grown a little quieter. Engrossed in the novel, she hadn't noticed her mother walk up beside her; and when she spoke, it startled her.

"Sorry," her mother said. "I didn't realize you didn't see me walk up."

Addison dog-eared the page and closed the book. If her dad had been here, he would have called her out on that. "That's what they make bookmarkers for," he would always say. Reading was one of the few things she and her dad had in common. They both loved to read, especially mysteries. It was actually her dad who had piqued her interest in Agatha Christie, the queen of mystery novels.

"Who was that on the phone?"

"That's what I was coming to tell you. It was Pastor Bryce. He wants to bring the new youth pastors over so we can meet them."

"Ooh, Mom," she said, moaning.

"I know, but what could I say?"

"I just don't want them to try and pressure me into going to church and the youth meetings. I'm just not ready."

"Let's just cross that bridge when we get there," Kyndal said as she turned and walked into the kitchen.

Addison returned to reading as another round of laughter rang out from upstairs.

CHAPTER 16

BUT FOR THE GRACE OF GOD

Isaac Darnell sat in the parking lot of Faith Hospital trying to muster enough courage to go in and see his friend. Since learning of Tyler and Addison's accident, he had not had a single drop of alcohol. As he sat alone staring at the steering wheel, he thought about the events of that horrible night.

Tim Olsen, another of his college buddies, had also been at the party. Since he was a designated driver for several of them, including Isaac, Tim had refrained from drinking any alcohol.

"Besides, my mom and dad would kill me if I came home with alcohol on my breath," he had told Isaac upon volunteering to be the designated driver. As they had not seen the need for him to stay on campus when he could live at home rent-free, Tim still lived with his parents.

The night of the party, Tim had left after hearing the blare of sirens. He had returned about fifteen minutes later and given Isaac and the other partygoers an update. He said while driving past the wreck, he had immediately recognized Tyler's blue Mustang, but not the other car involved.

It wasn't until a few minutes later that they learned the identity of the person in the second car. Apparently, New Haven had started a phone tree asking members to begin praying for the two young people. One of the members had texted someone at the party about the request and gave the identities of those involved. Isaac, as drunk as he was, remembered feeling sick to his stomach upon hearing the news about Tyler and Addie. As a matter of fact, he had thrown up shortly afterward. As word of the wreck began to spread to the party-goers, they had started leaving the party as if they were trying to beat a forest fire that was ready to engulf them. Most went the opposite way of the accident in order to prevent running into the patrolmen.

The next day, upon hearing Tyler had been released from the hospital, Isaac had texted him to inquire about his and Addie's condition. That was when Tyler told him about Addison's leg. A few days later, he had gone to visit Tyler at home, but only after Tyler informed him that his parents had gone to the grocery store. Isaac, upon arriving at Tyler's home, noticed he appeared to be more in bad shape emotionally than he did physically.

"Have you been to see Addison?" Tyler asked.

"No. What about you?"

Tyler had shaken his head and then told him how he had tried to see Addison in the hospital, but she had refused to see him.

Finally, after mustering enough courage, Isaac tapped lightly on the hospital door leading into Tyler's room. Not getting an answer, he slowly opened the door and made his way in. He was a little surprised to see the pale-blue walls and the navy-blue curtains that were pulled back letting in the light of a new day. The huge window overlooked a dogwood tree, which he thought would be beautiful once in bloom. He had expected the room to be rather stark and not so calming, like most hospital rooms. Though there was no sunlight coming through the windows on this side of the building, the room was flooded with so much natural light the overhead lights weren't even necessary. He heard soft and soothing worship music being piped into the room.

Directly across from Tyler's bed hanging on the wall was a picture of a guardian angel watching over two children as they crossed a broken and unsafe bridge. If Isaac remembered correctly from an art class he had once taken, the painting was called *Heilige Schutzengel* in German by the artist Lindberg. The combination of soothing colors, natural light, worship music, and the painting created a relaxing atmosphere to the room, giving off a sense of peace.

Isaac turned his attention to Tyler. The head of his bed was slightly elevated, and his solid cream-colored hospital blanket had been tucked neatly around his body covering him from the waist down. His arms lay outside the covers by his sides with not so much as a flicker of his long slender fingers. The light-blue hospital gown complimented his dark-black hair, and Isaac thought, *Tyler really did favor Elvis.*

Now as Isaac sat watching the almost lifeless Tyler, he could hardly believe the turn of events that had taken place in just a matter of weeks. A week after Isaac had visited Tyler, he had texted Isaac and asked him to visit Addison in the hospital. *She won't see me*, he had texted. *Tell her I'm sorry for everything, and if there was any way I could trade places with her, I would.*

Isaac doubted she would have wanted to see him either, but he should at least have had the guts to try. Isaac leaned forward in the chair and rested his elbows on his knees, beating both of his fists several times against his forehead.

"Why didn't I just do as he had asked?" he said aloud. However, he knew exactly why he didn't go see Addie. He was carrying around too much guilt himself, especially after hearing she had lost her leg. After all, it was his party, and he was the one who had sent Tyler for more beer.

He would give anything not to have run into Addie and Laney that day at Fletcher's Groceries. Had he not, Addie would be okay now and, more than likely, Tyler.

Lately, he felt as if he ruined everyone and everything he touched. He blamed himself for what had happened that night. He had gotten off no worse for the wear while others had ended up paying the price. He knew he was popular with the college crowd as well as with the high school students. He had selfishly used that popularity to manipulate others and to have a good time. His knuckles turned white as he clenched his fist hard against his forehead. He was not a praying person, although at the moment it entered his mind to do so. He had heard once the only prayer God heard from a sinner was the prayer of repentance.

"Well, I'm definitely a sinner," he mumbled. So if that were true, there was no need to pray and ask God to help Tyler and Addie.

He wasn't ready to ask Jesus into his heart. No way would God accept someone like him. He would have to clean his life up before he could ever ask Jesus to save him. To be truthful, he wasn't sure he could ever clean up his life enough to ask for God's forgiveness. He was too much of a screwup; he was just no good.

He looked up as he heard Tyler's mom and dad walk through the door. He felt his muscles immediately tense into a knot. Tyler had told him on the day he had visited him at home that his parents had learned he had been the one to send him for more beer. Tyler said his father had been livid.

"You mean he knew you were stone drunk, and he sent you out for more!" his dad had shouted. According to Tyler, it had taken several minutes before his mother was finally able to calm him. Isaac stood slowly and faced them for the first time since the accident. He could see Bryan Morris's ears turning red around the edges.

"What are you do—" he started to shout as he moved angrily toward him.

Rebekah quickly grabbed her husband by the arm. He stopped, but Isaac noticed Bryan's cold, piercing blue eyes were still locked on him. Rebekah spoke calmly, but he could tell it was all she could do to compose herself as well. He saw her jaw tighten as she gripped her husband a little harder than she meant to.

"It was very kind of you Isaac, to come see Tyler, but we would like you to leave now…please," she added as an apparent afterthought.

He felt paralyzed. His head was telling his feet and legs to move, but he was frozen.

"Now!" shouted Bryan Morris, taking one step closer to him. Rebekah tightened her grip. The loud, harsh voice of Bryan Morris was enough to get his feet moving. He couldn't say a word. He just nodded his head then eased past Rebekah Morris while keeping his eyes on her husband.

"Don't come back!" he heard Bryan Morris say as he reached for the door. Never before in his life had he been so glad to get out of a room.

* * * * *

It was ten o'clock sharp when a knock sounded at the front door. Addison was still sitting in her favorite chair where she had been for the last hour reading. Her mother came from the kitchen drying her hands with a dish towel. She had just finished cleaning the kitchen after making a cherry cobbler for the arriving guest. Her mother invited Pastor Bryce and the Scobies in and motioned for them to have a seat. The aroma of the homemade cobbler made Addison's mouth water as she sat trying to size up the new youth pastors.

Pastor Bryce did the introductions then took a seat on the sofa. She listened as her mother and Michael talked about the weather. Why was it, she wondered, did people always talk about the weather when they didn't really know what to say to one another? Michael and Jennifer Scobie looked to be in their early thirties. From what Addison was sensing, both appeared to have magnetic personalities, a plus when it came to working with young people.

Michael was tall with short dark-brown hair and dark-brown eyes that were set close together. He had a slightly long nose and was quite handsome, she thought. He seemed the quieter of the two, but then it was always that way when there were women in a room.

Now that the weather had been discussed and the ice broken, her mother and Jennifer sat talking to each other as if they had known each other for years.

Addison turned her attention to Jennifer Scobie. She had red highlights scattered throughout her long brown hair, which she parted to one side. Her bangs partially covered one of her eyes, but her beautiful brown doe-like eyes still stood out. She was petite and considerably shorter than her husband, who looked to be at least six feet tall, if not a little taller.

She watched with interest as Jennifer pulled out a picture of a little girl and handed it to her mother.

"This is our daughter Grace. She turned two earlier this month."

"She's absolutely beautiful!" exclaimed her mother as she took the picture. "Look, Addison," her mother said, bringing the picture over to her. "Isn't she adorable?"

"She sure is," Addison remarked as she looked at the picture her mother was holding in her hand. Grace was dressed in a pink dress with a matching pink bow attached to curly blonde hair. She had big brown eyes like her parents and a sweet, innocent smile. Addison thought she resembled her father a little more. When she said nothing further, her mother returned to her seat next to Jennifer and handed her the picture.

"Where is she?" her mother asked. "You should have brought her with you."

"Grace can get a little rambunctious sometimes," Jennifer explained. Smiling, she returned the picture to her wallet. "Maggie was kind enough to keep her for a while." Kyndal suddenly remembered the cherry cobbler.

"Listen, I've made a cherry cobbler. You can have dessert ala mode if you like."

Her mother stood as Jennifer and Pastor Bryce offered to assist her in the kitchen, leaving Addison at the mercy of Michael Scobie.

They sat smiling at each other in the awkward silence. Unfortunately, the weather had already been discussed, so what was there left to talk about? She cleared her throat just to break the silence; not to mention her jaws were getting slightly sore from holding an almost-constant smile. After what seemed an eternity, but was actually only a few seconds, Michael Scobie finally broke the tense silence.

"I hear you've been through quite an ordeal these past few weeks," he said, leaning forward, giving her his full attention. She was relieved to see compassion in his eyes and not pity.

"I guess you could say that," she answered solemnly. To her surprise, she watched as he came and knelt in front of her to get eye level. For a few seconds, he just looked at her with a serious expression and didn't say anything. He seemed to be studying very carefully as to what he should say next.

"You know, Addison, I'm guessing you are a woman of your word."

She wasn't quite sure how to respond to that statement. There had been times in her life she had been unable, for one reason or other, to keep her word to someone, but she had always tried. "I...I've always tried to keep my word," she said, not sure where he was going with this conversation.

"Good," he said, nodding. His eyes seemed to have softened a little, but were still serious. "I want your word, Addison McNeely, that you will attend the youth meeting Sunday evening. Will you give me your word you will come?"

Here it was—that awful feeling of being pressured into doing something she really didn't want to do.

"Yes, I-I guess I can," she said hesitantly. *What? Did I seriously just say yes! Where was the pressure? What the heck was I thinking? Obviously, I wasn't thinking*, she concluded as the questions ran through her mind. Michael Scobie had asked only one question and had only asked it once. She had caved quicker than a building being blasted by dynamite! *Geez Louise!*

"Great! I know God has something for you. You just wait and see," he said excitedly.

She wasn't sure what had made her agree to come. For a brief moment, she visualized herself bent over and kicking her own rear end.

He smiled and patted her on the hand. "Jennifer and I look forward to seeing you there." Smiling, he stood and made his way to the sofa as the rest of the gang returned from the kitchen. Jennifer joined her husband on the sofa.

"Honey, Addison has just agreed to come to the youth meeting Sunday night," he told his wife as she took a bite of the cherry cobbler.

"That's wonderful!" she exclaimed, quickly swallowing and turning to Addison with a wide toothy smile.

Kyndal had just handed Addison a bowl of warm cobbler when Michael blurted out the news. Addison looked at her mother and noticed her raised brow and the question mark in her large brown eyes. Addison had been so adamant about not going. The fact that she had agreed to go was a surprise to both mother and daughter.

The next half hour was spent discussing the new ideas the two youth pastors had for the New Haven youth group. Addison felt a little more relaxed around the two by the time they left. They really did seem like a nice couple who had a heart for young people. Even her mother seemed to enjoy their company.

Maybe Sunday wouldn't be bad after all. If nothing else, she would at least see how her peers would react toward her and the artificial leg. Maybe it would psych her up for what she was going to have to face when she returned to school after the holidays. This could be sort of a trial run, she thought.

She certainly wasn't going so she could hear about how God cared and how He will always be with you in times of trouble. No way could she stay and listen if they started speaking on that subject matter. She felt the anger begin to build inside of her, but that was nothing unusual. Over the past few weeks, she had felt angry much of the time. Why had God let this happen? She just couldn't get past that question. One thing was for sure: just because she had agreed to come to the meeting didn't mean she had agreed to stay for it all. She could leave at any time, which is probably what she would do.

That night, she went to bed once again feeling angry with God, Tyler, and Isaac. To be honest, she felt angry with the whole world. It just wasn't fair what had happened to her—and God could have stopped it all.

* * * * *

Sunday night rolled around sooner than she had anticipated. Alayna arrived early and knocked on the door. Kyndal jerked the door open and, without saying a word, turned to Addison, who was standing at the end of the sofa.

"Yes, you are going! You gave Michael Scobie your word!" Alayna came through the doorway. She wasn't sure whether to close the door behind her or leave it open for running purposes.

"I'm not going. I've changed my mind!" Addison plopped down on her dad's favorite chair, crossed her arms over her chest, and pouted her lips.

"Tell her she's going!" her mother said, turning to Alayna, finally acknowledging her presence. Alayna's mouth moved, but nothing came out.

"Tell my mother I'm not going!" Addison yelled, looking at Alayna.

Kyndal closed her eyes and took several deep breaths. "See if you can talk some sense into her," she said as she stomped upstairs. Alayna closed the door then came and stood in front of Addison.

"I just can't face people my own age. I just can't. I'm not ready," Addison said, frustrated at having made the promise to go.

"Listen, Addison, you'll be going back to school after the Thanksgiving holiday. Maybe it would be easier if you faced some of those people now."

"I've already thought of that, but I just can't face so many people at one time. It's just too much to ask."

Alayna sighed. "Look, Addison, most of the people in our youth group are Christians. Some of them even came to see you while you were in the hospital. They've already seen you."

"Yes, but my stump was covered with sheets and blankets. It wasn't like they really saw me without my leg. I just can't stand the thought of everyone staring at me and this dang fake leg!" More anger, if that was possible, began to burn deep inside her. "I'm just so angry right now!" she said through gritted teeth as she fought to hold back the tears. "I'm angry with God, Tyler, Isaac, but mainly at myself for going to that stupid party! Why didn't I listen to you?" she said, looking at Alayna.

Alayna looked into the pain-ridden face of her friend. "Addison, please don't do this. You can't go back and change things. You've got to move forward."

"Alayna, you, Mom, everyone, none of you understand!" She felt the warm steady flow of tears falling uncontrollably down her cheeks.

"Maybe I don't fully understand, but I'm your best friend, and I am in this with you. We will get through this together. Besides, Addison, you are a special and valuable person. You need to understand that your worth is not measured by a body part. You are loved by your family, your friends, me, and—whether you believe it or not—God." Reaching into her shoulder bag, she fished out a tissue and handed it to Addison. "I love you, Addison McNeely," she said as she reached and gave her best friend in the whole world a comforting hug.

Addison wasn't sure why, but somehow her friend always seemed to make things appear a little better than they actually were. Alayna was right. At least she would be facing a group of peers who liked her and looked up to her—or at least they had in the past.

"Maybe you're right," Addison said as Alayna released her hold.

The two walked to the foot of the stairs.

"Mom, we're gone!"

Kyndal came and stood at the top of the stairs. Smiling, she blew her daughter a kiss. "Thank you," she mouthed to Alayna as the two, along with Ayson, who had come bounding down the stairs, turned and headed out the door.

CHAPTER 17

THE LOVE OF GOD

Alayna prayed for the Lord to give Addison strength as they pulled into the parking lot of New Haven Church of God. After letting Addison out at the sidewalk leading to the youth building, she drove away to park the car. The large white youth building was separate from the main church, giving the youth more room for their activities. As it was a relatively large group of teens, the separate building enabled the youth to practice their music with guitars, keyboards, drums, and other instruments without disturbing other classes.

As Addison walked slowly toward the youth building, she saw the Scobie duo standing at the entrance to the building greeting each young person as they entered. There were about five steps leading into the building. Jennifer Scobie started to make her way down the steps to assist Addison, but she assured Jennifer she could manage without any help. She was so thankful Wyatt had helped her practice on the stairs. Alayna and Ayson caught up to her just as she stepped onto the last step. When they entered the building, several of the youth ran and hugged her.

"Did you like the flower we sent you?" Yvonne asked.

"Did you notice they were pink carnations?" asked Matilda.

"When are you coming back to school?" Steve asked.

The questions were coming faster than she could answer—when the inevitable happened.

"Can we see yer artificial leg?" Brian Walsh asked in his normal, long-drawn-out Southern accent. Everyone suddenly fell quiet and looked at Brian with their jaws dropped. They knew he was used to just blurting things out without thinking—but still. Beckah Joy Roth elbowed him in the ribs.

Irritated, Alayna spoke up, "Brian, how can you ask such a stupid question as that?"

"Well, I jus' wanted to see one. I ain't never known anyone that had one."

Beckah Joy elbowed him again, only this time a little harder. He rubbed his rib area and was about to say something when Michael and Jennifer entered the room. They noticed everyone gathered around Addison and saw Brian rubbing his side.

"What's going on?" Michael asked, moving closer to the group of young people.

"Brian just asked Addison to see her artificial leg. He can be so stupid sometimes," said Beckah Joy.

"First of all," said Michael, "we don't call each other stupid. Second of—"

"Well, what else do you call someone who asked a question like that?" Beckah Joy interrupted.

Beckah Joy Roth had the most baffled look on her face and was so sincere in her question that Addison burst into laughter. Beckah Joy looked even more baffled in trying to figure out what was so funny. Addison couldn't stop laughing. Her uncontrollable laughter was contagious. Soon a loud roar of laughter was heard from everyone in the room, except Beckah Joy, who was still trying to figure out what was so funny. When the laughter finally died down a few seconds later, Addison went and sat in one of the metal folding chairs. She rolled her jeans leg up and called for Brian to come see her artificial leg. She thought she would feel self-conscious as everyone gathered around her; but to her surprise, she didn't. Thanks to Brian and his so-called stupid question, the ice had been broken. If only it would go this well at school. In her heart, she knew it wouldn't.

After everyone finished looking at her leg, she rolled down her jeans leg and settled in with everyone else to hear what Michael and

Jennifer Scobie had to say. Addison listened as Michael spoke from Isaiah 43.

"God has promised when we pass through the waters, He will be with us, and the rivers they shall not overflow us. When we are walking through the fire, we shall not be burned, nor shall the flame scorch us, for He is the Lord our God."

Addison had heard teaching on this scripture before, but for some reason, it really seemed to sink into her spirit for the first time. She didn't even feel resentful at what he was saying.

He continued, "Jesus never promised we would not go through tough seasons in our lives, but He did promise to be with us and to help us through those seasons. Just remember we—*you*—are more than conquerors through Jesus Christ."

At that moment, Jennifer began to speak, and although Addison knew Jennifer was addressing the group as a whole, it was as if she were speaking directly to her.

"Just be assured when your faith does come under fire, God will always make a way out. God is good and faithful, and He is for you, He is not against you. His love for you is unwavering, no matter what."

Michael then asked the group to turn to another scripture, Psalm 30:5.

"Addison, would you please read this scripture for us?" he asked.

She had intentionally not brought her Bible, and Alayna had forgotten to bring hers.

"Here, use mine," Matilda whispered, handing the pink engraved Bible to her. She took the Bible and began to read aloud.

"For His anger endureth but a moment. In His favor is life..." She could feel her voice beginning to crack. Could it be that God was no longer angry with her for going to the party and for hitting Karlie? Was He even angry to begin with? Maybe He had been more disappointed. Swallowing the lump in her throat, she continued reading. "Weeping may endure for a night, but joy cometh in the morning." Without realizing it, she spoke aloud while continuing to stare at the scripture, "Lord, please let my morning come soon."

Jennifer came and knelt in front of her and whispered two simple words: "It will."

Addison looked up into the understanding eyes of someone who had apparently had her own share of weeping nights for whatever reasons. Later, she found out Jennifer had gone through two miscarriages before getting pregnant and carrying Grace.

As their eyes met, Addison burst into tears. She had never cried so much in her life as she had the past month or so. Michael asked everyone to gather around her as he laid hands on her and began to pray. She wasn't sure what was happening, but Addison knew the Lord was doing a work in her as she felt the weight of anger and guilt being lifted. Mostly, she felt God's love. She remembered feeling that same kind of overwhelming love on the day she had surrendered her life to the Lord. Some of the other young people were crying as well as they prayed for her.

Before she realized it, the two youth pastors were going from one young person to another and praying over them. It occurred to her as she watched her peers, some weeping bitterly, that she was not the only one going through something. Others were going through trials of their own. She wasn't the only one walking through the fire.

The devil had continually thrown his fiery darts at her and had eventually bound her with doubt, anger, unforgiveness, and even hate—but mostly he had bound her with the fiery dart of fear. Having not put on the whole armor of God as He had instructed her to do as a Christian, the fiery darts had accumulated into a raging fire that had totally engulfed her. But what Satan had meant for her undoing, God was using to make her stronger. She realized God was walking with her through this fiery trial, and instead of coming out destroyed, she was coming out victorious. God was using the fire to burn away the spiritual ropes that had her bound, especially that of fear—fear of an unknown future.

After praying for her, Brian requested prayer for his alcoholic father. Matilda requested prayer for a cousin hooked on cocaine. Yvonne was requesting prayer for her mother and father who were contemplating divorce. Charles and Steve, twin brothers, were weeping bitterly after finding out the day before that their mother had just been diagnosed with breast cancer. Charles also had an unspoken request. The prayer requests went on and on as prayer went up, and they released their faith. How could she have been so self-centered to think she was the only one going through something? She watched as the two youth leaders wept along with the young people God had placed in their care. They truly care, she thought. She and Alayna were the last to leave before time for the main service to begin in the sanctuary.

"You go on ahead to the sanctuary," she told Alayna. "I'll be there in a minute."

Alayna gave her a curious look but did as she asked.

"Mr. and Mrs. Scobie," Addison began, "I—"

"Please call us Michael and Jennifer," Jennifer said with a warm smile.

Smiling, Addison nodded. "Okay, Jennifer."

"Now, what were you saying before I so rudely interrupted?"

Addison shifted her weight to her good leg before continuing, "I just wanted to say, I'm glad I came tonight."

Jennifer reached and took her by the hand and gave it a squeeze. "I'm glad you came too."

"Ditto," said Michael, giving her a smile. He reached and closed the door, locking it behind them. The three made their way to the main sanctuary, Jennifer with her arm around Addison's shoulder. As if he knew what she was thinking, Michael spoke up.

"It will be all right. Everyone will be so glad to see you back."

Addison had not planned on staying for the main service and had told Alayna as much before arriving at the youth meeting. That had been the reason for the puzzled look on Alayna's face when Addison had told her to go on ahead to the sanctuary. It was not until she experienced such a presence of God in the youth meeting that Addison decided to stay. She limped slowly up the steps leading into the sanctuary.

Michael was right. She was greeted, kissed, and hugged so many times by her church family she did not feel uncomfortable at all. No one seemed to pay any attention to her limp, nor did they ask about her artificial leg.

One particular scripture from the book of Romans stood out as Pastor Bryce delivered the message the Lord had placed on his heart for the service. There has to be some good to come out of this, she thought, as she listened to the scripture concerning all things working together for the good of them who love the Lord.

During the invitation, Addison made her way to the altar. She asked the Lord to forgive her for being angry and self-centered.

"Please, God," she prayed, "do let some good come from this. Direct my path and use me for Your glory."

At the end of the service, Maggie lead the congregation in an old hymn. Addison stood up from the altar, raised her hands, and began to sing. This time, she not only sang from her lips but from her heart. She truly wanted to surrender all to Jesus. She wanted to surrender every area of her life to the One who had died for her and saved her, to the One who wanted a personal, intimate relationship with her, to the One who loved her, and loved her unconditionally. Months ago, she had made the decision to make Jesus her Savior; tonight she made the decision to make Him Lord as well. She wanted Him to be Lord over every area of her life, not just a few areas of her life.

Alayna slid from behind the pew and joined her friend at the altar. "Thank You, Lord," she whispered as she reached and put her arm around Addison's waist. Alayna smiled. She was smiling because she knew in her heart that everything really was going to be all right.

* * * * *

Today had been the busiest and most tiring day Addison had experienced except for the day she returned home from the hospital. She was completely exhausted by the time she arrived home. As she opened the door, she noticed her mother sitting in front of the fireplace working a crossword puzzle with Chip snuggled on her lap. Her mother removed her reading glasses and looked a little nervously at her as she came through the door.

"How did things go?" asked Kyndal. Addison moved toward her mom and bent down, giving her a kiss on the forehead.

"It went great, Mom. It really did," she said, smiling. She could see the relief in her mother's face.

"You want to tell me about it?"

"Maybe later," Addison begged off. Seeing the curiosity in her mother's face, she added, "I promise to tell you all about it tomorrow. I'm just so exhausted right now. It's been a really busy day."

"Okay, honey," her mother said, smiling, "Good night."

"Good night, Mom. Good night, Chip."

Chip opened his eyes and raised his head upon hearing his name, then lowered his head again and closed his eyes. He gave her mother's hand a nudge with his cool wet nose. Kyndal slid her glasses on and returned to her crossword puzzle as she began to rub her spoiled but loveable fur baby behind his soft velvety ears. Addison climbed the stairs and knocked on her brother's bedroom door.

"It's open!" he yelled. Ayson, who had run ahead of her as soon as they arrived home, was sitting on the edge of his bed, thumbing through a guitar book.

"Good night, little brother," she said.

He glanced at the digital clock sitting on his nightstand. "Already?" he asked, looking a little surprised that she would be going to bed so early. "It's not even eight thirty."

"Yeah, well, sleep can call at any time. See you in the morning," she said as she closed the door.

"Night, sis," he told her as he returned to thumbing through the book.

Entering her room, she sat on the edge of the bed, removed her artificial leg, and placed it on the chair next to her bed. After changing into her favorite silky knit nightgown, she laid her head on the soft down pillow and closed her eyes. It was amazing the peace one felt when they truly turned every burden and care over to the Lord. The peaceful feeling reminded her of the scripture in First Peter, where the Lord says to cast all our care on Him because He cares for us. That was the last thing she remembered as a much-needed and restful sleep overtook her. That night, Addison slept the best she had slept in a very long time.

CHAPTER 18

THE MYSTERY UNFOLDS

A few days later, a loud clap of thunder woke Addison from a sound sleep. Moaning, she focused her eyes on the red digital numbers of the clock beside her bed. It was 6:35 a.m., much too early to be up. She had been sleeping in her own bed now for a few days, and it felt good.

Moaning and not wanting to get up, she rolled over and covered her sleepy eyes with her arm. She could feel a slight headache coming on.

"Sinuses again," she mumbled. Giving up on going back to sleep, she threw back the warm blanket. She reached and grabbed her artificial leg. After attaching it, she slid into the soft pink bedroom slippers lying next to the bed. "It would be nice just to jump out of the bed like everyone else," she mumbled again. "But those days are long gone." She sighed.

As she made her way down the hall to the upstairs bathroom, she slid her arms into her thick, slightly bulky robe. She popped a sinus pill in her mouth and washed it down with the water she had poured. She debated whether or not to go back to bed, but then decided to head downstairs to make a cup of hot chocolate instead.

Just as she was taking the large mug of hot milk out of the microwave, another loud clap of thunder startled her and almost caused her to drop the mug. As she added the chocolate mix to the hot milk, she peered out the kitchen window into the backyard.

The large oak trees swayed rapidly back and forth as the strong wind whipped through their branches with ease. She was always amazed at how the wind was able to twist, bend, break and even uproot a tree. The rain pelted noisily against the windowpanes as she watched dark clouds move across the gray sky. She shivered at the thought of being out in the cold November rain. At the same time, she wondered how her mother and little brother could sleep through the loud claps of thunder.

Turning off the kitchen light, she made her way to the living room. She turned on the tiffany-style floor lamp and took a sip of hot chocolate. The delightfully rich chocolate instantly warmed her insides as she sat and snuggled comfortably into the chair.

Her eyes fell upon the unfinished crossword puzzle lying on the end table. She picked it up, took another sip of chocolate, and began to fill in the blank squares. A half hour later, Ayson bounced down the stairs in his football pajamas and stood next to her.

"What's a three-letter word for 'sense of self'?" she asked without looking up. She knew the word, but she also knew her little brother liked to think he knew something she didn't.

"That's easy. Ego," he said, smiling triumphantly.

"What are you two up to so early in the morning?" Both turned when they heard the cheery sound of their mother's voice. Addison couldn't figure out why, but her mother had seemed to be in a lot better spirits for the past couple of weeks.

"I'm helping Addison work a crossword puzzle," Ayson said, quickly snatching the crossword out of her hand.

"Hey!" she yelled as she grabbed for the paper. She missed as he tucked the paper under his arm and took off to the kitchen.

"I'm hungry. What's for breakfast, Mom?" he asked as he ran past his mother, giving her a quick peck on the cheek.

The lights flickered off then back on as a long rumbling of thunder caused the windows to vibrate, which in turn caused Chip to jump onto Addison's lap. She felt him shiver. "It's okay, little buddy. Nothing is going to hurt you," she assured him. Not convinced, he buried his entire body under the warm throw she had laid across her lap. The rain had not let up, and from the looks of things, it would not be letting up anytime soon.

"I'd better get the battery-powered lanterns out of the closet," her mother said, "just in case." After giving it some thought, she added, "I think I'll light a fire in the fireplace too."

Finishing a warm breakfast of bacon, buttered grits, eggs, and toast, Ayson ran upstairs to get ready for school. Having gotten his tooth fixed a few days earlier, Addison could tell her brother was feeling better. Her mother made her way upstairs to get ready as well. Being it was her day off, she was taking Ayson to school.

The rain was still coming down hard, and the wind had let up very little. There had been a few reports of power outages on the opposite side of town, but so far, the McNeely home had been fortunate. However, Therapy Inc. had not been so fortunate. While her mother and brother were getting ready, Wyatt called from his cell phone and informed her that her therapy appointment had been rescheduled for the next day.

"If it's not back on by tomorrow, I'll give you another call."

"Thanks, Wyatt."

As she hung up the phone, she felt a little disappointed—and it wasn't because she would be missing the therapy exercises. She informed her mother of the therapy cancellation as she and Ayson came down the stairs and lifted their raincoats from the coat rack.

"Bye, sis!" he yelled.

"Please be careful," she told them as they made their way to the door.

"We will" her mother said.

"Please, Lord, keep them safe," she prayed as she grabbed her Christie novel from the coffee table and plopped down on the sofa.

The warm glow of the flickering yellow flames in the fireplace illuminated the room, giving it a cozy and welcoming atmosphere. As she watched the yellow flames dance their way around the burning logs and listened to the soothing sound of the crackling wood, she felt herself becoming sleepy. The heavy pelting of rain wasn't helping her to stay awake either. She had always loved the relaxing sound of the rain and the fresh earthy smell it left in the air. Hard as she tried, she was unable to stay awake and finally nodded off to sleep along with Chip.

* * * * *

She awakened a short time later when she heard the door open and saw her mother and Ayson walk in.

"School's out of power," Ayson said with a huge smile on his face as their mother talked to someone on her cell phone.

"He's doing just fine. Thanks for checking on him. Yes, we still have power. Yes, noon Thursday. Talk to you later," she said as she put away her phone.

"Who was that, Mom?"

"Dr. Steelman," Ayson said as he pulled off his raincoat, draped it over the coat rack, and ran upstairs. He obviously had no curiosity, Addison thought, as to why Dr. Steelman would be calling and checking on him. It was happy-dance time as Chip followed her brother upstairs. Her brother might not have been curious, but she was.

"Why is Dr. Steelman checking on Ayson?"

Her mother cleared her throat, hung up her coat, and then began to smooth out her sweater and dress slacks. She didn't look at Addison as she answered, "I happened to mention to Noah—I mean Dr. Steelman—at work the other day that Ayson had a toothache," she said as she continued to smooth out invisible wrinkles.

Addison knew her mother well enough to know she was purposely avoiding eye contact with her. "Mom, please stop smoothing out wrinkles that aren't there and tell me what is going on. There is something you're not telling me."

Her mother stopped fidgeting and came and sat next to her on the sofa. She sighed and looked down at the gold wedding band that had been on her finger for almost twenty years. She began spinning it round and round on her finger. Still looking at the band, she finally answered.

"I've asked Noa—Dr. Steelman, to join us for Thanksgiving dinner Thursday." Only when she didn't hear a response did she look into the confused face of her daughter. "Well?"

"Well, what?" Addison asked, not knowing quite what to make of her mother's news.

"What do you think about my asking him to join us?"

"I'm not sure what I think. I mean, this is so unexpected." Now it was her looking at the gold wedding band on her mother's finger. Her mother was still subconsciously turning it around and around. Addison had always known this day would come, but she just wasn't prepared for it at the moment. She thought she would have more time to adjust to the idea of her mother being in a relationship with a man other than her father. Of course, she had already had four years to get used to the idea. If she wasn't used to the idea by now, she probably never would be. The sound of her mother's voice interrupted her thoughts.

"If it bothers you, I can call and ask him not to come. I'm sure he will understand."

"What about his family? Doesn't he want to spend Thanksgiving with his family?"

"The only family Noa—the only family Noah has," she began again, this time not backing away from referring to him by his first name, "lives hours away from here." Still getting no response from her daughter, she continued. "He can't go home because he is the surgeon on call for the hospital on Thanksgiving Day."

Now Addison understood the change she had seen in her mother lately. The mystery was solved. She had liked the change and wondered why it was so sudden, but had decided at the time not to ask her mother any questions. The atmosphere at home had been much more pleasant, and she hadn't caught her mother crying as often when she didn't think anyone was watching.

She was about to tell her mother to ask Dr. Steelman not to come because she just wasn't ready to see another man sitting at their family table. *Don't be selfish, My daughter.* It was that inward voice again, the gentle voice of the Holy Spirit. *You've trusted Me with your life, Now trust Me with your family.*

"Addison!" she heard her mother calling. "Are you listening to me?"

"I'm sorry, Mom, I was just thinking."

Her mother gave her a half-hearted smile and then reached and gave her hand a gentle squeeze. "I'll call him and tell him not to come."

Addison could hear the disappointment in her mother's voice and see the sadness in her eyes. "You'll do no such thing," she said, a lot more cheerful than she actually felt. "It will be nice to have company for Thanksgiving dinner."

Her mother's face lit up immediately, and a long overdue sparkle was seen in her eyes. Addison tried to convince herself it was from the lighting in the room, but she knew better.

"You're sure you're okay with this?" her mother asked, needing reassurance.

"I'm sure, Mom," she said with as much of a smile as she could muster. Her mother reached and hugged her tightly before standing and kicking off her shoes.

"What about Ayson?"

"Oh, he's okay with it, especially after he found out Noah plays the bass guitar."

Of course, he does, thought Addison. If her mother saw her give the eye roll, she ignored it. She started to ask when her mother had talked to Ayson about Dr. Steelman, but decided to let it ride. Apparently, her brother was okay with the situation, and she might as well be okay with it too.

The lights flickered off, but this time, they did not come back on. Her mother reached and turned on the battery-powered lanterns. Ayson and her mother played chess by the lanterns, and Addison resumed reading her Christie novel—again.

She only had three chapters left, and she was no closer to figuring out who committed the murder than when she had first begun reading. It was easy to finger the murderer in some novels she read, but not an Agatha Christie mystery. Of all the Christie mysteries she had read—and there had been many—only once had she ever guessed the murderer correctly. If the truth be known, it had probably been a lucky guess.

A little over three hours later, the power was finally restored. The angry winds outside had died down, and the cold November rain had turned to a light drizzle. The sky outside had lightened up to match Kyndal's mood. She had hummed golden oldies love songs off and on all morning. Addison knew it was because Dr. Steelman was coming to Thanksgiving dinner.

"Mom," Ayson had complained earlier while playing chess, "you're distracting me. I can't concentrate."

Addison had initially thought her mother was humming to distract Ayson during his move in the chess game too, but then noticed her mom had continued to hum even when it was her turn to move.

Things were changing in the McNeely household. Addison wasn't quite sure how she felt about all the changes, but she would just have to trust the Lord. She still had to face her peers at school next week. She tried not to think about going back, but sometimes the only way she could distract herself was to read her Bible.

Usually school was out Thursday and Friday for Thanksgiving, but according to the local news, because of the storm, the schools were going to be out for the rest of the week. Although there had been no report of tornadoes, the high winds had done a lot of damage to the community. Some homes were still without power. Trees were down in many areas; some of which had fallen on cars and houses. One huge oak tree that had been standing at the high school for years, even when Kyndal and Josh had attended the school, had been uprooted. Fortunately, when it fell, it had missed the school. Addison felt a pang of sadness over the uprooting of the huge oak that had stood for so many years to give a much-needed shade during the hotter days of school. According to the news, another six feet over, and it would have landed on the cafeteria. The unfortunate thing was, the tree had landed on a power line. There had been no reports of any deaths in the community, although one man did end up in the hospital with a broken hip after a tree fell into his living room. It was reported he had been looking out the window when the tree began to fall toward the house. As he took off running, he fell over a chair breaking his hip in two places, the tree barely missing him.

Addison closed her novel and thought about the upcoming Thanksgiving dinner. She could still hear the evening news, something about several wrecks, but the reporter's voice grew faint as she drifted off into a somewhat troubled sleep. She was just getting ready to pour the giblet gravy in Noah Steelman's lap when her mother woke her for supper.

"Ah, Mom, just when I was getting to the good part," she muttered, still half asleep.

"What good part?" her mother asked, giving her another hard shake on the shoulders. "Wake up, Addison. It's time for supper. You're dreaming."

Finally awake, her mouth began to water at the inviting aroma of her mother's homemade chili beans.

"What in the world were you dreaming about?" her mother asked as they headed toward the kitchen.

"Nothing important," she answered, smiling again at the thought of pouring giblet gravy onto Noah Steelman's lap.

* * * * *

Tuesday morning, Shannon and Addison made their way to her therapy appointment. Everything went well, and Wyatt complimented her on the progress she was making, especially on the stairs. However, for the first time, she felt a little distance between the two of them. He was nice and helpful enough, but something was different. He was much quieter than usual and more businesslike. *Had she said something to upset him?*

"Great job today, Addison," he said as he sat on the steps and began his paperwork.

"Thanks."

"Okay…well, see you next Monday after school," he said without looking up.

"Sure thing. See you then. Have a nice Thanksgiving, Wyatt," she said as she slowly turned to walk away.

"Thanks. You too," he said, this time looking up briefly before returning to his paperwork. He watched Addison leave through the glass double doors. "Wyatt Kingsley, you're such a jerk," he said aloud as he let out a discouraged sigh.

CHAPTER 19

THE VISITOR

Alayna, Addison, and Ayson returned to the McNeely house after Alayna had taken Addison to her last counseling session with Dr. Davenport. Running upstairs alongside Ayson, Alayna was eager to accept a challenge "Squirt" had tossed her way regarding one of his video games.

Addison dropped onto the sofa and then texted her mother to give her an update on the discharge. Dr. Tillie—as Addison had taken to calling her, but not in the doctor's presence—had not wanted to discharge her quite yet, but Addison had insisted she didn't need any further counseling. Before discharging her, the doctor had wanted to see how she would deal with returning to school, but Addison felt she would be ready to face whatever might be thrown her way. At least she prayed she would. She looked at the business card the doctor had given her in case she was to need further services. Carefully, she slid the card into the envelope along with the signed discharge papers Dr. Tillie had discussed with her. Her mother was not happy that she wanted to stop therapy sessions, but reluctantly gave in, knowing it would do no good to try and force her. After texting her mother and informing her that Dr. Tillie would call her and go over the discharge papers with her as well, she popped a peppermint in her mouth.

She heard the sound of laughter coming from Ayson's room. A few minutes later, Alayna came bouncing down the stairs.

"You know, Squirt is pretty good at those video games. I didn't beat him even once," she said, standing with her hands on her slim hips.

"Sit down a minute," Addison said, patting the seat next to her.

Alayna noticed the serious look on Addison's face as she sat next to her friend. "What's wrong?"

"Do you know who is coming here for Thanksgiving dinner?"

"I hear Dr. Steelman is coming."

"Who told you?" Addison asked, a little surprised that Alayna knew, and even more surprised she had not mentioned it.

"My mom told me," she said, reaching into the candy dish on the coffee table and taking out a piece of peppermint. "I think that is *sooo* cool," she said as she unwrapped the peppermint and tossed it into her mouth.

Addison sat staring at her friend in disbelief. Alayna noticed the troubled look on her face. "What?" she asked.

"Don't you think my mom is jumping into this relationship a little too soon?"

"No, do you?" she asked, sucking on the hard piece of candy. But before she could answer, Alayna said, "I thought you were okay with this."

"What makes you think that?"

"My mom says your mom says you were okay with it and that you gave the okay for Dr. Steelman to come." Addison frowned as Alayna kept talking, "From what I understand, your mom was going to tell Dr. Steelman not to come, but you stopped her."

"It's just, it's…it's going to be hard seeing my mom with someone other than my dad at our dinner table."

Alayna reached over and squeezed her hand. "Your dad would not want your mom to be alone for the rest of her life. You know he wouldn't."

Addison sighed. "I know."

"Did you know he was a Christian?"

"No, I didn't. How did you find out?"

"I overheard Pastor Bryce and Maggie talking at church the week before last. Maggie was shopping in Fletcher's Groceries and recognized Noah. She walked over and started a conversation with him. In the course of the conversation he mentioned he was a Christian and that he had been visiting several churches in the area. He told her he had not, as yet, felt led to attend any one particular church on a regular basis. Maggie invited him to visit our church."

Addison's eyes lit up for the first time concerning Noah Steelman. "You know something," she said excitedly, "maybe God is going to use Dr. Steelman to reach Mom."

"Maybe," said Alayna, tossing another piece of peppermint into her mouth. "Oh yeah," she continued, "he lost his wife and little girl in a car accident a few years ago." She held up her hand. "Before you ask how I know, Dr. Steelman told your mom, who told my mom, who told me."

They were interrupted by the ringing of Alayna's cell phone.

"It's Trevor," Alayna said.

Addison listened to bits and pieces of the conversation but couldn't put anything together as to what the conversation might be about. A minute later, Alayna hung up. "It's Tyler! The doctors brought him out of the medically induced coma," she said excitedly. "They believe he is going to be just fine."

Addison felt a flood of relief flow through her. If it was the last thing she did, she was going to see Tyler, but what if this time it was he who didn't want to see her? It was just a chance she would have to take.

Alayna continued, "Trevor said the doctors told Tyler's parents he still had a long road ahead of him with rehab and counseling, but he was going to be all right. Mr. Morris says the medical staff taking care of Tyler at Faith Hospital is calling him a miracle."

"Thank God he is going to be okay," Addison said. "How did Trevor find out all this?"

Alayna frowned fondly at her friend. "Honestly, Addison, you and your never-ending questions of who and how."

"What can I say?" she said, smiling. "I'm of the curious sort."

"Yeah, well, you know what happened to the cat for being so curious." Jokingly, she tilted her head to one side, crossed her eyes, and stuck out her tongue as she made an imaginary cut with her finger from one end of her throat to the other.

Both girls laughed, causing Alayna to almost choke on the piece of peppermint she was sucking on. She coughed up the piece of candy just as there was a loud knock at the door. Before either could get up to answer, Ayson came running from the kitchen, excited that Caleb was coming over and spending the day with him. Upon answering the door, he just stood staring at the person standing in front of him.

"Who is it?" Addison asked, rising slowly to her feet when she saw her brother's reaction. He turned and faced Alayna and his sister. Before he could answer, they heard the familiar voice.

"It's me, Isaac." Isaac Darnell stepped hesitantly inside the doorway. "May I come in?"

Both girls stared at each other for a few seconds before Addison finally invited him in. Ayson shrugged, closed the door, and ran back into the kitchen to finish his snack. Addison motioned for Isaac to sit in the chair across from them as she and Alayna took a seat again on the sofa.

"I'm sorry I haven't called or come by before now," he said, taking a seat on the edge of the chair. Neither Addison nor Alayna could seem to find their voice. "The truth is, I've been too ashamed to face you, Addie." She could tell this was as awkward for him as it was for them. She knew it had taken a lot of courage for him to be here. She had to give him credit, though; at least he was trying.

"I understand," Addison said, finally finding her voice.

Isaac looked around. "Is your mother home? I would like to apologize to her as well."

"No, she had to work today, I'm afraid." Right now she was *so* thankful her mother had returned to work. She breathed a silent, *Thank You, Lord.* Isaac showing up like this would have been a disaster.

Isaac looked around the room again, mainly from the lack of anything else to say. "Nice home you have."

Addison thanked him, but knew he was just being polite. Isaac's parents lived in a three-story home in an elite part of town. The

McNeely's humble home was nowhere near the Darnell's league when it came to homes, especially with its outdated décor.

"Addie, it's been difficult, but I haven't touched a drop of alcohol since all this happened," he said, looking at the floor.

Until then, Alayna had not spoken a word. "Yeah, well, you're not the only one who's been going through something difficult."

Isaac didn't look up. "I know," he said, barely above a whisper.

Alayna started to make another comment, but Addison placed her hand over Alayna's hand, looked at her, and shook her head. Alayna sighed and reluctantly gave in.

Addison swallowed the lump in her throat. "It wasn't your fault, Isaac. I made the choice to go to the party. Alayna tried to talk me into not going, but I wouldn't listen. I wanted to be part of the big college scene with all you popular football players and your friends." She was beginning to tear up as Isaac looked up at her.

"Addie, it *is* my fault. I'm the one who sent Tyler to the store for more beer. I messed up your life and his," he said, shaking his head and rubbing his hands through his blond hair. "I wish there was some way I could undo things, but there isn't."

"Isaac, I'm going to be all right. You've got to stop beating yourself up over this. I forgive you."

The words shocked her about as much as they shocked Alayna and Isaac, but she realized at that moment she truly meant them. She really had, with God's help, forgiven him. She tried to explain. "The one thing the Lord has been showing me through His Word is that we all have choices to make. But more importantly, we have to take responsibility for those choices. We are human, and we will make mistakes, but God can turn those mistakes around and use them for our good and for His glory. God is a forgiving God, and He loves us no matter what we've done. Like one of our youth leaders said, God's love for us is unwavering."

Isaac started to tear. "I went to see Tyler in the hospital, but his parents asked me to leave. Mr. Morris was really angry with me. If it hadn't been for his wife, he would have probably decked me, not that I wouldn't have deserved it. If they can't forgive me, I don't see how God can."

Addison leaned forward. "Give them time, Isaac. They are good Christian people. They'll come around."

"I just hope when the doctors bring Tyler out of that coma that he will be okay," he said, leaning back in the chair.

"You mean you haven't heard?" Alayna asked, surprised.

"Heard what?" he asked, sitting straight up. Having thought the worst, both girls watched as a moment of fear crossed his face.

Alayna quickly explained, "It's good news, Isaac. The doctors brought Tyler out of the coma early this morning. His doctor says he's going to be okay with some counseling and rehab."

To their surprise, he burst into tears. They looked at each other, thinking the same thing: here was this popular, "tough" football star crying like a baby.

There was another knock at the door. Ayson came running again from the kitchen. Isaac was trying hard to compose himself as Ayson opened the door and invited Caleb in. He slammed the door shut, and the two ran upstairs, never bothering to acknowledge anyone as they heard Caleb's mother drive away. Addison could tell Isaac was grateful the two boys had not paid him any attention.

"Well, I guess I had better be going," he said, starting to stand to his feet.

"Wait!" Addison said, motioning for him to remain seated. "What you said about God not being able to forgive you, I just want you to know that He can, and He will. All you have to do is ask Him, and I'm not just talking about what happened with Tyler and me. He will forgive you for every sin you've ever committed. Jesus died for you so you could come into a right relationship with the Father. He can change your life, your attitude, and your destiny if you will allow Him."

Isaac looked at the floor again as if he were truly contemplating what she had just said. She continued to speak as she felt led of the Holy Spirit. "The Bible tells us in the book of Romans that all have sinned and fall short of the glory of God."

Isaac looked into the compassionate eyes of his friend, a true friend.

"You're no better or worse than anyone else," Alayna added, starting to feel a change in her attitude toward him.

"I don't know how to ask Him for forgiveness. I've really never prayed before," he admitted, a little ashamed.

Addison took him by the hand. "If you're ready to make Jesus the Lord of your life, we'll help you."

"Yes, yes, I'm ready," he said as he began to cry again.

"Then repeat after me." So as to make him feel more comfortable, Alayna repeated the prayer of repentance along with him. When they had finished, all three were crying and hugging one another.

"You need to come to church Sunday," Alayna said. "You're welcome to sit with us."

He nodded and promised he would be there. "Keep me posted as to what is going on with Tyler," he said as he walked toward the door. "I would like to go see him, but his parents may be there, and I don't want to cause any further trouble." Both agreed to keep him informed. "If there is some way you can let Tyler know I have been asking about him, I would appreciate it."

"Can you believe it?" Alayna squealed after Isaac left. "We actually led someone to the Lord." They gave each other a high five. Isaac Darnell was pretty much the focus of their conversation for the next hour.

Later Kyndal called and said she was having to work over for about an hour or so and would be home as soon as she could. Just as Addison put down the receiver, Sarah Garrison called and said she would pick Caleb up before time for supper.

Of course, he wasn't ready to leave when his mother arrived to get him; but then again, he never was.

"I believe he would let your mother adopt him," said Sarah as she went to the foot of the stairs and yelled again for her son. Sarah Garrison was on the short side, a little plumb and had the same fiery red hair as her son. Caleb definitely favored his mom, right down to the blue eyes and freckles.

"Maybe I had better go up and get him," said Addison as she started toward the stairs. She was halfway when both boys came running down the stairs.

"Stop running, Caleb Garrison!" his mother warned. Addison smiled and noticed Mrs. Garrison was waiting for her to say something to her brother for running, but she just didn't feel like going there. Sarah Garrison gave a slight grunt as she and Caleb made their way to the front door.

Soon afterward, Alayna left, still on cloud nine over Isaac accepting the Lord. For the moment, the house was back to being peacefully quiet.

Kyndal arrived home fifteen minutes later. Addison had already started dinner.

"We're having spaghetti and a salad," she told her mother as she came into the kitchen. "I thought since we would be having such a large meal tomorrow that we could keep it simple tonight."

"Spaghetti is fine," her mother said, dropping her exhausted body into the kitchen chair. "Boy, am I tired." Chip ran and stood on his hind legs as he laid his front paws and head on her mother's knee. She reached down and pulled him to her chest, giving him several kisses on the top of his head before setting him back on the floor. He lay at her feet, licking one of his paws.

"Why did you have to work over tonight?" Addison asked as she tossed the salad.

"One of the nurses had a flat tire on the way to work, and she had to get it fixed before she came in."

Addison, in all honesty, was only half-listening. Her mind was on Isaac. "Mom, one of the most exciting things happened today."

"Really?" her mother said, kicking off her shoes. "What happened that was so exciting?"

"Isaac Darnell came by today, and Alayna and I—"

"Isaac Darnell!" her mother exclaimed, sitting straight up in the chair. "What was he doing here? I don't want him to ever step foot in this house again! Do you hear?"

Addison had expected her mother to be upset, but she was genuinely stunned at her mother's shocking reaction. She stopped stirring the spaghetti sauce then reached and turned off the burner. She turned to face her mother. "Mom, what is wrong with you? He just came by to apologize. He even wanted to apologize to you in person."

"I don't want his apologies. I want him to stay away from my family!"

Addison didn't think she had ever seen her mother so angry, except for when her dad had passed away. Her mother had been so angry with God and even with the doctors. She was still mad at God.

"Mom"—she sighed—"if I hadn't been where I wasn't supposed to be, I would still have two good legs today, but I chose to go to the party."

"How can you stand there and take up for those two? Whether you went to the party or not is beside the point. Tyler Morris should not have been drinking and driving, and Isaac should never have sent him for more beer knowing the drunken state he was in."

"But, Mom, Isaac was drinking too. He wasn't thinking straight himself," she said as she drew up a chair and sat next to her mother. "We've got to forgive, Mom. No one meant for me to lose my leg. I could have lost my life, but God was gracious and chose to spare me."

Her mother shook her head. "I just don't get God sometimes. I'm thankful He spared your life, but He could have spared your leg as well. After all, He *is* God. There is supposed to be nothing too hard for Him. Why did you have to be the one to pay for what they did?"

Addison shook her head. "I don't know, Mom, but no one understands all things at all times. Even God's Word tells us not to lean unto our own understanding." She took her mother by the hand. Softening her voice, she said, "Mom, Alayna and I led Isaac to the Lord. He says he has not had a drop of alcohol since the accident."

"And you believe him?" her mother asked, standing and going to the sink to pour herself a glass of water. She noticed her mother's hand shaking as she placed the glass to her lips.

"Yes, I do," Addison said as she stood and headed back to the stove and turned the burner on. Her mother turned to say something else when Ayson burst through the kitchen door.

"I'm hungry. What are we having for supper?"

"Spaghetti!" Kyndal and Addison yelled in unison, both with an edge of irritation in their voices. Ayson started to back slowly out the door. He knew he had walked in on something he didn't care to know about. He had gotten used to living with nothing but moody women for the past few years. They were either crying or yelling; it was always one of the two.

"Call me when it's ready," he said almost out the door.

"It's ready!" they yelled again in unison.

For a second, Ayson stood looking at the two women. "Women!" he mumbled, of course not loud enough that they could hear him; he wasn't crazy.

After dinner, Kyndal decided to start some of the cooking ahead for the next day. Addison could tell her mom was bone-tired. She wanted her mother to enjoy tomorrow and not spend all morning cooking, so she offered to help. Her mother gladly accepted. That was another way she knew how tired her mother was; usually she would have refused any help. Neither of them mentioned Isaac or Tyler the rest of the evening.

One good thing about Thanksgiving dinner was Dr. Steelman had offered to bring the turkey and dressing. Somehow Addison couldn't picture him as a cook. The man was just full of surprises, she thought—surgeon, musician, and cook all rolled into one. It was almost 10:30 p.m. before the two headed for the comfort of their beds. At least a great majority of the cooking was done, Addison thought. Now her mom would be able to get a good night's sleep instead of staying up half the night trying to figure out how she was going to get everything done.

* * * * *

Addison was asleep as soon as her head hit the pillow; her mother however, was having trouble falling asleep. It wasn't the next day's preparation of food that was bothering her. It was Isaac Darnell and Tyler Morris. She had no room for forgiveness, no matter what her daughter said. As far as she was concerned, neither one of the young men deserved forgiveness, not God's and certainly not hers. She wondered if forgiving Tyler and Isaac was something Josh would have done. As a Christian, would he have been able to forgive them, especially knowing their irresponsible actions had cost his daughter her leg, her joy, her happiness, her future? But she already knew the answer. Her husband would have forgiven them with open arms.

"Just as God forgives us with open arms," he would always say. She just didn't understand any of this Christianity stuff. Whatever happened to an eye for an eye? After an hour of tossing and turning, she finally drifted off to sleep.

CHAPTER 20

THANKSGIVING DAY

Addison awoke the next morning to the aroma of fresh homemade cranberry sauce, candied yams, and a mixture of other mouth-watering aromas. She glanced at the digital clock. She could hardly believe her eyes. No way had she slept till 8:30 a.m. She yawned, stretched, and reached across the foot of the bed for her robe. Ten minutes later, she was down stairs barging through the kitchen door.

"Mom, why didn't you get me up to help you?"

"There really wasn't that much left to do," her mother said as she lifted the lid from the green beans and gave them a stir. "Do these beans taste too salty to you?" she asked. She scooped one out of the pot and handed it to Addison.

"Taste just right to me," Addison said, smacking her lips together.

"I'm sure glad we decided to do the pumpkin and sweet potato pies last night," her mother said as she plopped down in one of the kitchen chairs.

"I can't wait to dig into them," Addison said as she pulled up a chair and sat next to her mother. "Everything smells delicious," she said, inhaling deeply to take in as much of the smells of Thanksgiving as possible.

Three hours later, Addison and Ayson watched as their mother came down the staircase. She was dressed in casual attire wearing light-brown khaki pants and a dark-brown long-sleeved pullover sweater. She had pulled her dark hair up and placed a gold flowered decorative hair clip slightly to the side.

"Mom, you look real nice," Ayson said. "But you need to lose the hair clip."

"He's right," Addison agreed as they entered the kitchen and returned bringing bowls of food to the dining table.

Kyndal reached up and felt the clip. "But I thought—"

"Don't think, Mom. Just trust us and lose the clip," Ayson said nonchalantly as he eyed the bowl of candied yams he had just placed on the table.

"Don't even think about it," his mother said, giving him a look with a raised eyebrow. He gave her a smile and returned to the kitchen to bring the remaining food to the beautifully set table. Their mother had brought out their best china, something she had not done in a long time.

"You don't think I'm too underdressed, do you?" she asked as she felt for the clip and removed it from her hair.

Addison reached and smoothed out a section of hair where the clip had been. "No, Mom, you're not underdressed. You look really nice. Besides, today is a day of eating comfort foods and being comfortable," she said as Ayson came through and set a bowl of corn on the table.

Kyndal tensed when she heard a knock on the door.

"You look fine, Mom. Loosen up," Ayson said as his mother hurried to answer the door.

Both watched as their mother nervously opened the door. Kyndal and Noah Steelman briefly looked at each other and then at their own clothes. Noah was dressed in light-brown khakis and a dark-brown long-sleeved button-up shirt. They both laughed. The fact the two of them had dressed almost alike made their mother appear a little more relaxed.

"At least I dressed appropriately," he said as he stood holding a bouquet of mixed flowers in his hand. He handed the flowers to Kyndal. "Beautiful flowers for a beautiful lady," he said.

Kyndal blushed slightly and took the flowers. "They're lovely," she said. "Thank you."

He brought her flowers? Just how serious was this relationship? Addison frowned.

Noah turned toward Ayson. "Hey, buddy. Do you think you can give me a hand with the turkey and dressing?"

"Sure," he said following Noah to his car.

Her mother smelled the flowers and then looked at Addison as if she was trying to read her reaction to the flowers. Kyndal appeared a lot younger today, and she was glowing with happiness. Addison saw the sparkle in her mother's eyes for the second time in two days.

"They're lovely, Mom. I'll get a vase." Addison ran water into a clear vase and arranged the flowers before returning to the dining area. She placed the arrangement in the middle of the dining-room table, a gesture that seemed to please both her mother and Noah.

When they had all gathered around the table, Noah asked if any of them minded if he said grace. No one objected. Usually Addison and Ayson blessed their own food silently as their mother wasn't one to say grace. Noah took Kyndal by the hand and reached for Addison's. She took his hand, noticing his strong grip as she reached for Ayson's hand. Until that moment, she had forgotten as a family how they too used to join hands while her father gave thanks. She listened as Noah asked the Heavenly Father not only to bless the food but to bless those who had prepared it. She felt her eyes begin to water as she remembered her dad praying a similar prayer at mealtime.

"Amen," she heard Noah say as she quickly let go of his hand and brushed away a tear. "Well, who's ready for some turkey?" he asked, smiling, as he stood to carve the golden-brown bird.

"That used to be Daddy's job," Ayson said softly and with unmistakable sadness as he managed to give Noah a weak smile. Caught off guard by the comment, mother and daughter just looked at each other speechless, and then looked at Noah, not certain what his reaction would be.

Noah looked at Ayson, understanding how he must have felt. "And I bet your dad was awesome at it. I'm sure he did a much better job than I will, but if it's okay with you, may I give it a try?" He gave Ayson a warm smile as if to say, *It's okay, buddy, I understand.*

This time, Ayson gave Noah a huge smile. "Sure!"

"Okay then, who's ready for some turkey?" he repeated again as he rubbed the stainless steel of the huge fork and knife together, making an almost irritating screeching sound.

"Me!" said Ayson as he held out his plate. Noah carved a slice of the juicy turkey and placed it on Ayson's plate.

"Who's next?" he asked as he carved another slice of turkey then placed it on Addison's plate. Before long, they were all enjoying a delicious home-cooked meal with all the trimmings.

Overall, the discussions at the dinner table went well. Ayson mostly talked about music, and her mother and Noah discussed the different countries they would like to visit. Thanks to Ayson, their dad's name had come up a few more times, but Noah was a trooper and taken it all in stride. Addison was sure he had thought about Taylor and Angie and the few Thanksgivings they were blessed to have spent together.

After dinner, Noah offered to help their mother with the dishes. She objected, but he had insisted. Addison and Ayson cleared the table and brought in the dishes to be loaded into the dishwasher. Their mother put the food up, and Noah loaded the dishwasher. The whole routine reminded Addison of an assembly line, but the task was complete in no time.

Everyone decided to wait on coffee and dessert as they gathered in the living room to watch some of the parades on television. In addition, Noah kept them entertained by telling some of his boyhood adventures. Addison was actually surprised to find the doc had quite a sense of humor. She had never seen him outside the doctor role. He really is quite human, she thought as she laughed at one of his tales. He proceeded to tell them how, as a teenager, his biggest goal in life was to be a rock musician. His parents were relieved when he finally changed his mind and decided to become a surgeon. His expression turned serious.

"If I had not turned my life over to the Lord when I did, there is no telling where I would be today. It wasn't until I started seeking His direction for my life that I decided to go the way I did."

Addison noticed her mother shift uneasily in her seat. No matter where they were, anytime anything remotely religious came up, her mother would become uncomfortable.

"By the way, Kyndal, you and your family attend New Haven, right?"

Kyndal shifted uncomfortably again. "The children attend," she said, looking over at the commercial on the TV.

"Oh, I thought all of you attended," Noah said, looking a little puzzled. "Do you attend somewhere else?"

Now their mother was really becoming antsy. "No," she said, her eyes never leaving the TV.

Noah Steelman didn't miss a beat. "Well then, what do you say we all go together this Sunday? I met Maggie Peters at the grocery store the other day, and she asked me to visit New Haven."

Addison was bursting inside with joy. Let's see you get out of this, Mom, she thought.

"Yeah, Mom, that would be nice," piped up Ayson. "You haven't been to church in years."

Addison saw her mother flinch and turn red, then noticed Noah trying to stifle a grin.

Not sure of what else her son would say, Kyndal quickly agreed to go. "I would love for all of us to go together," she said to Noah, who at the moment was still attempting to stifle a grin.

"You'll like it," Ayson told him excitedly, "It's a real neat church. My friend Callaway plays the drums at church, and I'm going to be playing the guitar. My best friend Caleb is learning to play the bass guitar. Maybe you could teach him a few things, Doc," he said, looking hopefully at Noah.

"I'd love to," Noah said as he let out a groan upon hearing his cell phone alert him to a message. "It's the hospital," he said after checking his message. "Maybe I can handle this with just a phone call. Do you mind if I use your landline phone instead of my cell?" he asked, standing. Kyndal led him to the phone in the hall and then returned to her seat. "I see," they heard him say to the person on the other end of the receiver. "I'll be there in about fifteen minutes." Addison saw the disappointment in her mother's face.

"I'm sorry," Noah said, returning to the living room. "Duty calls."

"You didn't even get to eat dessert," her mother said in protest. "How about I fix you a plate to go?"

"That would be nice," he said as he reached for his jacket and headed for the door.

"Could you please help me, Addison?" asked her mother as she made her way to the kitchen. A minute later, they returned and handed Noah a paper plate filled with various pies wrapped in aluminum foil.

"What about your dishes and your turkey and dressing?" her mother asked as a last-minute thought.

"I'll get them later," he said as he thanked her and reached to gently squeeze her hand.

* * * * *

Kyndal stood in the doorway and waved as Noah blew the horn and pulled out of the driveway. She smiled as she thought of the wonderful day she had just had with Noah and the children, but it had ended too soon. She wished every day could be like today. It wasn't until she watched him drive off that she realized just how lonely she had been. She had her children and a few friends, but it just wasn't the same.

She simultaneously felt feelings of happiness and guilt. When she had first started talking to Noah in the hospital, it was all related to Addison and her recovery. Later, they had casually started talking to each other about other things, including the death of her husband and the death of his wife and daughter. She finally got the impression—call it woman's intuition, if you will—that he actually enjoyed her company. Before long, he had started asking her to join him for lunch at the hospital cafeteria, and she had asked him to Thanksgiving dinner. She knew in her heart Josh would not want her to spend the rest of her life alone. However, she felt having feelings for someone else was the same as betraying him. She knew that was crazy, but this was how she felt. She wondered if he was feeling the same way about Taylor.

Later she continued to think about Noah as she dressed for bed. She felt so mixed up inside. The fact he was a Christian was not helping.

"Are you going to let me fall in love with someone else just to snatch them away from me too?" she asked God as she pulled her yellow floral gown over her head. Her feet felt cold, so she left her socks on and hurriedly climbed into bed, pulling the blankets around her shoulders.

Now, to make matters worse, she had promised to go to church with him and the children. But a promise was a promise; at least that was what she had told Addison when she had tried to back out of going to the youth meeting after promising Michael Scobie she would go. No way could she back out now.

"Why do all the good ones have to be a Christian?" she asked aloud as she turned on her left side and fluffed her pillow. She shivered at the thought of walking through church doors. She had not been inside a church since Josh's funeral. The only reason she had gone then was out of respect for his beliefs. She closed her heavy eyelids and was glad that, for once, sleep came easy.

* * * * *

Thanksgiving dinner had gone better than expected. Addison finished brushing her teeth and made her way to the bed to remove her artificial leg. She couldn't wait until Sunday. Her mom had actually promised to go to church. She prayed a quick prayer.

"Lord, please don't let her change her mind and come up with some excuse not to come." She shivered at the thought of her mother going through church doors. It had been years since her mother had been to church. Addison laid her artificial leg on the floor next to the bed and then pulled the comforter over her shoulders. Turning onto her left side, she fluffed her pillow and closed her eyes. Soon she was fast asleep.

* * * * *

Noah Steelman pulled off his blue surgery mask and threw it in the trashcan. It had been a long day. It was getting late when he settled down on the couch in the doctor's lounge. His stomach let out a long, loud growl reminding him that he had not eaten since dinner with Kyndal and her family. He went to his locker and pulled out enough one-dollar bills from his wallet to get a deviled egg sandwich from the vending machine. He washed it down with a stale cup of hot black coffee from the break room that tasted at least a day old. He suddenly remembered the plate of desserts. He walked weirdly to the refrigerator where he took out the paper plate, then unwrapped the sweet potato and pumpkin pie.

"Mmm," he said as he bit into the potato pie. It was one of the best he had ever eaten. He had really enjoyed spending the day with Kyndal and her children; however, he was a little surprised to find Kyndal did not attend church. He knew when he first met her she had been mad at God over Addison, but he thought the anger would have passed by now. He remembered how angry he had been with God over the loss of Taylor and Angie, but he had eventually gotten over that anger. As a matter of fact, if it hadn't been for his faith in God, he would have probably gone crazy. At least Kyndal had agreed to go to church with him and the children Sunday. He had really grown fond of her, but their relationship was something he was definitely going to have to pray about, not that he hadn't been praying already. He swallowed the last bite of potato pie when he heard the page overhead.

"Dr. Noah Steelman, please call extension 1633, Dr. Steelman, extension 1633." He all but dragged himself to the phone located on the wall next to the vending machine and dialed the extension.

"Please let this be something I can handle over the phone," he mumbled. It was.

After he hung up, he settled again on the couch, leaned his head back, and closed his eyes. Better grab some shut-eye while I can, he thought, but he had a feeling his day wasn't over. He was right. He had barely closed his eyes before he received another page. This time, it could not be handled over the phone.

CHAPTER 21

ANOTHER SURPRISE VISITOR

Caleb and Callaway came over the next day to practice music with Ayson for Sunday. Noah stopped by just long enough to pick up his dishes and give Caleb a few pointers on the bass guitar. Kyndal could tell Noah had had a long night from the way he constantly rubbed his red puffy eyes and from his sluggish gait. Before leaving, he complimented Kyndal on her "delicious," pies and Addison could see her mother was pleased.

Addison sat on the sofa and decided to call her best friend to make some plans for Saturday. To her surprise, Alayna said she would not be able to come over, giving no explanation. Addison decided not to pursue the issue.

"I hear your mom is coming to church Sunday." There was a slight pause before she added, "Your mom told my mom, who told me." She chuckled.

"We'll see if she goes through with it," said Addison.

"Okay, well, see you Sunday. Gotta hang up now," she said, hanging up rather abruptly.

Addison sat staring dumbfounded at the phone, wondering what was going on with her BFF.

* * * * *

Saturday came, and Addison had not heard from her best friend. Since she had nothing else to do, she decided to finish her Christie mystery. Two hours later, she finished reading and once again had failed to guess the murderer. Now what was she going to do? Ayson was busy upstairs as usual, and her mother had been cleaning, dusting, and serenading them all day with the golden oldies as she worked.

Isaac had texted wanting to know if she had heard anything else about Tyler. *No*, she texted back. *Will probably hear something tomorrow at church.* She was glad Isaac had texted instead of coming over or calling on the home phone. Her mother had still not budged on him coming over. "Absolutely not," she had said when Addison tried to bring it up again.

The phone rang, and she heard her mother telling someone that four o'clock would be fine. Noah must be coming over again, Addison thought as she picked up the remote and began channel surfing. For a Saturday, there sure wasn't anything on TV worth watching, she thought. She finally stopped on the cooking channel.

"Addison, you're going to have a surprise visitor," her mother said, sticking her head around the living-room doorway.

"Who is it?" she asked, turning down the volume on the TV.

"What part of *surprise* do you not understand?" her mother asked as she rolled her eyes.

Her mother went back to singing an oldies song Addison had never heard. Alayna must have changed her mind, she thought, but why not just say she was coming? After a while, she concluded it wasn't Alayna. She wouldn't be so secretive. She glanced at her faded blue jeans, which were purposely designed that way, and her garnet and black Carolina Gamecock shirt. She hoped she was appropriately dressed for her surprise visitor.

She returned to watching the cooking channel where the host of the program was preparing a home-made banana pudding and promising it would be the best you would ever sink your teeth into. Her mother finished cleaning and dusting and headed upstairs to take a shower.

"I think when I get done with my shower, I am going to make us a coca-cola cake."

Addison could already feel her mouth start to water. She glanced at the clock and noticed it was already half past three. She was getting more curious by the minute as to who her surprise visitor might be. At exactly four o'clock she heard a knock on the door. Her mother was in the kitchen and yelled for her to get the door. Moving as quickly as she could, she made her way to the door. Opening the door, she was pleasantly surprised at who was standing on the other side.

"Wyatt!" she exclaimed. "What are you doing here?"

"I hope it is okay that I came," he said, not sure if she was glad to see him or not from her question, and especially after the way he had acted the last time he had seen her.

"Of course, it is," she said, moving to the side and motioning him in. He stepped in and waited for her to close the door. "Have a seat on the sofa," she added, motioning toward it.

Wyatt sat on one end of the sofa, and she sat on the other end. At least two other people could have sat between them.

"Looks like we're not just on opposite sides of the sofa," he said, pointing to his shirt.

She had been so surprised to see him she had not even noticed what he was wearing. He had on dark-colored blue jeans and an orange Clemson Tiger shirt. Both the Gamecocks and Tigers were South Carolina teams, but big rivals.

"I always knew there was something not quite right about you. Now I know what it is," she joked.

"No, you didn't just say that!" Wyatt said as he pretended his feelings were hurt before they both burst into laughter. They were still laughing when her mother came through the kitchen door.

"Hello, Wyatt," she said, smiling.

Turning to look at Kyndal, he returned her greeting and couldn't help but notice how much younger she looked than when he had last seen her.

"Do you like coca-cola cake?" she asked, coming around to stand in front of him.

"Love it!"

"In that case, you'll just have to stay and have some. I'm getting ready to make one." She turned and smiled at her daughter, who was all smiles as well.

Kyndal looked at Wyatt and frowned. "Ummm, I need to find one of Josh's old shirts."

Addison looked at Wyatt and shrugged. "What can I say? You're in Gamecock territory."

Kyndal smiled as she returned to the kitchen and started to hum again. It was then it occurred to Wyatt why Kyndal McNeely appeared younger. She had seemed a lot happier at work too, always smiling and humming. He had heard the rumors going around the hospital regarding Dr. Steelman and Kyndal. That had to be the reason for her youthful appearance and sunny disposition.

"I hear your mom has been going out with Dr. Steelman lately," he said.

"Well, I don't know if I would call it going out," Addison said, her expression turning serious. "Is that what people are calling it?"

Wyatt could have kicked himself in the rear end. "I...I..."

Someone rapped on the door.

"Whew! That was close," Wyatt mumbled while breathing a sigh of relief.

Ayson came running down the stairs and opened the door. It was Callaway. He and his mother had stopped by to pick Ayson up. Afterward, they were going to swing by, pick up Caleb, and then head to the church to practice their music. Addison was glad they were practicing somewhere else for a while. The music, as good as it was, could get on one's nerves after a while, especially when you heard the same thing over, and over, and over.

"Bye, Mom. Bye, Addison." Then noticing Wyatt for the first time, he yelled, "Bye, Wyatt." As usual, Ayson slammed the door shut just as his mother yelled from the kitchen doorway.

"Love you. Don't slam the do—"

Addison turned back to Wyatt.

"I just wanted to stop by and see you," he said before she could bring up their previous subject. "I know you are starting back to school Monday."

Why in the world did he have to bring that up? She had been try-ing not to think about it for days.

"Yeah," she said, her mouth raised in a half smile. She didn't want him to know she was bothered by the thought of going back to school as much as she was. Wyatt realized Addison was trying to sound and appear braver than she really felt. She didn't fool him. He had gotten to know her better than she thought he had. Reaching into his left pant pocket, he moved closer to her and pulled out a folded sheet of paper.

"I've got something for you," he said, handing her the paper. "I hope it helps."

Addison took the paper and began unfolding it. It was a list of scriptures. She scanned the scriptures quickly and then looked at Wyatt. "You did this for me?" she asked, a little surprised. She also felt deeply touched he had taken the time.

"Sure, why not?" He shrugged, as if it was no big deal. But it was a big deal to her.

"Do you do this for all your patients?"

He smiled. "Just for the ones who need it," he said. Actually, he had never done this before. He had prayed for patients, even quoted scriptures to them as he felt led of the Lord, but he had never taken the time to write scriptures down and personally deliver them. Come to think of it, this was the first time he had ever felt led to do such a thing.

"Thanks, Wyatt. I really appreciate this," Addison said as she refolded the paper and placed it in her jeans pocket. "I'll be sure to read every one of them tonight before I go to bed." Then she asked, changing the subject, "Did you hear about Isaac Darnell?"

"Yes, I did. He posted on Reddit. He said you and "Laney""— Wyatt made bunny-ear air quotes—"led him to the Lord."

"I haven't been on social media lately," she said, looking away. "Too many people asking questions about my accident and surgery." She forced a smile.

Wyatt slid closer to her and gently turned her face toward him. He looked into her pained face. "People don't mean anything by it, Addison," he said, his hand still resting softly on her cheek. "They really don't. There are a lot more people out there who care about you than you think."

"That's very kind of you to say."

"I mean it, Addison, or I wouldn't say it."

"Who's ready for some cake?" Kyndal asked, coming through the kitchen door. "It will be ready in about ten minutes."

The sound of her mother's voice caused both of them to jump. Wyatt quickly removed his hand from her face.

"Sure, Mom, we're ready. Be there in ten," Addison said, turning toward her mom, who was still standing in the doorway.

Wyatt cleared his throat. "Like I was saying, Addison, that was really good news about Isaac, wasn't it?"

Addison, without a word, closed her eyes and sighed. Way to go, Wyatt! she thought. Her mother, at hearing Isaac's name, turned and went back into the kitchen.

* * * * *

Kyndal sat at the kitchen table with Chip at her feet waiting for the cake to finish baking. She had been cleaning all morning but really didn't feel as tired as she thought she would. She had a new burst of energy, and she knew it was because of her feelings for Noah Steelman. Earlier in the day when she had been dusting furniture and pictures, she dusted the large family portrait. She had felt the sadness engulf her as she looked at the loving and smiling face of her husband.

The day before, she had met Maggie and Shannon for lunch. It had been a long time since she had spent quality time with her friends, and she had finally confessed to them her true feelings toward Noah.

"I'm not sure if he feels the same way," she had told them. "I know he likes me, but I'm not really sure how much he likes me."

"From what I understand from one of your coworkers who comes into the restaurant, you're the first woman he has shown any interest in since his wife and child passed away," Shannon informed her as she bit into her burger.

"I really like Noah a lot," Kyndal said. "But I still love Josh. I don't know if I will ever get over him."

"You're not supposed to," Maggie told her, taking her by the hand.

"I also don't think Noah would expect you to," Shannon said, taking a big swallow of her chocolate milkshake. "I'm sure he will never get over Taylor."

Maggie raised an eyebrow and looked at Shannon. Shannon, however, was busy dipping a curly fry into a blob of ketchup and was oblivious to Maggie's raised eyebrow or anyone else for that matter. At that moment, Kyndal remembered why she had always been so fond of Shannon. It was her honest, direct way of saying things. A person never had to wonder where she stood on things. Kyndal had not had much of an appetite. She sat and moved her food from one place in her plate to another. Maggie tried to be a little more tactful than Shannon when she spoke about relationships

"A heart can love more than one person, Kyndal. You'll never be able to replace the love and memories you have of Josh, and he will never be able to replace the love and memories he has of Taylor—and that's okay because you're not supposed to. You two can still love each other with all your hearts and make wonderful memories of your own, and there's nothing wrong with that."

Her friend's wisdom had brought comfort to her that day, and from time to time, she recalled those words, like now.

She was suddenly jolted from her thoughts as she heard the beeping of the oven timer.

"I love the smell of fresh baked deserts," she said aloud as she took a deep breath and removed the cake from the oven. "Come and get it!" she yelled a few minutes later.

Addison and Wyatt came through the door, laughing.

"Mmm, smells good," Wyatt said as he sat in one of the kitchen chairs. Kyndal cut the cake while Addison gathered the silverware.

* * * * *

For another hour, they enjoyed one another's company before Wyatt announced he needed to be heading home. Addison felt so confused. The other day during therapy, Wyatt had seemed so distant; and now out of the blue, he showed up at her home acting, as if nothing was wrong. *And they say women are fickle.* She walked Wyatt to the door. After he left, she helped her mother clear the table.

"You're still going to church tomorrow, aren't you?" Addison asked as she placed the dishes in the dishwasher.

"I promised, didn't I?" Kyndal answered, rather irritated at the question. Addison said nothing further. They heard the front door slam.

"I'm home!" yelled Ayson as he started running up the steps. They heard a pause and then heard him start back down the steps. "Hey! Is that cake I smell?" he asked as he burst through the kitchen door.

Addison made her way upstairs and, feeling full, decided to put on a pair of sweatpants. At least they had an elastic waistband and would give her a bit more breathing room. Not being as active as she normally had been, she was positive from the fit of her jeans that she had put on a few extra pounds.

Upon taking off her blue jeans, she heard the rattle of paper in her pocket. She sat on the edge of the bed and pulled out the scriptures Wyatt had given her. She reached and took her Bible from the nightstand next to her bed. She smoothed out the wrinkled paper and read the first scripture reference.

"Philippians 4:13: 'I can do all things through Christ who strengthens me,'" she read aloud. She continued to go down through each scripture reference and read them aloud. "Proverbs 3:5: 'Trust in the Lord with all your heart, and lean not on your own understanding. In all your ways acknowledge Him, and He will direct your paths.' Second Corinthians 12:9: 'My grace is sufficient for you, for My strength is made perfect in weakness.'" She read the last scripture, not exactly her favorite: "Matthew 5:44, 'But I say to you, love your enemies, bless those who curse you, do good to those who hate you, and pray for those who spitefully use you and persecute you.'" She would definitely need to have those scriptures with her when she returned to school on Monday. She folded the paper and laid it next to her Bible on the nightstand.

She made her way to the bay window across from her bed, and pulling back the curtains, she looked out at the growing shadows. Nighttime was fast approaching, and so was Monday.

Later, Addison made her way downstairs and sat in the over-sized chair. She pulled out her cell phone and tried to call Alayna. It went to her voice mail. Addison sighed. She hung up the phone and turned on the TV. A short time later, she heard her mother on the phone ordering a large pepperoni pizza.

The local weather channel was calling for more severe weather Sunday afternoon. It has been an unusually rainy season, she thought as she turned it to the Lifetime movie channel and settled into the chair, pulling a Gamecock throw over her.

"Mind if I join you?" her mother asked, entering the room.

"Not at all," she said. "I'll join you on the sofa, and we can share the throw. I think this movie is going to be a chick flick," Addison said.

Her mother reached and grabbed the box of tissues from the end table and sat the box between them. Fifteen minutes into the movie, they were plucking tissues from the box and wondering why they hadn't opted for a comedy instead. Chip lay in between them to one side of the box of tissues, looking at them each time they pulled a tissue.

"Ohhh, isn't that so sweet, Chip?" said Kyndal, pulling a tissue from the box—tears and sniffles.

"Ohhhh, isn't that just so sad, Chip?" said Addison, pulling a tissue from the box—more tears and more sniffles. Chip wasn't sure what was going on with all the tears, tissues, and sniffles, but he had had enough. He jumped down and made his way to his doggie bed next to the fireplace. Giving a yawn, he closed his eyes and proceeded to cover his ears with his paws. Watching his reaction to their crying, the two women burst into harmonious laughter.

Someone knocked on the door. Kyndal, leaving with tissue in hand, went to answer. "Movie night," she told the young bewildered man as she wiped her eyes with the tissue, then reached for her purse sitting on the table next to the entrance. "Keep the change," Kyndal said as she closed the door behind the young man. "Pizza, anyone?" she yelled as she made her way to the kitchen. Swift running feet were heard coming down the stairs.

"Oh boy," Ayson exclaimed, following close on his mother's heels. "Pizza!"

Chip jumped up as well. Even he understood pizza.

* * * * *

Wyatt finally resigned himself to the fact that he was falling in love with Addison McNeely. But how did she feel about him? Should he tell her how he felt about her or just wait and see how things played out? He opted for number two—at least for the moment.

CHAPTER 22

THEN CAME SUNDAY

Sunday came, and true to her word, Kyndal attended the morning church service. Noah arrived in his silver extended-cab pickup and drove them to New Haven, where Shannon and her family were waiting for their arrival. The small group made their way to the third pew to the left where Patrick and Shannon Thomas sat on one side of Noah and Kyndal on the other. Addison sat next to her mother, followed by Alayna. Just as the music was beginning, Trevor Grant slid into the pew next to Alayna, along with Isaac.

Addison saw her mother's expression change when Isaac slid in the pew. She glared sharply at him, and for a moment, she thought her mother was going to say something. But then Jerry Ryder, the music director, asked everyone to stand and join in the congregational singing.

"Whew." Addison breathed softly as the music began.

Ayson smiled at them from the platform as he strummed his shiny red electric guitar. She saw her mother look at Ayson and noticed her expression soften as she smiled and looked proudly at her son. The congregation sung several praise songs before being seated. Pastor Bryce welcomed everyone, especially the visitors, before returning the service to Jerry for the choir special. After an uplifting song from the choir, Pastor Bryce returned to the pulpit, announcing he would be teaching on the poison of unforgiveness.

"Even when someone has wronged us," he began, "and does not deserve our forgiveness, we are to forgive them, just as our Heavenly Father forgave us when we didn't deserve His forgiveness."

Addison felt her mother squirm uncomfortably beside her.

Pastor Bryce continued, "Which of us has never wronged or hurt someone at one time or another? Can we cast the first stone? Matthew 6 sums it up like this. If we forgive those who have committed an offense against us, then our Heavenly Father will forgive us when we do the same against another. However, if we do not forgive others and hold unforgiveness in our hearts for a wrong committed against us, then our Heavenly Father will not forgive us."

"Amen," echoed several members of the congregation.

"Also, we are told in Ephesians chapter 4," Pastor Bryce was saying as he turned to the scripture in his Bible, "to be kind to one another, tenderhearted, forgiving one another, even as God in Christ forgave us."

Addison listened as Pastor Bryce red one scripture after another. "I had no idea there were so many scriptures on forgiveness," she leaned and whispered to Alayna.

* * * * *

As Kyndal sat listening to Pastor Bryce, she began to wonder if he had preached on the subject of unforgiveness because he knew she would be at today's service. Surely someone had to have mentioned she was coming. She leaned back slightly and looked around Addison at Isaac. He was wiping a steady flow of tears from his eyes. She could hardly believe what she was hearing as she turned her attention back to Pastor Bryce.

"Some of you may be wondering at this very moment how a person can forgive another who has wronged them, how they could even stand to be around that person who has caused them so much pain. I will tell you how. It is Christ in that person that gives them the strength to love and to forgive. With God, all things are possible, even the ability to forgive those who have wronged us."

What if the One who is supposed to be giving you the strength to forgive, Kyndal thought, is the one you cannot forgive?

As if knowing her thought, Pastor Bryce spoke up, "Some of you may even need to forgive God for a wrong you *think* He has committed toward you."

Kyndal noticed he emphasized the word think. She pulled at her dress as she continued to squirm uncomfortably in the pew. *Great, now he's a mind reader too!* She felt this was one of the longest sermons she had ever sat through, not that she had sat through many. She glanced at her watch: it had only been thirty minutes, but it felt much longer.

"Some of you are experiencing pain, loss, and suffering," Pastor Bryce continued. "In biblical times, it was customary for people experiencing these things to cover themselves in ashes to express those situations. Don't let those things harden your heart. I am here today to tell you that Jesus will give you beauty for ashes and joyous blessings."

A few more minutes passed before Pastor Bryce called the music director and the musicians to the platform. Kyndal watched as Ayson, Maggie, and Callaway took their places at their instruments and began softly playing. Pastor Bryce invited those who harbored the poison of unforgiveness to come forward for prayer.

"Jesus is the answer. Don't be ashamed to come forward," Pastor Bryce urged.

Kyndal was surprised at the number of people gathering at the altar. She saw Bryan and Rebekah Morris, arm in arm, making their way to the altar. Bryan was crying so bitterly she could see his entire body shaking. His wife was standing next to him, crying, as Pastor Bryce anointed them with oil and prayed over them. Kyndal was literally shocked at what happened next.

Isaac Darnell slid out of his seat and walked to the altar. He was crying about as hard as Bryan Morris. Just as Pastor Bryce finished praying for Bryan, Isaac walked up behind him and placed his hand on Bryan's shoulder. Bryan turned and looked into the face of Isaac.

Isaac, barely able to speak from crying so hard, finally blurted out the words he was trying to say. "I'm so sorry. Please forgive me!"

For a second, Bryan just stared at him with tears streaming down his face. All of a sudden, Bryan pulled Isaac toward him, and the two men hugged as they wept uncontrollably.

"We forgive you," Bryan said, still embracing Isaac. Rebekah wrapped her arms around her husband and Isaac.

What the heck just happened? Kyndal could not believe the Morrises could forgive Isaac! She certainly wasn't going to forgive him, ever! Neither was she going to forgive their son. She saw Addison pull a tissue from her purse and wipe a tear. She looked around. There were people all over the congregation crying. There didn't appear to be one dry eye in the whole church, except for hers. She had no tears left to cry, no compassion, nothing. She only felt numbness.

After everyone at the altar returned to their pews, Pastor Bryce asked the congregation to stand and repeat the Lord's Prayer.

"Our Father, who art in heaven, Hallowed..."

Kyndal had learned the Lord's Prayer when she was a young girl in church. She had never forgotten it, but today she would not recite it. She didn't care if the Lord forgave her sins or not. She was not ready to forgive Him or those who had hurt her and her family. She would never promise to come to church with anyone again. She was glad when Pastor Bryce finally dismissed them. On the way out, Pastor Bryce took her by the hand and gave her a warm and friendly smile.

"I'm so glad to see you, Kyndal. I had no idea you were coming today. What a wonderful surprise!"

"You mean no one told you I was coming?" she asked, genuinely surprised.

"No, but I'm glad you did. Please come again anytime."

Kyndal, Shannon, and their families made their way to the parking lot and discussed where to eat lunch. Usually they would go to S&Ps Homecookin' Restaurant after church for the lunch buffet, but Shannon and Patrick had decided a few weeks ago to close the restaurant on Sundays. Although Sunday was usually their busiest day, they had prayed and felt the Lord had led them to close the restaurant on the Lord's Day. It had been a difficult decision, but they felt it was the right decision. Now all their employees had the opportunity to go to church with their families.

"What about Clark's Country Diner? At least they have a variety of foods to choose from," asked Patrick.

"Is Clark's okay with everyone?" asked Shannon.

Everyone nodded in agreement and made their way to their vehicles. Patrick led the way to the restaurant.

"I thought Pastor Bryce preached an awesome message today," Noah said as he pulled onto the main road behind Patrick. "It's one we could all use from time to time."

Addison and Ayson spoke up in agreement.

Kyndal made no comment. "It's been a while since I've eaten at Clark's," she said out of the blue. Addison knew her mother was trying to change the subject. "It was pretty good from what I remember," her mother continued.

"What do you suggest?" asked Noah, changing the subject.

"I would suggest either the fried chicken or the meat loaf," her mother answered, looking relieved.

"How did I do today, Mom?" Ayson asked, leaning slightly forward from the back seat.

"You did great," she said, turning to look at him.

"You sure did, buddy," said Noah, looking back at him in the rear-view mirror.

Addison was about to agree, but instead she screamed, "Dr. Steelman, watch out!"

As their vehicle approached, the traffic light the light turned green. However, a driver coming from the right of them decided to try and beat the light. Noah blew his horn as he swerved and tried to keep the black Tahoe from colliding with them. The screeching tires and the blowing of horns caused chills to run up Addison's spine. Images flashed through her mind, reminding her of the night of her accident. The three passengers braced themselves for the collision. Fortunately, Noah was able to swerve and slam on the brakes, allowing the SUV to narrowly miss them. As the black Tahoe raced past them, the tinted window on the driver's side rolled down, and a bearded man wearing dark glasses turned toward Noah and made an unkind gesture with his finger. Addison was trembling uncontrollably.

"Is everyone all right?" Noah asked, his voice a bit shaky.

Kyndal looked around. "We're all right, just a little shaken."

Noah looked in both directions before proceeding on through the light.

Shannon and her family were waiting outside the diner when they pulled into the parking lot.

Alayna noticed the color drained from Addison's face and the faraway look in her eyes. "What's wrong with you?" she asked. Ayson quickly rushed to tell them about what had happened.

"You should have seen Dr. Steelman," he said excitedly. "He could be a race-car driver."

"Hardly," Noah said, smiling down at Ayson.

Ayson grinned. He really liked Dr. Steelman. Shannon and Alayna gathered around Kyndal and Addison. After a few minutes, Patrick convinced his wife that everyone was okay and that they had better go in if they didn't want to wait to be seated. He held the door as everyone made their way into the restaurant. Then out of the blue, Ayson exclaimed, "I think he was the Mafia!"

What?" Shannon and Kyndal asked in unison, turning to stare at Ayson.

"Well, the man was wearing dark glasses, and aren't black Tahoes with tinted windows the type of vehicles the Mafia drives?" he answered with wide but serious eyes.

This caused everyone to burst into laughter—except for Noah.

"No, that would be more like what the FBI would drive. The Mafia would be more inclined to drive a Mercedes Benz G class, or a Cadillac Escalade, possibly a BMW X5."

Almost as quickly as the laughter erupted, it stopped, everyone now turning their attention to Noah, who was looking down into the satisfied face of his little buddy.

Alayna finally asked the question the rest of them were wondering. "Should we be worried?"

"Maybe," Noah answered with a smile and a wave of his hands for the ladies to go ahead of him and the other men. Addison caught him give a quick wink to her overimaginative brother as she made her way past them to the hostess patiently waiting to seat them.

*****

After a delicious variety of fried chicken, meat loaf, corn, mashed potatoes, broccoli casserole, and green beans, they made their way back to their vehicles to head home. Addison felt herself tense somewhat as she stepped into the truck, but she was determined not to let her accident paralyze her for the rest of her life. Until today, she had done pretty well. For some reason, it had not occurred to her until their near miss that she could be involved in another wreck in her lifetime.

Noah stayed about an hour after dropping them off and then left.

Addison went upstairs to read her Bible. She read scriptures on fear, especially Second Timothy 1:7. She read it aloud, remembering Michael Scobie's words that faith comes by hearing and hearing by the Word of God.

"For God has not given us a spirit of fear, but of power, love and of a sound mind." Addison continued to recite the verse over and over as she laid her head on her pillow. Tomorrow she would have to face her classmates and Karlie Adams.

"Give me strength, Lord," she prayed as she closed her eyes and drifted peacefully off to sleep.

*****

That night, Noah lay in bed with his hands folded under his head, staring at the ceiling. He had really enjoyed the service at New Haven. However, he was beginning to doubt more and more his relationship with Kyndal. He had really felt the moving of the Spirit during the invitation, especially when the Morrises forgave Isaac. Noah knew it had taken a lot of courage for Isaac to ask for forgiveness. He had noticed, however, that Kyndal seemed unmoved at all by the service. He had seen her at the hospital be warm and compassionate with patients, but this morning at church, she appeared cold and almost stoic.

He felt so mixed up in his feelings. A part of him felt he was starting to fall in love with her, but at the same time, he could not see himself with such a bitter person. He knew she had been hurt by the death of her husband, and naturally so, but when would she ever move on? Could she ever move on? Maybe she could never love him. Maybe she would only have room in her heart for Josh, leaving no room for him. He knew in his heart he would always love Taylor as well, but he also knew his heart was big enough to love again. He removed his hands from under his head and rolled over onto his side. He reached and turned off the light. He knew what he had to do.

* * * * *

As Bryan and Rebekah Morris prepared for bed that night, they gave thanks once more to the Lord for giving them the strength to forgive.

After church they had returned home, grabbed a sandwich, and then headed to Faith Hospital. They had stopped and picked up Isaac on the way and arrived at the hospital to find Tyler sitting in a chair. He had tried to speak as his parents entered the room, but was only able to make a few sounds. They reached and hugged him.

"We have a surprise for you," Rebekah told him.

Bryan walked to the door as Tyler looked on with a curious look on his face. His dad opened the door, and Isaac stepped in holding a helium-filled "Get Well" balloon with Tyler's favorite chocolate candy bar attached to the end of the string. His parents watched as Tyler's face lit up. He tried to get words to come out of his mouth, but only nonintelligent sounds came forth.

Isaac noticed the frustration on Tyler's face. "It's okay, Tyler. I know you're glad to see me. I'm glad to see you too."

"We'll be back shortly," Bryan told Tyler. "We're going to see if we can speak with Dr. Linski."

Tyler nodded his head and turned back to Isaac.

"I brought you your favorite candy bar," Isaac said.

Tyler shook his head and pointed to the feeding tube in his stomach, indicating he could not eat the candy.

"You will soon," said Isaac as he pulled up a chair and took a seat next to his friend. At the moment, Tyler was being fed through a tube in his stomach as the bullet had nicked the part of the brain that affected speech and swallowing. Isaac turned serious.

"I came to see you once when you were still in a coma."

Tyler shook his head acknowledging he knew of his visit. Isaac assumed Tyler's parents had told him about the visit.

"I guess your parents told you about everything that day."

Tyler shook his head no and pointed to his ears.

"You heard us?"

Tyler nodded. Isaac had heard people in comas could hear what was going on around them, but he had forgotten that until now. "So you heard your parents send me away?"

Tyler nodded and then gestured with his hand pointing toward Isaac and then toward the door his parents had just left through. He shrugged and had a puzzled expression on his face. Isaac knew he was wondering how he happened to be here with his parents. He could barely hold back the tears.

"They forgave me, Tyler, and I'm asking you to forgive me too." He could hold back the tears no longer. Tyler's arms were weak, and he was a little awkward in doing so, but he managed to get one of his arms around Isaac. He tried to speak.

"Ah-ah-ah." He sighed then finally forced out the word, "I..."

Isaac pushed Tyler back from him. "You said the word *I*, Tyler! You said *I*!" Isaac jumped up and threw his arms and hands up in the air. It might have been about the simplest word a person could utter, but it was a start. He was still yelling when Tyler's parents and Dr. Linski entered the room. Isaac turned to face them when he heard them enter.

"He said the word *I*. He said *I*!"

Rebekah Morris burst into tears, but it was tears of joy. Arthur Linski looked first at Isaac and then at Tyler. Tyler, at the moment was attempting the biggest lopsided grin Dr. Linski believed he had ever seen.

"That's great news," he told Tyler. He sat in the chair Isaac had been sitting in earlier. "I believe you're going to be just fine, Tyler. It may take a while, but with a lot of hard work and a lot of patience, you're going to make it just fine." He informed Tyler and his parents that he would need to continue physical therapy and speech therapy. "He still has a long road to travel," he informed, them looking at Bryan and Rebekah. "And he will need all the support you can give him."

Tyler's muscles were weak and needed strengthening, but everyone could tell his determination was strong. Today's visit had been the most encouraging visit Bryan and Rebekah had experienced. They had dropped Isaac off at his home later that afternoon and then returned to church that night. It had been a blessed day, and they were grateful they served a good and merciful God.

* * * * *

Kyndal pulled her granny nightgown, as the children called it, over her head and walked to the bathroom to brush her teeth. She looked in the bathroom mirror as she swished the water around in her mouth and rinsed out the toothpaste. As she dried her mouth, she continued to stare at herself in the mirror. Don't fool yourself, she thought. You're never going be happy again. She noticed she appeared a little older tonight, older and sadder. She could not face herself in the mirror any longer. Tonight she walked with a newfound weariness toward the dark-oak sleigh bed and sat on the edge. She kicked off her bedroom slippers as she thought about the day's events. She thought of Isaac and the Morrises. She just didn't understand how they could forgive him. She would never forgive Isaac or Tyler.

She threw her legs onto the bed and pulled the blanket over her. Since her weekend to work was coming up, she had tomorrow off and would be able to drive the children to school. She was glad with it being Addison's first day back.

Then there was Noah. She rolled over on her side and punched her pillow. She had noticed he acted a little different after the morning church service. He had been quiet during lunch at Clark's and not very talkative once they had reached the house. Even though his body had been sitting in her living room, she noticed his mind appeared to be elsewhere. He seemed a little distant toward her. Maybe it's just my imagination, she thought as she rolled onto her opposite side. But what if it wasn't? Kyndal yawned and later fell into a troubled night of tossing and turning.

CHAPTER 23

BACK TO SCHOOL

Kyndal awoke the next morning to find she had kicked her blanket and comforter onto the floor. Her legs were hanging partly over the bed with only the top half of her body on the bed. Not bothering to hoist her lower body back onto the bed, she slid to the floor next to the bed and pulled her knees to her chest. She placed her head in her hands and dozed off without realizing it. She jumped when she heard the buzzing of the alarm clock fifteen minutes later. Kyndal groaned feeling as if she had been in a wrestling match all night and came out the loser, probably looked like it too, she thought. Pulling herself up, she walked around to the opposite side of the bed and turned off the annoying buzzer.

She stepped into the blue bedroom slippers lying next to the bed and slid her arms into the long sleeves of her matching robe, then headed downstairs to start breakfast. As she entered the kitchen, she had a gut feeling it was not going to be one of her better days.

* * * * *

The buzzing of the alarm clock woke Addison from a restful sleep. She rolled over and yawned as she turned off the alarm. Ayson ran past her bedroom door and banged on it.

"Get up, sleepyhead!" he yelled.

She let out a sigh as she sat on the side of the bed. Since she had not been going to school, she was not used to getting up quite this early.

Ayson banged on the bedroom door again. "Hey, sis, are you up!" At least some things were back to normal.

"I'm up," she answered. "Be down in a minute."

Even through the closed bedroom door, she could smell the inviting aroma of coffee and bacon. She heard the sound of Ayson's footsteps as he ran down the stairs; following behind was Chip. Her brother was always running. She wasn't sure if he even knew how to walk down a flight of stairs. She envied his energy and his two good legs. Of course, she couldn't blame him. If she had two good legs right now, she would be running up and down the stairs every chance she got. Ayson had always been a morning person. He could stay up late with the owls and still get up with the rooster the next morning.

She slid on her artificial leg and bedroom shoes, and headed downstairs where she was greeted by Chip.

When she entered the kitchen, her mom was scooping up a fried egg from the frying pan and placing it in Ayson's plate. "You want fried or scrambled?" she asked as Addison took a seat at one end of the table.

"Scrambled will be fine," she said through a yawn.

Ayson was spooning grits onto his plate. He sat with no shirt on and was wearing short-legged baseball pajama bottoms.

Addison grabbed a piece of buttered toast from the dish in front of her and looked at her brother. She thought about how much he reminded her of their dad. Their dad liked to sleep without a shirt on as well. However, unlike her brother, their dad would at least wear a shirt at the meal table.

It only took a minute for her mother to scramble the eggs. As her mother emptied the eggs into her plate, Addison noticed her mother looked a little tired. She had dark circles under her eyes, and she kept yawning.

"Mom, you've got to stop all this yawning. You're making me yawn," Addison said as she gave another wide yawn.

"Sorry," her mother said as she returned to the stove to cook another scrambled egg. "I didn't sleep well," she said as she broke a couple of eggs into a bowl. She grabbed the whisk and beat the eggs together and poured them into the hot frying pan. It was an unusually quiet meal; no one seemed to be in the mood to talk.

Forty minutes later, they were headed out the door. Kyndal dropped Ayson off at the middle school first then headed to the high school. Addison felt her heart beat faster and faster as they approached Iron City High. Her hands were beginning to sweat.

Kyndal noticed the look of dread in her daughter's eyes. She reached over and took her daughter by the hand. "You're going to have a great day today," she said, smiling.

Addison forced a smile. "Of course, I will," she told her mother.

Kyndal gave her daughter's hand a squeeze as she pulled in front of the school. Addison reached to get her bookbag from the floorboard of the car.

"Look," her mother said.

Addison looked at her mother, who nodded and was looking at something out Addison's window. Addison turned to see Alayna, Trevor, and several other students from her youth group running toward the car. She felt a flood of relief. At least she wouldn't have to go in alone. She had never been so glad to see her friends.

She had expected to get a lot of stares and to see a lot of whispering, and she was right. Slowly she made her way to the front of the school with everyone's eyes following every step she took. Her most awkward moment came when she began walking up the steps to the main entrance. Knowing everyone's eyes were on her made her more nervous, but she was determined to conquer those steps if it was the last thing she did. With narrowed eyes, she glared sharply at Alayna when she started to assist her by taking her arm. Alayna was familiar with that look and backed off. Beckah Joy was on the other side of Addison as they climbed the steps. She was about to take Addison by the other arm when she noticed the look Addison gave Alayna. She backed off as well.

Brian Walsh and Trevor were following close behind talking about an English paper that was due by the end of the week. Addison knew these steps by heart and knew there were eight steps before getting to the top. Carefully she climbed each step one by one. *Two more to go*, she counted silently. She could hear the whispers and feel everyone's eyes on her as she neared the top. With one step to go and feeling pretty good about herself, she made the mistake of looking up. Just as she was about to put her foot on the last step, she looked up and stared straight into the glaring eyes of Karlie Adams.

Addison heard Maddie Watkins, who was standing next to Karlie, let out a loud gasp as she threw her hand over her mouth and looked on with sheer panic. Karlie had so rattled Addison she missed the step and fell backward. She heard Karlie let out a satisfied laugh as she fell back into the arms of Brian and Trevor, almost knocking them off balance. However, they were able to catch her with the aid of Alayna and Beckah Joy. She heard others gasp as her peers looked on helplessly. Finally, she regained her balance. Alayna let go of her and headed straight for Karlie. Trevor grabbed her by the arm and shook his head. She ignored Trevor as she pulled away from him and continued toward Karlie.

"No, Alayna!"

Alayna stopped and turned to look at Addison, who stood shaking her head. "Let it go," she said softly as she started up the steps again. This time, because she was so shaken, she let her friends help her as they started once more up the steps. She stopped when she heard Maddie screaming at Karlie, "This isn't funny!"

Karlie stopped laughing and stared at Maddie in disbelief.

"You're a cruel person, Karlie Adams!" Maddie continued. "You're just plain ole cruel!" Maddie turned and walked off, leaving Karlie standing with her mouth wide open and her face beet red. Now it was Karlie everyone was staring at. Addison could tell not only had Maddie's outburst embarrassed Karlie, but her words had cut deep and hurt her as well. Karlie glared at Addison for a second, then turning her nose up, she quickly turned her head and stomped inside the building. Addison assured her friends and a few concerned classmates that she was fine.

She was about to go through the school doors when she heard her phone alert her of a text message. She must remember to turn her phone off once she was inside the building, she thought, as she reached into her pocket and pulled out her phone. It was a message from Wyatt. It simply read, *Praying for you*, but it was enough. She smiled as she pressed the keys on her phone. *Thanks, I need it.* She pressed the send button and then turned the phone off as she entered Iron City High for the first time in weeks.

Overall, everything went pretty well until her last class. Mr. Zendaye, her English teacher, had asked her to drop some papers off at the main office. He had told her since there were only a few minutes left before the bell rang, she need not bother to return to class. She suspected he could have asked any number of students to deliver the papers or taken them himself, but he had asked her for a reason. She knew he was giving her the chance to beat the crowd. At the end of the day, everyone was in a rush to get home or to some kind of practice. Students were always bumping into one another in the crowded hallways.

She delivered the papers to the secretary and asked her to give them to the school principal. She was about to go outside and wait on her mother when she decided to go to the restroom instead. Her artificial leg was bothering her a little, and she wanted to readjust it. This was the longest she had worn the leg since she had gotten it. She was about to enter the restroom when Karlie Adams came through from the other side, almost hitting her with the door.

"Oh, excuse—" Karlie was about to apologize until she saw it was Addison. Karlie pushed past her as Addison entered the restroom. She was about to enter one of the stalls when Karlie came bursting back through the door.

"I mean, I guess you think people are going to feel sorry for you," she told Addison. "Well, I got news for you. People aren't going to like you any better now than they did before."

Addison had not been aware of anyone not liking her. She had always gotten along with most people, except for Karlie and her little handful of followers. She decided to make no comment and started for the stall again. "Aren't you going to say anything?" Karlie asked in a somewhat irritated voice.

"What do you want me to say?" Addison asked, fixing her eyes directly on Karlie. She could tell her piercing stare was making Karlie a little uncomfortable. Karlie was the first to look away and, for some reason, changed the subject.

"I heard you and Alayna have gotten Isaac Darnell involved in all this religious junk."

"It's not junk, and it's not religion. It's real, and it's called Christianity."

"Well, whatever it's called, it's all over school about Isaac."

Addison looked at Karlie, her expression softening. She really did feel sorry for her. "Look, I don't know why you don't like me, but I—"

"I'll tell you why I don't like you," Karlie said, moving closer to her. "I mean, you think you're better and smarter than anyone else."

Had she really come across that way to people, or was this just the way Karlie felt?

"You think you're the most beautiful girl in the whole school. Well, you're no better or smarter than anyone else, and you're definitely not the most beautiful girl in school."

Addison had never seen so much hatred in a person's eyes. Karlie continued to move closer and closer toward her. "I mean, as a matter of fact, you're not even pretty!" She wasn't sure what Karlie was getting ready to do. She definitely couldn't outrun her. Karlie stopped inches from Addison's face. "As a matter of fact, you're nobody. Do you hear me, Addison McNeely? Noooobody!" Addison could almost see the sparks of hatred shooting from Karlie's eyes. Her voice and words were cold and harsh. "I mean, no one is ever going to want you now. You'll never be desirable to anyone." She laughed.

Addison would never have thought Karlie's words could cut so deep, but they did. She wanted to push past Karlie and run as fast and as far away as she could. Karlie stood stone-faced staring at her as if daring her to say anything. This time, it was Addison who looked away just as the dismissal bell rang. It was like music to her ears. Karlie stepped back and smiled.

"See you later, Ms. Nobody. By the way, who's having the last laugh now?" she said, emphasizing the word laugh.

"Okay, maybe I deserve that last comment," said Addison, having remembered Karlie's unfortunate mud bath.

Karlie didn't respond, but turned haughtily and walked out the door, leaving Addison feeling bewildered and alone. She heard a hubbub of laughter and voices from the hall as students passed by the closed door. At the moment, she could not bear the thought of facing anyone, so she remained hidden until the crowd thinned.

She was still standing in the middle of the restroom when two girls she didn't know came through the door laughing and talking. When they saw Addison they stopped in their tracks. One girl leaned over and whispered something to the other; then without another word, they turned and left, leaving her alone once again.

"Why didn't Mr. Zendaye deliver his own stupid papers?" Addison mumbled as she made her way into the hallway, now filled with only a handful of students.

A couple of guys looked her way and then quickly made their way to the outside doors. The way everyone looked at her and scattered when she was near made her feel as if she had the plague. She knew the real reason they acted that way was because they had no idea what to say to her, but still. She let out a defeated sigh as she made her way to the car where her mother and Ayson were waiting.

"How did it go today?" her mother asked, a little uncertain when she saw Addison's face.

"Don't ask," she said as she burst into tears.

"I bet it has something to do with that wicked witch Karlie!" Ayson said angrily.

Kyndal faced Ayson and gave him a brief lecture on why it was not nice to refer to someone as a witch. However, truth be known, she was thinking the same thing. She turned to face Addison. "What did—"

"Mom, if you don't mind, I don't want to talk about it right now," Addison said, trying to choke back more tears as her mother turned the key and started the engine. The ride home was quiet except for the occasional sniffling coming from Addison. Kyndal pulled into the driveway wondering if she should take the next day off from work to take Addison to school, but she knew her daughter would never stand for it.

Upon entering the house, Addison ran as fast as she could and headed upstairs to her bedroom. She fell across the bed and burst into more tears.

* * * * *

Kyndal sat her purse on the sofa and sat next to it kicking off her shoes. She wanted nothing more than to run upstairs and throw her arms around her daughter, but she knew it would not do any good. Addison was the type of person who needed to have space when it came to things like this. Eventually, her daughter would talk to her and let her into her private little world, but not before she was ready. She leaned her head back on the sofa and resigned herself to waiting for that time.

She heard Ayson rambling through the fridge and kitchen cabinets looking for something to snack on. She closed her eyes and tried to think of what she was in the mood to fix for supper.

"Hey, Mom!" Ayson yelled. "Can we have pork chops for supper?"

"That was easy," she mumbled, getting up from the sofa. "Sure, why not?" she answered entering the kitchen.

Supper was about as quiet as the ride home from school. Afterward, Addison helped her mother clear the table and put away the dishes. The little conversation they did have consisted mostly of unimportant small talk.

Kyndal watched the news later as the children headed to their rooms to tackle their homework. After supper was one of the times she missed Josh the most. The two of them would sit for hours and talk about the day's events, their children, and about their future together. She looked down at her wedding band and swallowed the lump in her throat.

Grabbing the remote from the end table, she turned on the TV to the weather channel. The bad weather initially called for had changed course and was now going to miss them. There would continue to be cold weather, but no rain. Kyndal dosed off before too long and dreamed of Josh as the remote slid from her hand onto the sofa.

CHAPTER 24

YOU CAN THANK ME LATER

Alayna picked Ayson and Addison up for school the next day. Addison yawned as she slid into the front seat of the car and snapped on her seat belt. A few minutes later, Alayna dropped Ayson off at Carolina Middle School then headed to the high school.

"Now that Ayson is not here, do you want to tell me what is going on with you?" Alayna asked as she pulled out of the student drop-off lane onto the highway.

"What do you mean? There's nothing going on with me."

"Yeah, right," Alayna said sarcastically, rolling her eyes.

Addison was quiet as she sat staring out the window, but not really seeing anything. She was too busy wondering what kind of day was ahead for her at school.

Alayna turned up the worship CD she had been listening to before arriving earlier at the McNeely home and let the subject drop. Alayna turned into the student parking lot and pulled into a parking space. She started to put the car in park when it occurred to her that she may have parked a little too far for Addison to walk.

"I'm sorry," she said, starting to back out of the parking space. "I forgot."

"No," Addison said quickly, "it's all right. I can walk. It's not that far." She grabbed her bookbag and opened the door. Once she started walking, she realized it was a little farther to the school than she had realized, but she wasn't about to say anything. She was a little slow, but otherwise she was making it okay. It took about five minutes for them to reach the foot of the steps that led to the main building. Her thoughts flashed back to the day before, making her feel a little anxious. Today there was only Alayna. There were no Brian and Trevor to catch her from behind if she lost her footing.

Alayna decided to take a chance. She leaned forward and whispered into Addison's ear, "Do you need me to help you up the steps?"

Addison shook her head. She glanced at the group of students gathered on the sidewalk and the small narrow porch at the top of the steps. They were all staring at her, and she knew what they were thinking. They were thinking the same thing she was: could she make it up the steps without falling?

"Come on, Addison," she said, encouraging herself. "You do this all the time at home." At least she did not see Karlie's face as she scanned the faces of the curious onlookers. However, she did see Maddie Watkins staring down at her from the top of the steps, her emerald-green eyes wide with anticipation. Addison took a deep breath.

The fact that everyone was so quiet made her even more nervous. The only sound resonating through the uncomfortable silence was from a weather worn wind chime located on the overhang of the porch. The cool November breeze created a soft and soothing yet subtle melody as it blew through the long bamboo tubes. Addison carefully made her way up the steps with all eyes upon her. Once again, she felt as if she were a bug under a microscope. Alayna walked close beside her but dared not touch her. Addison grabbed one side of the handrails as she slowly took one step at a time. It took her a few minutes, but she finally made it to the dreaded last step. She paused and took a deep breath again. *Just one more step—you can do this.* Placing her right foot on the last step, she finally raised herself onto the narrow porch unscathed.

She could still sense everyone's eyes on her, but did not turn around. She kept her eyes forward as she and Alayna started to enter the building. Then she heard someone clap their hands. She turned and saw Maddie clapping and smiling a genuinely friendly smile.

Then she heard another person clap. One by one, she heard more and more of her classmates clapping for her.

"Way to go, Addison!" Jonah Medley yelled before placing his fingers to his lips and giving a loud whistle.

At first, she felt almost mortified at the attention. She felt her face flush. But then as she looked into the warm and smiling faces of her classmates, she began to feel a wave of relief rush over her as she heard more whistles and cheers. She looked at her best friend, who was clapping and cheering as well between brushing away a tear. Maybe it wasn't going to be such a bad day after all. Smiling, she threw her hands over her head and interlocked her fingers. She waved her hands over her head the same as a victorious boxer who had just won a championship fight. In a way, she felt she had won a fight, a fight of self-confidence.

As the day wore on, she became aware she wasn't getting near the attention and stares she had gotten the day before. Who would have thought God would use Maddie Watkins, one of Karlie's best friends, to smooth the path?

Cheer practice was immediately after school to prepare for the championship game. The Wildcats would be playing their last game Friday in Ellenton, a town about fifty miles away. If they won against the Ellenton Gators, they would be state champs for the first time in three years. Addison was staying after school to watch practice. She was glad Karlie wasn't at school today to make her feel uncomfortable while she watched. Sarah Garrison was picking Caleb and Ayson up after school and then taking them to see a movie.

The bell rang as Addison sat in her last class. She would give the other students time to rush through the crowded halls. She felt a cold shiver as she thought about the day before and the incident with Karlie. A few minutes later, she bid Mr. Zendaye goodbye and headed to the gym. She decided to use the north end of the gym as there were fewer steps and she was beginning to tire. Alayna had a history class last, which was located farther from the gym, but she was already in the gym and dressed in black shorts and a gold T-shirt when Addison entered through the double doors.

The squad was now two cheerleaders down. She had not been replaced, and Karlie would be missing the last football game, or at least that was the rumor. She wondered what could be wrong with Karlie that she would have to miss the game.

Coach Redmond saw Addison sitting on one of the lower bleachers and waved to her as the squad ran warm-up laps around the gym. She blew her coveted silver whistle and held up three fingers, indicating the number of laps left, and then made her way to where Addison was sitting. Addison had missed Coach Redmond and her warm personality. After the coach gave her a heartwarming hug they mostly made small talk until the last lap was made.

Alayna waved as Coach Redmond gave Addison one last hug then turned to walk toward the squad. She blew the whistle as she waved her arms in the air, motioning for the girls to gather around her. Alayna and Maddie were discussing something as Maddie stood holding her left side. Addison doubted she would ever need to hold her side again from running so hard. The girls gathered around their coach and listened for the specific cheers she wanted the squad to practice.

Finally, after an hour of sweat-breaking practice, Coach Redmond allowed a ten-minute water and bathroom break. Alayna and Maddie ran over and said something to the coach. Ten minutes later, the girls were in formation for another cheer.

Coach Redmond motioned for Addison to come and stand next to her. When she had first motioned toward the bleachers, Addison had turned around and looked behind her. She thought maybe someone else had slipped in behind her to watch the practice. Seeing no one else around, she realized the coach was motioning for her. She once again felt all eyes upon her as she made her way to the coach.

"Wait here," she said as Addison came and stood next to her.

Addison turned toward the squad of onlookers when she heard some of them giggling. Less than twenty seconds later, her coach returned and held out a set of black-and-gold pom-poms. Addison gave her a confused look.

"Take these and get into formation," Coach Redmond said, smiling.

"But I can't—"

"You still have your lungs and your arms, don't you?"

Addison looked at the cheerleaders and then at her coach. "Yes, but—"

"Then get into formation."

Before she could protest further, Coach Redmond blew the whistle, and the squad started performing one of their familiar cheers. She walked over and stood next to Alayna, who was concentrating on her cheering as if nothing was out of the ordinary. Addison felt elated as she joined her fellow cheerleaders in cheer after cheer. She was even able to do some of the cheers that had simple leg movements.

A half hour later, practice was over, and the squad gathered around, congratulating her on a job well done. She thanked the squad and Coach Redmond for letting her practice with them and then held the pom-poms out in front of her toward the coach. Coach Redmond gave her a somewhat puzzled look.

"Why are you giving those back to me?" she asked.

Addison noticed the team looking at her with as much of a puzzled look as the coach had.

"You might need them."

"No. You'll need them Friday night for the game."

"The game!" Now it was Addison who gave a puzzled look as her jaw dropped open.

Coach Redmond pushed the pom-poms back toward her. "If you can cheer here, you can cheer on the field. See you Friday—as long as it is okay with your mother and your surgeon clears you," she added.

Addison stood staring after her coach as cheerleader after cheerleader came by and patted her on the back, offering their congratulations and "welcome backs." She could hardly believe she was back on the team, and she couldn't wait to tell her mom and Ayson. She even wanted to tell Wyatt, but in person.

"It was unanimous," Alayna told her. "The team voted, and it was unanimous."

"Whose idea was it?"

"It was mine, but you can thank me later. Right now I'm starving. Let's head for home."

* * * * *

Addison's family was excited about the news of her getting to cheer in Friday night's game. Even Chip seemed to have picked up on her excitement as he yelped and danced in circles around her feet.

"Mom, can I go to the game Friday night with Caleb and his parents?" asked Ayson as he settled on the sofa next to his mother. "Mrs. Garrison said it was okay for Callaway and me to ride with them."

"Sure," his mother said, reaching into the candy dish on the coffee table and grabbing a couple of mints. "Just make sure you behave yourself," she said, offering him a mint.

"Nah, I'm good," he said, running to the phone to call Caleb. "Thanks, Mom," he added.

"I'm going to start supper now," she told Addison as she grabbed another piece of candy and made her way to the kitchen.

Addison didn't even notice her mother speaking to her. She was in the middle of texting Wyatt and asking if he could stop by on the way home from work the next day. She pushed the send button on her phone and then turned on the TV while she waited for a response.

* * * * *

Wyatt read the text from Addison several times. He reluctantly sent back a message saying he could not make it. He just didn't think he could face her right now, maybe never. He was starting to have serious feelings toward her, but he felt sure her feelings toward him were one of friendship only. He had tried several times to tell her how he felt, but had backed down every time. He eventually concluded that she had become dependent upon him during her rehabilitation, and that was all. He had thought long and hard about their relationship and finally decided it was best to keep his true feelings to himself—and his distance. Seeing her, knowing she did not feel the same way, only made it hurt worse.

* * * * *

Addison's heart sank as she read the text from Wyatt. He gave no explanation as to why he couldn't come. The text was actually kind of direct and to the point. There was no warmth in it at all. The text simply read, *Can't make it.* There was no apology, no explanation, nothing. She debated whether or not to text him and let him know about being on the cheerleading squad again, but then decided against it.

Later that night, she had a terrible dream. She dreamed she was cheering at the game and suddenly lost her voice. She couldn't yell, and then she lost all movement in her arms and hands. She was just standing on the field looking like a fool as the crowd roared in laughter.

"You're nothing!" the crowd roared, "A nobody!" Then to make matters worse, her artificial leg gave way, and she hit the ground. Karlie was right, she thought, as she lay paralyzed on the field. Even Alayna and Maddie were laughing at her. Coach Redmond was shaking her head and repeating over and over how she had made a mistake in letting her back on the squad.

"Someone please get her off the field!" Coach Redmond yelled. The crowd roared even louder with laughter. A woman in the stands started yelling, "Get her off the field! She's too hideous to look at!" She looked up and saw Wyatt. He was joining in with the crowd.

"She's too hideous to look at! Too hideous to look at!" he was yelling.

Drenched with sweat, Addison awoke and sat straight up in the bed. She threw back the blanket and reached for her crutch next to the nightstand. She hobbled to the bathroom and poured a glass of water. She looked in the mirror and could have sworn she saw her own reflection laughing at her.

She returned to bed and tried to sleep, but all she could do was dream the same terrible dream over and over. It was only after she pulled her Bible from the nightstand and read for a while that she was able to get a few hours of sleep.

* * * * *

She awoke the next morning and decided to text Wyatt about being back on the cheerleading team. *Congratulations,* he texted back. *You will have to tell me all about it!* Although she knew it was foolish, she was feeling a little angry with him for having laughed at her in her dream, or should she say nightmare? *I will,* she texted him. *Also, thanks again for the scriptures. They really helped me to get through this first week of school.* Her heart sank as she stared at his response. *No problem. What are friends for? Gotta get to work. Talk to you later.* She had finally gotten the answer to how Wyatt felt about her. They were just friends; at least that was how he felt about her.

Fighting back tears, she made her way downstairs where her mother was waiting to take Ayson and her to school. Addison would be glad when she could drive again, but with so much going on, she and her mother had not had the time to look for another car.

Alayna was waiting for her when they pulled in front of the school. No one seemed to pay them any attention as they made their way up the steps. She liked it that way. At least she was finally getting a little normality back in her life.

"I've got to stop off at the office," Alayna said. "See you in trig class this afternoon." Alayna started to enter the office then stopped and turned to face her. "Where's your duffle bag for cheer practice?"

Addison began stuttering as she tried to answer without causing a scene. "Yeah, well, about that, I, ah…"

"What?" Alayna asked, irritated at it taking her so long to answer.

"I'm not practicing today," she finally blurted out.

Alayna walked back to where she was standing. "What do you mean you're not going to practice? You have too if you're going to cheer Friday night. You know how coach is about people not show-ing up for practice."

Addison looked down at the floor. "I'm not sure I want to cheer Friday night."

"What!" Alayna started to say something else, but glancing at her watch, she changed her mind. "I don't have time to discuss this with you right now. We'll talk about it over lunch."

Before Addison could protest, Alayna turned and walked into the office. Addison looked at her watch. She had three minutes to get to homeroom before the tardy bell rang. Throwing her hands up, she sighed and headed down the hall toward homeroom. She didn't want to have to discuss anything with her friend, but she knew she had no choice because of Alayna's persistent attitude. Usually she looked forward to lunch, but today—not so much.

Later that day, they stood in the lunch line trying to decide what to eat. Both finally opted for the grilled chicken salad and the sugar-free strawberry gelatin cup. They found an empty table in the corner of the lunchroom. Alayna sat her tray down a little roughly.

"Now what is this about you not wanting to cheer in Friday's game?"

Addison sat across from Alayna and told her of the dream. "It was so real. Maybe it is an omen that something bad is going to happen."

Alayna reached and tore open a packet of light ranch dressing and drizzled the dressing over her salad. "Don't be ridiculous!" she said, continuously stabbing her fork into the salad.

"Are you going to eat it or stab it to death?" Addison asked, nodding toward the salad.

"Funny," Alayna said, narrowing her eyes at Addison. "There," Alayna said, taking a bite of salad. "Satisfied?"

Addison smiled. "Yes," she said, taking a bite of her own salad.

"You're just trying to change the subject," Alayna said.

Before now, Addison had not told Alayna about the incident with Karlie. She proceeded to tell Alayna, hoping she would understand a little better. Alayna wiped her mouth with her napkin and laid it on her lap.

"You mean to tell me you're going to let someone like Karlie Adams define who you are and let a stupid dream dictate what you do in life?" She could hear the anger rising in Alayna's voice, but she wasn't sure if Alayna was mad at her, Karlie, or both. Alayna picked up her fork again before continuing, "You're coming to practice today," she said adamantly. "There is nothing further to discuss. Call your mom and have her drop off your duffle bag."

Addison gave a defeated sigh. "Okay, you win. I'll do it." As the saying goes, sometimes you just have to choose your battles.

Alayna smiled and patted herself on the back. Addison was about to call her mother when an announcement came over the loudspeaker.

"Attention, cheerleaders," announced Coach Redmond. "Today's practice has been canceled. Practice will resume tomorrow immediately after school. Again, today's practice has been canceled and will resume tomorrow immediately after school."

Addison and Alayna looked at each other.

"Don't say a word," Alayna said as she opened her gelatin cup. "You're still going to practice tomorrow." Alayna sucked the tasty squiggly dessert off the spoon and into her mouth.

To Addison's relief, the rest of the day was uneventful.

* * * * *

When her mother picked her up from school, Addison could tell her mother had been crying again. Her eyes were red and puffy. Wait for it, Addison thought. Wait for it.

"Allergies," her mother said when she noticed her daughter looking at her.

Yep, that was it—the excuse her mother always gave when she was caught with red, puffy eyes. Addison just nodded but knew from the flushing of her mother's face she was not telling the truth. Ayson was in the back seat working on his homework, oblivious to anything else.

Arriving home Addison rushed upstairs and changed out of her school clothes. Years ago, she and Alayna had promised not to keep secrets from each other. It was time she confided in her friend about her true feelings for Wyatt. She also wanted to find out why her best friend was acting so strange lately.

CHAPTER 25

SECRETS REVEALED

Later that night, Addison was finding it hard to sleep.

Monday would be her last day of therapy. She had mastered walking, climbing stairs, and how to safely get in and out of the shower, which in her opinion had been the hardest to master. Until yesterday, she had been sad about Monday being her last day, but now, knowing how Wyatt really felt about her, she was glad. She would still have to see him at church. A while back, she had invited him to visit New Haven, and he had continued to attend. It was going to be hard to see him, but what choice did she have? Sure, she could start attending another church, but she loved New Haven and her youth group too much to do that.

Sleep escaping her, she decided to text Alayna. *Are you still up? If so, call me or text me.* It was only a little after 9:00 p.m. She was almost certain Alayna was still up. Pulling the blanket over her head, she thought about Wyatt and waited for Alayna to return her text. An hour later, she fell asleep, wondering why Alayna had not called or at least responded to her text. Usually, Alayna didn't go to bed until ten o'clock on a school night, except on rare occasions. Maybe tonight was one of those occasions, Addison thought.

It was sometime in the night when she awoke and realized she had fallen asleep and left the lamp on. Alayna had probably texted back by now, she thought. She sat up in bed looking for the cell phone that had slipped from her hand when she had fallen to sleep. She finally located it lying next to the pillow beside her. She checked her phone and was disappointed to find no text from her best friend. Alayna didn't call, text, or come over as much as she used to. Why had she acted so secretive over the last couple of weeks? Addison turned the lamp off and rolled on to her side, wondering what was going on with her friend.

* * * * *

Alayna heard the ding of her cell phone alerting her she had a text. Rolling over in the bed, she closed the book she had been reading. Propping herself on one arm, she read the text from Addison. She sat straight up in the bed. She was about to respond to the text when she received a call. She looked at the name and answered the phone. By the time she hung up, it was almost ten thirty: too late to call her friend. She rolled over and was soon fast asleep, but not before wondering how she was going to tell her best friend about the secret she had been keeping from her.

For the past couple of weeks, she had been feeling a little guilty because lately she had been ignoring her best friend, and quite intentionally at that. She didn't want to hurt her friend, but she was afraid of how Addison might react upon hearing her secret. Years ago, they both had promised to never keep secrets from each other. Right now she was breaking that promise, at least until she could find a way to break the news to Addison.

It seemed she had just drifted off to sleep when she awoke to the buzzing of the alarm clock. She moaned as she read the bright-red numbers on the clock. She couldn't believe it was already half past six in the morning. She reached for the snooze button but had second thoughts after remembering she had to pick Addison and Ayson up and drive them to school. She also made another decision: she was going to tell Addison her secret.

Suddenly she remembered the text from Addison. She hoped Addison would not be upset that she had not called or returned her text. Jumping out of bed, she ran to the closet and pulled out a pair of jeans and a red-and-black striped long-sleeved button-up shirt. Upon leaving her bedroom, she reached and grabbed the black knitted scarf

241

lying on her dresser and wrapped it around her neck. Forty-five minutes later, she pulled out of the driveway and headed for the McNeely home.

* * * * *

Ayson was watching from the bay window when Alayna pulled up. Yelling for Addison, he grabbed his bookbag and ran out, slamming the door behind him. Two minutes later, Addison joined him and Alayna in the car.

"Before you say anything about me not texting you back last night, there's something I need to tell you," Alayna said as soon as Addison got in the car. Ayson unfastened his seat belt and leaned forward. Alayna turned and looked at Ayson, then back at Addison. "After we drop Squirt off, that is." Ayson rolled his hazel eyes and sat back in his seat, fastening the seat belt for the second time.

Surprisingly, Addison didn't appear to be upset that she had not returned her text. But then again, Alayna could see her friend's mind seemed to be miles away at the moment. They rode in silence as both were occupied with their own thoughts. Even Ayson seemed to be lost in his thoughts.

The drive to Carolina Middle School seemed to take forever. Addison couldn't wait to tell Alayna about Wyatt. She wondered what it was Alayna had to tell her. Alayna finally pulled in front of the school where Caleb was waiting under the covered sidewalk. Ayson unfastened his seat belt and grabbed his bookbag as he swung the door open and exited the car.

"See you later, squirt!" Alayna yelled.

Ayson looked back and waved as he made his way toward his friend.

"Okay, Addison, tell me why you wanted me to call you last night," Alayna said as she drove off.

Addison cleared her throat and confided in her friend about her true feelings for Wyatt. "I've fallen in love with him," she said, still staring out the car window.

Alayna wasn't really surprised. She had noticed how Addison's eyes lit up when she talked about him. "I thought maybe you had," Alayna said, glancing toward her friend.

"Too bad he doesn't feel the same way," said Addison, never turning away from the window.

"How do you know? Have you told him how you feel?"

"No," said Addison, finally turning and facing Alayna. "But he made reference yesterday to us as being friends," she said, emphasizing the word *friends* and making bunny-ear air quotes with her fingers. Alayna pulled into the parking lot designated for the senior class only and turned off the engine. "Enough talk about me. What was it you wanted to tell me?" Addison asked.

Alayna hesitated. This wasn't going to be easy, especially with all Addison had going on with Wyatt. "Well I...I...well, I've been seeing someone," she blurted out before she changed her mind, not that Addison wouldn't have hounded her until she did tell her.

Addison's mouth flew open. "You've what?" she asked when she was finally able to speak. "Why haven't you said anything?"

Alayna could tell from her friend's voice she was a little hurt that she had not said anything before now. "Well, to be honest, I just didn't want to hurt you."

Addison felt a little confused. "I don't understand."

"Well," said Alayna a little hesitantly, "you were so down on yourself thinking no one would ever want you. I just couldn't say anything."

Addison felt hurt her friend had not confided in her until now, but she really did understand. After all, she was just now confiding in Alayna about her feelings for Wyatt. She reached and hugged her best friend tightly. "Believe it or not, I would have probably done the same thing had it been the other way around." Then it occurred to her as she released her friend. "But who are you seeing?"

Alayna felt relief take over as she gave her friend the good news. "It's Trevor. I'm seeing Trevor Grant. I was on the phone with him last night, and it was late when we hung up. That's why I didn't return your text."

"Alayna, that's great! But I wouldn't have thought that in a million years! I mean, I always felt he had a crush on you, but you never seemed to give him a second thought."

"I guess I've gotten to know him better through the youth meetings and through everything that happened to you," she said, looking away from Addison upon the last part of her comment. Addison reached and touched Alayna's hand to let her know she understood. She looked at Addison and smiled. "Trevor really does love the Lord, and so do I," she continued. "We just kind of connected, first about you and then the Lord. Before long, we found we had the same interest in a lot of other things—even chess."

Both girls laughed when Alayna mentioned chess. That was one game Addison had no knowledge of no matter how many times Alayna had tried to teach her.

"I'm really happy for you, Alayna. I really am."

"Thanks," she said as she reached and gave Addison another quick hug, relieved that the secret was out.

"Alayna," she said somewhat hesitantly, "please don't tell anyone how I feel about Wyatt, not even your mother."

"But why not say anything?" Alayna saw a saddened expression come over Addison's face.

"Because although I have fallen in love with Wyatt, I'm pretty sure the feelings aren't mutual. Like I said, he just referred to us last night as friends."

"Why not just tell him how you feel?" Alayna asked, wondering exactly what to say.

"Are you crazy!" exclaimed Addison.

Alayna was about to say something when the warning bell sounded.

"We had better hurry to homeroom before we're tardy," Addison said as she opened the door.

* * * * *

Three minutes later, Addison sat in homeroom thinking of everything that had recently transpired. She was glad she had finally confided in Alayna as to how she felt about Wyatt.

"Earth to Addison!" she heard someone say as she was shaken by the shoulder. She looked up into the face of Matilda Rogers from her youth group.

"Sorry, Matilda, I was just thinking about someone—I mean something."

"No explanation needed," she said. "But did you hear about Karlie Adams?" Addison could tell from the expression on Matilda's face it was something serious.

"No, I haven't. What's wrong?" The tardy bell rang just as Matilda whispered something. "What did you say?" she asked after the bell stopped. "I couldn't hear you."

Matilda leaned closer. "She was in a one car wreck. She ran off the side of the road and hit a tree. One of her legs is broken."

It wasn't exactly what had happened to her, but listening to what had happened to Karlie made Addison cringe as it brought back unwanted memories. Addison listened as Matilda continued.

"They are keeping her in the hospital for a few days for observation to make sure there are no other injuries or any internal bleeding."

Addison wasn't sure why Matilda had bothered to whisper the news about Karlie since by the end of the day, it was the talk of the entire school. The whole squad was talking about Karlie as Addison and Alayna entered the gym.

"After the way she treated you, I bet you are happy to hear that," said Louanne.

"Of course not!" exclaimed Addison, shaking her head. Addison had to admit a part of her wanted to be happy at the news, but she knew it was just the devil trying to get her to focus on the wrong Karlie had done to her. She asked God to help her not to have those feelings and committed to praying for Karlie instead.

Coach Redmond blew the whistle, turning everyone's attention to practice and a new cheer. Fortunately, it was a short and rather repetitive cheer, seeing how she only gave them one practice to learn it. Addison went through the motions of cheer after cheer, but her thoughts kept turning to Wyatt...and Karlie Adams.

CHAPTER 26

LOVE—SOMETIMES A COMPLICATED THING

Kyndal had been pulled from the ER to ICU due to staffing needs and was charting on the grumpy old man in room 12. Bruce Weathers, a regular at the hospital, had thrown his food tray in the floor again, claiming the nursing assistant who brought his tray in was trying to poison him. Bruce, as he preferred to be called, had been admitted with a diagnosis of uncontrolled blood sugars. He also had a diagnosis of Alzheimer's. Unfortunately, the combination of those two diagnoses fueled his confusion and paranoia. It had taken Kyndal nearly ten minutes to convince Bruce he needed to eat, and almost that long to calm the nursing assistant. Finally succeeding, she ordered another tray and personally delivered it to his room when it arrived. Kyndal had just finished charting on him when she heard Noah being paged to call the ER. Her eyes began to swell with tears.

Kyndal had not seen or spoken to Noah on a personal level in almost a week. The last nonprofessional conversation was after they had finished eating lunch one day in the cafeteria. It was then he had told her he did not think their relationship was going to work. He hadn't offered any explanation but said he would like to remain friends. She had not pressed him for a reason, mainly because the news had come as quite a shock. At the time, she had not known what to say or how to respond. As far as she knew, they had been getting along extremely well. She had simply nodded when he gave her the news, but did manage to tell him she did not believe she could be just friends, at least not yet. He said he understood, then left the table with her staring dumbfounded into her leftover chicken salad. Since that day, their conversations had been strictly business with casual hellos when passing in the halls.

It was not until a few days later that it occurred to her that maybe the change in Noah had come about because she was not a Christian. As strong as her feelings were for Noah, she was not going to become a Christian just to hold on to him. Once again, God had taken away someone she loved and cared about. Until Noah, she never believed she could possibly love another man other than Josh McNeely. Now, once again thanks to God, she had lost him too.

It was getting time for her two o'clock med pass. Two hours from now, she would be home, kicking off her shoes and taking about an hour rest before starting supper. She was thinking maybe tuna casserole. It would be quick and easy.

"At least something in my life would be easy," she mumbled as she went to answer the call light to room 12.

* * * * *

Noah left room 1 of the ER. He had been so busy keeping up with the fast pace of the ER he had not had a chance to eat lunch. Finally, most of the patients had been seen, and one of the other ER doctors offered to cover for him so he could eat lunch.

As he headed to the cafeteria, he hoped they were serving some of his favorites. He looked at his watch and noticed it was getting late. He knew the cafeteria would be closing soon. One thing he had learned as a doctor was to eat a big breakfast in case you had to eat a late lunch, which was usually the case. Today had been an exceptionally late day. Even his large breakfast had not been enough to hold him. He looked at his watch again. He had five minutes to get to the cafeteria before it closed and reopened again at four thirty to serve dinner. He barely made it through the door as Gideon Banks, the dietary manager, stepped to the door to lock it.

"Cutting it close, aren't you, Doc?" Gideon asked as he locked the door behind him.

"First chance I've had to get here. You have anything left worth eating?"

Gideon grunted and scratched his head. "Very little, Doc, especially this late in the game. Take a look and see what you can find."

Denise, Alene, and Carl, three of the dietary workers, were just starting to put away the leftovers from the hot bar.

"You're a little late, aren't you?" asked Denise.

"Just a little," he answered as he grabbed a tray and utensils and started down the serving line. "What do you have left?"

"Not much of anything," answered Alene.

He noticed there was no meat loaf or chicken left. There was spaghetti sauce left, but no spaghetti noodles. There was a handful of corn left, no green beans, and one spear of broccoli. There were mashed potatoes left, but nothing to go with them.

"You have any hamburgers left, Carl?"

"Afraid not, Doc," he answered, shaking his head. Noah looked at the salad bar, which looked a little skimpy as well. He wasn't really in the mood for a salad, but it looked as if that was his only choice.

"Guess I'll have a salad," he told Denise, a little disappointed. He could feel his appetite leaving.

Carl heard the disappointment in his voice. "I tell you what I'll do, Doc," he said, placing his hand on Denise's arm to keep her from fixing the salad. "How about I fix you a nice juicy cheeseburger and some fries? At least it will be something warm and will only take a few minutes."

"Gee, that would be great, but are you sure?"

"Of course, I'm sure. If I wasn't, I wouldn't have offered. Besides, I owe you one for taking out that aggravating gallbladder of mine."

Noah thanked Carl and felt his appetite returning. His empty stomach even let out a growl of approval. He started to head for a corner table when Alene caught him off guard.

"How are you and Nurse McNeely doing? She sure is a sweet little thing."

"Well, we've sort of…called it quits for now," he said hesitantly. He turned and headed again for the table, but not before noticing Denise nudge Alene in the side and whisper something in her ear.

"Well, how was I supposed to know?" he heard Alene say as she wiped her hands on her apron and turned to enter the kitchen located behind the counter. "No one ever tells me anything!" It wasn't long before Carl brought out a mouthwatering cheeseburger and piping-hot fries.

"Thanks, Carl, this sure hits the spot," Noah said after blessing his food and taking a big bite out of the burger. He reached for a napkin as the juices ran onto his fingers and plate. Carl smiled, feeling pleased that the doc was satisfied with the hot meal. He turned and headed back to the kitchen to help the women.

Noah would have enjoyed his lunch a lot more had Kyndal not been on his mind. He truly loved her and couldn't understand why God had allowed him to fall in love with someone who wasn't a Christian. He felt confused and frustrated.

Since Taylor's death, Kyndal was only the second woman he had been out with. The first was a nurse he had worked with while living in Georgia. He and Karen had only been seeing each other for a short while when he broke it off, and she moved to another town. Some said he was the reason for the move, that he had broken her heart. He had never been serious about Karen, but he enjoyed her company. There had been no chemistry between the two of them as far as he was concerned, but after a few weeks, he could tell Karen was interested in having a more serious relationship. To keep from hurting her any further, he had broken off the relationship and resigned himself to being alone—that was until Kyndal McNeely entered his life. He couldn't help but keep asking the same question over and over. Why would God allow him to fall in love with someone who wasn't a Christian? He took another bite of the juicy cheeseburger. He hadn't tried to fall in love with her and hadn't even wanted to. It just happened. He felt like a big heel when it came to the way he had broken things off with her. He had not even been man enough to offer her an explanation.

"Jerk," he mumbled as he dipped a crispy fry into ketchup and then popped it into his mouth. He wondered if she had put together the reason for the breakup. Taking a sip of his tea, he tried not to think about Kyndal for the remainder of his break. He had just woofed down the last bite of the cheeseburger when he heard his name being paged overhead. Gideon stopped wiping down the tables when he heard the page and came to unlock the cafeteria door.

"Next time, call ahead, Doc, and I can put you back a plate. We can always heat it in the microwave when you get here if we need to."

"Thanks, Gideon, I'll do that," he said as he stepped into the hallway, almost knocking Kyndal off her feet. He heard the door lock behind him. *Why couldn't I have been just a few seconds later coming through that door?* he thought as he grabbed hold of Kyndal to keep her from falling. For a few seconds, they stood staring at each other, saying nothing.

"Are you all right?" he finally asked.

"I'm fine," Kyndal said, staring into his eyes. *Why does she have to look at me with those sad but beautiful brown eyes?*

"Excuse me," he said, releasing her arms. "I have to go."

"I know," said Kyndal softly, still looking into his eyes. Somehow he didn't get the feeling they were talking about the same thing. He hurried off, leaving her to watch him as he rounded the corner.

* * * * *

Kyndal looked at the tubes of blood in the biohazard bag she was carrying. Before almost being knocked off her feet by Noah, she had been on her way to deliver a stat blood to the lab. Talk about bad timing, she thought. She hurried to the lab while wondering at the same time why love had to be so complicated.

* * * * *

Noah could not get out of sight fast enough. He could sense Kyndal's eyes following him as he sped up the hall as fast as he could. It was going to be hard running into her like this, but there was no way he could avoid it. With both of them working at the hospital, it was bound to happen every now and then. The thought had even crossed his mind to move again, but he couldn't keep moving every time something uncomfortable happened in his life. He had really liked New Haven Church of God, but he wasn't sure when Kyndal might show up. He knew it would be awkward for the both of them if they showed up on the same Sunday, maybe even for Addison and Ayson.

"Lord," he prayed as he rounded the corner, "I need your Holy Spirit to guide me. Tell me what to do." At that moment, he clearly heard the Holy Spirit.

Pray, then be still, and know I am God. An overwhelming peace came over him.

"Thank You, Lord," he said as he entered the intensive care unit, but he still couldn't help but wonder why love had to be so complicated.

* * * * *

Wyatt sat in front of his computer preparing to take one of his online courses for physical therapy. However, his mind was mostly on Addison—again. He wasn't exactly sure when he had fallen in love with her, but it seemed almost as far back as when she had thrown her Agatha Christie book at him. A smile played across his lips as he remembered that day and her cute red face when she realized she had thrown the book at the wrong person. Regardless of when he had fallen in love with her, the point was, he had. He had come close to telling her how he felt the night he had been at her house, but it just didn't seem to be the right time. On the other hand, when would be the right time? He had meant to try and stay away from her as much as possible, but he wasn't doing too well with that. He hated admitting it, but the thought of not seeing or talking to her was almost more than he could bear. He was hopelessly in love with someone who only saw him as a friend, and that hurt.

As he powered up his computer, he wondered if he was the only one who felt love was a complicated thing.

CHAPTER 27

GOD'S HAND IS NOT SHORTENED

Isaac sat in the chair next to the bed of his friend in the rehab unit of Faith Hospital. Tyler had been making real progress toward his recovery. He was now able to move all of his extremities, and except for occasional stuttering, he was able to speak much more clearly. At the moment, the two of them were watching a college football game. Isaac shifted slightly in his seat.

"Tyler," he said as he turned off the TV, "I need to talk to you about something."

"W-what about?" Tyler asked.

"I believe you know I got born again a few weeks ago," Isaac said, a little uncertain how Tyler would react to what he was about to say to him.

"Yes, that's g-great," Tyler said, trying his best to get the words out. "B-but if you're going to try and get me t-to accept Jesus, d-don't." Tyler said and turned the TV back on.

Isaac reached and turned it off again. "Why do you say that?" he asked, a little surprised at Tyler's abruptness "Look what God's brought you through, Tyler. You could be dead right now." Isaac was determined to give Tyler the opportunity to accept Christ before he left today.

He noticed Tyler's eyes begin to water. "I d-don't know why I'm not dead. I s-should be. I don't deserve t-to be alive. Look what I did t-to Addison."

"Tyler, Addison is okay," he said as he looked steadily into his friend's eyes. "She is not mad at you, and neither is God," he continued. "Addison has forgiven you, and if you will ask, God will forgive you too."

Tyler grabbed hold of the sheet and clenched it with his fist. "How can Addison not be mad at me? I have r-ruined her life. I can't g-give her back her leg!"

"You didn't ruin her life, Tyler. I mean, I know her life has changed, and you're right, you can't give her back her leg. But God is helping Addison through this, and He can help you too."

"God c-can't forgive me," he began to sob. "W-what I've done is…is unforgivable. Besides, I'm not even s-sure God e-exist!" he said, sobbing even harder.

Isaac was determined not to back down. He had to reach his friend with the help of the Holy Spirit. "Are you one-hundred percent sure He doesn't exist?" Isaac asked, emphasizing the words *one-hundred percent* and *doesn't*. He moved his chair even closer to Tyler's bed.

Almost instantly, Tyler stopped crying. The question was so unexpected that it caught him off guard, as if someone had suddenly walked up to him and slapped him in the face.

"No. I'm n-not one-hundred percent s-sure He doesn't exist," he answered.

Isaac could sense Tyler was really contemplating the question, so he continued, "Tyler, the day you die, you will surely know that God exist. However, if you die without Him, it will be too late. There will be no turning back. All hope will be lost. The time for repentance will be lost. Tyler…you will be lost…for all eternity. "Please, Tyler," Isaac pleaded, "don't risk going to hell for all eternity."

The tears started flowing again as Tyler listened to the words of his friend. Wiping his eyes, he looked at Isaac. "Will God really forgive me after everything I've done?"

"God forgave man for crucifying His only Son. Don't you think He can and will forgive us for anything else we have done? But we have to ask for His forgiveness. He not only forgives us, Tyler, but loves us—unconditionally."

Isaac reached in the bedside table and took out the Gideon Bible, opened it, and moved in closer.

"First John tells us if we confess our sins, that He is faithful and just and will forgive us our sins and will cleanse us from all unrighteousness."

Tyler turned toward Isaac as he continued to read.

"The book of Isaiah informs us that the Lord's hand is not shortened that it cannot save and His ear heavy that it cannot hear." He offered the bible to Tyler. "Here, you read it."

For a few seconds, Tyler stared at the Bible being held out to him, then slowly reached for it and began to read. When he finished reading, Isaac took the Bible, closed it, and returned it to the drawer. He continued to tell of God's love and forgiveness. Less than five minutes later, Tyler bowed his head and asked for forgiveness of all his sins.

"Now, God, if You c-can use me, t-take my life and do s-something with it," he added. Tyler knew God had forgiven him, and he could feel the weight of every burden he had ever carried being lifted. He had never felt so much love and acceptance.

"Knock, knock," they heard Dr. Arthur Linski say as he knocked on the door and entered the room without waiting for an answer. As soon as he entered the room, he could tell from the serious looks on their faces that the young men had been in some sort of deep discussion. "I'm sorry. Am I interrupting something? I can come back in a few minutes if you'd like."

"No, n-now is fine, Dr. Linski," Tyler answered with a smile.

* * * * *

Arthur Linski noticed Tyler appeared to be a little more at peace than usual. He usually had a frown on his face, and seldom did he ever see Tyler smile. He had even thought of prescribing some antidepressants for Tyler, but was trying to hold off. He also knew Tyler had been beating himself up over the girl who had lost her leg in the accident. He closed the door behind him as he entered the room. Tyler could contain himself no longer; he had to tell someone.

"Dr. L-Linski, I just ask Jesus to f-forgive me and to c-come into my h-heart," he said, smiling.

"That's wonderful news, Tyler," he said as he shook Tyler's hand. Now he knew why the noticeable change in the young man's countenance. He bent and placed his stethoscope over Tyler's chest and listened to his heart and lung sounds. He also examined the area of Tyler's head where a "bone flap" had been attached using a metal plate and screws. Eventually, the plate would be removed once the bone knitted together.

Dr. Linski pressed on Tyler's abdomen and then placed the stethoscope over his abdomen. The doctor listened intently as he moved the bell of the stethoscope from one area of Tyler's abdomen to another. Dr. Linski smiled as he raised and removed the stethoscope from his ears and let it hang from his neck. Placing his hands in his pockets, he continued to smile at Tyler.

"Young man, how would you like to go home this week?"

"Y-You mean it?" Tyler asked with an even bigger smile on his face.

"I sure do. But you'll still have to continue outpatient therapy for a while—and counseling. However, the way you're going, you should be through with both in no time."

There was another knock at the door. Bryan and Rebekah Morris entered the room. They greeted Dr. Linski and the boys.

"I believe your son has got some great news for you two," said Dr. Linski. On his way out, he smiled and patted Bryan's shoulder. Closing the door behind him, Arthur Linski paused on the other side feeling pretty good. He knew now, given the decision Tyler had made to follow Christ, that Tyler Morris and his family were going to be all right.

CHAPTER 28

GAME TIME!

Game time finally rolled around. Shannon was to pick up Kyndal and Ayson, and then stop by and pick up Callaway and Caleb before heading to the playoff game. There had been an attempted break-in at the sporting goods store the Garrisons owned so now they were unable to take the boys to the game. Arrangements had been made for Caleb to ride with the Thomases and then spend the night with Ayson. Although Pastor Bryce and Maggie were going to the game, Callaway had wanted to ride with the other two boys. If she knew anything at all about her son, Kyndal knew Callaway would be spending the night as well.

Pulling up to the McNeely home, Shannon blew the horn. Ayson was the first out the door dressed in a heavy coat. He had a toboggan over his head with the hood of the coat pulled over the toboggan. Kyndal came out seconds later carrying cushions and blankets. Shannon couldn't help but laugh as she watched Kyndal approach the car. She looked as if she was expecting a blizzard. Seeing his mother's arms were full; Ayson jumped out of the car and opened the back of the SUV.

"Thanks for helping me carry all this stuff," his mother remarked sarcastically shoving the cushions and blankets into the vehicle.

"Sorry mom. I didn't know you were bringing so much junk...I mean stuff," he said when she looked at him with narrowed eyes.

"Where's Patrick?" Kyndal asked as she jumped in the front seat and snapped her seatbelt in place.

"He's at home in bed with a bad sinus infection. He didn't want to get out in the night air." Shannon pulled out of the driveway and made her way to the Peter's home.

"See you at the game!" Maggie yelled from the doorway as Callaway jumped into the back seat. "Sure you don't mind if Callaway rides with you?"

"No problem, Maggie!" Shannon yelled as she waved and pulled out of the driveway. She headed to pick up Caleb. Fifteen minutes later everyone was settled in and on their way to the championship game.

* * * * *

Addison was a little nervous about cheering at the game. It was her first game since the accident, and she was afraid of making a total fool of herself, especially after the dream. She knew she was going to be self-conscious with everyone staring at her. People had watched her cheer before, but she didn't have an artificial leg then. She was already feeling awkward, and the game hadn't even begun. Alayna saw the apprehension in her friend's face.

"You're going to do fine," she said as they boarded the activity bus. Addison barely heard her teammates belting out cheers as the bus pulled out of the school's parking lot.

Staring out the window, Addison's thoughts drifted to something Michael Scobie had taught on a few Wednesdays before from the book of Matthew. It had been on her mind for the better part of the day. Although there were several parts to the scriptures, it was a certain part that had been on her mind:

> I was sick, and you visited Me. I was in prison, and you came to Me.
> When did we see You sick or in prison and come to You? the righteous will ask.

The King will answer and say to them, "Assuredly, I say to you, inasmuch as you did it to one of the least of these my brethren, you did it to Me."

She had been so busy earlier she had not had much time to think on the scriptures as she would have liked. Now that she had a little time to relax, she decided to think on the scriptures and see what the Lord was trying to say to her. She didn't know anyone in prison, and the only person she knew in the hospital was Tyler, and she had heard he was coming home this weekend. By the time she would be able to get to him, he would be home. Plus, she and Alayna had visited him already.

There had been some touching moments that Saturday when they had driven to Faith Hospital. It had been against her mother's wishes; however, she had not stopped them from going. Tyler's room had been filled with tears and hugs that day. She had told Tyler she had forgiven him, and although he seemed relieved that she had, he still couldn't understand how that was possible. She and Alayna had tried to explain to him about the love and forgiveness of God before they left, but he had not been too receptive. Besides, she could tell he had not yet forgiven himself.

Returning to her previous thoughts, she concluded she did not know anyone who was actually sick. So what was the Lord trying to say to her? *There's one more person*, Addison heard the Holy Spirit say.

"I don't know anyone else," she whispered. By now, the cheerleaders were cheering so loudly not even Alayna sitting next to her heard her speak. Then it hit her like a Jethro Gibbs smack on the back of the head. She could have sworn her heart skipped a few beats.

"Not Karlie Adams!" she said louder than she intended.

"What?" Alayna asked, leaning closer to hear her.

Addison shook her head. "Nothing!" she shouted over the deafening noise.

Putting her silver whistle to her lips, Coach Redmond finally stood and faced the noisy cheerleaders. She blew as hard as she could, causing everyone to place their hands over their ears. Even the bus driver winced and placed a hand over one of his ears. The shrill sound of the whistle was worse than the noise the cheerleaders were making, but it did get everyone's attention.

"Quiet please! Save your voices for the game," Coach Redmond said as she sat again and buckled her seat belt. She began leafing through the leather-bound book of cheers as she shoved the whistle hanging from the chain around her neck into the top of her jacket.

Addison heard the low drone of voices as the bus merged onto Interstate 85. The long ride to Ellenton was relatively quiet. If the squad even started to get a little loud, Coach Redmond would give a quick blow of the whistle, cuing them to quiet down. It took fifty minutes from the time the bus pulled onto the interstate until they pulled into the parking lot of Ellenton High.

Addison felt the butterflies in her stomach multiply as the large crowd of fans from both teams piled into the stadium. Along with the rest of the squad, she made her way quickly to the end field where Coach Redmond started them on warm-up exercises and stretches. A few minutes later, the stadium was packed on both the home and visitor sides.

Addison and Alayna barely heard someone calling their names. It was their moms, Ayson, Callaway, and Caleb. Following not far behind were Pastor Bryce and Maggie. Every one of them was waving excitedly as they made their way to the concrete bleachers. Addison and Alayna waved and giggled when they saw Shannon reach and give Caleb's red hair a quick tousle. Both girls jumped when coach blew her whistle.

"Three minutes, girls!"

Three more minutes, and they would be running onto the field followed by their beloved Wildcats.

The Ellenton Gators' cheerleaders lined up on the opposite side of the field. The green-and-yellow pom-poms were waving furiously over their heads as they prepared to cheer their Gators onto the field. The noise intensified as the Gators' fans stood and roared as the football team ran onto the field between two rows of cheerleaders as the Ellenton band played their fight song.

Next it was time for the Wildcats to be led onto the field by the Wildcats' cheerleaders. Addison wished they had made two rows for the football team to pass between like the Ellenton cheerleaders, but leading the Wildcats onto the field was the way ICHS had always done it. Addison stood to the side. There was no way she would be able to run onto the field in front of the team without being trampled. To her surprise, she was lifted into the air. Jonah Medley and Alan Stellar had lifted her onto Trevor's shoulders. The cheerleaders and Trevor ran onto the field. The Wildcats' fans let out a loud roar, along with ear-splitting whistles as the Iron City band struck up their team's fight song. Addison held on tightly to Trevor with one hand. In the other hand, she shook black-and-gold pom-poms over her head as she cheered for the ICHS Wildcats following behind. Reaching their side of the field, Maddie and Alayna helped Trevor lower her from his shoulders.

"Thanks, Trevor," she said as he gave Alayna a wink and ran to join his teammates.

Addison turned to Maddie.

"Thank you," she said as Maddie reached and gave her a quick hug.

"Anytime," Maddie said. "I'm glad you're part of our squad again."

The fans on both sides of the field stood for the national anthem and for a moment of student-led prayer for the safety of both teams and for sportsmanship to be displayed between the two teams.

Cheers went up again as the announcers started naming the Gators' cheerleaders as they cut cartwheel after cartwheel from one end of their lineup to the other. More roars came from the crowd as the names of the Gators' starting lineup were called.

Next it was time for the Wildcats' cheerleaders to be announced. Alayna and her teammates cut flips head over heels from one end of the lineup to the other as their names were called, and the fans stood cheering. When it was Addison's turn to be announced, she threw her pom-poms over her head and took off running as fast as she could. Not only were the Wildcats' fans standing and cheering, but the Gators' fans stood and cheered as well. Apparently, news of her ordeal had spread to the opposing team. Chalk one up for social media. The roars going up were almost deafening. She was so touched by the Ellenton fans' kind gesture she turned and gave them a wave of her pom-poms. It took a while for the crowd to settle; then they announced the Wildcats' starting lineup as more roars, whistles, and claps went up.

By the end of the 17–14 game, Addison was totally exhausted; and fortunately for her, the dream had been just a dream. The Wildcats had fought hard and fierce in overtime, but it had been the Ellenton Gators who had taken home the championship trophy in the end. It had been a tough loss for the Wildcats and their fans. The Wildcats seniors had played their last football game for Iron City High, and the senior cheerleaders had cheered their last high school football game. It was an emotional time for all involved, not so much for the loss but for a chapter closed in their lives. Even the rough and tough senior football players were unashamedly shedding a few tears.

Addison and Alayna would love to have ridden back with their parents, but it was school policy that they ride back on the activity bus. Every one of the cheerleaders was so exhausted Coach Redmond didn't have to blow her prized silver whistle even once. Most everyone slept, except for Addison and a couple other cheerleaders. She tried to sleep, but her mind kept going back to what she felt the Lord had spoken to her earlier; plus, Alayna had leaned over on her shoulder, making her a little uncomfortable. She started to wake Alayna, but hated to, so she decided to think on other things and not think so much about how uncomfortable she was.

Had the Holy Spirit really told her to visit Karlie in the hospital? Wasn't it enough she was praying for Karlie and trying to forgive her? She kept trying to tell herself she had not heard the Holy Spirit correctly, but deep inside, she knew she had heard Him loud and clear. She also knew why the Holy Spirit was directing her to go. It wasn't so much for Karlie as it was for her. She knew God wanted to get rid of any pride she had involving Karlie. To visit Karlie and be nice to her would definitely mean swallowing her pride. She could feel herself wanting to gloat over the fact that Karlie hadn't been able to cheer in the last football game of her high school career. She didn't want to feel that way, but a part of her couldn't help it. Karlie had been so mean to her. Even so, it was wrong, and she had really had to struggle with that lately. She asked for forgiveness for feeling that way and asked for God's help in dealing with those feelings. She would deal with the Karlie issue later.

She let her mind drift to Wyatt Kingsley and wondered why he had not responded to her text letting him know about the Wildcats' heartbreaking defeat. She had just given into sleep when the driver hit a deep pot-hole, jarring most everyone awake, including Alayna. It was just as well since they were only about fifteen minutes from the school. Addison glanced at her watch: it was almost 12:15 a.m. No wonder Wyatt hadn't answered her text. It had been a little after eleven when she had texted him. Alayna rubbed her eyes.

"Are we home yet?"

"Almost. We've got about another fifteen minutes."

Alayna leaned her head on Addison's shoulder again. "Wake me when we get there," she said, yawning and closing her eyes.

Fifteen minutes later, the bus pulled into the parking lot of Iron City High. The football team had not yet arrived, but Alayna wanted to stay and see Trevor before leaving. Addison threw her duffle bag in the back seat of the car and settled down in the front passenger seat. Leaning the seat back, she was about to tell Alayna to wake her later when she heard the bus carrying the football team pull into the graveled parking lot. Getting out of the car, Alayna made her way toward the bus parked in front of the "Wildcat Den" entrance located under the gymnasium.

Cheers and yells reverberated from the waiting parents and football fans as the players exited the bus one by one, each with their heads hung low and their shoulders slumped in defeat. It had been a tough loss. and all the cheering in the world would not help them feel better at the moment. She saw Trevor slowly making his way toward Alayna.

Addison glanced at her watch again. It was getting late even for a night owl. She leaned her head back and closed her eyes. If she didn't get home soon, her mother would begin to worry.

Five minutes later, Alayna opened the door and slid into the driver's seat. Addison opened her eyes and raised the back of the seat.

"How's Trevor doing?"

"A little down, but give him a couple of days, and he'll be back to his old self," Alayna said as she put the key in the ignition and turned the switch.

Fifteen minutes later, Alayna pulled into Addison's driveway. They mumbled their goodbyes as Addison grabbed her duffle bag and closed the door. Her friend drove off and tooted her horn once as she guided the car onto the dark highway. The porch light had been turned on, causing little flying insects to gather around the white light. She unlocked the door and softly closed it behind her. She wasn't surprised to see her mother waiting. Wrapped snuggly in a Wildcats throw with her feet tucked under her in the family's favorite chair, her mother looked up from the book she was reading.

"I thought you would be home before now," she said as she straightened her legs and set her feet on the floor.

"Alayna wanted to wait and see Trevor before leaving," Addison said as she dropped her bag on the floor then plopped beside her mother. She leaned her head on her mother's shoulder. "I'm so tired." She yawned.

"I bet you are." Kyndal reached and removed the gold-and-black ribbons and elastic band from her daughter's hair, allowing the long straight hair to flow freely over her daughter's shoulders. "Sweetheart, you did great tonight," she said as she ran her hands through her daughter's hair, smoothing out a few tangles.

"Thanks, Mom, but could we wait and talk tomorrow?" she asked as she yawned again, causing her mother to yawn as well.

"Sure thing," she said as they both eased their way out of the oversized chair. Addison walked wearily up the stairs while her mother performed her nightly ritual of making sure every light was off and all doors were locked.

CHAPTER 29

MAKING AMENDS

It was late when Addison woke the next morning. She checked her phone and read Wyatt's text. *Tough break*, he had texted earlier regarding her message of the Wildcats' loss. *Call me when you get up*. The inviting aroma of breakfast filled the air as she made her way toward the kitchen. Her mother was talking to someone on the hall phone.

"I know, Shannon," she heard her mother say. Addison wasn't sure, but she suspected their conversation had something to do with Noah.

She swung the kitchen door open. She was so hungry and used to eating way before now. Reaching for a biscuit, she broke off a piece and gave it to Chip. He gulped it down in one swallow and then sat next to her foot, looking at her as if to say, *More, please!* Who could resist those big brown puppy eyes? Chip did his usual happy dance when he saw her reach and break off another piece of biscuit before tossing it his way. She wondered why there was only one plate on the table instead of two, until it occurred to her that Ayson and his two friends were meeting at the church early to practice for tomorrow's church service.

Pouring herself a glass of cold milk, she thought about when she would visit Karlie in the hospital, not that she really wanted to. Her mother came through the door just as she swallowed her last bite of cantaloupe.

"Good morning, sweetheart," her mother said as she made her way to the coffeepot.

"Morning, Mom," she answered as she set down her glass. I might as well get this over with, Addison thought.

After Kyndal took a seat at the table, Addison shared with her how she was feeling led to go to the hospital to see Karlie. Being familiar with the animosity between the two, her mother tried to reason with her.

"Addison, you know Karlie is not going to want you there. Why put yourself through her abuse?" Kyndal held the cup of steamy hot coffee to her lips and blew. "You know she's only going to put you down as usual."

Addison let out a long sigh. "Because, I've got to be obedient to what I believe the Lord is telling me to do," Addison said as she watched her mother give an eye roll. "Mom, can I please borrow the car?"

Her mother purposely ignored the question. "Why would the Lord tell you to go visit someone who couldn't care less whether or not you visit them, and probably prefers you didn't?"

Addison shrugged as she rose from the table. "I just know this is something I have to do. Please, Mom. Let me do this."

"First, Isaac, then Tyler, now Karlie," her mother said. "I just don't understand you." She let out an exasperated sigh. "The keys are in my purse," she finally added with a slight edge to her tone.

"Thanks, Mom," Addison said as she bent and gave her mother a kiss on the cheek.

Kyndal didn't understand, but she knew when Addison had her mind set on doing something, it was hard to talk her out of it, especially if she felt it was something the Lord wanted her to do.

"I'm going upstairs to get ready," Addison said as she placed her dirty dishes in the sink. "I'll be home before dinner."

Kyndal sat blowing and staring into her cup of hot coffee as her thoughts turned to Noah Steelman.

* * * * *

Addison called Wyatt before leaving for the hospital. They talked briefly about the game then she asked him to say a prayer for her as she was going to see Karlie. It wasn't long before she was headed toward the hospital and praying silently for God to help her. She parked the car as close to the hospital as possible. All the handicapped spaces were taken, but fortunately, the rest of the parking lot wasn't too full, so she was able to park close to the building. Entering the blue-and-black mingled carpeted lobby, she stopped at the information desk to inquire of Karlie's room number.

She stood outside the door of room 226 for a good five minutes before she finally summoned enough courage to knock on the partially closed door. She felt her heart racing, and the palms of her hands were beginning to sweat as she knocked on the door.

"Come in," she heard Karlie say.

Taking a deep breath, Addison opened the door and entered the room to find Karlie sitting in bed with the head of her bed raised. She was texting someone when she looked up and saw Addison. Addison could see the surprise on Karlie's face as she slowly made her way to the foot of the hospital bed.

Now she knew how Tyler must have felt those many weeks ago when he had attempted to visit her in the hospital. At least Karlie hadn't thrown a book at her, not yet anyway.

Karlie didn't say a word but continued to text. After a few seconds, she finished texting and laid her phone on the table next to her bed. She still didn't acknowledge her but instead just lay in bed, staring at Addison.

"May I sit down?" Addison asked, nodding toward the chair at the foot of the bed.

Karlie gave a light shrug. "Whatever," she said as she looked stoically at Addison.

Addison had not felt this uncomfortable in a long time as she inched toward the mauve-colored chair and sat down. She desperately wanted to run as fast as she could from the room, but it was too late. Besides, her legs felt like rubber bands, even her artificial one. She was so nervous she almost wished one of the nurses would come in and tell her she had to leave for one reason or another.

Finally, Karlie spoke. "Why are you here, Addison McNeely? Did you come to gloat because I didn't get to cheer in my final game as a senior, and you did?" she asked, showing very little emotion.

"No, I, uh…just…thought I would come by and see how you were doing," she answered, shifting uncomfortably in her chair. Her mouth and throat were so dry she felt her tongue was starting to stick to the roof of her mouth. The dryness made her cough. She placed her hand over her mouth and coughed for what seemed an eternity. Karlie rolled her eyes and nodded toward the pitcher of water next to her bed. Addison grabbed a paper cup and filled it halfway with water. She drank the cool water and was finally able to compose herself. She could have sworn she saw a slight smile, a very slight smile, play across Karlie's face. Maybe it was more of a smirk. But if it was a smile, she was sure it was because Karlie could see how uncomfortable she felt and was enjoying it to the max.

"Why?" she finally spoke with a tone of irritation.

"Why what?" Addison asked, already forgetting the conversation that had taken place prior to her coughing spell.

Karlie rolled her eyes again. "I mean," she said with a little more irritation, "why do you want to see how I am doing?"

"Karlie, can't we just put things behind us?" Addison asked in an exasperated voice. "Look, if you don't want to be friends, that's okay, but we ought to at least be civil to each other." She was so wishing she was anywhere but in this hospital room with Karlie.

"Why?" she asked again.

What was it with all the whys? Karlie sounded like a little two or three-year-old child with all the whys. Addison decided to turn the table. "Why not?"

"Because I don't like you, that's why not," she said with a slight smirk.

"Got to give you one for honesty," Addison said with a halfway smile. Did Karlie almost smile? Addison slid further back in the chair. "That day in the restroom at school, you told me I thought I was better than you, but that's not true. I don't think I'm better than anyone," she said, trying to make Karlie understand.

"Maybe you don't feel that way now," she said, "now that you're only a half person and a cripple." This time, she gave one of those irritatingly full-blown Karlie smirks, no doubt about it.

Addison felt her temper starting to get the best of her. *Love your enemies*, she heard the Holy Spirit say. *Bless them and do good to them.* It was all she could do, but with the help of the Holy Spirit, she was able to hold her tongue.

Addison stood and looked Karlie directly in the eyes. "Karlie, if I've done anything to offend you I'm asking you to forgive me. I'm going to pray and ask God to completely restore your health, and if there is anything you need, let me know."

She noticed the smirk on Karlie's face begin to fade. Karlie was silent as Addison made her way to the door. Placing her hand on the knob, she turned and smiled into the confused face of her enemy. "Get well soon, Karlie." Karlie turned away from Addison as she pulled the door open and then closed it gently behind her.

Glancing at her watch, Addison noted she had spent a little over twenty minutes with Karlie, but it felt much longer. She was glad she had obeyed the Holy Spirit and visited Karlie, but she was glad the visit was over.

During lunch, she told her mother about the visit.

"I really don't see what was accomplished," her mother said, taking a bite of her sandwich.

"I'm not sure if anything was accomplished either, but I obeyed the Holy Spirit. That's what's important. Now the rest is up to Him."

Addison heard a low grunt as her mother poured herself another glass of iced tea. They ate in silence for the remainder of the meal until Addison excused herself and made her way upstairs.

The past few weeks of school had flown by. Three more days, and they would be out for Christmas break. She was so ready. She had better call Wyatt. She was eager to tell him about her visit with Karlie. Why was it, she thought, did she still want to share every detail of her life with Wyatt Kingsley when he had made it perfectly clear he only wanted to be friends? She was hopelessly in love with him—that was why.

* * * * *

The next three days of school were uneventful. The teachers seemed to have their mind on the upcoming holiday as well. Work in the classroom was light, and no one was giving homework. Karlie had been discharged from the hospital the day of Addison's visit, but she would not be returning to school until after Christmas.

Lately, Addison had noticed her mother's sad countenance as she cleaned house. Heartbroken and a little angry, she had stopped her melodic singing, and the sparkle in her mother's eyes had faded. Addison had tried on several occasions to talk to her mother about Noah, knowing he was the reason for the change, but she had refused to open up about her feelings. Earlier when Ayson asked why Noah wasn't coming around anymore, her mother had all but brushed him off.

"We've decided to take a little break for a while," she had told him.

Of course, Ayson wasn't satisfied with that answer.

"Why?" he asked.

Her mother had put him off further by saying it was a grown up thing, and both had left it at that. Addison tried to think of something less depressing like the upcoming holiday. Christmas was a busy time of year, and unlike most people, she was one of those who loved all the hustle and bustle of the season. A couple of days earlier, she and Alayna had fought through the crowds and finally finished their shopping.

Both had taken part-time seasonal jobs on the weekends over the last three weeks at one of the local department stores to earn a little cash for Christmas. Their only job was to wrap gifts, which she was thankful for, given her amputation. At least she could sit while wrapping gifts.

Between her work and Wyatt's work, they had hardly seen or spoken to each other except when she saw him at church on Sunday night. On the day of her last therapy session, she could have sworn she had seen some disappointment in Wyatt's face that she had finally been discharged due to meeting her goals, but then again, it was probably her imagination.

Now she sat on the edge of the bed staring at the presents she had carefully chosen for her family and friends. She knew Ayson would like the computer game she had bought; after all, he had dropped enough hints over the past few weeks. She wasn't sure about her mother. If she thought about it too long, she would end up returning half of what she had bought. I can be so indecisive sometimes, she thought as she reached and grabbed a roll of shiny red foil wrapping paper and scissors. She had picked out a ruby necklace with matching earrings for her mother. Of course, they weren't real rubies; she couldn't afford that. Carefully she cut and folded the paper over the boxes. Next she reached for the green foil paper lying next to her scissors. Green was Alayna's favorite color, so she would have her present wrapped in green.

Addison thumbed through the writing journal she had bought for her best friend. Laying the lavender-colored journal aside, she picked up the next gift she had bought for Alayna. It was a picture of them in a silver "Best Friends Forever" frame. The copied photo had been taken a few years earlier at Myrtle Beach when their families had vacationed together the summer before she and Alayna entered seventh grade. It was one of the best vacations Addison could remember having. She smiled as she looked at the two of them with their arms around one another with big goofy smiles on their faces. The blue-green ocean and blue sky with its billowing white clouds in the background almost appeared to meet and become as one, kind of like the two best friends. Alayna had always felt more like a sister than a best friend.

As she stared at the picture, she could almost hear the caw of the seagulls and smell and taste the salty air of the ocean spray. She wiped away the lone tear running down the right side of her face as she remembered her dad being the one to snap the picture.

"Say cheese!" he had told them as they posed for the camera.

"Cheese!" they yelled simultaneously as her dad snapped the picture, capturing a moment in time that would forever be in her heart.

"I'm never going to get done with my wrapping if I don't stop reminiscing," she said aloud. She smiled as she touched the photo one last time before carefully wrapping it and placing the box beside her. She had just finished wrapping the last gift when her cell phone rang. She was surprised to see it was Wyatt.

"Did you hear about Karlie?" he asked with excitement in his voice.

"No, I haven't. What about her?" Addison wondered what in the world could be going on with Karlie now.

"She gave her heart to the Lord."

"You're kidding me!" Addison was glad she was sitting down. "Do you know any details?"

"According to what she posted on social media, Tyler and Isaac came to visit her after she came home from the hospital. Anyway, Tyler started testifying of how God had spared his life and that he had invited Jesus into his heart. Between the testimonies of the two of them, she made the decision to give her heart to the Lord."

Addison was barely able to comprehend what she was hearing. "You mean Karlie? Karlie got saved?"

"Yep, and that's not all," Wyatt continued. "She mentioned how you had come to see her in the hospital even though she had bullied you horribly at school."

Addison was speechless. All she could think about was how she had recently been saved, followed by Ayson, Isaac, Tyler and now Karlie.

"It's spreading like wildfire!" she exclaimed.

"Seems that way," Wyatt said. "But I can't talk any longer. Gotta get back to work."

They said their goodbyes. She immediately phoned Alayna and gave her the news.

"I don't believe it!" Alayna exclaimed.

"Believe it!" Addison said, excited about the news.

The following Sunday, Karlie Adams walked down the aisle of New Haven and made a public profession of faith. She also wished to join the church, as did Tyler and Isaac. Karlie stood next to Tyler and Isaac as the congregation lined up to offer them the right hand of fellowship. When Addison came to her and reached to shake her hand, Karlie grabbed her and pulled her toward her. She hugged her as hard as she could.

"I'm so sorry," she told Addison, still clinging to her.

"It's okay," Addison told her.

She let go of Addison and looked at her. "Please say you forgive me, Addison," she said with an almost pleading look in her eyes.

"Yes, I forgive you, Karlie. Now I need to ask for your forgiveness."

"But there's nothing to forgive," she said, not understanding.

"Oh yes, there is. You wouldn't believe the thoughts I have had toward you. I didn't want to have bad thoughts, but I did."

Karlie smiled. "Then I guess we'll just have to forgive each other."

Addison returned the smile as they hugged again.

"Friends?" asked Karlie.

"Friends," replied Addison.

After church, Karlie asked to speak to Addison in private.

"I just wanted to let you know why I acted the way I did toward you in school. I mean, I hate to admit it, but I was jealous."

Addison was truly surprised. "I don't understand, Karlie. You are one of the most beautiful girls in school."

Karlie gave a self-conscious smile. "Thanks, but there's more than just beauty on the outside. I mean, you're beautiful too, Addison, but more importantly, you're beautiful on the inside. Everyone likes you, and that made me jealous."

Addison stood looking at Karlie, not knowing quite how to respond. Finally, she responded by saying the only thing that came to mind. "I'm sorry, Karlie. I had no idea."

Karlie reached and hugged her. "There's nothing to be sorry for. I just wanted you to know why I behaved the way I did and to once again say I'm sorry. I'm glad we can be friends now," she said, releasing Addison from the hug.

"Me too," said Addison as they locked arms and made their way to the others who were waiting.

That night, Michael and Jennifer Scobie added one more person to their youth group. Addison thought about something she had heard years ago. She looked at Alayna as they each slid into the seat of Alayna's car.

"You know something, Alayna?" she asked.

"What?" asked Alayna as she reached for the seatbelt and strapped it across her chest.

"I was just thinking. If every Christian in the world could reach just one person and lead them to Christ, revival really would break out."

Before pulling onto the main highway, Alayna stopped and looked thoughtfully at Addison. "Yeah, I guess it would. That's something to really think about."

CHAPTER 30

THE LETTER

The Christmas holiday had come and gone as well as just about the whole school year. Life was changing for Addison and her friends. In a little over four months, she and her classmates would be graduating from ICHS. She would miss high school but was looking forward to college. She had finally gotten another car, a blue Honda, and was grateful for that small miracle. Since Alayna and Trevor were still seeing each other, she wasn't seeing quite as much of her best friend as she used to, but Addison understood. Times change, circumstances change, people change.

The one thing that had not changed, however, was her love for Wyatt, who had been coming to New Haven for a while now. She saw him every Wednesday and Sunday, and they spoke often. At church events, he always seemed to make his way over to her, and they would have a great time fellowshipping with each other. On occasion, the two of them would stand around and talk after church, sometimes for an hour after everyone else had left. Addison had noticed on several occasions that Wyatt had started to say something to her, but then changed his mind. At least three different times she had questioned him as to what he had wanted to say.

"Never mind, I'll tell you later," he would always answer.

Tonight was one of those moments. The two church vans had just pulled into the church parking lot after returning from a youth retreat over the weekend. Wyatt had agreed to drive one of the vans while Michael Scobie drove the other. She had made a point to ride on the one Pastor Scobie had driven. The more she fell in love with Wyatt, the harder it was to be around him knowing the love wasn't returned. It was getting much harder to be just friends. As she exited the van, Wyatt approached her and asked if she would like to grab a bite of dessert at one of the local restaurants. She thought it a bit unusual as they usually just hung out at the church afterward, but she agreed.

"How fickle can you be?" she said softly to herself as she headed for the little blue Honda. "You wouldn't ride the van in order to avoid him and then you agree to meet him for dessert!"

Before pulling onto the highway, she called her mother to let her know of her plans and that Maggie would drop Ayson off. "That's fine, but don't stay out late," her mother told her.

Addison promised to be home by ten o'clock, being the next day was a school day.

Having reached her destination before Wyatt, she waited in the car with the motor running and the heater on until she finally saw him pull in. The cold midthirties weather was probably why Wyatt had wanted to meet inside the restaurant instead of staying at the church with the cars running to stay warm.

"Duh, ya think!" Addison said aloud, rolling her eyes at her own self as she exited the car and joined Wyatt. They hurried into the restaurant, leaving a trail of white clouds as their warm breath hit the damp and cold night air.

The two welcomed the warmth inside the restaurant as they ordered and slid into a booth opposite each other. Both had the strawberry cheesecake and coffee. They mostly talked about the winter retreat and how well Alayna and Trevor seemed to be getting along.

"Why didn't you ride my van?" he asked after they had finished their dessert.

"Just didn't." She shrugged. She was glad he didn't ask anything further. He was starting to shift uncomfortably in his seat. She knew what was coming. Sure enough, he cleared his throat and told her he needed to tell her something.

"Okay, what do you need to tell me?" She knew what else was coming.

"You know, it's getting late," he said, glancing at his watch. "We'll talk later." Getting up from the table, he started for the door as she followed. The air had turned even colder as they stood outside shivering. "Brrrr!" he said, blowing warm air into his hands before shoving them into his coat pocket. "Well, see you Wednesday," he said.

"Sure," she said, disappointed and wondering what he had wanted to tell her. She turned to walk toward the car, but took only a few steps before stopping and turning back to face him. "No, Wyatt Kingsley!"

Wyatt had started to walk away as well, but upon hearing her words, he stopped and turned. Addison noticed the puzzled look on his face. She was not going to let up. Not this time. She had wondered for months about what it was that he wanted to tell her. There were times she felt Wyatt liked her as more than just a friend, but she didn't know for sure. Maybe he did love her, or maybe he was trying to tell her he would be moving away soon—whatever it was, tonight she was not letting him off easy.

"Wyatt Kingsley, we're not leaving here until you tell me what it is you have been trying to tell me for the past few months."

"Seriously?" he asked. "Do you know how cold it is out here?"

"Yes, I do, so you had better talk fast!"

Wyatt saw the determination in her face. He reached and pulled her away from in front of the door as a couple hurriedly approached, trying to get inside the warm restaurant.

"Addison, couldn't we just talk about it some other time?" He still had her by the arm and tried to guide her toward her car, but she pulled away and stared straight into his eyes.

"No, we will talk about it now!" she said defiantly.

He looked deep into her determined eyes. He could not keep it to himself any longer. "Addison McNeely, I...I love you."

For a few seconds, neither could tear their eyes away from each other. She almost pinched herself to see if she was dreaming.

"I love you too Wyatt Kingsley," she said softly as they held each other close. Neither seemed to notice the cold anymore.

* * * * *

Of course, Addison couldn't wait to tell her best friend. Alayna was elated about the news and had already begun planning their double dates. Her mother was equally excited about the news, and Ayson—well, Ayson was Ayson. Upon hearing the news, he said one simple word: "Cool."

Addison felt as though her head was spinning. She had finally gotten her permanent leg a month earlier, and now she was getting ready for graduation, then college—and now Wyatt was in her life as more than just a friend. Life was good, but she would be lying if she said she didn't have days that she would look at her leg and regret the day she went to that party. But if there was one thing she had learned, it was to shake off the regret as soon as it came. She could not let a past mistake or regret control her future. She had also learned to lean on Jesus, without whom she would not have been able to get to this point in her life. She had had many disappointments and knew she would have more, but she also knew she would have Jesus by her side—always. Yes, God was good; and unbeknownst to her, she would soon see His hand move in the life of her family once again.

* * * * *

The past few months had been extremely emotional for Kyndal. Addison's graduation had come and gone, and soon her daughter would be attending college. She was glad Addison had chosen to attend the local college, but could hardly believe her little girl was now a young woman getting ready to start a new chapter in her life. Where had the years gone? Even Ayson was growing up too fast, but she supposed all parents felt this way about their children and their fleeting childhood.

She placed her hands on her hips and looked at the overcrowded closet she was about to tackle. Even though it was a walk-in closet, there was still not enough room. Over the past few years, she had continued to pile things into the closet, but had never taken anything out. Josh's clothes still hung on the left side of the closet and hordes of boxes were stacked upon the shelves. She couldn't even remember what was in half of them. It had been five years now since his death, and she had finally resolved herself to the fact that she needed to clean out his stuff, especially the clothes. She knew there were people who could use them. She decided to tackle the boxes first. As she stepped on the metal footstool and reached for what looked like a shoebox, she accidently knocked off something beside the box. She heard it fall to the floor beneath her. Holding the shoebox, she carefully stepped off the stool. She placed the box on the floor and sat next to the item that had fallen. It was her husband's Bible. She remembered placing the Bible on the top shelf a few days after his death and vowing never to open it. But it lay open now, and there was an envelope in it. Oddly, the envelope was addressed to God. She picked up the envelope and started to place it back in the Bible, but curiosity got the best of her. Why would Josh be writing a letter to God? she thought as she sat on the closet floor. Slowly she reached in and pulled out the letter. Tears began to fill her eyes seeing the familiar sight of her husband's handwriting. She blinked tightly to clear her eyes and began to read.

Dear God,

I'm certain You know what this prayer is about. Really, Lord, I'm not sure why I am writing my prayer in letter form, but it is just something I feel led to do. As You know, I couldn't ask for a better wife and mother than Kyndal. You truly blessed us when You allowed her to be a part of our lives. She's funny and smart and loving, everything a man and his children could ask for. But, Lord, the god of this world has blinded her. Please let her come to understand that greater love has no one than this, than to lay down one's life

278

for his friends. Reveal to her through Your sweet Holy Spirit that You are her friend and You loved her enough to lay down Your life for her. Lord, I know I don't have many more days to be with my precious family, and I would gladly lay down my life for them. I love them that much, but it is not my blood that can save. Only Your blood can do that, and there is no other name under heaven by which we must be saved. Lord, I'm not giving up on Kyndal, and I know You won't either. Let her feel the love You have for her. Wrap Your loving arms around my precious wife and let her know You will always be with her. Help her to come to understand that You will never leave her nor forsake her or our children. Help her to come to know you as her Lord and Savior.

When this earth as we know it has passed, Lord, I want to see my beautiful wife again, but I can only do that if she accepts you as her Savior. Kyndal needs You, Lord, just as I do. She just doesn't know it yet. Help her to see that need, Lord. Open her heart to You. I love You, Lord, and please help Kyndal to love You too. Lord, I pray this prayer for my precious children as well. Take care of my family, Lord. I know You will. In Jesus's name, I pray, amen.

Kyndal wiped away the tears and gently folded the letter, holding it close to her heart. Something was happening. She finally understood what Josh and her children had been trying to tell her. Burying her hands in her face, she asked the Lord for forgiveness. She asked him to change her and to be the Lord of her life. She had never felt so free, so happy. The heaviness and bitterness that had plagued her for years had lifted. She had heard people say that when they gave their heart to God, it felt as though they were engulfed in liquid love. Until today, she had never understood that. Tears were still flowing, but now they were tears of joy as she smiled and lifted her hands toward heaven. She knew her life would never be the same. She also knew in her heart, at this moment, Josh McNeely was rejoicing in the presence of the angels.

CHAPTER 31

JESUS CALLING

Addison looked at the faces of the students she had been addressing. She had definitely gotten their attention, or should she say the Holy Spirit had. The students were quiet as she bent and picked up the artificial leg from the gymnasium floor and reattached it to her stump. Standing, she smoothed her pant leg and made her way to the podium as all eyes followed her.

"So now you've heard my testimony," she said as she took a moment to swallow the now lukewarm water next to the podium. "I pray after today that each one of you will think twice before drinking alcohol and especially drinking while driving. But I also don't want to leave here today without giving you an opportunity to accept Jesus as your Savior. God does not want any of us to perish." She kept looking into the faces of the students. She could feel the Spirit of the Lord moving as she asked Pastor Bryce to give the invitation.

She watched as numerous students left their seats and came to stand in front of the podium. Some chose to kneel; most were crying. She still felt there were more who needed to come and give their hearts to the Lord. She saw some of the students in the bleachers looking at their watches; some were beginning to fidget in their seats.

"God says in Second Corinthians that today is the day of salvation," Pastor Bryce was saying. "None of us are promised tomorrow."

Addison and Pastor Bryce watched as a few more students responded. There were probably a hundred or more students who had responded, but she still felt there were more who needed to respond to the invitation. She felt the Holy Spirit inside her grieve as she watched some of the students laughing and talking as other students prayed and asked God for forgiveness and repeated the sinner's prayer. She could hardly believe their disrespect and indifference to the precious moving of the Holy Spirit. She watched as two students started down the bleachers before another student with blue-spiked hair pulled them back into their seat.

"Surely you don't believe all this Jesus stuff," the boy with the blue hair yelled as one of the young men stood up again and made his way to the gym floor to join Pastor Bryce. "Jesus freak!" he yelled as he broke out in laughter.

As the young man made his way to the gym floor, he turned and motioned for the other young man who had started to come with him earlier. "Come on, Tommy!" he yelled.

Addison saw Tommy start to get up and rejoin his friend until the young man with the blue hair said something to him and laughed. Tommy looked at his friend then dropped his head. Tommy's friend waited a few seconds then continued making his way to the front of the podium. Pastor Bryce finished praying with the students who had gathered on the gym floor.

Addison stepped again to the podium. She was thankful for the many souls that had been won today, but she felt there were still more that needed to come. Many of the students were still standing in the middle of the gym. She listened as she heard them pray and weep for family and friends.

"Don't let anyone keep you from coming to the Lord today," she said as she looked toward the young man who had started to come forward. He saw her look his way and hung his head again. She began to cry as she looked around the gymnasium. Her heart was heavy. "Today Jesus is calling you to make the decision to follow Him. He loves you. Don't turn Him away," she pleaded. "Remember," Addison said as she gave one last plea to those who needed to repent, "no one is promised tomorrow. The Lord could come back this very day."

A handful of students responded by making their way to Pastor Bryce, but Tommy wasn't one of them. Two days later, she heard Tommy was dead. He had been killed by a hit-and-run driver while riding his bike.

EPILOGUE

Today, just four weeks after the FCA meeting, Addison and Alayna had put on their black cap and gown and walked across the stage of Williamston College. Later, their two families, along with Wyatt, were meeting at Wilson's Steakhouse to celebrate the graduates' accomplishments. It had already been an exhausting day, and the day wasn't over. Addison held her left hand out and smiled as she admired her 1-carat princess solitaire engagement ring. She had one more big event coming up: her wedding. It had been a hectic few weeks between college graduation and wedding planning, but it was all beginning to fall into place. She kicked off her shoes and threw her cap and gown on the sofa, then went and sank into the love seat. She thought about her friends and how things had changed since high school and her accident. Except for Alayna and her, most of her friends had gone their separate ways. She had received a degree in counseling and guidance and already had a job lined up at Carolina Middle School as a guidance counselor starting in the fall of the upcoming school year. She and Wyatt, who was now a physical therapist, would be getting married in June.

Two years ago, her mother and Noah had finally tied the knot, and all three of them had moved into Noah's four-bedroom farmhouse. It was located in the country in a picturesque setting of large oak trees and flowers. Addison's favorite part of the landscape was the large oval pond surrounded by weeping willow trees which could be viewed from the wrap around porch. On warm breezy days, it seemed as if the willow trees were waving as they gently swayed in the wind as she sat on the porch soaking up the surrounding beauty. She would miss this place once she was married. However, last year Wyatt had bought her old homeplace, and that was where she and Wyatt would be living. Over the past year, they had tried to do some updates to the house, but it had been slow going. Her mother had even left the furniture, including the floral monstrosity. After the wedding, Addison was looking forward to moving in and giving the home a woman's touch. Wyatt had definitely not been one for decorating.

Alayna had graduated from the nursing program and was working at the local hospital as a tech until she could take the state board. After passing the boards, she would be transferring permanently to the ER as an RN. She and Trevor, however, were no longer together. Trevor had moved away from the small town of Iron City to Charleston, South Carolina, to pursue a career in dentistry. The long distance between them had been hard on their relationship. The breakup had been mutual with no animosity, and they remained good friends, still keeping in touch, mainly through social media. Alayna had recently met a local police officer named Jonathan Silvers. They had met one night when Jonathan brought a prisoner into the ER for medical assistance. Jonathan was a Christian and attended Living Word Baptist Church in Indianville. Alayna had visited Living Word a few times, and Jonathan occasionally visited New Haven. Alayna and Jonathan appeared to really hit it off, and Addison had the feeling the relationship might get pretty serious. If it did, there was a good possibility Shannon Thomas could end up with a little redheaded, blue-eyed, freckled-faced grandson if he ended up looking like his father.

As life would have it, Beckah Joy Roth's family had moved to Charleston as well. The Roths had moved closer to Beckah Joy's grandmother, who was in the early stages of Alzheimer's. Beckah Joy also had an uncle who pastored a small church in the city. A few months ago, Trevor had started attending the church. It was then that he learned of the Roths having moved to Charleston. He and Beckah Joy started dating shortly after and seemed very happy together. She was studying elementary education and would be graduating college within the next two days.

Giving a long exhausted sigh and rubbing Chip, who had curled up next to her, Addison thought about the rest of her friends and family. Isaac Darnell and Karlie Adams fell in love and married after Isaac completed college with a degree in religion. Karlie became a dental hygienist. Six months ago, they felt the Lord calling them to the mission fields, and they moved to Africa and started a church and an orphanage.

Maddie Watkins was still single with no love interest as she was studying to be a doctor and said she had no time for serious relationships.

A few months after Addison's mother had given her heart to the Lord, she made amends with Bryan and Rebekah Morris, and of course, Tyler and Isaac. It had taken the help of the Lord, Pastor Bryce, and Maggie, along with much prayer and soul searching when it came to forgiving Tyler and Isaac, but she was finally able to truly forgive.

"I can't believe the heaviness that has been lifted and the peace I feel since forgiving them," she had confided to her children one night after supper.

It was shortly after that she and Noah started seeing each other again. Noah had asked Kyndal to forgive him for being a jerk concerning the way he left her hanging after he broke up with her without any explanation. Her mother eventually forgave him for being a jerk, and well, the rest is history. It had been an emotional roller coaster for her mother.

Addison remembered the day her mother had finally decided to remove her wedding band. She and her mother had cried as her mother carefully removed the ring she had worn for almost twenty-three years and placed it in her jewelry box. She said she would always love Josh McNeely, but it was time to let go of the past and move on. Noah was a true gentleman and understood how hard it had been for her to remove the ring. He had never once asked her to remove it even when they had been dating. He knew it had to be in her timing; no one understood that better than he did. Her mother had also learned that she had room in her heart to love again. The two were good for each other. Her mother was singing again, and to Addison, it was the most beautiful sound on earth.

Even her little brother and his friends were growing up fast—and tall. Now that he was taller than Alayna, she had stopped referring to him as "squirt," much to Ayson's delight. He, along with Callaway and Caleb, had joined a local gospel group and were playing and traveling to different churches as school allowed. He had another year of high school left but was already making plans to major in music at the local college. He wanted to become a worship leader wherever the Lord may lead. He wasn't exactly sure how everything would play out, but he was praying and trusting the Lord to give him direction in his life.

After a few months in jail, Tyler Morris went back to college and is currently in the process of becoming a Christian psychologist. He and his cousin Jude are still on probation, but it could have been much worse. Addison had gone to court and spoken on Tyler's behalf, which she believes helped him to get a reduced sentence. Physically, Tyler still has some occasional stuttering, but other than that, there appears to be no residual side effects from the gunshot wound. He is frequently invited to various churches and events to give his testimony, and on occasion, Addison and Tyler are invited to speak together. He particularly has a heart for young people, and on numerous occasions, he has assisted the Scobies' with the youth at New Haven. This turns out to be especially helpful since Michael and Jennifer are expecting another child any moment. Grace Scobie can hardly wait to meet her new brother, Michael Gabriel Scobie Jr.

Life definitely had not turned out like any of them expected, but then again, it seldom does. The Lord had opened doors and closed doors. It had been a walk of faith for each one of them and would continue to be, as each new chapter in their lives unfolded. Each had walked through the fire in their own way, but true to God's word, He had never left them in the fire to walk alone. He had walked with them and brought them out stronger than before they had gone in. Addison knew there would be more times of walking through the fire, but she also knew she would never be alone in her time of need.

* * * * *

June rolled around, and Addison's big day had finally arrived. She paced nervously at the back of the church as she and Ayson waited for the music to begin that would send them down the aisle to her beloved. She gave one last check in the hall mirror. Turning from front to back and front again, she was pleased with the dress she had chosen. The white trumpet/mermaid sleeveless tulle dress with V neck and sweep/brush train really did flatter her figure. The Japanese Akoya white pearl necklace and matching earrings her mother had worn when she married Addison's dad only added to the beauty of the dress. The chignon hairstyle with the leaf-motif chignon wrap comb and the barely-there wedding veil completed the look. She had chosen sage green for her maid of honor's and bridesmaid's dresses, which really complimented Alayna's auburn hair and blue eyes. She and Wyatt had decided on a deep-gray tux with a white vest for the groom and deep-gray tuxes with sage vests for the groomsmen. All her bouquets had a mixture of sage, peach, silver, and white flowers mixed with darker greens. It had been both fun and stressful planning the wedding, but she was glad the day had finally arrived.

It meant the world to Addison that Isaac and Karlie had returned from Africa for her wedding. It meant even more that Karlie had agreed to be one of her bridesmaids, along with Maddie. Wyatt's dad was his best man, and except for a touch of gray around the ears, he and Wyatt could have passed for twins, even down to the dimpled chin. Wyatt's younger brother, Franklin, with his blue eyes, dark hair, and oblong face favored their mother. He, along with Alayna's boyfriend, Jonathan, whom Wyatt had become good friends with, made handsome groomsmen.

Turning to look at Ayson in a traditional black tux, Addison again noticed how much he favored their dad, and even more so now that he was older. Ayson was truly handsome, and she was so proud to have him walk her down the aisle.

Finally, "Here Comes the Bride" rang out from the piano, cueing Addison and Ayson to begin their entrance. Ayson looked at his beautiful and radiant sister. Smiling, he took her by the arm, and they began their entrance into the sanctuary. Soon her brother would let go and place her hands into the strong and safe hands of her soon-to-be husband—the same way her daddy had let go of his little girl so long ago and placed her into the strong and safe hands of his Savior.

"I love you, Daddy," she whispered. At that moment, she could have sworn she felt a kiss upon her cheek—a kiss from heaven.

AFTERWORD

How about you? Have you accepted Jesus as your Lord and Savior? Jesus is the way, the truth, and the life. No one can come to the Father except through Jesus (John 14:6). Jesus is the *only* way to heaven. Jesus could return any minute. If you would like to invite Jesus to be a part of your life, repeat this prayer from your heart:

> Dear Heavenly Father, I confess that I am a sinner. I repent of my sins and ask You to forgive me and to cleanse me now from all unrighteousness. Wash me in Jesus's blood. I believe Jesus is the Son of God who died for me and then arose. I trust Jesus and make Him not only my Savior but the Lord of my life. Thank You, Jesus, for dying for me. Father, take my life and do something with it. I thank You, Father, for Your forgiveness, mercy, and grace. Thank You for hearing my prayer and cleansing me from all unrighteousness through the blood of Your Son, Jesus. In Jesus's name, I pray. Amen.

If you prayed this prayer and are truly repentant, the Lord will take your life and do something with it. If you have not yet made up your mind, let me ask you one more question in closing: Where will you be one second after your heart stops? Will you be in heaven, or will you be in hell, a place where all hope is lost? There will be no turning back. That is something to think about. It is *your* choice—*you* choose. Jesus has done everything possible for you to have eternal life. On the cross, He spoke the following words: "It is finished!"

Jesus was the ultimate sacrifice. Don't be left behind. If you prayed the above prayer, remember God the Father desires to have a personal and intimate relationship with you, so much so that He sent his only Son to die for you. Get in a Bible-believing church, buy a Bible, read it daily, and start your amazing journey with the Lord of your life!

ABOUT THE AUTHOR

Bonita M. Hullender is a retired registered nurse. She resides in South Carolina with her husband and best friend, Joel, along with their Chihuahua-mix fur baby Chip. She feels blessed to have three wonderful sons, three beautiful daughters-in-law, and eight precious grandchildren. In addition to her love of writing, she loves to read. When she was a teenager, she read every Nancy Drew and Hardy Boys mysteries the library had. As her love of reading grew, so did her desire to write a novel, but only recently did that desire become a reality. She also has a love for music and enjoys playing the piano for her own entertainment and playing the alto saxophone in her church's orchestra.

CPSIA information can be obtained
at www.ICGtesting.com
Printed in the USA
BVHW071004150521
607358BV00005B/228